SALVATION

BOOK THREE OF THE SUBVERSIVE TRILOGY

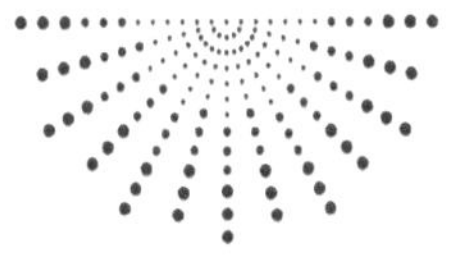

RAENA ROOD

ONE FOUNDATION PUBLISHING, LLC

SALVATION

BOOK THREE OF THE SUBVERSIVE TRILOGY

By: Raena Rood

"We are hard pressed on every side, but not crushed; perplexed, but not in despair; persecuted, but not abandoned; struck down, but not destroyed."
--2 Corinthians 4:8-9 (NIV)

For my parents…
From saxophones to figure skates to word processors.
Thank you for letting me dream big.
This one's for you.

PROLOGUE

Standing in front of the full-length mirror in his dressing room, Pastor David Ogden stared at his reflection, which was perfect in every way. But when he tried to force his signature megawatt smile onto his lips, his facial muscles rebelled against him, refusing to comply.

He was really nervous tonight. He *never* got nervous.

He couldn't see the crowd yet, but their energy flowed through his veins like blood, making him feel immortal, like a vampire. Five-thousand people waited for him in the auditorium of Elevation Ministry Center. They'd paid exorbitant ticket prices for the honor of attending the Friday evening service, which was broadcast live to six-million viewers in the U.S. alone.

The audience had come for a show, and Ogden intended to give them a show.

Stepping back from the mirror, Ogden took an appraising look at his body. At forty-six, he was in perfect physical condition, thanks to a diet high in organic proteins and vegetables and low in complex carbohydrates and sugars. He ran three miles a day, lifted weights with a personal trainer three days per week, and suffered from none of the aches or pains common to people his age. His teeth were bleached white and arrow-straight, and the small but solid muscles that rippled beneath the fibers of his perfectly creased suits met the approval of the beautiful women he invited into his bed.

But regardless of his flawless exterior and excellent physical health, lately he couldn't seem to stop thinking about death.

It wasn't hell he feared, of course. He wasn't a fool. Even during his brief stint as a Christian minister for the uneducated masses, he'd known that such fantastic concepts as heaven and hell had been invented to control the small-minded. No, what he feared was death itself—or more precisely, the inevitable undoing of all his hard work. Even his fame and power and money could not save him from it. On those long nights when sleep eluded him, even the comforts offered by the fresh-faced young women from his audience weren't enough to distract him from the thoughts of the long, dark sleep that awaited him.

If he was lucky, he might have another thirty or forty good years remaining before he blinked out like a lightbulb that had burned too brightly. Yes, his legacy would continue through his books and teachings, but those, too, would eventually fade away, lost to the indifference of time.

It was unavoidable.

These days, the only thing that occupied Ogden's thoughts more than his eventual death was the auburn-haired young woman. The one who'd attacked the local compliance office and broadcast her seditious message to the world.

"Gemma Alcott."

Ogden rolled her name around on his tongue, testing it like a food he might decide to spit out. The world knew her name because people from Alcott's hometown had recognized and identified her on social media, for all the good it had done. The Task Force had offered a reward for information leading to her capture and to the capture of the other subversives involved in the attack. There had been a few leads, but according to Ogden's contacts within the Federal Bureau of Compliance, none of those leads had borne any fruit.

No one knew where Alcott and her friends were hiding.

Or perhaps the people who knew were keeping their mouths shut.

When Alcott had filmed herself wearing that upside-down Task Force patch on her shoulder, she couldn't possibly have known that her video would go viral. Or that it would garner millions of likes and retweets and shares. Or that the thousands of subversives in detention centers would hear her promise of salvation through the speakers in their cells. By the time each of the major social media sites got around to deleting her video from their platforms, the damage had already been done. Alcott had become a hero to both the subversives and the sympathizers. And in the months following the broadcast, the daily number of renunciations began a slow but steady decline.

Ogden's broadcast ratings had also slipped.

Just a little. But they *had* slipped.

Now, Ogden equated Miss Alcott with death.

Sweat coursed down his chest, and his armpits itched like crazy. They always itched when he got hot. The room's thermostat hung on the wall beside the couch, and Ogden walked over to it and punched the down arrow until the display read sixty degrees. Earlier, he'd ordered his personal assistant, Tara Wilkinson, to crank the air conditioning in the auditorium up as high as it would go. "I want to see my breath," he'd told her, only half-kidding. Tara had raised her eyebrows at this order— it was only the first week of May, and the nights were still chilly —but she'd nodded briskly and scurried off to find a maintenance worker.

A knock sounded on the door.

"Yes," he called out. "Come in."

The door swung open, and Tara appeared on the other side,

as she usually did on the rare occasions that Ogden thought of her. Although she was in her early thirties, which put her at the high end of his preferred age range for women, he didn't find her at all attractive—at least, not compared to the women he typically entertained. Tara was a mousy brunette who wore no jewelry except for an ugly gold locket, and she always wore her hair the same way: slicked back into a too-tight bun perched high atop her head, like a ballerina. But unlike a ballerina, all of Tara's skirts were neutral-toned and hit below the knee, and her blouses were too large, giving her an overall shapeless appearance, like a depressing brown amoeba.

Also, she always had a lemon-flavored cough drop in her mouth, even when she wasn't sick, and that both annoyed and disgusted him.

"Good evening, Mr. Ogden." Tara remained outside of the dressing room, thankfully far enough away that he only got a slight whiff of her overpowering, drug-store brand, freesia-scented body wash. The woman's eyes darted from his face to the clipboard in her hands. She always carried a clipboard around with her, although Ogden couldn't for the life of him understand why. He rarely gave her anything to do and certainly nothing that required taking notes. "We're ready. You're on in five minutes."

"Yes, Tara. Thank you." His eyes lingered on the chipped beige polish on her fingernails, and he tried to keep the disgust he felt from working its way onto his face. "I'll be there in a moment."

Their eyes met again, and Tara surprised him by holding his gaze for a few seconds longer than usual. Her lips parted slightly, her mouth dropping open as if to say something. The woman rarely spoke, so Ogden leaned forward, eager to hear what she had to say.

But the moment passed.

Tara uttered a quick, "Okay," and then eased the door shut

behind her, leaving Ogden to wonder if he'd imagined the whole thing.

✝

Five minutes later, David Ogden clutched his gold microphone to his chest and stepped onto Elevation's stage to a thunderous applause. He extended his arms to either side of his body, the stream of light from the spotlights making him glow brighter than Moses after his encounter with God on the mountain. He took his customary bow, and on the way back up, he discreetly turned his head to glimpse at himself in one of the three Jumbotrons.

Handsome as ever.

His megawatt smile had returned with a vengeance.

"Thank you." Ogden gestured for the audience to sit, but they continued to clap. Normally, he reveled in the admiration of his fans. Consumed it like food. But tonight, he wanted to keep things moving. "Thank you all for coming. Please take your seats so we can begin."

The audience ignored him, stretching out the applause for another thirty seconds. Ogden knew it was thirty seconds because he was counting them off in his mind. He wasn't an anxious person, but tonight, his stomach hurt, his undershirt was soaked with sweat, and his armpits were driving him crazy.

"Thank you," he said for the third time. "Ladies and gentlemen, please take your seats."

Finally, the clapping died down. What followed was a thunderous shuffling sound, like the beating wings of a thousand birds, as the audience lowered themselves into their cushioned seats. Thousands of faces gazed expectantly at Ogden, waiting to be entertained and to have their guilt appeased.

He raised the microphone to his lips. "Good evening, ladies and gentlemen. Thank you for joining our Friday evening broadcast. I'm Pastor David Ogden of *Elevation Ministries*, and as always, we're coming to you live from Harrisburg, Pennsylvania. Tonight, I want to talk to you about hope. Folks, it can be difficult to have hope sometimes, can't it?" He allowed the audience a moment to nod or voice their assent. "Especially when the world seems to be spinning out of control. It's difficult to feel hopeful about our nation when there are so many people actively working to destroy everything we've—"

"Ogden!"

He stopped speaking and scanned the audience for the person who'd interrupted him. "Yes? Who called out?" He brought a hand up to shield his eyes from the glare of the lights. "I'm having trouble seeing you. These lights are very bright."

At first, he saw nothing but the usual canvas of blank faces staring back at him. Then, a few rows back from the stage, a young woman rose from her seat, thick auburn hair flowing unhindered down her back. Unlike everyone around her, she hadn't dressed for the occasion. Instead, she wore a gray utility jacket, faded jeans with holes in the knees, and a pair of scuffed, black Army boots.

A black facemask covered her nose and mouth, and she wore an upside-down Task Force patch on her left shoulder. She stopped directly beneath the main platform, only a dozen feet from the stage.

Although there were five-thousand people in attendance, the auditorium was perfectly silent. Ogden could sense the crowd holding its breath, waiting to see what would happen next.

"I'm sorry we have to do this," the woman said, her voice muffled by the mask. "But you've left us no choice."

Ogden walked to the edge of the stage and knelt. "I know who you are. You're the young woman who attacked the compliance office last fall, aren't you? Gemma Alcott. Is that your name?"

He was close enough to the young woman that his microphone picked up her words clearly. "Lots of people are going to die tonight," she said, "but you're going to die first."

The young woman reached inside her jacket, pulled out a pistol, and aimed it at him.

Slowly, Ogden rose to his feet, but he didn't move away from the edge of the stage. He couldn't afford to portray weakness or fear in this moment—not with the world watching him. "Miss Alcott, whatever you're planning to do tonight, I assure you, it won't solve anything. It will only make your situation worse. I couldn't help but notice that patch on your shoulder. If it's truly freedom you desire, there's only one way to find it." He put a hand over his heart. "And that's by letting go of the things that are keeping you in chains."

"I'm sorry," the young woman said, "but this is the only way."

She pulled the trigger.

Ogden felt the impact like a fist slamming into his left shoulder. He dropped his gold microphone and stumbled into the podium. Gripping it with both hands, he dipped his head to survey the damage to his shoulder. Bright-red blood erupted from a single hole in his perfectly creased suit.

For the first time onstage, Ogden didn't have to act. The pain was tremendous.

The auditorium erupted into chaos. Terrified screams filled the room as Ogden's most devoted followers abandoned their seats—and their leader—and ran for their lives. The aisles filled with people dashing for the exits, dragging their families along with them. Those who moved too slowly were shoved to the side. Several people fell to the ground and did not make it back up before the crowd surged over them.

Still clutching the podium, Ogden searched the floor beneath the stage for the young woman with the auburn hair, but she was already gone, swallowed up by the crowd.

An explosion of pain rolled through his shoulder, and he clutched it and moaned, sticky blood spilling through his fingers. All around him, the room blurred, as if he was viewing it from underwater, and then he lost his grip on the podium and crumpled to the floor.

Running footsteps. The distinct sound of heels clicking on the stage. And then Tara, his assistant, loomed over him, her eyes widening as she took in the wound on his shoulder and the blood on his hands.

She slipped her hands underneath his armpits and tried to lift him, but she wasn't strong enough, and his body sank back onto the stage.

"Come on, David!" she shouted. "Stand up! We need to get out of—"

A violent blast rocked the building, tossing Tara to the ground like a rag doll and rattling the fillings in Ogden's molars.

An eerie silence enveloped the auditorium. Still clutching the base of the podium, Ogden watched as the members of the audience who hadn't made it outside yet stopped running and stood in the aisles. They backed away from the exit doors as smoke drifted into the room. A few people even returned to their seats—as if by doing so, they could turn back time.

Then, on the other side of the exit doors, the screaming began.

CHAPTER ONE

"You don't have to run anymore. It's safe here."

Gemma Alcott sat across the table from a couple who'd knocked on the front door of Letty's Book Cellar a half-hour earlier. They were requesting sanctuary for themselves and their teenage daughter. They'd taken a chance by hitching a ride to Winter's Dam with a long-haul truck driver, but twenty minutes into the ride, the burly man had rolled up his sleeve and showed them the tattoo on his right shoulder: two intersecting swords that formed a flaming cross hoisted atop a pair of shoulders.

"Really?" The father's tired blue eyes filled with tears. He clutched his wife, and they both started to cry. "Oh, thank you, God. Thank you, Father."

Gemma pushed a box of tissues across the table toward the couple. Then, she excused herself from the table and escaped down the hallway to Letty's old office. Watching these emotional scenes play out—especially between families—always made her uncomfortable. While they cried, she found a box of cookies and began arranging them on a plate.

The Sanctuary was gone, destroyed by the Task Force the

previous fall. But Letty's signs were still out in the world, luring weary subversives to Winter's Dam with the promise of safety. Only the dead woman herself knew the location of every sign, so finding and removing all of them would've been an impossible task. This meant that someone had to remain at the bookstore to help any subversives who might show up, and Gemma had volunteered for the job.

She returned to the table a few minutes later, carrying a plate of Lotus Biscoff cookies. She always handed out those cookies to new arrivals. It was her own little tribute to Letty, who had once given an entire bag of them to Gemma, claiming that she didn't like them. That had turned out to be a lie, because when Letty died, she'd left behind a seemingly endless supply of them. When those had eventually run out, Gemma had walked down to Fallon's Grocery and bought ten more bags.

"Here," she said, placing the plate on the table next to a pile of crumpled tissues. "You guys could use a little sugar therapy."

The man pushed the tissues aside and pulled the plate closer. Then, he and his wife each tentatively picked up a cookie. They'd given their names as Andrew and Catherine Bowler, originally from Altoona, and they'd claimed to have been in hiding as subversives for nine months prior to stumbling across one of Letty's signs inside an abandoned church. They definitely appeared to be a family who'd been living a rough life off the grid. Their faded and filthy clothing, their mosquito-bitten arms, and their sun-scorched faces were all evidence of too much time spent outdoors without proper shelter.

Their daughter, Taren, hadn't said a word since their arrival at the bookstore. Although she was almost six feet tall and heavyset, her clothes were still two or three sizes too big for her. Her chestnut hair reached all the way to her waist and contained knots as big as a man's fist. Gemma guessed the young woman's age to be about eighteen or nineteen—approximately the same age Gemma had been on the night the Task Force had dragged her parents out of her life.

Instead of sitting at the table with her parents, Taren walked among the rows of books, running her hand reverently along their spines.

"We didn't know what to expect when we found your flyer hanging in that church," Andrew Bowler continued, taking a small bite of his cookie. "We were just trying to find a safe place to sleep for the night. But this..." He opened his arms as if to embrace the bookstore. "This is truly amazing. God bless you for helping us."

The flyer wasn't Gemma's—it was Letty's—but she didn't bother to correct him. So far, the couple hadn't brought up the old woman on the flyer, and Gemma had no desire to discuss Letty's violent death with strangers.

"So, where will we be staying?" Catherine Bowler glanced around the dreary bookstore. "Not in here, I suppose?"

"Actually, you'll be staying with some locals," Gemma replied, absently twisting her emerald engagement ring around her finger. She kept her palms against the table so the Bowlers wouldn't see the scars on the underside of her wrists—tiny slashes from when she'd had to free herself from Mullen's restraints in the coal mine. "Sympathizers. I won't get into specifics, but last fall, the Task Force ruffled quite a few feathers here in Winter's Dam, and that led to many of the locals offering space in their homes to hide subversives. I think it's their little way of fighting back."

Andrew Bowler nodded, but the relief in his eyes had faded a little. "Okay. So, who are they? The people taking us in, I mean."

"An elderly couple in town—the Courtneys—have agreed to house you indefinitely. I spoke with Eva Courtney on the phone after you first arrived. She said they're already housing two other subversives in their spare bedrooms, but they have space for you in their attic."

Catherine Bowler gave her husband a weary look. "The attic?"

"It's the only space available," Gemma rushed to say, although that wasn't entirely true. There were other openings in town. People usually volunteered a spare bedroom here and there, but if this family wanted to stay together, the Courtneys' attic was their best option. "From what Eva told me, it sounds like a nice-sized attic, it's clean, and they've already set up beds for you. There's a bathroom at the base of the stairs—you'll have full use of that—and Eva said you're welcome to join them for meals. All they're asking for in exchange is that you help around the house and the yard. They're getting older, and keeping up with the place is becoming a chore."

But Catherine Bowler was already shaking her head. "We don't even know these people, Andy. I thought we'd be staying..." Her voice trailed off. "I'm not sure what I thought."

Andrew Bowler put an arm around his wife's shoulders. "We'll be okay, honey. They must be nice people if they're opening their home up to strangers. Besides, we've spent most of the last nine months sleeping in tents. I think the attic will be a wonderful change of pace." He glanced at his daughter, who'd just appeared at the end of a row of bookshelves. "What do you think, Taren?"

The young woman glanced up at the sound of her name but did not answer. Instead, she disappeared into the next row, as if trying to escape from the question.

"She won't let me cut her hair," Catherine Bowler whispered to Gemma. "Not since we left our home. She also doesn't like how it feels when I brush it. I try, of course. I even brought a Wet brush along—the kind that doesn't pull the hair—but she still puts up a fight. So, I don't bother anymore. Back home, she used conditioner in the shower, but out in the woods, we didn't have those luxuries." After a brief pause, she added, "She has autism."

Gemma stopped twisting her ring. They sold shampoo and conditioner at Fallon's Grocery, but that would mean seeing Teresa, which would be uncomfortable. But it might also mean seeing Gavin, which would be much, much worse.

Still, if there was anything Gemma could do to help these people, she needed to do it.

"I'll see if I can rustle up some conditioner for you," she said. "I'll drop it by the Courtneys' house tonight or tomorrow."

The woman's face softened into a smile. "Thank you so much. We'd really appreciate that."

"You're very welcome," Gemma nodded. "Also, I should mention that, according to Eva Courtney, you'll be the only people living in the attic right now. But there are six beds up there, so others may join you in the future."

"We're just thankful for the shelter," Andrew Bowler said. "If others come along, we'll welcome them with open arms. But if you don't mind me asking, where is the other woman? The one whose picture is on the flyer?"

And there it was. The question Gemma had been dreading since the Bowler family had stepped inside the bookstore. People always asked about Letty. It was inevitable. By the time their journey brought them to the bookstore, Letty had become an almost mythological figure to them. "She..." Gemma's voice came out sounding gruff, and she cleared her throat before continuing. "Unfortunately, Letty passed away last October."

"Oh, no!" Catherine Bowler pressed a hand against her chest. "We've been praying to meet her since we found the flyer. Did she fall ill?"

She didn't fall; he kicked her, Gemma nearly said as her mind filled with the image of Letty's crumpled body at the base of the cellar stairs. Another victim of the redheaded soldier, Mullen, and his unquenchable hatred for subversives and those who housed them.

But Mullen was dead now, too. He wasn't ever going to hurt anyone else.

Gemma couldn't tell Catherine Bowler about Mullen—where would she even begin?—but she also couldn't lie. So, she said what she always said whenever anyone asked about Letty. "Her death was very sudden and unexpected."

Usually, people took the hint and left it at that, but not Catherine Bowler. A strange sort of understanding settled over the woman's face, and she whispered, "Did someone kill her?"

Tearing her eyes away from the woman, Gemma grabbed a cookie from the plate and bit into it. The cookie disintegrated on her tongue, flooding her mouth with the taste of cinnamon and caramel. She didn't like Lotus Biscoff cookies anymore—not since the day she'd eaten an entire bag while visiting Letty—but she needed something in her mouth so she had a reason not to answer Catherine Bowler's question.

Thankfully, Taren Bowler saved her by emerging from the row, clutching a hardcover book against her chest.

"What've you got there, Tare-Bear?" her father asked. "We aren't supposed to take anything from the bookstore, sweetheart."

He was right. The bookstore wasn't open for business anymore, as evidenced by the "Store Permanently Closed" sign hanging in the front window. But if Taren Bowler wanted a book, she could have a book.

Gemma rose from her seat and moved closer to the girl. Not *too* close, but close enough to see that the book she was holding was *Wuthering Heights.* "I read that one back in high school," she said, nodding at the book. "I wrote a book report on it for my senior English Lit class. My teacher gave me B on my report, and when I asked him why, he said it was because he hated the book. He called it..."—she lowered her voice an octave and donned a haughty accent—"nineteenth-century gothic garbage." Both Andrew and Catherine Bowler chuckled at this, and

Gemma shifted back into her own voice. "I thought it was romantic."

Taren kept her eyes low, not acknowledging anything Gemma had just said.

"Anyway, it's true that the bookstore isn't open anymore, but you can treat this place like a library and borrow another book when you've finished with that one. We've got plenty to go around."

Taren finally lifted her eyes to meet Gemma's, and the corner of her mouth ticked into a ghost of a smile that vanished as quickly as it had appeared. She muttered a quick, "Thank you" in a hoarse voice before returning her gaze to the ground.

"You're welcome."

A single honk came from outside the store.

Gemma jogged to the door and eased it open far enough to see a blue Kia idling in the parking lot. She gave Eva Courtney a quick wave and held up her index finger to indicate that the Bowlers would be out in a minute. Then, she returned to the family. "Eva Courtney is here. I told her you didn't have a vehicle, so she's going to drive you back to the house."

Andrew Bowler rose and pushed his chair underneath the table. "How nice of her." But he looked anxious. They all did.

As the family headed for the door, the hardcover book in Taren's arms reminded Gemma of something she'd nearly forgotten. "Before you go, do you guys have a Bible?"

Catherine Bowler's eyes widened. "A Bible? Of course not. We haven't even *seen* a Bible in years. The soldiers confiscated every Bible when they raided our church four years ago. They detained our minister and three of the elders that day."

"I'm sorry to hear that." Gemma knew what it was like to lose people you loved to the detention centers, those godforsaken bottomless pits from which few ever emerged. "But if you don't have a Bible, I'd like to give you one as a gift."

"A gift?" Andrew and Catherine Bowler replied in unison. Even Taren looked interested.

"Sure. Hold on a second."

Out of the thirty-three Bibles that Gemma had carried out of the coal mine, only five remained in the bookstore. She had gifted the rest to various subversives prior to their departure for their new homes in Winter's Dam. The Bibles that hadn't yet been given away remained hidden in plain sight among the thousands of other books on Letty's dusty shelves, their specific locations known only to Gemma. If the Task Force ever raided the bookstore, she could imagine them ransacking Letty's office and upstairs apartment, but she doubted they would think to toss the shelves, remove the dust covers, and check each book individually.

She jogged halfway down the aisle and made a sharp turn into the history section. *Right side. Second shelf from the top. Four-teenth from the left.* A book about Civil War generals. Locating it easily, Gemma pulled the book off the shelf. Underneath the fake dust cover that featured competing images of Ulysses S. Grant and Robert E. Lee was a timeworn, leather-bound King James Bible.

Returning to the front of the store, she handed the Bible to Andrew Bowler, who clearly didn't understand why Gemma was giving him a history book. Then, he flipped it open, and as he paged through the book, his hands started to shake. "Wow," he mumbled to himself. "I'd almost forgotten how delicate the pages are in these old Bibles. I'm afraid I'm going to rip them."

The sound that emerged from Catherine Bowler's throat was somewhere between a laugh and a squeak. She tossed her arms around Gemma's shoulders. "Thank you," she said, fresh tears spilling down her face. "You've done more for us today than you'll ever know."

"It's nothing. Really."

Andrew Bowler gently closed the Bible and studied Gemma

as if he wasn't sure what to make of her. He tapped a finger on the leather cover. "How?" he asked, his forehead wrinkling in curiosity. "How did you get this?"

Gemma hoped the smile she offered him in response was answer enough.

✝

After the Bowler family left, Gemma spent the rest of the afternoon tidying up the bookstore. She dusted shelves that didn't need dusting and swept floors that didn't need sweeping. The tiny half-bath at the end of the hallway was spotless, having just been cleaned two days prior, but Gemma cleaned it again. It was there, while kneeling on the stained linoleum with a toilet brush in one hand and a bottle of Scrubbing Bubbles in the other, that she began to cry.

The tears came without warning, as they often did.

These random crying jags were becoming more frequent, and when they happened, Gemma could do nothing but ride them out. She rested an arm on the toilet lid and buried her face in the crook of her elbow, her nostrils filling with the smell of citrus-scented toilet bowl cleaner.

The days were bad enough, but the nights were awful. The detention centers plagued her dreams, gruesome and endless nightmares where terrible things happened to her parents and her friends from the Sanctuary. Taylor also showed up in her dreams, but he wasn't Taylor anymore. The Task Force had reprogrammed him into a cold, emotionless killer, and he was always chasing her. Always trying to catch and hurt her.

Unlike normal dreams, these nightmares did not fade from her mind after a few minutes or hours. They haunted her thoughts all day long until she eventually crawled into bed, drifted off to sleep, and dreamt of fresh horrors.

She dreaded sleep.

When Gemma had no more tears left to cry, she picked herself up off the floor, washed her face at the sink, and left the bathroom. She slipped into one row of bookshelves, took a hidden Bible off the shelf, and began reading where she'd left off the day before, in the book of Joshua. Reading the Bible always made her feel better, even if sometimes she had to force herself to do it. But no matter how hard she tried, she couldn't get her mind to focus today.

After reading the same paragraph for the third time, she closed the Bible.

Taking up Letty's mantle in Winter's Dam hadn't been an entirely selfless decision. She couldn't bring herself to leave the town because it was the last place she'd seen Taylor. If he was still alive, and if he ever escaped from the Task Force, the Sanctuary would be the first place he would go. When he discovered the Sanctuary burned to the ground, his next logical step—and Taylor was very logical—would be to reconnect with Letty.

He had no way of knowing that Letty was dead.

Taylor occupied Gemma's thoughts most days. Often, she stared at the front of the bookstore, envisioning the door swinging open and Taylor stepping inside. She'd spend hours imagining every detail of their reunion, from the fresh scars Taylor would have from the injuries sustained during his time in captivity to his voice when he spoke her name for the first time in months. Part of her believed that if she pictured Taylor clearly enough in her mind, she might actually conjure him up.

But that wasn't reality.

The reality was…when people left Gemma, they never came back.

She glanced at her watch. Almost three o'clock. Sophia would be home in an hour. The eleven-year-old couldn't attend school with the other kids in town, but a local retired schoolteacher—Abigail Sherman—had agreed to homeschool her on

Tuesdays, Thursdays, and Saturdays. After Mrs. Sherman drove Sophia home, Gemma and the young girl would retreat upstairs to the two-bedroom apartment they shared with Brie and Max.

During the day, Brie and Max worked for Claude and Lizzy Fishman at the butcher shop. They came home each night in blood-stained clothes, drained and grumpy from long days spent deboning, trimming, and packing beef. But the job kept meat on their dinner table, where they otherwise would've had none. However, they both refused to cook after working all day, forcing Gemma to handle the domestic duties, including the cooking. While Gemma was an excellent baker, she was a horrible cook. Out of necessity, Sophia had become quite the little chef. She spent her non-school days perusing the cookbooks in the bookstore and making frequent trips to Fallon's Grocery for ingredients.

Gavin lived across town with the owner of Fallon's Grocery, Todd Fallon, and Todd's daughter, Teresa. He earned his keep by stocking shelves after-hours at the store. According to Sophia, Gavin and Teresa were *a thing* now—whatever that meant. On the few occasions that Gemma had seen Gavin around town, she'd thought he'd looked happy—certainly happier than he'd ever been with her.

She *wanted* to be happy for him—she knew she *should* have been happy for him—but she just couldn't manifest any positive feelings.

All she felt for Gavin was anger.

The sound of a vehicle pulling into the parking lot caught Gemma's attention.

Although the bookstore shared its parking lot with the convenience store next door, after nearly six months at Letty's, Gemma knew how it sounded when a car pulled up to the convenience store and when one pulled into a spot next to the bookstore.

Was it more Christians seeking shelter? Prior to the Bowlers, the most recent group to show up at the bookstore had arrived almost three weeks earlier. Two groups in one day was unheard of. Maybe it was just an old customer passing through town, one who didn't realize that the bookstore had closed since their last visit.

Or maybe it was the Task Force.

Or maybe—a quiet and treacherous voice whispered in her mind—*it was Taylor.*

Each of these possibilities went through Gemma's mind as she made her way to the front door, her right hand slipping underneath her oversized cardigan to touch the butt of the revolver she always wore on her right hip when she was alone in the bookstore. She'd found the gun on the top shelf of Letty's closet not long after moving into the woman's apartment—yet another thing she hadn't known about Letty.

Outside, a car door slammed.

Gemma peered through the glass, but she couldn't see the vehicle from her vantage point, and she wasn't about to open the door to get a better view. If it was a bookstore customer, she hoped they would decide that no one was home and leave.

If it was the Task Force, it was already too late.

Footsteps climbed the porch steps—only one set, and definitely not the heavy boots favored by the Task Force. These sounded more like flip-flops, which ruled out any subversives on the run. Moments later, a dark-haired woman wearing a yellow sundress and white sweater appeared on the porch, heading for the front door. The woman had a very chubby baby in her arms and a massive diaper bag slung over her left shoulder.

The diaper bag had cows all over it.

With a gasp, Gemma released her grip on the revolver and fumbled nervously with the lock, suddenly unable to figure out how the stupid thing worked. She unlocked the door and yanked it open just as the woman and baby boy appeared on the other side of the glass.

"Addie!"

CHAPTER TWO

They stood in the middle of the aisle, embracing and crying, with Weston squished between them like the cheese in a sandwich. He even smelled a bit like cheese. Based on the body-shaking giggles coming out of his adorable, snaggle-toothed mouth, Weston seemed to enjoy the hug as much as Addie and Gemma.

"I can't…believe…you're here." Gemma's chest hitched with each word, as if her body were trying to suck the words back inside.

"Oh, quit your brutzin'!" Addie scolded, even though she was crying as hard as Gemma. "You're getting snot all over my baby."

But Gemma couldn't help it. The emotions bubbled out of her like water in a hot spring. Addie was actually *here*, in Winter's Dam, and she no longer looked like a walking corpse. Her pale skin had returned to its natural color, and she appeared to have regained the twenty pounds she'd lost while breastfeeding Weston at the Sanctuary. She also smelled incredible—a mixture of floral body spray and lavender shampoo.

And then there was Weston. Nine months old and as round as a basketball. Back at the Sanctuary, Taylor used to call him

Tank—partly to annoy Addie and partly because it was true—and the little guy had grown into the nickname. The one-piece denim jumpsuit he wore made him look like a baby farmer. The only thing missing was the straw hat and a piece of hay jutting out of his mouth. He had very little hair yet, only what amounted to an old man's comb-over, but what little hair he possessed was the same dirty-blond as his father's. He watched Gemma with slate-gray eyes so wide they took her breath away.

Once you got past the faint odor of cheese, Weston smelled wonderful. A delicious combination of baby powder, and diaper cream, and that wonderful baby-sweet fragrance common to all little heads. Gemma brought her nose close to Weston's comb-over and took a discreet sniff.

Releasing Gemma from the hug, Addie gave her a bemused smile. "Did you just smell my baby's head?"

"I might have. Is that a problem?"

Addie snorted laughter. "Would you take him for a minute? I need a break after that drive." She handed Weston off to Gemma, who would've passed out from shock if she hadn't been holding a baby. Back at the Sanctuary, Addie didn't like to let anyone—including Kyle—hold Weston, but now she was passing him off to Gemma like a squirming sack of flour.

She's free now, Gemma realized. *She's not afraid that someone's going to take him anymore.*

Addie dropped the diaper bag on the floor and collapsed onto one of Letty's cushioned reading chairs. She stretched her legs out in front of her, her arms dangling off the armrests. It wasn't a very ladylike way of sitting—especially in a sundress—but it was *very* Addie.

"So, where's Kyle?" Gemma asked, bouncing Weston on her hip. But when she heard milk sloshing around in his tummy, she stopped bouncing him. "He didn't want to come with you?"

Addie's left foot began to shake, and she crossed her slender legs, one flip-flop bobbing over the hardwood floor. "He's working today. He got a job at a hardware store in Strasburg. His boss is a real jerk, but it's a steady paycheck. He had a hard time finding work with that stupid yoke on his ID," she said, referring to the yoke symbol on the identification cards of any Christians who'd renounced their faith.

"We're praying that we can save up enough money to afford our own apartment this summer," Addie continued. "Being back on the farm with my folks hasn't been easy. They don't like Kyle."

"Really? Why not?"

Addie shrugged. "They think he's the reason I stayed away for so long. And they're right. There's no way I would've stayed at the Station if Kyle hadn't been there. When I showed up on their doorstep with a husband *and* a baby, my daddy was mad enough to spit nails. But my momma got all heated and told him he better not scare us away. So, he just keeps his distance."

"But I'm sure they're in love with Weston, right? He's their first grandchild."

The flip-flop bobbed even faster. "They love Weston. Even my daddy does. But Kyle..." Addie shook her head. "Daddy won't speak to him. My momma is a little friendlier, but not much."

Addie sounded disappointed, as if living a normal life wasn't turning out to be everything she'd hoped it would be. She no longer had to fear the Task Force or having Weston taken away from her, but it seemed like she'd exchanged one form of imprisonment for another.

The question slipped through Gemma's lips. "Do you regret it?"

Addie gave her a hard look. "Regret what?"

"Renouncing."

The flip-flop stopped bobbing up and down, and Addie's face grew red. "I hid from the government for years, Gemma, and I delivered my first baby in a disgusting, bug-infested cabin. I almost lost my husband and my baby to the Task Force *on the same day.* Yes, I stood in front of those cameras, and I lied to the world about my faith. But God knows my heart. He knows I lied to protect my family." She slid forward in her chair. "Do you think I'm going to hell for renouncing?"

"Absolutely not! I don't think that at all. I'm just curious how you're doing."

Addie's expression relaxed a little. "Renouncing was the best thing for our family, Gem. Did I want to do it? Of course not. But when people you love are in danger, there's just no other choice."

Gemma nodded, unsure of what else to say. She looked to Weston for inspiration, and he offered her a toothy grin, bubbles oozing from the corners of his lips. Then, he grabbed a fistful of her hair and pulled it toward his mouth.

Addie sprang out of her seat and gently freed Gemma's hair from Weston's vise-like grip. Then, she held out her arms for the baby. "No, honey. We don't know where Auntie Gemma's hair has been."

After she surrendered Weston to his mother, Gemma realized her forearm was damp. "He's very wet, isn't he? He's a very damp child."

Addie rolled her eyes. "First, he's teething. And two hours strapped into a car seat took care of the other end." With Weston balanced on one arm, she gestured at the diaper bag. "Could you grab me the changing pad and a diaper? This little stinker is soggier than a wet-bottom shoofly pie."

Eager to leave the renunciation conversation behind her, Gemma dug into the cow-covered diaper bag, retrieved the items, and handed them to Addie. Then, she leaned against a bookshelf and watched as Addie undid the buttons lining the inner thighs of his denim jumpsuit to reveal the most water-logged diaper Gemma had ever seen.

"He isn't potty-trained yet?"

Addie pulled the diaper out from under Weston's bottom,

rolled it into a tight little ball, and secured it with its own tape. "He's nine months old, Gem, *and* he's a boy. I'll count myself lucky if he's potty-trained by middle school." She held the balled-up diaper out to Gemma. "Here."

Gemma took a step away from the soggy diaper. "What am I supposed to do with it?"

"You could have it bronzed for posterity, but I'd recommend just throwing it away."

Reluctantly, Gemma took the still-warm diaper from Addie and rushed down the hallway to the restroom, holding the diaper out in front of her the entire way. She tossed it into the trashcan and made a mental note to empty the trash before she went upstairs for the evening.

Returning to the front of the store, she found Addie re-buttoning Weston's pants. Only then did she notice that her best friend's fingernails were no longer chewed down to the quick, as they'd been the last time Gemma had seen them. Now, they were freshly manicured and painted a pale blue. Gemma cast a self-conscious glance at her own stubby fingernails, which had seen no nail polish in years.

"So, did Kyle know you were coming to see me today?"

"I didn't mention it to him," Addie said, shaking her head. "He wouldn't have wanted me to come. My momma and daddy wouldn't have liked it much either, so I just told them that Weston and I were going to run a few errands this afternoon. Momma's making chicken and waffles tonight at six, so I should leave here by four."

"Four?" Gemma's eyes dropped to her watch. "That's in twenty minutes! Why would you drive all this way just to turn around and go home? And what about Sophia? She'll be devastated if she doesn't get to see both of you."

"Then don't tell her." Addie's voice was flat and unemotional. She put Weston on all fours in the center aisle while she folded up the blanket and stuffed it back into the diaper bag. The baby rocked back and forth like a car revving its engine, a line of drool plummeting from his mouth to the wood floor. "But I'm not staying. I only drove up here to find out what you're going to do now—after last night."

"Last night? What are you talking about?"

"You haven't heard? Don't you watch the news?"

Suddenly, Gemma wished Addie hadn't come to visit, because something bad was about to happen. She could feel it in her bones, like an approaching storm. "What happened last night?"

After Addie finished zipping up the diaper bag, she removed a cell phone from one of the bag's side pockets and swiped with her index finger until a video appeared on the screen.

"Watch this," Addie said, handing the phone to Gemma.

And then she hit play.

✝

The Elevation Bombing.

That was what the news was calling it.

Gemma watched the report with one hand clasped over her mouth, partly because she couldn't believe what she was seeing and partly because she thought she might be sick. She'd thought the worst was over when Ogden got shot. That had been bad enough. But she never could've prepared herself for what happened next.

"Tragically, those audience members who escaped the auditorium had no way of knowing they were rushing into a trap."

Footage shot from various outdoor security cameras showed a delivery truck parking in front of the building's main entrance at exactly nine minutes after seven. At seven-fifteen, approximately the same time the masked woman was shooting David Ogden, two men got out of the delivery truck and casually strolled away.

"Both men wore masks that covered most of their faces. Also, like the female shooter, they wore upside-down Federal Task Force patches on the shoulders of their uniforms."

When the delivery truck exploded, hundreds of Ogden's followers had already made it outside of the building. A stillshot of Elevation's exterior showed the aftermath: the powerful blast had blown out most of the front windows and caused a partial collapse of that section of the building.

"The resulting explosion claimed the lives of forty-seven people. Countless others remain in the hospital with shrapnel injuries. Miraculously, David Ogden appears to have survived the assassination attempt. As of this morning, he remains hospitalized in stable condition with a single bullet wound to the right shoulder."

Addie reached across Gemma's body to pause the video. "We don't have to watch the rest. I can just give you the highlights."

"I can take it."

Addie didn't look so sure, but she hit play.

"According to early reports, no one has claimed responsibility for the bombing, but government officials suspect that the individuals responsible are part of a group of militant subversives. The proximity of last night's bombing to the Pennsylvania compliance office that was attacked by subversive extremists last fall suggests that the same group orchestrated both attacks. Sources confirm that high-ranking members from both parties of Congress will be in closed-door meetings with the president today to discuss how best to deal with this growing subversive threat."

Those words echoed through Gemma's head. *Closed-door meetings. Growing subversive threat.*

"Turn it off," she whispered. "Please. Turn it off."

Addie turned off the phone and slipped it inside her diaper bag. "So? What are you going to do now?"

"What do you expect me to do?"

When Addie bent over to pick up the diaper bag, her hair fell into her face, and Weston grabbed a handful and stuffed it inside his mouth. Addie didn't bother to stop him. "Many people are dead, Gemma. I know it wasn't you who shot David Ogden, but the girl was obviously trying to look like you. Why would someone do that?"

The answer was obvious. "To frame me."

"Exactly. Things were bad enough before, but imagine what might come your way now. Unless..."

"Unless what?" Gemma asked, twirling the chain of her cross necklace around her fingers.

"Unless you turn yourself in right now. Tell them you had nothing to do with it. And then renounce."

A soft scraping sound came from overhead. Probably a low-hanging branch scratching the roof or a bird's wings flapping against one of the front windows. Birds flew into those windows all the time. But Gemma's eyes darted to the massive bookshelves on either side of the center aisle. She imagined them slowly inching their way across the wood floor, moving a little closer whenever she looked away, intending to trap her and crush her.

"But I had nothing to do with the bombing," Gemma protested. "If I turn myself in and renounce, I'm only going to look guiltier. Even if I thought they'd believe me, I can't turn myself in because I could never renounce."

Addie tugged her wet hair out of Weston's mouth, but he snagged it and pulled it back in. "The Task Force is coming for you, Gemma. It's not a matter of *if* but *when.* And these people..." She gestured over her shoulder at the front door, and, beyond that, the town. "I know they protected you after your little stunt at the compliance office, but they will not protect you forever. You're going to become too much of a liability."

No. That wasn't true. The people of Winter's Dam would never turn her in. Not only because they were decent people, but because turning her in would expose them as sympathizers. How would the residents of the town explain all the subversives who were currently hiding in their attics, spare bedrooms, and basements?

"You don't understand, Addie. These people are in as deep as I am."

"No, they're not!" Addie cried, startling Weston, who released her hair and whimpered. "Don't you see what's happening? Don't you feel the noose tightening around your neck? I'm not even in your position anymore, and I can still feel it. This isn't a fight you can win, Gemma. The world isn't going to just wake up one day and realize that Christians aren't the enemy. You've been lucky so far, but eventually, your luck is going to run out. And on that day, you're going to realize that you're not fighting the good fight. You're fighting a losing battle."

Weston's whimpers gave way to angry howls, and when Addie bounced him up and down on her hip to quiet him, he only screamed louder. He'd gone from perfectly content to a full-blown meltdown in a matter of seconds.

He was his mother's son.

"Come on, baby. It's spritzing outside. We better get home."

Gemma glanced at the store's front windows and saw that it was raining.

Addie slung her diaper bag over her shoulder and headed for the front door. "I hope you make the right decision, Gem. I'll be praying for you."

"Thank you for coming to see me," Gemma called after her. She meant it, despite how the visit was ending. "Take care of that little boy. And tell Kyle I miss him, too."

Addie paused, one hand on the doorknob, and turned to face Gemma. "My granddaddy used to have a saying, and I think it applies in this situation. He used to say, 'When a person slaps you on the back, he might be trying to help you swallow something.'"

With that final parting blow, she left the bookstore.

Sadness expanded inside Gemma's chest, inflating like a balloon until she had to grab onto the nearest bookshelf to keep herself upright. She hadn't felt so hopeless since the Task Force had ripped Taylor out of her life. Even when Addie and Kyle had left their group to renounce, Gemma had mourned their loss but accepted it.

But this was something entirely different. This felt final. Like it might very well be the last time she ever saw her best friend. Because as much as Gemma wanted to believe that it was nothing more than saying the words necessary to survive, renouncing had changed Addie into a person she hardly recognized.

And something greater than distance separated them now.

CHAPTER THREE

Max and Brie knew about the bombing.

Gemma saw it on their faces the moment they walked into the apartment in their red-stained clothing. But they said nothing. Not in front of Sophia. Likewise, Gemma didn't mention Addie's visit and hasty departure. She hadn't decided whether to tell Max and Brie, but she definitely would not tell Sophia. The girl would be devastated if she knew she'd missed a chance to see Weston.

At five-thirty, they gathered around the kitchen table and consumed a bland dinner of baked chicken and rice in near-perfect silence. Even Sophia was quieter than usual. Despite not being around other kids her own age, Sophia enjoyed school, and she seemed to thrive in Winter's Dam. She rarely talked about her mother anymore, and she never mentioned the Station or the Sanctuary.

When Gemma couldn't take the silence any longer, she said, "So, how was your day, Soph? Did you learn anything interesting?"

Sophia used her index finger to push rice onto her fork and then shoveled the bite into her mouth. "We talked about World

War II today," she said, meeting Gemma's eyes for the first time. "About how Adolph Hitler came to power in Germany. Mrs. Sherman said he took over the media first, which made it possible for him to control everything that was being said about him, good or bad. If anyone disagreed with him, he shut them down—or worse. He didn't want the German people thinking for themselves. He wanted to *tell* them how to think."

Gemma glanced at Max and Brie, who both looked equally uncomfortable with the conversation. Brie put her fork down and took a long sip of water, while Max pushed a piece of chicken around his plate.

"He also released films about how terrible the Jews were," Sophia continued. "How they needed to be exterminated in order for Germany to succeed. One film compared them to rats. So, that was how the people saw the Jews...as disease-carrying rats who needed to die. By telling those lies about the Jews, Hitler was able to kill six million of them before the good guys stopped him. And I just...I can't stop thinking about something Mrs. Sherman said."

When Gemma couldn't bring herself to speak, Max took over.

"What did she say, Soph?"

Even though she'd only eaten half of her dinner, Sophia put her fork down and pushed her plate away. Then, she wrapped her hand around the glow stick she still wore around her neck. "She said that history has a way of repeating itself. That if something worked once, eventually someone will try it again. They'll change it up a little, so it's not obvious what they're doing. But it'll still be the same evil, just wearing new clothes."

Max looked to Brie for help, but instead of jumping in, she grabbed her knife and cut her bite-sized chicken chunks into even smaller pieces. "That's probably true," he finally said.

"But what if someone tries to do that to us?" Sophia demanded, looking at Max with pleading eyes. "What if someone like Hitler tries to convince the world that Christians need to be killed and not just locked up forever in detention centers? Do you think people would go along with it? They would, wouldn't they?"

A loud clang came from the white box on the wall above the stairway, startling them all.

Someone was ringing the doorbell to the bookstore.

Max shot out of his seat and jogged over to the closet. He grabbed the revolver from underneath a blanket on the top shelf, tucked it inside his waistband, and disappeared downstairs.

Mullen, Gemma thought.

But it couldn't have been him, because Mullen was dead. She'd heard about his death on the news a few weeks after she and Sophia had escaped from the mine. A local hunter had found Mullen's abandoned pickup parked on the old access road near the lookout tower on Dragon's Back Mountain. When the police ran the plates, they'd discovered that the truck was registered to a Task Force soldier who'd gone AWOL two weeks earlier. A subsequent search of the mountain led them to the collapsed entrance of the mine. One of the police officers had a father who used to be employed as a tour guide at the mine, and he knew about the location of the emergency egress ladder.

Two days later, they'd pulled Mullen's body out of the vertical shaft known as the Wishing Well. The fall had broken almost every bone in his body, but somehow, he'd survived it. The medical examiner had listed Mullen's official cause of death as dehydration, and he'd estimated that the Task Force soldier had survived for at least two days at the bottom of that shaft, unable to move.

It had given Gemma no satisfaction to learn that Mullen's death had been pure agony. Even someone as awful as him didn't deserve to die like that.

Gavin appeared at the top of the stairs, trailing behind Max like an afterthought. When he saw them gathered at the dinner table, he quickly removed the Phillies ball cap from his head and held it in front of his stomach. He'd cut his hair short, so it appeared much darker than the blondish-brown mop to which she'd grown accustomed, and he'd put on at least twenty pounds —most of it muscle—since moving in with Teresa and her father.

It angered Gemma to see Gavin looking so good. So healthy.

Max returned to his spot at the table. "You hungry, buddy? You want some chicken and rice?"

"No, I'm not hungry at all," he said, glancing uneasily around the tiny apartment, looking everywhere but at Gemma. "I had a really late lunch. They've been keeping me pretty busy at the store."

Gemma took a sip of water and set the glass on the table with a purposeful thump. "How's Teresa? Is she keeping you busy, too?"

For the first time, Gavin's gaze fell upon Gemma. Anger burned within those green eyes of his, but there was something else there, too.

Guilt.

"Teresa's good," he replied, crushing his ball cap in his hands. "She wanted me to find out if you guys need anything. Are you still good on supplies?"

"We're fine."

Gemma stared at him, drilling him with her eyes, searching for the truth he kept so well hidden from her. But what she *really* wanted to do was scream at him, to demand that he admit what had really happened back at the high school when he'd left Taylor behind.

Gavin had claimed that he'd closed the door to the tunnel because the Task Force was coming. That holding it open for another second would've compromised their entire mission.

But Gemma *knew* he was lying. She saw the truth in his eyes every time he looked at her. As a Christian, it was her responsibility to forgive him. She understood that. But how could she forgive someone who refused to admit what he'd done?

A heavy silence settled over the room like a weighted blanket.

Finally, Sophia began to gather the empty plates. "Should I do the dishes?"

"We'll do them together later." Gemma patted her on the arm. "Why don't you go to the bedroom and read for a few minutes? I think Gavin has something he wants to tell us."

Sophia's body tensed, and some of the color left her face. "Why don't you want me to hear?" The girl had experienced so much trauma in her life. Now, whenever adults asked her to leave a room, she knew it meant something bad.

Gemma would not lie to the girl, but she also didn't want Sophia to worry—not until there was something to worry about. "Something happened yesterday that might affect us. I promise I'll tell you about it later tonight, when we're doing the dishes. But I just need you to give us a few minutes to figure things out."

Although she still looked worried, Sophia seemed satisfied with this answer. With a quick nod, she padded down the hallway to the bedroom she shared with Gemma.

After Sophia closed the bedroom door, Brie turned to Gavin. "Please just sit. You're making me nervous."

But the only available chair at the table was Sophia's empty seat, which was right next to Gemma.

The pained expression on Gavin's face suggested he would've preferred the cold floor to being forced into such close proximity with his ex-girlfriend, but he stepped toward the table. As he lowered himself into the chair, Gemma leaned away from him and crossed her arms, trying to put as much distance between them as possible.

Max folded his hands in front of him, his expression serious.

The jagged scar on the left side of his face was fading, but if the cries that echoed from his room at night were any indication, his memories of being a prisoner of the Task Force were as vivid as ever. "I take it everyone heard about the bombing."

Gavin nodded. "It's all Teresa's dad could talk about. Obviously, he's worried about what this means for the town. Whoever did this is obviously trying to frame us."

"Not us," Gemma interrupted. "*Me*. They're trying to frame me." She pushed away from the table and stood, banging her knee against one of table legs hard enough to make the glasses rattle and her eyes water. She grabbed her half-empty plate and retreated to the kitchen, where she hovered over the stainless-steel sink, her eyes dropping to the emerald engagement ring on her left hand.

Her heart ached for Taylor. Every part of her ached for Taylor.

Seeing Gavin only reminded her how much she missed him.

"I'm sorry, Gemma." Gavin's voice drifted to her from the other side of the room. "I know how you must feel."

She dropped her plate into the sink, where it broke into three large pieces.

"Don't."

"Don't what?"

Gemma whipped around so fast that he shrank away from her. "Don't say you know how this feels. You don't know how this feels."

He lowered his eyes to the floor and said nothing.

But Brie and Max continued to watch her, as if they knew she was about to drop another bomb on them. So she did.

"Addie thinks I should turn myself in."

Max's eyebrows bunched together. "You talked to Addie?"

Casting a glance toward the closed bedroom door, Gemma lowered her voice. "She stopped by the bookstore this afternoon. She brought Weston with her. Apparently, no one knows she came to see me—not her parents or Kyle. She said they wouldn't have approved."

Her eyes traveled from one face to the next, and all of them —including Gavin—were looking at her in disbelief. Slowly, the disbelief gave way to hurt. None of them had seen Addie in months. They probably hadn't expected to ever see her again.

"I don't get it." Brie shook her head. "She and Kyle left right after the Task Force raided the Sanctuary. How did she know where to find you?"

Leaning against the sink, Gemma bowed her head and forced the confession from her lips. "I called her. This was months ago now. Her mother answered. When I asked to speak with Addie, her mother sounded really suspicious. She wanted to know who I was. I couldn't tell her the truth, obviously, but I knew her caller ID would show the bookstore's number, so I pretended to be Letty. I just started babbling about how Addie had recently ordered a book online from my store and that I needed to talk to her about a problem with the order."

Gavin dropped his head into his hands. "Gemma, I can't believe you called her. Do you know how big of a risk that was? What if Addie's mother had looked the bookstore up on the internet and came across Letty's obituary?"

"But she *didn't.* She believed me, and she put me on with Addie. We didn't talk very long. I told her about Letty because I thought she had a right to know, and then I told her I'd decided to stay at the bookstore to help any other Christians who might show up. She didn't say much in response. Just a lot of one-word answers. I think her mom was in the room. But I just wanted Addie to know where we would be, in case—"

"In case what?" Brie demanded, her face turning crimson. "In case she decided that life on the run with us is better than life on the farm with Ma and Pa Kettle? Don't be stupid, Gemma. I mean, did you honestly think she was going to come back after everything that's happened?"

"She came back today."

"And yet she's not dining with us tonight."

"But she couldn't stay," Gemma offered weakly. "Her family was expecting her home at a certain time. Plus, our conversation didn't end on a pleasant note. I upset her when I said I wouldn't consider turning myself in and renouncing. She thinks the people in town are going to turn on us."

"She's got a point," Max said, speaking up for the first time. "Don't get me wrong, I love living here, but at some point, we're going to have to accept that we can't stay forever. I'm not saying we should renounce, but we can't stay in Winter's Dam much longer. Bad things happen when we overstay our welcome."

"I agree," Brie said. "We've already been here too long. All we're doing by staying is putting these people in more danger."

Gavin brought a hand to his temple. "No way. You guys can do what you want, but I'm *not* leaving. Not when I have nowhere to go and every reason to stay. Whatever happens to me from now on is up to God, but I'm not leaving." Then, as if that settled the matter, he stood up, popped his hat on his head, and walked toward the stairway.

The sound of his footsteps faded as he disappeared downstairs.

Max spread his hands on the table, palms up. "So, Addie thinks we should turn ourselves in and renounce. Brie and I think we should leave Winter's Dam before the Task Force finds us. And Gavin thinks we should stay forever." He turned his attention to Gemma, who still hadn't moved from her spot at the sink. "What do you think?"

"I think we need to stay." Gemma felt the truth of the words as soon as they left her lips. "Christians are going to keep showing up. Someone needs to be here for them."

"Even if that means endangering everyone in this town?" Brie asked in a soft voice.

In that moment, God brought the sun-scorched face of

Taren Bowler to Gemma's mind. The young woman in over-sized clothing, with a fist-sized knot in her hair, clutching a well-worn copy of *Wuthering Heights* against her chest.

"I'm sorry," she said. "You guys need to do what's best for you. But I can't leave. Not as long as the bookstore is standing."

Later, after Brie and Max went to bed, Gemma called Sophia to the kitchen to wash the dishes. Then, she explained—in the best way she could—about the Elevation bombing and what it might mean for their group. Without hesitation, Sophia agreed they should stay in Winter's Dam, whatever the consequences.

"People need our help," she said, accepting a wet plate from Gemma and using a dishrag to wipe off the soapsuds. "Besides, I like it here. It feels like home."

Later, when Gemma crawled into the queen-sized bed she shared with Sophia, she lay awake for hours, staring at the back of the girl's head. Fiery-red curls spilled across her pillow, and the streetlight outside the window cast its glow on Sophia, illuminating her like some kind of slumbering princess who'd fallen under the spell of an evil sorcerer. A spell which would keep her imprisoned inside a lonely tower for the rest of her days.

Only, in this fairy tale, there was no Prince Charming.

No one was coming to rescue her.

Help me, Father, Gemma prayed. *One day, help me break the spell.*

She rolled away from Sophia and closed her eyes. One hand drifted up to clutch the silver cross that hung over her heart.

Help me set her free.

CHAPTER FOUR

Tearing his eyes away from the anchors of *The Today Show*, David Ogden used his uninjured arm to grab the glass of freshly squeezed orange juice from his bedside tray. Bringing the juice to his lips, he winced as the stringy liquid slid down his throat and settled in his stomach with the rest of his subpar breakfast.

Not cold enough, he decided, settling back into his stack of pillows. *And way too much pulp.*

Despite her supposed years of experience working with celebrities like himself, Ogden's recently hired personal chef—an obese woman named Esther with a military-style buzz cut—still hadn't mastered the art of properly juicing an orange. Nor had she learned how to make over-easy eggs that didn't leave snail-trails of slime on his plate. He could've gotten a better breakfast from any of the greasy spoons in downtown Harrisburg.

The half-eaten tray of food sat next to him on the bed, a visible memorial to an extremely disappointing morning. He'd consumed the bacon (not crispy enough) and the whole-wheat toast (slightly stale, too much butter), but the eggs remained on the plate, the yellow-orange gobs of coagulated yolk contrasting with his stark-white comforter. The sight made him want to gag, and he momentarily considered overturning the tray on the bed just to make a point. A childish tantrum, to be sure, but he could always claim it was an accident. He was still recovering from a gunshot wound to the shoulder, after all.

But overturning the tray wouldn't punish Esther; it would punish Lucy, his thin and energetic housekeeper. Lucy would be the one to spend the rest of her day sweating in the stuffy laundry room, struggling with various stain removers in a futile effort to get the yolk stains out of the comforter, while Esther lumbered around the kitchen without a care in the world, undoubtedly plotting new and ingenious ways to destroy Ogden's favorite meals.

With a heavy sigh, he picked up the remote, aimed it at the flat screen on the wall, and switched off the television, making Al Roker disappear in the middle of his weather report.

The lousy breakfast wasn't the only thing upsetting him today.

The morning news had said nothing about the bombing.

The evening news had said nothing last night, either. There'd been no discussion of Ogden's recovery from his gunshot wound. No interviews with survivors of the attack, breathlessly describing what they'd seen and heard in those crucial moments before the bomb exploded. No emotional profiles of the victims and their families. No debate about the government's response—or lack thereof—to the escalating threat posed by subversives. And no update on the ongoing repairs to Elevation Ministry Center.

Absolutely nothing.

Less than a month had passed since the bombing, and yet the country had already moved on, and that just would not work for Ogden.

The phone on his bedside table rang, a blaring intrusion into his morning. His first instinct was to hurl it across the room, but someone would come running, and he had an image to uphold. So, he leaned across his breakfast tray to grab the telephone, and in doing so, sent a stream of orange juice sloshing over the rim of the cup and onto his breakfast tray.

Thankfully for Lucy, none of it got on the comforter.

He brought the phone to his lips. "Yes?"

"Mr. Ogden?"

It was Tim Levins, his head of security. Ogden recognized the hoarse voice. Levins always sounded like he needed to clear his throat. He used to be an MMA fighter, and Ogden wondered if maybe the guy hadn't sustained some damage to his vocal cords back in his fighting days. But Levins had a neck like a tree trunk and knew how to keep his mouth shut, which were two things Ogden looked for when selecting his personal security detail.

"Ms. Grimes is here to see you," Levins continued, his voice like a tire driving over gravel. "Should I send her up?"

For the first time that day, Ogden felt like smiling.

"Yes, Tim," he replied, pushing his tray out of the way. "Please send her up."

Two minutes later, Lydia Grimes—Director of the Federal Bureau of Compliance and one of the most immoral women Ogden had ever known—breezed into his bedroom without knocking. Lydia was used to being one of the most important people in any room, so she didn't trouble herself with such frivolities as respectfulness and manners.

Although Grimes was attractive and unmarried, Ogden had never slept with her. She was older than he preferred—somewhere in her mid-forties, if he had to guess—but she clearly took pride in her appearance and worked out regularly. In the few years they'd known each other, Ogden had gotten the impression that Grimes was waiting for him to make a move on her. But he'd never done it. He couldn't say why, exactly. Only that there was something about the woman that just didn't sit right with him. Something obscene lurked behind those mud-colored eyes of hers. Something that frightened even him.

"Your security staff confiscated my bag, David," Grimes said, settling into the armchair closest to his bed and tucking a strand of caramel-colored hair behind one ear. "Do those goons of yours really think I'm going to sneak a gun in here and assassinate you?"

He gestured to the sling on his left arm. "Stranger things have happened, Lyds."

"Don't call me that, David. You know I hate that. I want my bag back."

"Relax. I'll take care of it."

He picked up the phone and punched in the number for his personal assistant, Tara Wilkinson. It was the only number he knew by heart.

She answered on the first ring. "Yes, Mr. Ogden?"

"Tara, I apologize for bothering you, but Lydia Grimes is visiting me this morning, and it appears that Tim Levins—in an overabundance of caution—took possession of her bag. Could you retrieve the bag from Tim and bring it up here promptly?"

"Yes, sir. I'll bring it right up."

"If Tim has questions, just have him call my room."

"Yes, sir."

He hung up the phone and gazed at Grimes, waiting for her to announce the true reason for her visit. She certainly hadn't driven all the way from Washington to Harrisburg because she was worried about his recovery. Grimes wouldn't have batted one of her fake eyelashes if the redhead's bullet had missed its mark and hit him squarely in the heart instead of the shoulder. In fact, she probably would've enjoyed it if he'd bled out and died on camera with the entire nation watching. That sort of public tragedy would've absolutely thrilled a contemptible woman like Lydia Grimes.

A wisp of a smile perched on her crimson lips. The woman rarely smiled, and Ogden had never seen her teeth. He wasn't sure she actually *had* teeth, but if she did, they were probably fangs dripping with blood.

"Why are you looking at me like that, David?" she asked, demurely crossing her slender legs in a ridiculous attempt to toy with him. "Like I'm a puzzle you're trying to solve."

"Oh, Lydia. You're a puzzle I solved long ago."

He couldn't help himself. The woman was like a viper lurking in tall grass, but she was still beautiful, and flirting was in Ogden's nature. "I was hoping maybe you'd driven all the way up here to bring me flowers. Or did Tim confiscate those, too?"

Her laughter emerged as a soft hiss, like air slowly leaking out of a balloon. "I don't bring men flowers. Men bring *me* flowers."

"Of course. How radically feminist of me."

Grimes uncrossed her legs and leaned forward in her chair, hands clasped on her lap. Her V-necked blouse dipped low, but not low enough to give Ogden a glimpse of anything interesting. "I had my driver take me by Elevation on my way here. The repairs are coming along nicely. It's crazy what little damage was actually done to the building itself," she said, a mischievous glint in her eyes.

This was one reason Ogden hated dealing with Grimes. This game she insisted on playing, where she didn't break character. It made him think Grimes didn't trust him any more than he trusted her.

"That's because of the truck's location when it blew. The structural damage to the building was minimal. Most of the issues were cosmetic. Easily fixable. All in all, I'd say we were very lucky."

The woman raised a hand to her neck, as if to clutch at pearls that weren't there. "Lucky? Forty-seven people are dead, David. I'd hardly call that lucky."

Give the woman an Oscar.

"You know what I mean, Lydia. The whole situation is tragic, of course." He pointed to his left shoulder. "Just look at me. A little farther to the right and I wouldn't be sitting here right now."

"Yes, well..." She waved him away as if he was being silly for bringing up his own injury. "Thankfully, your would-be assassin wasn't a very good shot. Perhaps all the lights and cameras threw her off?"

"Perhaps."

But the auburn-haired woman *had* been an excellent shot. The bullet had hit its target exactly as intended, and Lydia Grimes knew it. After all, it was Grimes who'd hand-picked the woman for the task. Ogden knew nothing about the identity of the female shooter, except that she was a soldier in the Task Force, she'd qualified as a sharpshooter, and she'd performed extraordinarily well on several highly classified operations.

The only problem? She was a natural blonde.

But a little hair dye had fixed that right up.

"So, when do you think you'll be ready to return to the stage?" Grimes asked, a little too eagerly.

He stretched his right arm across his chest to an itch on the left side of his neck. "As soon as I can, but I will not rush it. I don't want to broadcast my comeback show from some temporary location. That's why I've got my people working hard on the repairs. I need to get back out there, Lydia. On *my* stage. The country needs me."

"Oh, David," she said, her voice dripping sarcasm. "I question how our nation has survived this past month without your bottomless wisdom."

Anger coursed through Ogden's veins, and it took every ounce of self-control he possessed to keep his mouth shut. How dare this vile woman come into his house and speak to him in such a disrespectful manner? As if he was just some moron—

some dilettante—she was dragging along for the ride. *He'd* been the one to sacrifice here. *He'd* taken a bullet in the shoulder. *He'd* watched his building go up in smoke.

All in the name of progress.

Meanwhile, Grimes had sacrificed nothing. She hadn't even gotten her nails dirty.

He was opening his mouth to say exactly that when a tentative knock on his bedroom door interrupted the tense silence, preventing Ogden from saying something he'd regret. "Come in," he grumbled.

The door swung open, and Ogden's assistant, Tara, entered the bedroom, her sensible pumps sinking into the plush gray carpeting. The combination of freesia-scented body wash and lemon cough drops accompanied her into the room. She carried Lydia Grimes's leather satchel in her right hand.

"Here you are, Director Grimes," Tara said, her ugly locket dangling from her neck as she gave Grimes a respectful little bow. "I apologize for any inconvenience."

"It's about time." Grimes snatched the bag away from Tara and opened it up, as if checking to make sure nothing had been stolen. "What on earth took so long?"

A single strand of brown hair had broken free from Tara's signature ballerina bun, and she reached up and nervously tucked it behind her ear. "I apologize for the delay, Ms. Grimes." Although the delay was likely the fault of Ogden's security guys, it wasn't Tara's nature to throw anyone under the bus. So, she skillfully changed the subject. "Is there anything else I can get for you? A glass of water, perhaps? Or some coffee?"

Grimes gave her a hard stare. "You can disappear."

With a quick nod, Tara backed out of the room and closed the door behind her.

Ogden rolled his eyes. "Lydia, why do you have to be such a—"

"Careful, David," she cut him off, reaching into her satchel and pulling out a MacBook Pro. "That's no way to talk to the woman who's single-handedly turning you into a cultural icon."

Hearing Grimes refer to him as a cultural icon didn't give Ogden the warm, fuzzy feeling he would've expected. Instead, it made him feel like a dog sitting at its owner's feet, waiting for a bone that might never come. "That sounds wonderful, but how can you expect me to trust you? You're not known for playing nice."

That same unsettling, hissing laugh burst from her lips again. This time, it made Ogden think of steam coming out of a volcano. "Of course I don't play nice. You don't get to positions like mine—especially as a woman—by playing nice. But you can trust me, David. You and I work well together because we share a similar vision for this country."

"Yes, but my vision is very self-centered, Lydia."

"So is mine." Grimes crossed her legs again, but this time, there was nothing sensual behind the movement. Now, she was all business. "The current administration has proven itself to be too wishy-washy, too unwilling to take a hardline stance against the subversive threat. The events of the past few months have forced our president to step outside of his comfort zone regarding dealing with subversives, but it still hasn't been enough to quell the tide. Every month since that redhead and her friends raided the compliance office, renunciation numbers have continued to fall, and those appalling resistance symbols keep popping up in new places. A week ago, we found one on the sidewalk in front of the Capitol, for goodness' sakes! We're losing control. It's ingrained in our DNA as humans to follow strength, not weakness, and the public clearly perceives our government as weak. I'm a member of that government, David, and I'm many things, but I'm *not* weak."

Ogden pursed his lips thoughtfully. He knew exactly where Grimes was going with this speech because he'd heard it almost verbatim the first time she visited him two months earlier. But if she needed to get it out again, to rationalize what she wanted to do, then he would sit back and listen and nod encouragingly in all the right places. Because while Grimes thought she was playing him, he'd been playing her from the very beginning. Playing her like a fiddle.

"Can we drop the act, Lyds? It's just you and me here. Can't we stop with all this business talk and enjoy our victory? I think we've earned a celebration."

She gave him a wicked grin. "How should we celebrate, David?"

"Oh, I have a few ideas," he teased, swallowing back the bile that rose into his throat at the thought of being physical with this loathsome woman. "But we should probably keep our meetings G-rated until I've fully recovered."

Grimes stuck out her lower lip in a fake pout. "I suppose I can wait," she said with a wink. "To be honest, David, you've really impressed me over the past few weeks. There was so much that could've gone wrong with the bombing, and the risk of it being traced back to us was huge. But you executed everything perfectly. When you suggested taking a bullet in the shoulder, I thought you were crazy. I thought the bomb would be more than enough to accomplish our mission, and I saw no need for you to take such a personal risk. But you were right. That bullet turned you into a hero. Everyone loves you now. And do you want to hear the best part? Those forty-seven deaths have forced the president to act. Four days ago, he signed an executive order giving the Bureau of Compliance full authority to move forward with the next stage of our plan."

"Which is?"

Her lips parted, giving Ogden a glimpse of the twin sharp points of her incisors. Maybe the woman really was part vampire. "The unbindings began yesterday."

Ogden barked out a laugh. Laughter was inappropriate,

given the circumstances, but the whole thing was utterly ridiculous. "Unbindings? Is that really what you're calling them?"

"Laugh all you want, David, but language is very important in this situation. Public opinion is like a rubber band. Stretch it too far, and it snaps. You don't give the public the chance to decide for themselves if something is good or bad, moral or immoral. Most of them are too stupid to make those kinds of decisions. *Tell* them how to feel about it. Put it on a pretty little plate and feed it to them. You, of all people, should know that. Hasn't your entire career been built around telling little spineless jellyfish you call worshippers what to think?"

He ignored the insult, mainly because it was true. "But unbindings? That's how you've chosen to describe the execution of thousands of subversive detainees?"

"They're...not...being...executed," Grimes said slowly, as if speaking to a child. "They're being *unbound* from the dangerous religious views they refuse to give up. We also considered calling them liberations, but that seemed a little too on-the-nose, even for us. The only way to rid this country of the plague of Christianity once and for all is to capture all the roaches and kill them. All of that bloodshed might make your tummy hurt, but it's what needs to happen. When you're fighting an infection in the body, you eradicate it. You annihilate it. You don't allow little pockets of infection to grow and thrive because then the infection never really goes away. If left unchecked, a tiny little pocket of infection will destroy the whole body."

"And by pockets of infection, you're referring to the detention centers."

"Precisely," Grimes replied. "Ultimately, the roaches are being set free, which is what they want. If the public had any idea what those detention centers are really like, they would understand. I've been inside them, David. I've heard roaches in their cells, begging for death. Believe me when I tell you, we're showing them mercy by killing them."

"Lydia, I didn't know you cared so much about the roaches. How humanitarian of you. Remind me to nominate you for the Nobel Peace Prize."

"You're teasing, but I wouldn't be surprised if I get nominated." She gave him a little wink and flipped open her laptop. "Convincing the president that the unbindings were necessary was hard enough. Convincing the public will be even harder. The unbindings will continue no matter what, but in the long run, we're going to need the public on our side. That's where you come in. I need you back on the air ASAP. Because of the attack, the entire nation will tune in for your comeback broadcast. We have to make it spectacular. Something that will have people cheering and crying at the same time."

"You're not going to blow up my building again, are you?"

Grimes met his gaze over the top of her laptop, her eyes darkening with something akin to hunger. "Not unless you don't make good on your promise to me," she said. "When you're all healed up, we're going to have a *proper* celebration."

He smiled. "I wouldn't miss it for the world."

The MacBook remained on Grimes's lap, but she angled it so he could see the screen. "This was filmed yesterday at a detention center outside of Los Angeles. This center is the first of its kind to open in California and the first in the nation to begin the unbindings. As you watch the video, I think you'll agree that these unbindings are being accomplished with great care and compassion for the roaches—more than they deserve, in fact."

Ogden didn't want to watch the video, not because he cared about the subversives—he didn't—but because there was something distinctly unpleasant about *watching* the executions (try as he might, he could never think of them as *unbindings*). In his mind, it was comparable to watching a veterinarian put a dog to sleep.

Yes, sometimes sick animals needed to be put out of their misery, but that didn't mean he wanted to watch it happen.

In the end, however, his curiosity won out, and his gaze dropped to the screen. The video was jerky, probably filmed on an iPhone, and showed a sterile room with a main aisle and beds lining either wall. Probably an infirmary. There were detainees in every bed, their hands and feet secured with wrist and ankle restraints. Nearly all of them were elderly.

Lydia ran a fingernail along the side of the laptop, gently stroking the metal exterior. "We're starting with anyone who's been in a detention center for more than three years and hasn't shown significant progress toward reintegration. Then, we'll continue with the people who've been detained for two years, and so on. Anyone who has been detained for less than a year *and* is showing significant progress toward rehabilitation will be granted immunity until their next report. But let me just say...very few people fall into that category."

Ogden barely registered that Grimes was speaking. Instead, he focused all of his attention on the small, balding man in a lab coat who stood in the center of the aisle between the rows of bound detainees. "Ladies and gentlemen," the man was saying, "we apologize for the restraints, but you're still prisoners of this facility, and we have a responsibility to ensure that you're not a danger to the medical staff."

A danger to the medical staff? Ogden held back a laugh. Not only were most of the people on the screen elderly, but they were all hideously thin and looked as if they might blow away in a stiff wind.

"You're in the infirmary so we can help you. We're going to be administering a shot into your arm. You might feel a slight burning sensation at the injection site, but that will subside rather quickly, and then the pain will be over."

One detainee raised his head, thin strands of bone-white hair flowing over his pillow. "What is it?" he asked. "What's in the shot?"

"As you may or may not be aware, our nation's best scientists have been working diligently to develop a treatment for your condition. After years of research, they believe they've finally discovered a cure."

Ogden arched an eyebrow at Grimes. "A vaccine for Christianity?"

She winked at him. "Just watch, David."

The man on the screen pulled at his restraints. "Please. No cure."

Other detainees followed suit, and in a matter of seconds, the quiet infirmary had descended into chaos. Detainees writhed on their beds, struggling to break free from their restraints. But most were weak from malnourishment, and their strength gave out quickly. They slumped onto their beds, hair plastered to their forehead with sweat, sucking in air in heavy, hitching gasps.

Some of the detainees' lips began to move, and although Ogden couldn't hear what they were saying, he knew exactly what they were doing.

Praying.

Moments later, a mob of orderlies and guards flooded the room, surrounding the beds and holding the detainees down as the doctor went from bed to bed, injecting shots of potassium chloride into emaciated arms, and the detainees' prayers morphed into screams.

Ogden resisted the urge to cover his ears. Those deep, guttural screams. He feared he would hear them in his nightmares for years to come. It felt as if something was stuck in his throat. He swallowed, but it was still there. "Does the injection hurt?"

Of course it hurts, you idiot, Ogden chided himself. *Just listen to them.*

Grimes held her palm up in a *Who cares?* gesture. "The potassium chloride causes quite a bit of pain at the injection site. We don't knock them out like they do for death row inmates, since it saves money doing it this way. Besides, unlike on death row, there are no squeamish civilians around to witness the unbindings, so..." Grimes let her voice trail off and gave him a little shrug. "As you can see, it's all over quickly."

On the laptop's screen, most of the detainees had gone still, heads sagging, eyes and mouths hanging open. The doctor—who only a few minutes earlier had told the detainees they would receive a cure for Christianity—walked from bed to bed, checking for vital signs and rattling off times of death for the nurses to jot down on their clipboards.

Lydia closed the laptop.

The painful lump was gone, but now Ogden's throat felt like sandpaper. "Why, Lydia?" His voice cracked, so he grabbed the cup of room-temperature orange juice from his tray and took a long swig. "Why did you tell the detainees that the shot was a cure for Christianity?"

"We wanted to see how they would react. We wanted to see if they would fight."

Ogden gaped at her. "How they would react? I could've told you how they would react! Obviously, they were going to be upset, Lydia. You've been torturing them for three years, and they haven't renounced yet. These people will never willingly give up their religion. Never."

"Which is why the unbindings are necessary."

"I'm not arguing about the unbind—oh, for Pete's sake, let's just call them what they are. Executions. I don't care if you execute the roaches, Lydia. I really don't. Kill them all, if you like. But do it humanely. Don't be a monster. I mean, do you get some perverse pleasure out of making them suffer?"

"This isn't about making them suffer. It's about preserving the future of our nation. My goal is the same as yours. We both want to rid this country of the plague of Christianity. Yes, telling the detainees it was a cure wasn't a nice thing to do, but it was just an experiment. From now on, we're going to tell them that the shot contains a mixture of essential vitamins and nutrients to supplement the food they're being given. We're going to tell them it will make them feel better. They won't have any idea what's coming. Does that make you happy?"

Ogden said nothing in response. There was nothing else to say. He desperately wanted Lydia Grimes out of his house, and it relieved him when she took the hint and packed up her things.

"We'll talk again soon," she said, rising from the chair. "Take care of that arm, David. This country needs you."

And then she quietly slipped out of his room.

Ogden sank deep into his comforter and closed his eyes.

He didn't believe in hell, but if there *was* a hell, Lydia Grimes was headed there.

Then again, he thought, just before he drifted off to sleep, *I'll be right there with her.*

CHAPTER FIVE

Balancing on Letty's old stepladder, Gemma sprayed some cleaning spray on an old rag and wiped down the top of one bookshelf. There was only about a foot of space between the top of the shelf and the ceiling, and she had to duck her head to keep from bumping it. She'd spent hours cleaning the bookstore, but it had never occurred to her to clean the tops of the shelves. Apparently, the thought hadn't occurred to Letty either because Gemma had only cleaned two shelves so far, and her rag was already filthy.

No other Christians had shown up at the bookstore since the Bowler family, nearly a month earlier. According to Mrs. Courtney, the Bowlers and their daughter, Taren, were settling nicely into their new home in the attic. Whenever they joined the Courtneys for meals, Taren always brought her copy of *Wuthering Heights* to the table.

She'd already read it three times.

Gemma rarely hung out in the bookstore in the evenings, but she couldn't take being trapped inside that tiny apartment with Brie and Max, who were both still annoyed that she refused to leave Winter's Dam. They could've gone by themselves, of course, and if the decision had been up to Brie, they probably *would've* gone. But Max wasn't willing to leave Gemma and Sophia on their own, and Gemma loved him for that.

Something drew Gemma's attention to the store's front window, and she climbed down from the stepladder and went to the door. Through the glass, she saw thousands of white flakes blowing across the highway. The temperature outside had been hovering in the mid-fifties, but her first thought was of snow. *But snow in May?* Then, she remembered the ornamental pear trees in the backyard, and she realized that the white flecks blowing around the highway weren't snowflakes at all, but white flowers. The trees had been in bloom for weeks, and Gemma hadn't been able to walk within three feet of the trees without being chased away by an army of possessive honeybees.

Feeling breathless, she ran to the stairway and called Sophia down from the apartment. They rushed into the backyard and spun in circles, their arms outstretched toward the sky, trying to capture the delicate blooms in their palms. But the wind teased them, sending the flowers pirouetting like tiny dancers over their heads, just beyond their reach, before carrying them over the roof of the bookstore.

For those few precious moments, Gemma forgot about Taylor.

The guilt immediately overwhelmed her.

When the sky grew dark, Sophia retreated to the apartment to watch cartoons, while Gemma remained outside, wandering past the lush pear trees toward the small shed at the rear of Letty's property.

Next to the shed, hidden beneath a drab-gray car cover, was Taylor's Charger.

Since parking the vehicle beside the shed back in November, Gemma hadn't driven it or so much as looked inside of it. She couldn't drive without risking being pulled over, but that wasn't the real reason she hadn't gotten behind the wheel in seven months. It was because she'd locked too many memories of Taylor inside the Charger. She couldn't even look inside the vehicle without seeing herself in the passenger seat and Taylor behind the wheel, his right arm stretched across the center console, his fingers interlaced with hers.

She hurried past the Charger and opened the door to the shed. A Toro lawnmower sat just inside the door, a dense layer of dust coating its red surface. The building also housed a variety of snow shovels, well-used gardening tools, and a pile of empty planters stacked almost to the ceiling.

In the rear corner of the shed, Gemma knelt before a canvas dropcloth and pushed the fabric aside to reveal a navy-blue backpack. *Her* backpack. The one she'd carried everywhere at the Station. She unzipped the bag, removed its contents, and laid them out in front of her:

Her utility jacket with the upside-down Task Force patch sewn onto the left shoulder.

The Bible she'd found in the church basement in Ash Grove.

Taylor's Task Force radio.

Every so often, Gemma took a quick inventory of the backpack's contents to make sure that nothing had grown legs and wandered away, as her mother used to say. She couldn't really say why she'd singled out these particular items to be stored inside the backpack, or why she'd hidden them in the shed, except that each item had profound importance to her.

The jacket with the upside-down patch represented strength and rebellion—two things Gemma hadn't realized she was capable of until she'd stood in front of those television cameras and read the Bible aloud to the world. And, of course, the patch represented Taylor.

Who he used to be, and who he'd become.

Next, she picked up the Bible.

She had other Bibles now, but the one she'd found in the church basement felt as if it had been waiting for her to find it. Whoever had buried it at the bottom of that storage container had probably been trying to hide it from the Task Force. They would never know that, by hiding the Bible so well, they had played a crucial role in saving the life of a young woman they would never meet. Because, in that Bible, she'd found the hope to go on.

To endure.

Putting the Bible down, she turned her attention to the final item from the backpack.

Taylor's radio.

He'd lost it while saving Gemma from falling into the mine, and she'd found it six months later, still laying at the base of the escape ladder.

To Gemma, the radio represented hope. If she could find it again, after so much time, perhaps she could find Taylor some-day, too.

Clutching the radio to her chest, she bowed her head and prayed for a miracle. She couldn't go on like this forever, living a life that didn't include Taylor. She didn't just want him back—she *needed* him back. She needed to feel his arms around her again. To smell him. To touch him. To breathe him in like oxygen.

Not just Taylor, but also Oliver, Mia, Abram, her parents...

All of them.

She returned the items to the backpack, reburied it under-neath the heavy canvas, and retreated to the apartment. While Brie and Max had already withdrawn to their bedroom at the end of the hallway, Sophia had fallen asleep on the couch with *Looney Tunes* blaring on the television, one of Letty's patchwork quilts covering the bottom half of her body. Gemma settled onto the couch beside the girl, lulled by the normal sounds of the apartment—the clicking of the baseboard heaters, the hum of the refrigerator, the steady whirring of the overhead fan in the living room. Her eyelids grew heavy as Bugs Bunny used his superior wit and skill to outsmart a variety of villains and would-be assassins.

Outside the living room window, a small patch of white blossoms still clung to the uppermost branches of the pear trees, as if afraid to accept their fates. But then a strong gust of wind battered the trees, forcing the blossoms from the branches and sending them sailing through the air like dandelion seeds.

On the television, Bugs Bunny taunted one of the bad guys: "Of course you realize this means war."

Gemma pulled the quilt up to her chest and allowed her eyes to drift shut.

✝

A hand slammed over Gemma's mouth, startling her awake.

Mullen.

The dead soldier loomed over her in the darkened room, shattered bones rattling within withered flesh, decaying lips pulling away from his teeth in a lecherous grin, unable to give up the hunt even in death.

Panic seized every muscle in her body, paralyzing them as if she'd grabbed onto an electric fence. She tried to scream Sophia's name—to warn the girl to run—but the decomposing skin covering Mullen's hand blocked the sound.

Noise echoed in the hallway, the unmistakable sound of fighting in the back bedroom. Next came a loud thud, heavy enough to rattle the windows in their frames, followed by a grunt of pain that sounded like Max. She tried to lift her head to see what was happening in the hallway, but her dead attacker held her in place.

Fight, her mind insisted. *You have to fight. It's your only chance.*

She twisted her body and kicked her legs wildly, struggling to free herself long enough to scream. She couldn't help Max or Brie, but maybe she could still warn Sophia. Her right foot slammed into the coffee table, sending its contents—a pile of magazines, a half-eaten bag of Middlesworth potato chips, and Sophia's empty cup—tumbling to the floor.

"Knock it off!" her attacker growled.

His voice was a lot of things—deep, frightening, and unfamiliar—but it also wasn't Mullen's.

She stopped fighting long enough to look at her attacker, her short nails digging into his wrist—a strong wrist that definitely *wasn't* decaying. When her body relaxed a little, the man brought his face closer to hers, and for the first time, Gemma saw the black ski mask covering his face. Covering everything but his eyes.

She knew Mullen's eyes—she still saw them often in her dreams—and these weren't Mullen's eyes.

The man brought a finger to his lips, his meaning evident.

Be quiet.

Gemma lay beneath the stranger, paralyzed by indecision, her mind and body at odds with one another. Every instinct was telling her to kick, punch, and fight. To do whatever it took to free herself from her attacker's grip.

But something stronger than instinct kept her from fighting.

"We have to move," the man commanded, his voice barely more than a breath in her ear. He still hadn't loosened his grip on her mouth. "There's no time."

No time? What did that mean?

And why hadn't Sophia woken up yet? Why wasn't she screaming?

Gemma lifted her head to look at the far end of the couch.

Sophia was gone.

The quilt was still there, as was her pillow, but the girl wasn't. Then, Gemma's eyes drifted beyond the couch to the narrow hallway that led to the bedrooms. The door to the stairway was hanging wide open, and she could no longer hear the sounds of fighting coming from the back bedroom.

Max and Brie were gone, too.

Now that she wasn't fighting anymore, her attacker had relaxed a bit, so he wasn't expecting it when Gemma brought a knee up and slammed it squarely into his groin. He fell sideways, clutching himself, and she seized the opportunity, launching herself off the couch and sprinting for the kitchen table.

But her attacker was already coming after her. She could hear him. She grabbed one of the dining chairs, swung it behind her back, and smashed it into the man's left shoulder. He let out another angry howl of pain.

Gemma dropped the broken chair.

The revolver, her mind remembered. *In the closet. Top shelf.*

"Stop!" the man shouted, apparently no longer concerned about being quiet or about whatever perceived danger waited for them outside.

Gemma ignored him and ran for the closet. Throwing open the door, she went up on her tiptoes and shoved her hand underneath the blanket, blindly searching the top shelf for the gun. Finally, her fingers closed around a familiar metal shape and she yanked it free, using her thumb to cock the hammer just as the man grabbed her arms and wrenched them behind her back.

She pulled the trigger.

The bullet tore into the hardwood floor near her right foot, probably lodging itself into a bookshelf on the first floor. Then, the man twisted her arm in such a precise and terrible way that she had no choice but to release the gun. It clattered to the floor.

Instead of picking it up and killing her with it, the man kicked the gun away with his boot, sending it sliding underneath the couch. He shoved her against the narrow strip of wall between the closet and the stairway.

"Do you want to die tonight?" he spoke directly into her ear, his voice walking the line between a growl and a whisper. "Try to shoot me again."

She winced as steel handcuffs closed around her wrists.

"Letty Webb," he muttered, still holding her firmly in place. "Where is she?"

There was no point in lying. As Letty herself had once quoted Harriet Tubman, "I can't die but once." And Letty had already died. There was nothing more this man could do to her.

"She's dead," Gemma muttered.

"Dead?" the soldier repeated, as if he didn't understand the word. "Then who are you?"

Now would be a good time to lie.

But she was tired of lying. Tired of hiding. Tired of pretending.

"Gemma Alcott."

The soldier remained silent for several long seconds, still panting from the exertion of chasing Gemma around the apartment. Finally, he said, "The one who hijacked the renouncements."

It wasn't a question.

"Where are my friends?" she demanded, struggling uselessly against the man's ironclad grip. "Where did you take them?"

He yanked her away from the wall and pushed her toward the stairway. "Start walking."

They descended the stairway together, the man holding onto Gemma's upper arms. When they reached the bottom, he kept pushing her forward, past the dark bookshelves with their hidden Bibles and toward the front door, which hung open like a mouth ready to consume her.

The man jerked her to a sudden stop just before they reached the door. She turned to look at him, to find out why they'd stopped, but then something came down over her head—some kind of hood—and everything went black.

"What are you doing?" Gemma cried, unable to see anything through the thick fabric. She felt the edges of panic creeping closer as the soldier pushed her into the chilly night air.

Nothing remained but sounds and sensations. The faint rumbling of an idling vehicle. The breeze that tickled the tiny hairs on her arms. The tricky board in the middle of the porch that sank slightly beneath her feet. And Letty's old porch swing, playing a familiar creaky tune as the wind propelled it back and forth.

When Gemma reached the bottom of the porch steps, she heard the squeak of hinges as a car door opened in front of her. Then, before she could react, before she could even *think* of how to get away from the vehicle, the man grabbed her around the waist, lifted her up, and shoved her inside the vehicle.

The floor trembled beneath her hands and knees as the door slammed shut behind her. She reached out with her right hand, searching, and felt a foot. A *small*, bare foot.

"Sophia?"

"Gemma?" The girl's voice sounded like a song. A hymn of praise. "Is that you?"

Oh, thank God.

"I'm here, Soph." She wanted to cry, but she couldn't. She had to be strong for Sophia. "It's going to be fine. Don't worry."

"We're all here."

Max's voice reached out to Gemma like an extended hand, and her relief was so immense that if she could've found him in the darkness, she would've planted a kiss right on his lips.

"Brie's here, too. We're all okay." Max lowered his voice. "They got Sophia first. She was already in the van when they threw us inside. There are two guys, plus the one who grabbed you. I think we're in a cargo van."

Gemma heard the faint tremble in Max's voice, and she remembered how the Task Force interrogators had tortured him to get information about the Station. One of the worst things they'd done was suffocate and revive him repeatedly. And now here he was, in the back of a stuffy cargo van with a bag over his head. "Max? Are you okay?"

"I'm fine."

He didn't sound fine.

"Who are they?" Gemma wondered aloud. "Task Force?"

"If they are, they're not wearing uniforms," Brie replied, not bothering to lower her voice. "The two who attacked us were dressed in all black."

The vehicle rolled forward, turning right toward the highway.

"He asked me about Letty," Gemma muttered as the vehicle picked up speed. "He sounded surprised that she was dead."

"Letty?" Max asked. "Do you think someone from the Sanctuary gave her up?"

"I don't know. Maybe."

After murdering Letty, Mullen had tricked Kyle Hogue and Mike Yost into believing that he was a subversive so they would transport him to the Sanctuary. Once there, he'd shot both of them, either just before or just after calling in the location. But he hadn't stuck around to explain to the Task Force how he'd found the campground. He'd been too busy kidnapping Sophia and laying a trap for Gemma. The soldiers who'd raided the Sanctuary had no way of knowing that an elderly bookstore owner from Winter's Dam had funded the campground. Without that critical information, it was highly unlikely that they would've wasted any time sending the Christians from the Sanctuary to interrogators.

So why was Gemma's attacker looking for Letty?

Gemma braced herself against the side of the van, her shoulder pressed into Sophia's. "Or maybe these guys aren't with the Task Force at all."

"Who else would they be?" Brie asked quietly, as if she wasn't really expecting an answer, but Gemma responded immediately, her voice coming out sounding much stronger than she felt.

"I don't know," Gemma said. "But as soon as they pull over, we're going to find out."

CHAPTER SIX

Taylor Nolan was back in the White Room.

He'd thought up hundreds of other names for the room: Torture Chamber, Bloody Room, Hell's Doorstep, to name a few. But he'd finally settled on the White Room because it was the least scary of the potential names and because everything in the room was white. The tile floors. The walls. The plates covering the electrical outlets. Even the wooden chair in its center—the only piece of furniture in the room—was entirely white, including the screws that held it together. Whenever it was time to leave his drafty holding cell and go to the White Room, the t-shirt and elastic-waist pants the guards ordered him to put on were also stark white and stank of bleach. Even his skin had grown pale, as if his body was trying to camouflage itself so the interrogators could not find him in the White Room.

The White Room was disorienting. When Taylor entered the White Room, he wondered if the Task Force had figured out a way to suck all the color out of the world.

But when his interrogators arrived—*if* they arrived—the pristine world around him would become stained by at least two colors: the olive green of his interrogators' uniforms...and red.

Lots and lots of red.

These were not the same interrogators Taylor and the others had rescued Max from all those months ago. These men were harder. Smarter. Colder. Trained mercenaries. He wasn't even certain they *were* Task Force soldiers, despite the uniforms they wore to convince him otherwise. Their uniforms contained no nametapes or identifiable unit patches. Nothing but barren fabric clinging to bulging muscles, all set beneath the well-tanned faces of his torturers.

He sat on the chair in the middle of the room, his bare feet cold against the tile floor, staring at the windowless door and waiting for the interrogators to appear. He wished they were already there, because anticipating their arrival was worse than everything that came afterward.

Sometimes, the two men arrived quickly. Sometimes, it took them hours. Sometimes, they didn't show. Those days—the ones where they never showed—were both terrible and wonderful. Torturous hours spent imagining all the awful things they might do to him, followed by a flood of relief—a relief so tangible he could actually *taste* it on his tongue—when the door finally swung open and it was just another skinny Task Force guard coming to escort him back to his holding cell.

"Come on," he muttered to himself, willing them to show. If they were coming, he just wanted to get it over with. "Come on. Come on."

Taylor didn't know his interrogators' names, so he thought of them as Patches and Groot.

Patches was the leader of the two, although he was significantly younger than Groot, who had to be pushing fifty. Patches looked to be in his early thirties, and he wore his greasy, brown hair long—way too long to comply with Task Force regulations. He wasn't physically intimidating, either. If they hadn't handcuffed Taylor, he easily could've taken the guy in a fight. But Patches was dead behind the eyes. There was nothing there. No morality. No humanity. Nothing. He had a boyish face that somehow looked both innocent and maniacal at the same time. He was someone who could thrust a hunting knife into another person's throat and still be hungry for lunch. Taylor thought of him as Patches because scaly, red patches of skin littered his arms, particularly around his elbows. Psoriasis or something like it. He was always scratching at these patches, sometimes hard enough to draw blood.

Taylor had nicknamed the other interrogator Groot because the man was basically a walking tree trunk. Thick arms. Thick legs. Rock-hard body. There was nothing soft about the guy, not even his head, which was shaved bald. Unlike his namesake, Groot said nothing, which made him utterly terrifying.

Groot was present in the White Room for one purpose and one purpose only: to inflict pain. This usually involved suffocating Taylor with a plastic bag until he passed out, or using tiny knives—knives that looked almost comical in Groot's hands—to cut him. The guy left Taylor's face alone, for reasons known only to Groot himself, but he loved carving designs into the skin of Taylor's back, chest, and arms.

The worst of the cuts had occurred the first time they'd shown him the pictures—the ones in the manila folder. Shirtless and already bleeding, Taylor had lunged at Patches, almost snagging the sleeve of the guy's uniform before Groot heaved him back into the chair. In retaliation for this offense, Patches had grabbed the knife from Groot and slashed Taylor's chest from left to right, leaving a wicked scar that cut right across his heart.

Once, Groot had twisted Taylor's left kneecap in such a way that he couldn't walk for a week, but that hadn't stopped the guards from dragging him to the White Room for additional "sessions." Even now, his left knee still felt weaker than his right when he put weight on it. On more than one occasion, Patches had promised to relieve Taylor of several of his fingers, but he'd yet to follow through on that threat.

Unable to look at the door any longer, Taylor closed his eyes and thought of Gemma. Thinking about her brought him peace and pain in equal measure. He didn't know where she was, if she was free, or if she was even still alive. Sometimes, he imagined her sitting beside him in his holding cell, her hand entwined with his, chattering away about everything and nothing. He couldn't remember exactly what she looked like anymore, but he could still hear her voice clearly in his mind, and that was the only thing that kept him from losing all hope.

In his lowest moments, he imagined her falling into Gavin's arms again, finding comfort with him as she once had at the Station.

How long until she lost hope? Or had she already given Taylor up for dead?

The door to the White Room swung open.

Dully, Taylor opened his eyes. He fixed his gaze on the floor and worked his way up, searching for cutting implements. For tools and plastic bags. For anything that could hurt him.

But there was nothing dangerous.

Only Patches in the doorway, clutching the manila folder in his right hand, its edges wrinkled and worn.

Groot wasn't with him.

That had never happened before.

Without speaking, Patches opened the folder, removed the top photo, and tossed it to the ground at Taylor's feet.

In the photo, a blonde woman lay dead on the ground, a bullet hole in her forehead.

Susan Richardson.

A member of the Sanctuary's leadership council. Taylor hadn't seen Susan since the emergency meeting at the Camp

Mahantango trading post, just prior to Taylor and the others leaving for Winter's Dam to find Letty.

He'd seen the photo before. He'd seen them all before. But seeing Susan lying there, lifeless, still stung him in a way that Patches would never understand. He'd wanted so badly to protect the people at the Sanctuary. Not just Gemma. All of them.

But he'd failed.

More photos slid into Taylor's frame of vision, one after another, like he was clicking through images using one of those old View-Masters. All the photos had been taken at the Sanctuary after the Task Force raid. One showed the charred remains of a cabin. Another showed the dining hall, flames erupting from its roof. There were also photographs of bodies. Six people had died in the raid, including Susan. The killings were all justified, according to Patches. Every subversive killed had supposedly fired a weapon at the Task Force, forcing them to retaliate with deadly force. But Taylor didn't buy it. He'd known these people. Susan Richardson never would've pointed a gun at a soldier. She'd hated guns.

"See any friends of yours?" Patches asked, tossing more pictures onto the floor so that they overlapped one another. "Want to say a quick prayer for their souls?"

Gemma's not in any of them, Taylor assured himself. *She wasn't there during the raid. She escaped. Somehow, she got out.*

But then a new photo landed in front of him.

No. Not a photo.

A flyer.

The same flyer Gemma had found hanging on a bulletin board in the church in Ash Grove.

Letty's Book Cellar—New and Used Books in Winter's Dam.

Looking for a good book? We've got a towering selection!

Mention this ad to save 10 percent off your purchase.

Or visit our website and use our discount code: PV1810

"What's the matter, Nolan?" Patches asked. "You recognize this place?"

Working hard to keep his expression neutral, Taylor looked Patches in the eye and gave him a disinterested shrug. "Never seen it before in my life. Sounds like a good deal. Although you don't strike me as much of a reader."

Patches' eyes darkened, as they always did before he lost control. "Oh, I don't strike you that way, do I? Do I strike you more like *this?*" Then, he slapped Taylor on the cheek, a prissy slap with little power behind it, as if he were afraid of hurting his hand on Taylor's face.

"Walked into that one," Taylor muttered.

"You certainly did. Anyway, do you know what happened a few days ago?" Patches asked, his dead eyes sparkling unnervingly. "You'll never guess. Some colonel *finally* got off his fourth point-of-contact and gave our unit the go-ahead to interrogate the roaches we arrested at your old campground. And wouldn't you know it? One interrogator had a breakthrough last night when a roach spilled the beans about some old woman and a secret message on a flyer. He even told them where he'd seen the flyer—at a gas station in the middle of nowhere." Patches picked up the flyer and tapped Letty's photo with a slender finger. A crease cut through the center of the old woman's forehead. "We sent a few guys to that gas station this morning, and what do you know? They found this flyer hanging up on the bulletin board just inside the door. You don't recognize her, do you?"

Taylor shook his head. "I have no idea who that is."

"She's a *sympathizer.*" Patches scratched angrily at his right elbow, which was particularly inflamed today. "That's who she is. And she's the worst kind of sympathizer. She provided a refuge for subversives. You think that should go unpunished? Weren't you a soldier?"

"Even if this woman had something to do with the campground, what does it matter now? You've arrested all the subversives. You've destroyed their hideout. We're talking about one old woman here. What does she matter at this point?"

Patches continued to scratch at his arm, sending white flecks of skin drifting to the floor. "She matters because she might be in contact with other sympathizers. Or she might have another hideout somewhere—one we haven't found yet. Either way, she's going to be detained for questioning. We've sent a unit to Winter's Dam. Their orders are to bring the old woman in for questioning and to search the town for any other subversives."

Taylor wanted to lunge out of the chair at Patches. He wanted to throttle the guy, take the pistol that was strapped to his right hip, and shoot his way out of this facility. He wanted to get to Letty and warn her.

But if what Patches was saying was true, then it was too late.

"Anyway, that's why I came here today," Patches continued. "To give you the good news."

"Good news?"

"Yes. The higher-ups have determined that you're no longer of any use to us, so you're being transferred to a new location in the morning. That makes this our last meeting."

Patches looked regretful. Maybe even a little sad.

Like a kid about to lose his favorite toy.

"Transferred where? To the stockade?" Taylor had always known that when they tired of torturing him, they would transfer him to a military detention facility to await his court-martial. But he hadn't had a single hearing yet. He hadn't been offered a lawyer. Nothing.

Patches laughed as if Taylor had just told a funny joke. "The stockade is for soldiers, Nolan, and you're no longer a soldier. They dishonorably discharged you from the Task Force. You're a *subversive* now."

Taylor didn't know how to respond to that news. He wasn't even sure how he felt about it.

"Where am I being transferred?"

"Like I said, you're one of them now—a subversive—so you're being sent to a detention center. I'm not sure which one, but I doubt the location matters to you. Maybe you'll run into a few of the roaches you locked up. I'm sure they'll welcome you with open arms." The sadness vanished from Patches' face, and he looked downright gleeful at the thought of Taylor encountering people he'd detained. "By the way, since you're not technically a Christian, that means you cannot be rehabilitated, so there's no possibility of release for you. Ever."

Taylor's body sank deeper into the chair with each word, his hope deflating. What had kept him going during the interrogations—aside from thinking about Gemma—was the hope that he would eventually get his day in court. With a court-martial, they would have assigned him an attorney. He could've pled his case to a jury. He could've talked about how Colonel Carver went rogue in Ash Grove and about the murders he'd witnessed the Task Force committing in Winter's Dam.

Now, he would never have that chance. For Taylor, being sent to a detention center was the equivalent of a death sentence.

But his death would come slowly.

Patches knelt down to collect the photographs, humming quietly to himself. When he'd collected them all, he tapped them on his thigh until they were neat and even, and then he slid them back inside the folder.

All the while, Taylor watched him—this physical representation of every evil perpetrated by the Task Force—and he wanted to make Patches bleed the way Groot had made *him* bleed. He wanted to hurt the guy. He wanted to kill him.

He couldn't do anything with his hands...but his feet were free.

With Patches kneeling in front of him, and with no thought of the consequences, Taylor kicked his right leg out, his foot striking Patches in the lower jaw. The angle wasn't great, and the kick wasn't as hard as Taylor would've liked, but it was hard enough.

Patches fell backward onto the tile, the pictures tumbling to the floor. Reflexively, his hand flew up to his mouth, and blood flowed through his fingers. His eyes darted from the blood to Taylor.

"You're not much to look at without your oversized friend," Taylor said. He'd gotten a little taste of power with that kick, and it tasted good. "At first, I thought you were the brain and he was the brawn of this operation, but you're not the brain, are you? The Task Force probably couldn't find anywhere else to put someone as useless as you." And then, because Taylor couldn't control his smart mouth—even when his life depended on it—he added, "And for the love of all that's holy, put some cream on those rashes."

Patches' eyes darkened until they were almost black. Then, he lunged at Taylor with his teeth bared, as if to maul him to death. But instead of sinking his teeth into Taylor's neck, Patches punched him in the face. And it wasn't a prissy hit this time. This punch knocked Taylor off the chair. He landed on his side, his head slamming into the tile floor with a dull thud.

And there it was, the color he'd been expecting, spreading on the tiles in front of him one last time.

Red.

CHAPTER SEVEN

They'd been driving forever. Or what felt like forever.

Gemma shifted her body for the hundredth time, trying to find a position that would relieve some of the pressure on her back and shoulders, but she couldn't get comfortable. Not with her hands cuffed behind her back and Sophia's head on her shoulder. Each time she moved, Sophia let out an irritated grunt and scooted closer, and the entire process began again.

Even worse than the pain in her back was her stomach. She was feeling really sick, as if she might throw up. But she couldn't throw up. Not with the bag over her head. She focused on breathing slowly, trying to calm herself down, reminding herself, over and over, that she wasn't suffocating. She was getting plenty of air. Whatever the soldier had placed over her head was porous and easy to breathe through. There was no reason to panic.

Not yet, anyway.

She could feel Brie's legs pressing against her own, and there was something comforting about that—knowing that Brie was still there, even if Gemma couldn't see her.

"Are you guys awake?" she whispered. "Brie?"

"Seriously?" Max grunted. "You think we could sleep right now?"

Brie nudged Gemma's leg with her boot. "No one can sleep with you rutsching around." A sharp intake of breath followed the statement, and then Brie said, "Oh my gosh, I'm talking like Addie. If it weren't for these handcuffs, I'd slap myself in the face."

The voices of her friends made Gemma feel a little better. A little less alone. She desperately wanted to tear off her mask and see their faces. "Where do you think we're going?"

"Could be anywhere," Max replied. "I lost track of the turns a while back."

"Yeah, me too." The driver had taken so many turns that Gemma suspected he was deliberately trying to keep them from figuring out their location. But they'd been on a major highway for the last half-hour. The road was smooth, and the van was traveling much faster than before.

She could hear voices in the front of the van. *Raised* voices. Almost as if the men were having an argument. But she couldn't make out what they were saying. There had to be a partition separating the front and the back of the van.

"Gemma?" Sophia whispered. "I have to go to the bathroom."

"Honey, can you hold it? We're still on the road."

"No." The girl sounded on the verge of tears. "Please. I really have to go. I don't feel good."

Tilting her head toward the front of the van, Gemma listened for the sounds of fighting, but the men had grown quiet. "Okay," she finally said. "Just sit tight. I'll take care of it." Her own stomach troubles forgotten, she scooted over Sophia's legs and crawled toward the front of the van.

"Gem?" Brie asked. "What are you doing?"

"I'm going to make them pull over."

"Oh, cool. Just checking."

Since Gemma couldn't use her hands, she had to crawl in an awkward upright position, inching forward to keep from losing her balance and smashing her face off the floor. When her right shoulder bumped into the metal partition that separated the front and back sections of the van, she pressed her ear against the metal and listened for voices.

Nothing.

She screamed into the divider, "Hey!"

The vehicle swerved, the abrupt motion tossing her into the side of the van. But the driver quickly regained control, and then Gemma heard a metallic sliding just above her head.

"What's wrong with you?" It was the gravelly voiced man who'd attacked Gemma in the apartment. He sounded as if he was in the back of the van with her, which meant there was a window built into the partition. "Are you trying to get us killed?"

Gemma carefully worked her way back to her knees. "We have a little girl who needs to go to the bathroom. Unless you want a mess back here, I suggest you pull over."

The window slammed shut, and the muffled arguing resumed. But the argument only lasted for a few seconds before it grew quiet and stayed that way. Just when Gemma was considering screaming into the partition again, the van executed a quick left-hand turn and came to a stop.

"I hope you know what you're doing," Brie muttered as the driver killed the engine.

Moments later, the rear doors opened. Fresh air filled the van, and sunlight breached the black fabric covering Gemma's head—the first light she'd seen in hours.

"We're at a rest stop," the gravelly voiced man said. "We'll let you use the bathrooms, but we'll have to remove your handcuffs and hoods, obviously. Trust me when I tell you, it's not in your best interest to do anything stupid."

"No one's going to try anything," Max spoke up. "We appreciate you stopping."

The van sank a little as one man crawled inside, and Gemma gasped when someone grabbed the bottom of the hood and pulled it over her head. The sudden rush of light momentarily blinded her.

She couldn't see anything, but at least she could breathe again. Greedily, she sucked the cold air into her lungs. She hadn't noticed how much the bag had restricted her breathing until it wasn't there anymore. The thought that the men might force her to put it back on terrified her.

When her eyes adjusted to the brightness, she saw a man crouched in front of her. It was him. The one who'd attacked her in Letty's apartment. She recognized his eyes.

He wasn't wearing a ski mask anymore.

The man had dark hair and a lean build, and he appeared to be in his late thirties or early forties. He wasn't unattractive, but the deep lines etched into the skin around his eyes and forehead gave him a weathered appearance, as did the dark scruff covering the lower half of his face. He held Gemma's gaze for several moments before his eyes drifted to Sophia. "You need to use the bathroom, sweetheart?"

"Uh-huh," Sophia responded, squinting at the man. Her eyes still hadn't adjusted to the light. "Yes, please."

"I'll go with her," Brie offered. "I'm not feeling very well, either."

Gemma glanced at Brie and Max. Like Sophia, they were both barefoot and wearing only their pajamas. "Here," Gemma said, slipping off her boots. "Wear these and carry Sophia."

The man crouched in front of Gemma nodded to a younger man sporting a shaggy haircut and a patchy goatee. "Hirsch. Uncuff them both and go with them," he said. "Wait right outside the bathroom."

"Roger that."

A third man stood a few feet away from the van, dark-skinned arms crossed over his chest, his eyes fixed on the highway. "Just hurry up, man. I don't like stopping like this."

After Hirsch uncuffed Brie and Sophia, he glanced at Max. "What about you, partner? You need to go? Now's the time."

Max's eyes shifted to Gemma, his brow furrowing beneath his dark curls. He obviously wanted to protect Brie and Sophia, but he also wasn't comfortable leaving Gemma alone in the back of the van with a kidnapper. Finally, he said, "Nah. I'm good."

Hirsch gave him an indifferent shrug and then helped Brie and Sophia out of the van.

Gemma watched as they walked across the parking lot toward a beige-colored building. A bright-red sign with yellow lettering announced it as the Pilot Travel Center. Beyond the building, Gemma could see at least a dozen big rigs parked in a staggered line. Billboards lined the highway they'd been traveling on, nearly all of them advertising local adult bookstores and pleasure shops.

Gemma averted her eyes from the lascivious ads and returned her attention to the man kneeling in front of her. "Who are you?" she demanded, forcing a confidence she did not feel. "Where are you taking us?"

The man surprised her by answering right away. "I'm Clarke. The kid with the awful hair—the one escorting your friends to the bathroom—is Hirsch, and the strong-but-silent one over there is Ward."

"Clarke, Hirsch, and Ward," Gemma repeated. "You don't have first names?"

Clarke shook his head. "We don't use first names around here."

"Okay. So, who are you? Task Force?"

The lines in Clarke's forehead deepened. "I was never with the Task Force." He sounded offended by the suggestion.

"Some of my guys used to be Task Force, but they're not anymore."

Gemma caught Max's eyes over Clarke's shoulders, and his baffled expression reflected how she felt inside. Nothing was making any sense. "What guys? Who are you people? And what do you want with us?"

"We didn't want *you*," Clarke said matter-of-factly. "We were looking for Letty Webb. You said she was dead. What happened to her?"

Mullen happened to her.

"A Task Force soldier murdered her. Seven months ago."

Clarke's eyebrows shot up. "Really? So...why are you living in her apartment?"

She glanced at Max, looking for guidance. When he nodded, she said, "The five of us have been in hiding together for years. Along the way, we found Letty, and she kept us safe. After she was murdered, we had nowhere to go, so we stayed in her house."

Gemma intentionally omitted the fact that she'd spent the last seven months finding safe places for any subversives who showed up at the bookstore. Until she knew who this man really was and what he wanted, he didn't need that information.

"Okay," she said. "You know who we are. Now tell us what you want."

Clarke's head tipped back as if searching the roof of the van for answers. Then, he blew out a heavy breath and lowered his gaze to Gemma. "We weren't expecting to find anyone at the bookstore except Letty. Our intel was that Letty lived alone. Our intention was to remove her from the premises—by force if necessary—no later than zero-five-hundred hours. We didn't even have a physical description of the subject—only her name, the name of the town, and the name of the bookstore. That's it."

Questions danced around Gemma's head like sugar-fueled kids at a birthday party. She didn't know where to begin, so she settled on the most obvious question of all. "You wanted to get Letty out of the bookstore by five in the morning? Why? What was going to happen at five?"

Clarke passed a hand through his hair. "It's a long story."

"I've got time."

The slight flare of Clarke's nostrils showed Gemma that she was walking a dangerous line. This was a man she'd kneed in the groin and almost shot, after all. But instead of knocking her head into the side of the van, Clarke cleared his throat and began to speak.

"Last October, the Task Force detained a large group of subversives at an old campground near Winter's Dam. All the subversives were sent to detention centers, but several days ago, the Task Force transferred a few of the sympathizers apprehended during the detention to a special unit for temporary internment and interrogation."

"Interrogation?"

Goosebumps erupted on Gemma's arms. Clarke had to have been referring to Clyde and Lizzie Fishman, and Gerry and Melinda Tuttle. Both couples were sympathizers from Winter's Dam who'd worked closely with Letty to keep the Sanctuary supplied with food and medicine. After Gemma and the others had rescued them from the Task Force in Winter's Dam, the Fishmans and the Tuttles had decided to stay at the Sanctuary until things cooled down a little. They couldn't have known that the Sanctuary itself was going to be raided.

They'd been in a detention center for months, and now they were being interrogated, too? And the poor Fishmans had already lost their young son, Jason, to the Task Force.

Gemma stared at Clarke, tears blurring her vision. "I don't understand. How do you know all of this?"

"We have people everywhere," Clarke said. "Our group consists mostly of ex-cops and ex-military. People who lost their jobs when they refused to enforce the government's compliance orders against Christians. We've got guards inside the detention centers. We've even got active members of the Task Force working with us."

"Interrogators?" Max interrupted, a horrified expression on his face. "Some of your people are interrogators?"

"No," Clarke quickly responded. "Not interrogators. They're a different breed altogether. But we've got a few people in Operations and Intelligence, which is where the interrogators send their information. Those guys try to keep us informed of any upcoming operations. We can't rescue everyone, but if we get information on an upcoming raid, we try to get people out if we have enough time."

Everything came together at once for Gemma, like the last piece of a puzzle sliding into place. "Are you saying that the Task Force was going to raid the bookstore last night? That you got us out before they came?"

The question hung in the air for way too long. Long enough for Gemma to realize that she didn't really want to hear the answer.

"Not just the bookstore," Clarke finally replied, his face grim. "The whole town."

CHAPTER EIGHT

With her handcuffs removed, Gemma traced her fingers over the angry red slashes on her wrists, unable to think of anything but the people back in Winter's Dam—the locals who had willingly opened up their homes for Christians, despite having already experienced the wrath of the Task Force, and the Christians who'd come to the bookstore, searching for Letty and finding Gemma instead. When she'd told them she had a place for them, they'd all looked at her as if she were some kind of savior.

"You left them behind," Gemma muttered, uncertain if she was addressing Clarke or herself. Or maybe both. "You didn't even warn them. You didn't even give them a fighting chance."

Clarke glanced over his shoulder, giving her that intense stare of his, before continuing to unlock Max's handcuffs. "You don't understand," he said, shoving the cuffs into his pocket. "We had no time. There was no way to clear the whole town on such short notice, and warning everyone would've caused a panic. Can you imagine the chaos? We would've been lucky to get you guys out, much less everyone else."

Gemma glanced at Sophia, who'd returned from the truck

stop carrying a plastic bag filled with snacks and sodas, courtesy of Hirsch. But she wasn't eating anything. Instead, she was leaning against the side of the van, listening to the conversation between Gemma and Clarke. A year ago, Gemma would've asked the girl to go somewhere else for a few minutes, to shield her from the worst details of the conversation. But Gemma had given up on trying to protect Sophia from the terrible things happening all around her, partially because Sophia was a highly intelligent and intuitive child, and because she worried more if she *didn't* know what was going on. But the bigger reason Gemma had given up was because the world was a cruel place, and someday, Sophia would have to face it on her own.

Gemma couldn't protect her forever.

When she said nothing, Clarke continued, "Our target was Letty Webb," he said, his voice a strange combination of defiance and apology. "No one else. We didn't *have* to get you out of—"

"Let's go back," Gemma cut him off. "Right now. We have to go back."

Brie leaned against the rear door of the van, muscular arms crossed over her chest. "I hate to say it, but she's right. Those people put their lives on the line for us." Her eyes flitted to Gemma. "Plus, we have a friend in the town. We need to check on him."

Gavin.

Gemma had forgotten about Gavin.

"You can't help them," Clarke protested. "Don't you understand that? Whatever happened in Winter's Dam last night is already over."

"But what if your information was wrong?" Gemma offered. "What if there was no raid? What if they canceled it after your informant gave you the information? Couldn't that be possible?"

"Of course. Anything's possible. But—"

"Then we have to go back. If it were your friends back there, your cop friends and their families, and there was even a chance that you could help them, you would go back in a heartbeat. I've known you for ten minutes, Clarke, and I know that's true."

She wasn't flattering him. She already knew what type of man Clarke was: a sheepdog, alpha-male, protector type. That wasn't something a person could turn off and on at will. Once a sheepdog, always a sheepdog. In a strange way, Clarke reminded her of Gavin—an older, rougher version of Gavin.

She knew she'd finally gotten through to Clarke when his lips drew into a thin line—so thin they almost disappeared entirely from his face. He shot a look at Hirsch and Ward, who were standing a few feet away from the van, eavesdropping on the conversation.

Hirsch stuffed a bit of chewing tobacco into his lower lip and lifted his shoulders. "I've got nothing better to do today, boss."

Ward nodded in agreement. "Your call."

Gemma gave it one final push. "Please," she whispered. "Our friends are back there. Help them."

Clarke gave her a lingering stare, dark eyes squinting slightly, as if trying to look into her soul to figure out who she was.

Finally, he said, "If we leave now, we can be there in an hour."

✝

From her spot in the back of the van, Gemma couldn't see much as they drove into Winter's Dam, but she could smell the smoke.

Clarke had been right.

It was already too late.

The stench of smoke transported her back to Oliver's barn after Mullen had torched it with her friends trapped inside. To

Gemma, that smell represented destruction. It was one of the worst smells in the world. It embedded itself into everything, ruining even those items that the fire had not touched. It clung to clothing. It filled your nostrils and adhered itself to memory centers in your brain so that you could never forget it, not for as long as you lived.

Maybe that was why the Task Force loved burning everything.

Because people *never* forgot that smell.

Ward parked in front of the smoldering remains of the bookstore, and Gemma stepped out of the van. Max followed her, and they stared in silence at what had been their home for the past seven months. The second floor of the bookstore had been utterly destroyed—the fire must've originated on that level—but the first floor hadn't fared much better. The intense heat had blown out every window, and shards of glass littered the front yard. The roof had partially collapsed, one section drooping over the porch like a lazy eyelid. Gemma couldn't tell how much damage had been done to the bookstore itself, but any books not destroyed by fire would've almost certainly been ruined by the thousands of gallons of water the fire department had pumped into the structure to put out the flames.

"Stay in the van, Soph," Gemma whispered, breaking her own rule of no longer shielding Sophia from the harsh realities of the world, but she didn't really care. Sophia didn't need to see this. "Stay with Brie."

"Why can't I get out?"

Gemma jerked her head toward Sophia. "Stay. In. The. Van." The look on her face must've left no room for argument because even Brie didn't protest being told to stay put. She nodded and pulled a tearful Sophia into her arms.

Gemma and Max walked toward the center of town.

The destruction reminded Gemma of the chaotic path of a tornado. Not every house had been destroyed. Some remained untouched by the horrors of the previous night, while others had been reduced to skeletal frames of charred wood and melted vinyl siding. The Task Force appeared to have chosen which homes to destroy at random because not every torched house belonged to a sympathizer. The town's main drag, where the homes and businesses stood close together, had borne the brunt of the damage, as the fire had hopped between structures before it could be contained.

Neither Gemma nor Max spoke as they walked through the town, surveying the damage. Thick crowds of people stood in their pajamas and bathrobes, staring up at their ruined homes with hands clasped over their mouths. None of the homes were still burning, but the volunteer firefighters from Winter's Dam remained on the scene, trying to keep the fires from flaring back up. Two firetrucks were parked in the middle of Main Street, effectively shutting down the highway to any thru-traffic. One truck was pumping water into a house that appeared to be a total loss, while the other was parked in front of the remains of That Dam Diner. A group of firefighters had gathered outside of the diner, their smoke-stained faces grim with exhaustion.

"Why are there only two trucks?" Gemma asked. "Where are the fire departments from the nearby towns?"

"I bet the Task Force ordered them not to respond," Max muttered. "They made the town fend for itself."

Gemma didn't want to believe him, but he was probably right. Speaking out against the Task Force or acting in direct opposition to their orders was a surefire way to be labeled a sympathizer.

As Gemma and Max approached the crowd, several of the townspeople glanced up, their somber expressions hardening into disgust.

"Is everyone alright?" Gemma asked.

No one responded. Instead, they turned their backs on her,

as if she were a stranger and not someone who'd been living among them for seven months. *They don't want us here anymore,* she realized. *And who could blame them?* She felt Max's hand on the small of her back, gently urging her to keep walking.

"Let's go," he whispered. "We have to check on Gavin."

The stench of smoke grew worse the farther into town they went. Gemma didn't even notice the dirty looks she was receiving as she searched the faces in the crowd with increasing desperation. The nagging sense of worry in the back of her mind was exploding into full-blown panic.

She hadn't seen any of the Christians she'd placed in homes since taking over for Letty.

Not one.

"Gemma!"

Someone broke free from the crowd and jogged toward her, black soot smeared across his face.

"Gavin?"

She ran forward, meeting him in the center of the street, but she stopped short of hugging him. Even if she'd wanted to hug him, she wouldn't have done it because he wasn't alone. Teresa followed behind him like a lost puppy, her long, dark hair damp with sweat. Even with her red eyes and soot-stained face, Teresa was still beautiful.

Over the young woman's shoulder, Gemma could see the burnt-out husk of Fallon's Grocery.

"They detained Teresa's dad." Gavin sounded out of breath. "We weren't home, or I'm sure they would've detained us, too. We only got back a little while ago." His eyes briefly flicked to the ground, and Gemma decided not to push the issue any further. She had no desire to know where Teresa and Gavin had been or what they'd been doing during the raid. "The Task Force went from house to house, searching for subversives. Sounds like they found them all."

"All of them?" Gemma's heart dropped. Dozens of faces

flashed before her eyes, many of them children. She surveyed the buildings again—the ones that the Task Force had set ablaze. "Not all the houses that were burned belonged to sympathizers."

"Yeah. They didn't always set the sympathizer's house on fire. Sometimes, they torched their *neighbor's* house as punishment," Gavin said. "Supposedly to discourage people from turning a blind eye if their neighbors are breaking the law."

Teresa stood beside Gavin, not speaking, obviously in shock. He put an arm around her shoulders, and she clung to his waist, as if terrified that someone might try to take him away. Now that her father was gone, Gavin was all she had left, and she wasn't about to let him go.

Don't let yourself get too close, Gemma wanted to warn her. *In this world, everyone gets taken away eventually.*

Max ran a finger along the scar on his cheek. "Did anyone die?"

"A few people went to the hospital for smoke inhalation and minor burns. Nothing too terrible. But..." When Gavin's voice trailed off, Teresa clung to him even tighter and buried her face in his shirt. "There's a rumor that a family didn't make it out of one house, but we don't know anything for sure yet. It's possible they made it out and we just haven't—"

"Who?" Gemma grabbed his arm. "Which house?"

Gavin reluctantly met her eyes. "The Courtneys had a family staying in their attic. Two parents and a teenage girl. They'd only been in town for about a month..."

No.

No. No. No.

The faces of Andrew and Catherine Bowler—and their daughter, Taren—flashed through her mind.

"We don't know for sure that they didn't make it out," Gavin offered, trying to create hope where there was none. "It's possible they did and no one's seen them yet. All the fires started on the second floors of the buildings. The Task Force threw Molotov cocktails through the second-floor windows. But they ordered people to get out first. The Courtneys supposedly heard the parents having trouble getting their daughter to leave the attic. I guess she was scared, and she fought them."

A strangled moaning sound came from Gemma's throat.

"Stop talking, man," Max said, wrapping an arm around Gemma. "We don't need to hear any more."

When Gemma closed her eyes, she saw Taren huddled in the attic's corner, clutching the weathered copy of *Wuthering Heights* to her chest. She saw Andrew and Catherine Bowler kneeling over their daughter, coughing as smoke filled their lungs, pleading with her to leave, even as their only escape route went up in flames.

"I promised they'd be safe," Gemma whispered too softly for anyone but God to hear.

Then, she tore free from Max's arms and ran.

CHAPTER NINE

Gemma ran past the charred remains of the bookstore, her arms pumping as if she were trying to outrun the devil himself. She sprinted across the vast expanse of Letty's back yard, passing the ornamental pear trees and trampling their withering white blossoms into the mud.

Had it only been yesterday when she and Sophia had danced in the yard as petals whipped around them? It felt like a lifetime ago.

She came to a sudden stop, her eyes falling on the dilapidated wooden structure at the far end of the yard.

The Task Force hadn't torched the shed. The building was still standing, which meant that Gemma's backpack was safe. The Charger was still there, too, hiding under its protective cover. She hadn't lost everything.

She lunged forward and ripped open the door, half-expecting to find a soldier crouched in the darkness, waiting to pull her inside and kick the door shut behind her.

But the shed was empty.

She squeezed her body through the narrow pathway, heading for the canvas dropcloth.

Going to her knees, she pushed the dropcloth aside with a shaking hand.

Her backpack was still there.

She blew out a breath she hadn't realized she'd been holding, unzipped the backpack, and pulled out each item. The utility jacket with the Task Force patch. The Bible she'd found in Ash Grove. And, of course, Taylor's Task Force radio. It was all there, just as it should've been. Untouched. Waiting for her to return.

"Is that the jacket you wore during the renouncements?"

The deep voice startled Gemma. She spun around, the radio clutched in her hand, ready to hurl it at whoever had snuck up on her.

Clarke stood in the narrow walkway, his body wedged in between Letty's push mower and a bulk-size bag of black oil sunflower seeds. He wasn't a large man, by any stretch of the imagination, but from Gemma's perspective on the floor, he looked huge.

"Yes, it is," she muttered, carefully slipping her arms inside the sleeves, as if she were putting on a sacred religious tunic instead of an old jacket. The material felt stiff against her skin, and the jacket itself smelled like the interior of Letty's shed: slightly musty with an underlying hint of motor oil. But when she gazed down at the patch on her left shoulder—Taylor's patch—she drew strength from it.

Clarke nodded his approval of the jacket. "You know, most people would've been too scared to pull a stunt like that—especially on camera, in front of the entire world. You ticked off a lot of people."

"Good. That was my intention."

"Don't do that," he said, narrowing his eyes at her. "Don't turn something brave into something trivial. It took guts to stand in front of those cameras and read verses from the Bible. You don't see that kind of bravery anymore."

"That wasn't bravery, Clarke. That was stupidity. Don't confuse the two. I put everyone I love in danger."

He rubbed his forehead, as if nursing a headache. "Did you know people now use that symbol," he said, pointing at the patch, "to represent the rebellion? I never saw anyone using that symbol before you broadcast yourself wearing that jacket, but now I see it everywhere, spray-painted on train cars or on the sides of buildings. Whether you intended to or not, you started something back in November. Things are changing. People are ready to fight back." He opened his hands, palms up. "So, what do *you* want to do?"

She looked up at him. "What do you mean?"

Clarke walked to the back of the shed, bumping into the bag of sunflower seeds and spilling some of them onto the floor. He knelt in front of her. "You can't stay in this town any longer, right? And you can't return to your previous life at the Sanctuary. It seems like God has closed both doors, doesn't it? So, I'll ask you again. What do *you* want to do?"

Gemma thought of Taren. Of the choking smoke and intense heat. She hadn't deserved to die like that. No one deserved to die like that.

The words slipped from between her lips. "Take me with you," she said, meeting his eyes. "I'll do whatever you want. If your group is taking on the Task Force, I want to be a part of it."

Clarke jerked his thumb toward the door of the shed. "Right now, they have all the power. The Task Force. The government. But their grip on this country is faltering. Can't you feel it? It's like this low hum that's barely audible, almost like a vibration in the ground, but it's there. You just have to listen for it. The good people who call this country home are tired of watching everything their ancestors fought for go up in smoke—sometimes literally. They're ready for change. They just need someone to lead them. And I think you're the person to do it."

She pressed her lips together, her gaze dropping to the scars on her wrists. "I want to work with you, Clarke. I'll do whatever it takes to work with you. But don't ask me to be a leader. No one would follow someone like me."

He arched an eyebrow at her, but instead of growing frustrated, he looked amused. "I was a cop for fifteen years, Alcott, and the biggest lesson I took away from that job is people won't follow terrible leaders. They just won't. But thousands of people are already following you. You haven't seen it because you've been hiding away in this little town, but in the eyes of the rebellion, you became a leader the day you donned that jacket in public."

Gemma felt something catch fire deep inside of her. A tiny ember that Clarke had coaxed into flame. She wanted Clarke's words to be true. She wanted to do something important, not for the glory, but for the people she'd failed to protect along the way.

For the Bowlers. For her parents. For Taylor.

"Okay," she finally agreed. "So, what are we going to do first?"

"Exactly what you suggested when you hijacked the renouncements."

And then the corner of his mouth ticked upward into a half-smile that reminded Gemma so much of Taylor that her heart skipped a beat.

"We're going to liberate the detention centers."

CHAPTER TEN

Gemma's departure from Winter's Dam was as unceremonious as her entrance had been months earlier.

Just after ten in the morning, she threw her backpack inside the trunk of Taylor's Charger. Then, she climbed behind the wheel, cranked the engine, and put the town in her rearview mirror. She gripped the wheel with both hands and focused on the taillights of Clarke's cargo van, on the road unraveling in front of her, on the cars flying by in the opposite direction, their drivers smiling and carefree.

She focused on everything except the all-encompassing absence of Taylor.

In the passenger seat, Max stared out the window, not speaking but occasionally reaching up to push a limp curl away from his eyes. Brie and Sophia rode in the backseat. Brie was fast asleep, her head resting against the rear passenger window, her mouth drooping open. She'd gone to sleep almost immediately after they'd left Winter's Dam. Nothing rattled Brie.

Sophia was wide awake.

Gemma wondered if she would ever sleep again.

Gavin and Teresa were riding in the van with Clarke's men. They hadn't wanted to leave Winter's Dam, but they hadn't been given much of a choice. None of the townspeople wanted Gavin to stay in town any longer, not after the events of the previous night, and Teresa would not stay behind without Gavin.

Gemma was thankful the couple hadn't been injured or detained, but she was also thankful that they were riding in the van. Driving the Charger only seemed to exacerbate the anger Gemma felt toward Gavin, as if some part of Taylor still lived in the vehicle itself, so she was glad she didn't have to be trapped inside a vehicle with him.

Ninety quiet minutes later, Ward activated the van's turn signal.

A huge sign in the shape of a pentagon stood on the left side of the mostly deserted highway. Two letters—W and M—had been drawn on the sign in elegant cursive handwriting, the letters intertwined as if dancing.

Below the letters, the sign read: *Welcome to the Westbow Mall.*

Ward turned the van into the mall's parking lot, and Gemma followed, her eyes skimming over the large concrete building. The mall wasn't huge, by any means. From Gemma's point of view, it looked like one long rectangle, its boarded-up windows and rundown appearance indicating that it had been closed for some time. They drove around the right side of the mall and continued to the rear of the building.

Max peered through the windshield. "Clarke's headquarters is in a mall?"

"Perfect," Brie chimed in, fully awake. "Someone torched my house and destroyed most of my clothes, so I'd like to do a little shopping."

When they reached the back of the mall, Gemma noticed a wing jutting out from the building like an outstretched arm. A sign just below the roof read: Westbow Theaters. So, it was an old movie theater. The wing was painted cobalt blue and had a matching metal-encircled spire that stretched from its roof straight into the sky. Compared to the rest of the mall, which looked as if it hadn't been renovated in forty years, the movie theater wing—clearly a more-recent addition—looked downright futuristic.

Suddenly, the van turned left and disappeared down a short ramp. At the bottom of the ramp, the van's brake lights flashed as it came to a stop in front of a loading dock door. After a few seconds, the metal door began to rise. Ward drove through the opening and continued into what Gemma now realized was an underground parking garage.

Following the van into the small parking garage, Gemma quickly realized that the underground lot hadn't been intended for public use. It was too small. There was plenty of above-ground parking available in the mall's vast outdoor lot. Plus, Gemma had seen no signs in the parking lot directing customers toward the underground garage, which meant it had probably been used as parking for mall staff and employees.

The cargo van pulled into a spot near a concrete stairwell. In the neighboring space sat a rusty blue pickup truck that looked as if it had driven through every level of hell described in *Dante's Inferno.*

Gemma parked beside the pickup and shut off the engine. As she climbed out of the Charger, she heard the door to the parking garage lowering behind them.

The rear door to the van swung open, and Gavin jumped out. He turned and extended his arms to help Teresa down. Somehow, they both looked even worse than when they'd left Winter's Dam. Teresa remained next to the van, one hand on the door, surveying her surroundings with a dazed expression. She looked like a survivor of a nuclear holocaust, emerging into the world again after months spent underground. "Where are we?"

"The Westbow Mall," Clarke answered, gently moving her

out of the way as he stepped down from the van. "About twenty minutes north of Harrisburg. This place closed down five years ago. It's owned by some development company out of New Jersey now. They're going to tear it down in the next year or two, probably throw up a Wal-Mart or something in its place, but they haven't done anything yet. We've been here for three weeks, and nobody's bothered us. The lights are still on, and the toilets still flush."

"Sounds like heaven to me," Max said, climbing out of the Charger. "But what's with all the buses?"

Gemma frowned at him. *Buses?*

Noticing her confusion, Max gestured for her to turn around.

She hadn't noticed the buses before because she'd been so focused on following the van into the garage. But when she spun around and her eyes landed on them, she drew in a sharp breath.

On the far end of the garage, shrouded in darkness, a dozen bright-yellow school buses stood in a line, taking up most of the spaces in that section of the garage. Unlike Max, Gemma knew why the buses were there, and she knew how Clarke intended to use them, because he'd explained his plan to her—the Cliff's Notes version of it, at least—back in Letty's shed. Now, seeing the buses lined up like slumbering soldiers awaiting their orders made everything more real to Gemma, and it wasn't fear she felt, but excitement.

We're really doing this.

Clarke joined Ward and Hirsch at the front of the van. "We'll talk about the buses later. For now, let's get you guys settled upstairs. I hope you don't mind sleeping on cots."

Gemma and Brie exchanged a look. They'd used cots for two years back at the Station, and the ancient mattresses they'd slept on at the Sanctuary hadn't been much better. The beds in Letty's apartment—actual beds that included a mattress, box springs, pillows, sheets, and blankets—had spoiled them, but they knew how to make do with much less.

"Cots are fine," Gemma said. "We're far from picky."

As she followed Clarke and his men toward the stairs, she silently thanked God for giving them somewhere to sleep tonight. Clarke didn't *have* to bring them to the mall. They could've easily ended up spending the night in the woods, sleeping on the cold, hard ground, struggling to stay warm and dry.

But God had provided for them again, as He always did.

Gavin spoke up, a nervous edge to his voice. "We're going to stay down here for a few minutes, if that's okay." He dipped his head at Teresa, who now stood with her arms wrapped around his waist, her face buried in his sweatshirt. "She's not ready to go upstairs yet."

Clarke considered this for a moment before nodding. "No problem. When you're ready, just head up these stairs to the employee entrance. The door sticks a little, so give it a good push."

"Got it."

Sophia clung to Gemma's arm as they followed Clarke, Hirsch, and Ward up the stairwell. Brie and Max stayed close behind. The stairwell was dimly lit and smelled faintly of urine, and years of scuff marks discolored the light-gray concrete steps. Two flights up, they came to a windowless door with the words *Employees Only* scrawled in faded black lettering. There was no lock on it that Gemma could see. Clarke gave the door a hard shove, and it swung open.

Beyond the door was a bright hallway.

The left side of the hallway featured three doors, each with a window and spaced about twelve feet apart. Ward and Hirsch continued down the hallway, but Clarke stopped outside of one door and gestured to the window, which was covered with blankets. "These used to be the mall offices. One was the corporate office, one was the security office, and one was the first aid station. Now, these rooms are where most of us sleep, hence the blankets over the windows to keep the light out." He jabbed a finger toward the overhead fluorescent lights. "Most of the stores use regular light switches, but these lights are on an automatic timer that we haven't located yet. They shut off at zero-hundred hours and snap back on five hours later. Makes sleeping outside of those hours a little challenging. Anyway, it's already pretty tight in the offices, but you can grab a few cots and set them up wherever you want. There's plenty of room, obviously. You've got the whole mall. Any questions?"

"Yeah." Brie raised her hand. "Where can I get a Cinnabon?"

Clarke looked at Brie as if trying to decide if she was going to be trouble. "The stores are all empty," he said slowly. "You won't find anything but stained carpet, empty kiosks, and a dry fountain. And this mall never had a Cinnabon."

"Of course it didn't," Brie replied, chewing on her nails.

They continued down the hallway and stopped outside of two large bathrooms—a men's room and a women's room. Clarke pointed at the bathrooms. "There are a dozen toilets and sinks in each bathroom but no showers. We use the showers in the locker room of the security office, and we have a rotating schedule to use those. You're welcome to sign up." He gestured to a piece of notebook paper taped to the wall between the bathrooms. "This is the bathroom cleaning schedule. If you look, you'll see my name. I expect to see each of yours on there by the end of the day." He glanced at Sophia. "You too, young lady."

I'm still going to be cleaning toilets, Gemma realized. *Just a lot more of them.*

Brie visibly bristled at Clarke's order. "Um, there's absolutely no way I'm going to—"

"We have no problem taking our turn." Max grabbed Brie's

hand and offered Clarke an apologetic smile. "No problem at all."

Clarke's gaze lingered on Brie for a few more seconds. Then, he shook his head and continued around the bend in the hallway.

The moment Clarke disappeared from view, Gemma spun on Brie, anger flowing through her veins. "Knock it off! You're going to get us kicked out of here!"

"Would that be such a bad thing?" Brie shot back. "You're the one who dragged us here, Gemma, with literally no explanation why you believe we can trust these people. I mean, how do you know Clarke isn't secretly working *with* the Task Force?"

"Have you forgotten that Clarke is the only reason we're not in a detention center—or worse—right now? He rescued us last night. Why would he do that if he was working with the Task Force? Plus, I have a good feeling about him."

"Oh, you have a good feeling about him? Well, why didn't you just say so? Is it a *love* kind of feeling?" Brie batted her dark eyelashes at Gemma. "The guy has got to be pushing forty, though, which is a little old for you, but who am I to judge? Now that Taylor's dead, it's time to move on to the next guy. Because if there's one thing our little Gemma is good at, it's moving on."

"Brie, shut up!" Max shouted, his face beet red. "What's wrong with you?"

"You always stick up for her, Max!"

"I'm only sticking up for her because you're being awful right now! Why would you say something like that?"

"Stop fighting!" Sophia cried, covering her ears with her hands.

Gemma stood completely still, her right hand hanging at her side, her fingers gripping the stiff fabric of her jeans. She could feel the sting in her palm as if she'd already slapped Brie. It took every ounce of restraint she possessed just to keep her hand from flying at Brie's snarky, self-righteous face.

Taylor's dead. Taylor's dead. Taylor's dead.

"Get away from me!" Brie tore her hand out of Max's grip. "If I'm such a terrible person, then just get away from me!" She spun on her heels and disappeared around the corner.

Gemma glanced at Max, expecting him to rush after Brie, but he didn't. He didn't even look all that worried or upset. Instead, there was a hardness in his eyes—the same defiance Gemma had seen in the photos Carver had shown her back in Ash Grove. The ones taken after Max had endured days of torture at the hands of Carver's men.

That look made her just as proud now as it had then.

"Thanks," Gemma whispered. She didn't know what else to say.

"Don't mention it."

Sophia removed her hands from her ears and leaned close to Gemma. "What's wrong with Brie? Why is she so mad?"

Gemma brushed a strand of hair away from Sophia's eyes. "She's just stressed out. After last night, I think we could all use some sleep."

Together, the three of them continued around the bend in the hallway. Just ahead, Gemma saw where the corridor opened up into the mall's main concourse. There was an empty kiosk— the kind where vendors had once hawked earrings, or licensed NFL hats, or tiny remote-controlled helicopters—and beyond that, a darkened store with a closed security gate.

Sunlight streamed through a huge skylight, but after the artificial brightness of the interior hallway, the mall itself seemed positively dim. Dozens of empty storefronts butted up against the main walkway, but all identifying signs and markings had been removed, making it impossible to tell what each store used to be. All except for the department stores, which anchored each end of the mall. They were identifiable because their signs were huge and couldn't be removed. To Gemma's left was a Boscov's department store, and to her right, at the opposite end of the long walkway, was an old JCPenney.

"What's with all the cots?" Max asked.

He was right. There were cots everywhere. Hundreds of them. They occupied much of the space in the mall, leaving two narrow paths for walking—one on either side of the concourse. They also filled several of the vacant stores. Laying on each cot was a folded blanket and a pillow.

The mall looked like the sight of some future refugee camp.

Which was exactly what it would soon become.

Dozens of people milled around the concourse. Most were men, but a handful of women were present, and they were all too busy to worry about the three strangers who'd just appeared at the end of the hallway. Some carried cardboard boxes loaded with food. Others carried boxes of clothing. A small group had gathered around a rectangular folding table with papers strewn across its surface. Clarke stood at the head of the table, his arms crossed over his chest, like a general surveying his troops.

Although these people were all supposedly ex-police and ex-military, there wasn't a uniform in sight. Everyone was in civilian clothes.

Without asking, Sophia darted for one cot, grabbed a blanket, and clutched it against her chest. She glanced back at Gemma, and the tiny amount of comfort provided by the blanket had been enough to bring a smile to the girl's face.

With Sophia gone, there was no reason to keep the truth from Max any longer. "I didn't want to say anything in the car," she began, "but Clarke's people aren't just helping people like us. That's why there are so many cots. They've got some bigger targets in mind."

Max looked confused for a moment, and then his eyes widened. "The detention centers?"

Gemma nodded. "You can tell the others. Just don't say anything to Sophia yet. I'll talk to her about it."

Just then, a young woman walked past the hallway, a large cardboard box in her muscular arms. Her eyes flicked briefly to Gemma with little interest, but she only made it a few more steps before coming to a stop, the box sagging in her arms as she turned around.

Gemma couldn't believe it was her. It couldn't *actually* be her, could it? But there was a striking resemblance, for sure. The same slender but muscular build. The same scorpion tattoo on her left arm. The same dark-chocolate hair. But her military haircut had grown out, and she was now sporting a flattering pixie cut that softened the sharp lines of her face and made her appear distinctly more feminine than the Task Force soldier Gemma had met in Ash Grove.

The one who'd helped save her life.

"Dietrich?"

CHAPTER ELEVEN

The sleek black detainee transport bus rumbled up to the front entrance of Stovington Detention Center, kicking up plumes of dust and jostling its dazed passengers each time it passed over the slightest dip in the road. Occasionally, these jolts elicited a cry or moan from the human cargo, but one stern look from the armed guards at the front of the bus quieted them down.

As the bus groaned to a stop, Taylor slipped a finger between his wrist and the metal handcuffs that connected his hands to the leg irons. The sadistic Task Force corporal who'd put the handcuffs on him had made sure that the metal dug painfully into his wrist bones. After a two-hour bus ride, the dull pain had transformed into something more akin to agony.

The guards at the front of the bus began shouting orders at the passengers, forcing them off the bus. One by one, the detainees shuffled into the building, their hands cuffed in front of them.

Taylor couldn't stand up because he was the only detainee in leg irons.

He was also the only one in a Task Force uniform.

The others were still wearing their street clothes but that would change soon enough. During in-processing, the guards would force them to surrender their clothing and put on the standard-issue detainee uniform of khaki-colored pants and button-up shirts.

Before leaving his holding cell, the guards had brought him a Task Force uniform. *His* Task Force uniform. The one he'd been wearing when he was detained, rank and nametape still attached. The only thing missing was the patch he'd ripped off his uniform in Winter's Dam.

He assumed the uniform was a last parting shot from Patches.

Surviving inside a detention center with no hope of release would've been difficult enough...

But surviving inside a detention center as an ex-Task Force soldier would be impossible.

Once everyone else got off the bus, two guards returned for Taylor and unlocked his leg irons. Then, they grabbed his arms and escorted him off the bus.

"Welcome to your new home, soldier," one of them sneered.

In-processing took hours.

The guards spent the better part of that first afternoon moving Taylor from one empty holding cell to another, as if uncertain of what to do with him. He felt like the spud in a never-ending game of Hot Potato—no one wanted to hold on to him for too long for fear of getting burned.

The room he currently occupied had a door with a single, narrow window. Inside the cell was a wooden bench, a sink, and a metal toilet hidden behind a low privacy wall. He needed to go to the bathroom—badly, in fact—but he couldn't bring himself to use the toilet. Not with the guards watching him through the window. And they *were* watching him. He couldn't hear what they were saying, but every time they glanced at him and laughed, he fought the urge to flip them the bird.

Turning his back on the guards, Taylor reclined on the bench, putting himself out of their line of sight. Nothing about this new position—lying on his side with his hands cuffed—was comfortable, but he wouldn't give the guards the satisfaction of watching him anymore.

At some point, he must've dozed off, because he woke to a sharp, stabbing pain in his right arm. The moment his eyes popped open, Taylor realized two things—he was no longer handcuffed, and a beefy nurse with an extremely long chin hair was jabbing him with a needle. The urge to fight her was automatic, and if it hadn't been for the two guards holding him down—the same two who'd been laughing outside his holding cell earlier—he probably would've broken the needle off in his arm.

"What is that?" he demanded as the nurse pushed the plunger on the needle, sending clear liquid into his arm. Before she could respond, the pain hit him, and he clenched his jaw to keep from screaming. Whatever was inside of that needle *burned*. He could feel it winding its way through his veins like poison, seeking something to destroy. Was this injection going to kill him? What would happen when it reached his heart?

The nurse grinned at him—an icy grin, if ever there was one. "Just relax, honey," she said. "We're from the government, and we're here to help."

This elicited a chuckle from one guard. The other looked confused.

"The shot smarts a bit," Nurse Chin Hair continued, "but it's just a little something to make your transition easier, courtesy of Uncle Sam. We're patriotic here at Stovington, did you know that?" She glanced at the guards, who returned her smile with even bigger ones of their own. "We sure love our soldiers, don't we, boys? Especially the traitors."

"Please," Taylor mumbled, struggling to stay conscious, but his body and his mind were no longer on the same page. He could feel the mystery liquid following the intricate roadmap of his veins, relaxing each of his muscles until no fight remained in his body. While his mind screamed at him to kick, to punch, to do *anything*...his body felt warm and content, exactly as it had when he used to get drunk to forget about the things he'd done in the Task Force.

"You should thank us," Nurse Chin Hair informed him as she pulled the needle out of his arm. "You've got some tough times ahead of you. We're just trying to make you as comfortable as we can for as long as possible."

Taylor couldn't understand anything the nurse was saying. It was like she was speaking a foreign language. And the long black hair dangling from her fleshy chin distracted him. His mind was fuzzy, and he couldn't focus on anything except that hair. He kept his eyes on it, watching it bob up and down, convinced it was going to grow longer and wrap itself around his throat.

The nurse dropped the needle on a metal table. "This one's a fighter," she said, probably to the guards. "He should be dead to the world by now."

Dead. Finally, a word he understood.

"Can you give him another dose?"

"Nah. Just look at him. The lights are on, but no one's home."

The nurse leaned into his line of sight, that same evil grin still plastered on her lips. "Stop fighting, baby. You won't win. What's that old expression you Christians used to say?" She looked at the guards for help, but they only shook their heads. "Let go..."

Even in the hazy recesses of his drug-altered mind, Taylor knew the expression the nurse was searching for. He'd heard it uttered hundreds of times as a kid, usually from people who attended his church. But he'd heard nothing of the sort from his pastor father, because when it came to matters of faith, Joseph Nolan had never been a fan of feel-good, bumper-sticker slogans of Christianity. In fact, he considered them trite and meaningless, and although he'd lost congregants after stating as much during a sermon one Sunday, he'd never apologized or backed down from his position. At the time, Taylor had thought his father was too hard-nosed. Too stiff-necked. Too rigid and old-fashioned in his beliefs.

But Joseph Nolan had been right, because when the rubber met the road, those Christians with the feel-good bumper stickers plastered on the backs of their sedans and minivans had been among the first to renounce.

Just before Taylor's eyes drifted shut, the nurse's face lit up, and she snapped her fingers. "I've got it! Let go...and let God."

So he did.

CHAPTER TWELVE

"I couldn't stay in the Task Force. Not after what happened to you."

Gemma peered across the table at Amy Dietrich, formerly of the Federal Task Force. The two women occupied a booth inside one of the mall's empty storefronts—an old pizza parlor, the walls still painted in the red, white, and green color scheme. Dietrich had been one of Colonel Carver's soldiers back in Ash Grove. On the day that Taylor had killed Carver to save his own life, Dietrich had shown up at the church just as Gemma, Taylor, and the others were trying to escape. But instead of turning them in, she'd put her own career on the line by letting them go.

"So, you just left?" Gemma asked, bringing a Styrofoam cup of instant coffee to her lips. "You went AWOL?"

Dietrich gave her a quick nod. "I signed up because I wanted to make this country better. All my life, I'd been told that Christianity was bad. So, when the National Compliance Order went into effect and the government said that the only way to unite our country again would be to eliminate Christianity, I believed them. It probably sounds strange to you, but I honestly thought

I was doing the right thing. I thought I could *help* subversives by getting them into detention centers to be rehabilitated." She raised her eyebrows and gave Gemma a pointed look. "The real ones—the ones like you—never give up their faith."

Gemma shrank deeper into the booth, recoiling from the compliment. She didn't deserve praise, not from Dietrich or anyone else. "I'm not as strong as you think. The night of the town meeting, Carver held me on the balcony and made me watch as those people beat Taylor half to death."

Dietrich winced at the memory. "Sergeant Nolan. I can still see him standing up there. I thought they were going to kill him."

"You think I'm strong, but if Carver hadn't duct-taped my mouth shut, I would've confessed everything. About my group, our hiding place, everything. I would've told him anything—*literally anything*—if it meant those people would stop hurting Taylor."

"Sergeant Nolan was your boyfriend, right?"

Gemma extended her left hand, palm down, across the table. Because the little restaurant got very little natural light, the emerald stone on Gemma's finger appeared almost black. It reminded her of the mood ring she hadn't taken off for an entire summer when she was eight, until, one day, the stone had turned black and never changed back.

"He's my fiancé," she said. "We got engaged last fall."

Taking Gemma's hand, Dietrich examined the engagement ring. A sad smile found its way onto her lips. "What happened to him?"

Gemma pulled her hand away and tucked it underneath her leg. "I don't know. The Task Force captured him right after we got engaged. I haven't heard anything since. He'd been AWOL for six months at that point, so he could be in a military prison. Or he could be dead."

The look of dismay on Dietrich's face told Gemma that

those were both distinct possibilities. "I'm so sorry, Gemma. I wish I could tell you he's okay, but I don't know what they would do with him."

Tears slid from Gemma's eyes, but she quickly wiped them away. "I pray for him constantly. When I first wake up in the morning, whenever I think of him throughout the day—which is a lot—and when I go to bed at night. Prayer is all I have at this point."

The ex-soldier raised her cup to her lips, but she didn't take a sip. "So, you said you would've given up your friends to save Sergeant Nolan from the beating. But would you have renounced?" She crossed her arms on the table, seeming genuinely curious. "Would you have renounced your faith to stop the beating?"

Dietrich's question hit Gemma like a punch to the gut. She'd never thought of it that way before. Yes, she would've told Carver anything he wanted to know to save Taylor's life, but would she have renounced her faith to save him? When she imagined herself renouncing, it felt impossible, like cutting out her own heart with a dull scalpel.

But for Taylor? There wasn't anything she wouldn't do for Taylor.

"I don't know," Gemma finally said with a heavy sigh. She pulled her sleeve down far enough to wipe the remaining moisture off her cheeks. "I want to say I wouldn't have renounced, but I honestly don't know."

Dietrich pinched her lips together and nodded. "I saw a lot of things in the Task Force. I saw people refuse to renounce, even when it meant losing the most important things in their lives. On many occasions, I saw children ripped from their parent's arms. Sometimes, I was the one doing the ripping." Her voice broke, and she lowered her gaze to the table. "Anyway, after everything that happened with you, it was like something had woken me up. I finally realized that I was on the wrong side of this fight."

"So, you defected?"

"I went AWOL," Dietrich corrected her, finally taking a long sip of her coffee and following it up with a grimace. "And I'm not the only one, as you can see," she said, nodding toward the main concourse. "A few others from my unit went AWOL before I did, and none of the commanders seemed to care all that much. I guess they figured the AWOLs would turn themselves in as soon as their IDs expired and they could no longer buy food. Anyway, after I left, I reached out to one of the other AWOLs—a guy I trusted—and he was the one who connected me with Clarke. And now, here I am, raiding local donation bins after dark and stealing clothing for a bunch of subversives."

That brought a smile to Gemma's lips. "So, you're one of us now? Just without the religion."

Dietrich uttered a little laugh. She curled her fingers into a ball and gave Gemma a playful fist bump. "Subversives for life, my friend."

✝

After their meeting at the old pizza parlor, Dietrich brought Gemma and the others to an old store near the mall's central hub. Judging by the lingering smell of chocolate, Gemma believed the place might've once been a candy store. Now it was filled with boxes of secondhand clothing, each one separated by gender and size. Gavin and Teresa had grabbed some clothing from Teresa's house since the Task Force had only burned down the grocery store. But Gemma, Sophia, Max, and Brie had nothing to wear except for the clothing they'd been wearing the previous night, which, for everyone except for Gemma, was pajamas.

They dug through the bins in silence, taking only what they

needed. The clothing wasn't intended for them, after all. It was for the others. The ones who, God willing, they might soon help rescue.

After rummaging through the bins, the next order of business was to claim a few cots for themselves and find a place to sleep. Everyone agreed—including Gavin and Teresa—that their little group should stick close together for the time being. But the mall offices were already crowded, and although there were plenty of empty cots in the mall itself, no one wanted to sleep out there. It was too out in the open, too unprotected, especially for people who had grown used to sleeping in abandoned coal mines and isolated cabins. If the Task Force raided the mall, their group wanted to be somewhere deep within the building itself with easy access to an exit.

It was Max who'd suggested the old movie theater they'd seen as they'd driven up to the mall. He'd spent his summers working as a ticket-ripper at his local movie theater, and he seemed downright excited at the prospect of living in one for a little while. Plus, the theater had its own bathrooms, *and* it was set apart from the rest of the mall, which made them all feel a little safer.

After Gemma told Clarke where they were going, they headed for the movie theater. They walked through the empty mall in an awkward little train, with Max as the conductor, a flashlight in his hand. Brie trailed behind the rest of their group, her hands shoved deep into the pockets of her newly acquired blue jeans, a permanent grimace affixed to her face. She hadn't spoken to anyone since the fight in the hallway.

Gemma's eyes locked on Gavin's and Teresa's interlaced hands like a heat-seeking missile, and she tried unsuccessfully to tamp down the anger she felt. Ignoring Gavin and Teresa had been easy enough in Winter's Dam, but now Gemma had no choice but to bear witness to their blossoming romance, and frankly, the sight of it made her feel sick.

Not that she was jealous that Gavin had fallen in love, because Gemma had never truly been in love with him. He'd always been a stand-in for Taylor, which sounded harsh, but it was the truth. And her distaste for their relationship certainly had nothing to do with Teresa. Gemma loved the girl, and she would forever be grateful to Teresa for alerting the rest of the group that Gemma had driven back to the mine to rescue Sophia. If Teresa hadn't done that, Gemma and Sophia might not have made it out of the escape hatch.

The truth was...she hated seeing Gavin happy. That was the long and short of it. It killed her to see him so happy, because he'd stolen that same happiness away from her. He'd left Taylor behind in the school's basement, claiming that the Task Force was coming and that he'd had no choice but to lock the door. Only Gavin and Taylor knew if that was true, and Taylor was gone. But no matter what had actually happened that night, there was no getting around the fact that Gavin had decided to sacrifice Taylor's freedom to save his own.

Gemma tore her eyes away from those interlaced hands and tuned back in to what Max was saying. He was rambling on about the various places he'd found customers hiding in between showings during his box office days.

"The bathrooms rarely worked," Max said, more energized than Gemma had seen him in a long time. "Our general manager told us to check those regularly, particularly between shows. We also found people hiding in storage closets where we kept the cleaning supplies and old movie posters. Empty theaters were also a favorite. Occasionally, we found people hiding underneath the screens, behind decorative curtains. Can you imagine being so opposed to paying another seven bucks that you'd be willing to crawl back there and hide for half an hour?"

"That sounds like something Taylor would've done when he was younger," Gemma said, smiling as she imagined him crouched behind the screen with his friends. "Even if he had the money for a second show, he wouldn't have paid. I can totally see him hiding behind the curtain just to see if he could get away with it."

Max glanced at her, eyebrows raised. She never talked about Taylor, and no one else could talk about him, either. It was an unwritten rule. But gradually, Max's surprise gave way to a grin. "And if I'd stumbled across his hiding place, I bet he would've somehow convinced me to let him stay for the movie."

Gemma tapped the flashlight Clarke had given her against her thigh. "You would've been hand-delivering him free popcorn by the start of the previews."

When they reached Boscov's department store, they turned left into a short wing that jutted off from the mall's main concourse. A dry-as-a-bone wishing fountain sat at the end of the wing, directly beneath another skylight. The old entrance to the movie theater was located just beyond the fountain, its windowless double doors painted the same bleak-white color as the surrounding wall. A low metal bench stood next to the doors.

As their group skirted around the wishing fountain, Sophia grabbed Gemma's elbow and pointed at the empty concrete basin. Three marble tiers stood in the center of the basin, like cake plates stacked on top of each other. An elevated platform surrounded the fountain itself, and Gemma could easily envision parents sitting there, shopping bags at their feet, while their children tossed pennies into the water. When Gemma looked closer, she realized there were still pennies scattered on each tier.

"Oh, I almost forgot about the upstairs projection room," Max said, continuing to list all the theater's potential hiding spots. "We always kept the projection room locked at our theater. Only the projectionists and managers had keys. It wasn't just because of the expensive equipment, but also because, when it wasn't locked, some employees liked to sneak up there between shows and make out."

Gavin used his free hand to squeeze Max's shoulder. "You weren't one of them, were you, buddy?"

Max smirked at him. "No, I was a late bloomer. Anyway, I doubt the projection room is locked. What would be the point? There's nothing to lock up anymore. I'm sure whoever owned the theater took the equipment with them when this place shut down."

He tugged on the handles of double doors that led into the theater, and after a few hard pulls, the doors flew open, releasing a smell from within that was both damp and musty and smelled faintly of popcorn.

Max stepped through the doorway and directed his flashlight into the darkness, but even with the flashlight, it was difficult to see anything.

"Clarke said it's okay to turn on the lights, if we can find them." Gemma ran the beam of her own flashlight along the wall just inside the entrance, searching for the light switch she knew had to be there. "There aren't any windows down here, and the ones at the front of the cineplex are all boarded up."

And then she saw it—just to the right of the set of double doors, higher on the wall than she would've expected. A light switch. She went up on her tiptoes and flicked the switch into the on position.

Directly overhead, a series of fluorescent lights spaced at even intervals in the drop-tile ceiling flickered and then blazed to life, giving off a grim, yellow-tinged light. A long hallway stretched out in front of them, featuring the slightly elegant, slightly funky color scheme that Gemma associated with most modern cineplexes. The bottom halves of the walls were a pale-lavender color, while the top halves were bright-yellow. The tough industrial carpet, which featured red, purple, and yellow circles floating on a dark background, reminded Gemma of the bouncing ball screensaver on Letty's computer.

Max practically sprinted down the hallway, the beam of his flashlight bouncing off the walls. The others had to jog to keep up with him. He aimed his flashlight at the four doors along the right wall as he passed them. "Theaters nine, ten, eleven, and twelve. Can you believe this place had twelve theaters? Mine only had eight."

Sophia leaned close to Gemma. "Why is he so excited?"

"Max is in his happy place, Soph," she replied. But it was more than that. The cineplex represented Max's old life—the time before he'd gone into hiding. It was something familiar and comforting. A bit of normalcy and peace in a world that had gone insane.

Gemma understood because she'd found that kind of peace during those precious six months she'd spent with Taylor at the Sanctuary.

Pushing open the door to the last theater, Max directed his flashlight at the old exit sign to the right of the screen. "There are emergency exits in every theater. Those doors should only open from the inside, so we can get out quickly, but no one can get in."

They continued to explore their potential new home with Max as their overly enthusiastic tour guide. At the end of the hallway, just beyond the last theater, was another set of bathrooms, and then the hallway took a sharp right turn. After a dozen more feet, it took an equally sharp left turn into another hallway, where they found eight more theaters. The hallway emptied into the large lobby and concessions area, where hungry moviegoers had once crowded into lines to purchase nachos, slushies, hot dogs, and buttered popcorn.

The popcorn smell was even stronger now, and Gemma's stomach growled in response.

"Oh my gosh, this place is enormous!" Sophia skipped

through the empty lobby, where the color scheme was even brighter and more obnoxious than the hallway. "I can't believe we get this whole place to ourselves!"

"For the time being," Gemma said. She walked up to the concessions stand, leaned over the dust-coated glass counter-top, and peered into the kitchen area, but it was too dark to see much. There was probably a separate light switch in that area. Either way, there wouldn't be any food back there, not after all this time. But she would've given anything for a huge bucket of buttered popcorn. "Where do you want to set up camp, Soph? One of the theaters?"

With her arms spread wide, Sophia spun in a circle in the center of the lobby. She hadn't changed into her donated clothes yet, so she was still wearing her pajamas—the same peach-colored leggings and green muslin nightgown that Letty had given her for her birthday last summer. The nightgown billowed around her legs as she twirled. "Can't we all just sleep out here together? That would be so cool."

Gemma couldn't imagine anything *less* cool than being forced to spend all night with Gavin and Teresa. "The lobby is way too open, Soph. It'll freak me out, and I won't be able to sleep. Why don't we just pick one theater and sleep in there? There's plenty of room. We'll have our own little space."

Sophia stopped spinning and dropped her arms. Gradually, the light dissipated from her eyes as she retreated inside her herself. "Fine."

"What if I let you pick the theater? Would that make you happy?"

"I guess," Sophia replied with a shrug. "What about seven? That's my lucky number."

"Sounds good to me. Dibs on theater seven."

Max opened a door and shined his flashlight inside an old storage closet. "Hey Brie? Which theater do you want?"

Brie leaned against the old box office counter, her arms

crossed over her chest—a signature Brie stance. She locked eyes with Max, her glare sharp enough to cut glass. "I honestly couldn't care less."

"Cool, then I'll pick." Max tapped his chin thoughtfully. Then a smile lit up his face. "We'll take theater one. All the big-budget summer blockbuster movies—the ones with the most death, destruction, and explosions—go in theater one. That's perfect for us, babe."

Brie didn't crack a smile, but Gemma had to bite her lower lip to keep from laughing.

A few feet away, Gavin and Teresa leaned close together, quietly conferring with one another. Their discussion didn't look heated, exactly, but the next thing to it. Finally, with a frustrated shake of his head, Gavin said, "I guess we'll take theater twelve."

Gemma rolled her eyes. Of course those two wanted to stay in theater twelve. It was as far away from everyone else as they could get.

Passing a hand through his curly hair, Max said, "Man, I can't believe none of Clarke's guys claimed this place. It's outstanding. Like our own little world."

He was right. This really was their own little world. But if everything went according to plan, the mall would soon be filled with freed detainees. God willing, there would be so many of them that they would fill the main concourse, forcing Clarke to utilize the movie theater to house them all.

Like our own little world, Max had said.

Not for long, Gemma prayed. *Please, God, not for long.*

CHAPTER THIRTEEN

The world was pitch black. The color of oil and coal and death. Of ancient things buried deep inside the earth. Things that decay and rot.

Taylor rolled from his back to his stomach, a movement that required far more effort than it should've. When he made it to his stomach, he carefully pushed himself onto his hands and knees and hesitated for a moment, his palms pressing into the cold tiles, waiting to see if any consequences would come from rolling over. There wasn't any pain—at least not yet—but his muscles felt slow and uncertain, as if they'd forgotten their purpose.

The needle. He remembered the mystery liquid seeping into his arm. *The nurse must've drugged me. Knocked me out.*

But how long had he been unconscious?

Aside from his weakened muscles, Taylor didn't recognize any lingering effects from whatever drug they'd given him. His mind seemed to be working fine. He knew who he was, right down to his birthdate, social security number, and shoe size. He remembered arriving at the detention center and spending hours in a holding cell before Nurse Chin Hair and her two cronies had stabbed a needle into his arm. And he remembered Patches and Groot, although he would've been just fine with the nurse wiping *those* memories from his brain entirely.

He assumed he was inside a cell at the detention center, but as he searched his ink-black surroundings for something to focus on, something he could use to orient himself, his eyes didn't detect even the faintest hint of light. Not from a window. Not from a crack underneath a door. Nothing.

"Hello? Is anyone there?"

He slid his hands back and forth, searching his immediate surroundings for the metal frame of a bed or a desk. Anything recognizable. The thought occurred to him that he'd dedicated years of his life to detaining subversives and sending them off to detention centers, but he had no idea what the centers were really like.

A few years back, one of the major news networks had done a series about life inside of a detention center, and the cushy living conditions Taylor had seen in the report left him feeling disgusted. Subversives sharing rooms—often with their own family members—and dining together in a brightly lit dining hall. They could come and go from their rooms as they pleased, and aside from their mandated therapy sessions and re-education classes, they had no real responsibilities. The detention facility featured on the program even had an in-ground swimming pool and tennis courts. To Taylor, the place looked a lot more like a health spa than a prison.

But this place...this was *nothing* like the detention center he'd seen on the news.

He crawled forward, his hands and knees sliding along the tile floor in slight movements as he felt his way around the room. The top of his head found the concrete wall a fraction of a second before his hands did, and the resulting thump and flash of pain made him irrationally angry. Angry enough to hurl curses at the wall. The cursing made him feel better, but only for a few seconds, because when he stopped shouting, he heard something.

There was the faint sound of crying coming from the other side of the wall.

But it wasn't the ordinary sound of someone weeping. That Taylor could've handled. But these cries were different. These were half-cries, half-moans, and although they sounded almost inhuman, Taylor knew they were coming from a man. It was the worst thing he'd ever heard.

The sound of a human being in complete despair.

He scooted away from the wall, but the cries only grew louder, as if the person making those terrible sounds could sense that someone had finally taken notice of their anguish. Even when Taylor covered his ears with his hands, he couldn't block it out. It made him wish that the nurse would return with her needle and plunge it into his arm again just to make the sound go away.

He thought of a Bible verse from the Book of Matthew: *"Then the king told the attendants, 'Tie him hand and foot, and throw him outside, into the darkness, where there will be weeping and gnashing of teeth.'"*

Taylor's father hadn't been a fire-and-brimstone pastor. Joseph Nolan had rarely spoken of hell, and what it might entail, in any of his sermons. But it was the thread—or the backstitch, to use a sewing reference his mother would've appreciated— that joined everything together. He wove the certainty of hell for nonbelievers throughout every sermon he preached, even if he rarely spoke of it outright, because he truly believed the place existed and that the vast majority of people on Earth were headed there.

That had been one reason Taylor had freed himself from his father and his father's religion. Because despite the undertones buried within his father's sermons, Taylor hadn't been a believer in heaven or hell. Or life after death. Or God.

And that disbelief had a lot to do with his mother.

Taylor had been at her side when she'd passed away. After being discharged from the hospital to home hospice care, his mother had spent the last two weeks of her life in a hospital bed in their spare bedroom. Even now, huddled on the tile floor of his pitch-black cell with his hands clasped over his ears, Taylor could recall the medicinal and antiseptic smell of that room. But there had been something else there, too. An underlying odor that he eventually came to recognize as the stench of approaching death.

Over those final two weeks, different hospice nurses came and went from the house regularly. Most of them were friendly enough. They introduced themselves to him and tried to make him laugh, but Taylor ignored them. He didn't want strangers in his house. He didn't want to tell them about his day. He just wanted them to go away so his life could go back to the way it had been before the cancer.

On a cheerful Tuesday morning in mid-June, with the entire summer stretching out before him like a promise, Taylor had awoken to the sounds of birds chirping outside of his bedroom window and one of his neighbors firing up their lawnmower. His first thought was that it was going to be a beautiful day.

He'd only been awake for a few minutes when his father had knocked on his bedroom door and walked into the room without waiting for a response, a wrecked expression on his face.

Taylor assumed his mother had passed away, and his first emotion had been relief. He'd wanted it to be over—her suffering *and* his.

But then his father had uttered in a choked voice, "It's time," and Taylor's stomach had plummeted into his feet.

Still wearing his pajamas—a Phillies t-shirt and a pair of basketball shorts—Taylor had climbed out of bed and walked into the hallway without first brushing his teeth or using the bathroom. His father followed him into the spare bedroom, his large hand between Taylor's shoulder blades, urging him toward one of two chairs set up next to his mother's hospital bed. Her window, like Taylor's, was open to allow in the morning sunshine, but the birds were no longer chirping.

He sank into the chair and stared at his mother. She wasn't awake. She hadn't been for days, not since the pain had gotten so bad that the hospice nurses had drugged her into unconsciousness. She did not know that her son was by her side, and she never opened her eyes, not even when Taylor's father picked up her left hand and placed it inside Taylor's. It was already cold and lifeless, and it took every ounce of willpower that Taylor could muster not to let it go.

Joseph Nolan walked to the other side of the bed, took his wife's other hand, and recited the Twenty-Third Psalm.

Taylor had fixed his bleary eyes on the top of his father's head. Each word felt like a tiny pin jabbing his heart until he couldn't take it anymore.

"Not this one."

"What?" his father asked, barely able to lift his head.

"Not this one," Taylor repeated, defiance causing his voice to grow stronger. "This one makes her sad because it reminds her of funerals. You know that. Can't you read something else?"

Over the dying body of his mother, Taylor had watched the grief in his father's eyes transform into anger, but he'd refused to look away. He was only twelve, and he still had to live under his father's roof for at least six more years. But his mother was dying. She didn't love this particular Psalm, and Taylor would not allow it to be the last thing she ever heard.

Eventually, the anger in Joseph Nolan's eyes had fizzled, and he'd torn his gaze away from his son and brought it to rest on his wife. He'd brought a hand to her face, tears running down his cheeks as he tenderly touched the bandana she wore to cover her bald head.

When his father hadn't continued reading the Twenty-Third Psalm, Taylor had closed his eyes and recited one of his mother's favorite verses from Scripture. He felt his throat trying to close around the words, but he'd forced them out, anyway. For her.

"For I am convinced that neither death nor life, neither angels nor demons, neither the present nor the future, nor any powers, neither height nor depth, nor anything else in all creation, will be able to separate us from the love of God that is in Christ Jesus our Lord."

She died a few hours later, at one o'clock in the afternoon. After she passed, Taylor had returned to his sunlit bedroom, crawled under the covers, and prayed. He'd asked God to bring his mother back. To raise her from the dead, just as He'd raised Lazarus. Then he'd waited, convinced that his father would soon burst into the room and announce that God had answered his prayers. That his mother was awake.

But his father never came. Not even to check on him.

Eventually, two men had arrived from the funeral home. Taylor heard them in the hallway outside his bedroom, speaking in low, conspiratorial voices with his father. Then, and only then, had he allowed himself to cry. But his primary emotion hadn't been sadness but bitterness. It had already taken root inside his heart. Bitterness toward his father. Bitterness toward God.

A bitterness that would never leave.

Huddled on the floor of his cold, black cell, Taylor drew his hands away from his ears, steeling himself for the sound of those inhuman cries. But he couldn't hear anything. The person on the other side of the concrete wall had mercifully gone silent.

And then light filled his cell.

Blinding light...and grief-stricken voices.

His hands went to cover his eyes because the light was so

bright it hurt, and the thin flesh of his eyelids wasn't sufficient to block it out. He cringed against the floor, his hands covering his face, blindly bracing himself for whatever came next. Maybe an interrogator—the one responsible for the cries coming from the man next door—would burst into the room.

When nothing happened, Taylor worked his hands away from his face. It was a gradual process, but as his eyes adjusted, he realized it wasn't the lights themselves—because they were just normal fluorescents—but the lingering effects of Nurse Chin Hair's drugs that were making him so sensitive to the light.

When his eyes cleared, he saw the door.

It looked to be made of steel, and there was no way to open it from the inside. Three-quarters of the way up the door was the outline of a square. Most likely a food slot. There was no window or porthole in the door itself.

Then, he noticed the camera hanging above the door, aimed at him like a watchful eye. They'd encased it in a metal security cage, probably to prevent the occupant of the cell from tampering with it. A steady red light glowed at its base.

How hadn't he noticed that light before?

Who was watching him? And what were they hoping to see?

He pried his eyes away from the camera long enough to survey the rest of his room. It was narrow, only wide enough to accommodate a single metal bed with a thin mattress, a stainless-steel toilet and sink, and a small shower in the room's corner. A cheap toothbrush and tube of toothpaste sat on the corner of the sink, but there were no blankets or sheets on the bed. No soap or toilet paper. No towels. There wasn't even a curtain attached to the shower area. So, unless the powers-that-be hadn't delivered his amenities to his room yet—which he somehow doubted—if he showered, he would do it within full view of the camera.

His eyes returned to the toothbrush balanced on the edge of

the sink, and bitter laughter erupted from his mouth. Apparently, the detention center staff didn't value privacy or cleanliness, but they valued surveillance. And oral hygiene.

He finished his visual recon of the room, confirming what he already knew: the small window built into the door was the room's only window. The solid concrete walls virtually eliminated any hope of escape. Overhead, a metal grate covered an air vent in the ceiling, but unless he lost half his body weight or amputated a few limbs, there was no way he would fit through the vent's narrow opening.

Only then, after he'd seen everything there was to see, did he allow his mind to tune in to the voices—the ones being piped into his cell over the speaker system.

It took him a moment to realize he was listening to the voices of American citizens. Hundreds of them. All renouncing their Christianity before the entire world.

"My name is Janice Murdock, and I renounce my faith in Jesus Christ."

"My name is Chris Anders, and I renounce my faith in Jesus Christ."

Renouncements, he realized. *They force the detainees to listen to renouncements.*

Those lukewarm Christians who'd renounced immediately after the National Compliance Order went into effect had often used the opportunity to plug their businesses or websites. Back then, listening to renouncements had been a bit like watching one long block of commercials. But the people whose voices were being piped into Taylor's cell weren't like those people back in the early days. These people had held out as long as they could. Most of them sounded heartbroken. Some were crying so hard it was difficult to understand them. The renouncements went on forever, until Taylor couldn't imagine that there were any people left in the country who *hadn't* renounced.

Eventually, the lights went off, and the voices went silent.

Taylor didn't know what time it was or if he should have been asleep or awake, and that was probably the point. Alternating silence and darkness with bright lights and renouncements was likely torture for the detainees. Something designed to disorient them. To break down their minds and their bodies.

No, this place wasn't hell. But it was close.

With nothing else to do and nothing to see, he stared into the camera's unblinking eye.

And he waited.

CHAPTER FOURTEEN

A rough hand shook Gemma's shoulder, rousing her back to consciousness.

"Alcott."

The sudden dump of adrenaline tightened all of Gemma's muscles and brought her fully awake. She bolted upright, nearly slamming her head into Clarke's.

"What's going on?" She pushed the hair out of her face. "What are you doing in here?"

The ex-cop crouched beside her cot, the massive theater screen curving up behind him like a cresting wave about to crash over them both. "Meet me in the parking garage in fifteen minutes. We're going for a ride."

She glanced at the readout on her digital watch. It was just after six in the morning. "What? Why?"

"Because I want to show you something." He rose to his feet and then added, *"Just you."*

Gemma's searching eyes found the other cot. Before going to bed, Max had shown her how to dim the theater lights to their lowest setting so it wouldn't be completely dark, but they could still sleep. There was enough light for Gemma to see Sophia curled up on her cot, her chest rising and falling with the slow, steady breathing of sleep.

"What about Soph? I can't just leave her here. What if she wakes up alone?"

Clarke released a stiff breath. "Then get someone to stay with her, Alcott. Just meet me in the parking garage. Fifteen minutes." With that, he strolled purposefully up the handicapped ramp and out of the theater.

Reluctantly, Gemma rolled off her cot and threw on a tattered pair of jeans, a black tank top, and the Army-style jacket she'd liberated from the clothing bins. She dressed quietly, determined not to wake Sophia. The girl had slept the whole night with no nightmares, which was a good sign.

She exited the theater and found Max at the other end of the hallway, stretched out on a cot outside the entrance to theater one. "Why are you in the hallway?" she asked, nodding at the cot. "Don't tell me Brie made you sleep out here."

He yawned and stretched his arms over his head. Then, he rubbed at the scar on his cheek, as if to make sure it was still there. "She kicked me out."

Irritation washed over Gemma. Their group had enough things to worry about without Brie's dramatics. "I'm sorry, Max. Listen, do you mind staying with Sophia until I get back? I have to meet Clarke in the parking garage."

Max's eyebrows shot up. "The parking garage? Why?"

"He says he wants to show me something."

"You want me to come with you?"

She shook her head. "I'm supposed to come alone."

It was clear from the expression on Max's face that he didn't like the idea of Gemma going anywhere alone with Clarke, but he also knew there wasn't any point in arguing with her. They were guests in Clarke's house, and they had to follow his rules. "Don't worry about Sophia," he said, pushing himself off the cot. "I'll wait in there until she wakes up. Maybe I'll try to get a little more sleep." And then, because he couldn't help himself, he added, "Just be careful, okay? I'm not sure about that guy."

"Neither am I."

✝

Clarke leaned against the driver's door of the battered blue pickup truck, a paperback book open in his hands. When he noticed Gemma approaching, he stuffed the book inside his back pocket and gave her a critical look.

"You're five minutes late."

She frowned at him. "Late for what? What's so important at six-thirty in the morning?"

"You'll see. Get in."

Walking around the rear of the truck, Gemma pulled the passenger door open and winced at the discordant screech of the rusted hinges. Clarke's truck was jacked up higher than most pickups, and there was no running board, so she gripped the seat with one hand, the grab handle with the other, and then hauled her short body inside the cab.

"Your truck isn't designed for short people."

Clarke turned the key in the ignition. The engine sputtered for several seconds before groaning to life. The truck sounded like an animal that needed to be put out of its misery.

"Good thing I'm not short," Clarke replied, grabbing a pair of aviator sunglasses from the dashboard and putting them on. He shifted the truck into gear and drove it out of the parking garage.

Gemma twisted in her seat to watch the heavy door roll shut behind them, marveling at how deserted the mall appeared from the outside. It seemed impossible that dozens of people were hiding inside. And if all went according to plan, soon dozens would turn into *hundreds*.

Although it was still early, and the sun hadn't fully risen yet, the outside world seemed excessively bright to Gemma after the relative dimness of the mall. She had no sunglasses, so she pulled the truck's visor down, but even that wasn't enough to keep her from squinting.

The highway wasn't as deserted as it had been the previous day, but it was still far from busy. A few cars drove by in both directions, but none of the drivers even glanced at the mall or at Clarke's truck. They were too focused on their own ordinary lives—going to work, or the gym, or wherever normal people went at six-thirty in the morning. Gemma couldn't imagine living that kind of life. A life without fear. A life where she could be oblivious to everything happening around her without suffering terrible consequences.

As they drove down the exit ramp that joined up with the highway, a tractor-trailer blew past in the opposite direction, clearly exceeding the speed limit by *a lot*. Gemma stole a look at Clarke and saw the slight flare of his nostrils.

"You want to pull that guy over, don't you?" she asked.

"More than you know."

After fifteen minutes of driving south, the highway linked up with Routes 22/322 at a four-lane concrete bridge that crossed the expanse of the Susquehanna River. Just after the bridge, Gemma saw the Pilot Travel Center on the right side of the road. The same place where they'd stopped the previous day so Sophia could use the restroom.

As they drove past the truck stop, Gemma heard herself asking, "Why me?"

Clarke's fingers tightened around the steering wheel. "What do you mean?"

"Why am I sitting here with you? Why not someone else? Why not Max?"

Clarke gave her a sharp look. "Because you're the leader of your group," he replied. "Whether you like it or not."

Gemma wasn't sure how to respond to that, so she said nothing.

Just past an old-fashioned burger joint called the Red Rabbit Drive-In, Clarke veered to the right, exiting Route 22/322 and joining up with Route 11/15—a road that Gemma knew well. Her father had never enjoyed roads where people regularly drove twenty miles over the speed limit, so he'd avoided Route 22/322 at all costs. Route 11/15 had been his preferred road whenever they went to Harrisburg, but the road had its drawbacks. The lazy highway ran parallel to the Susquehanna River and featured several gas stations, a few greasy-spoon diners, and more than its fair share of adult novelty shops. For reasons Gemma had never understood, those stores sprouted alongside the well-traveled roadway like neon-coated weeds, choking out other businesses and giving the whole highway a grimy, polluted feel.

Twisting her body so she was facing Clarke, Gemma leaned against the passenger door. She hoped the rusty hinges wouldn't give way and send her tumbling backward onto the highway. "Doesn't the mall seem a little exposed to you?" she asked, aware she might have been walking a thin line with Clarke but not really caring. "Our group...we're used to staying in the mountains, far away from any big cities. There's a highway right outside the mall and Harrisburg is close. You really think it's a safe place to bring hundreds of detainees?"

Clarke's body stiffened at the question, and he responded without looking at her. "Absolutely. That's why we chose it. There aren't any windows to fortify, and they'd boarded up all the doors up before we got there. We had to reinforce them a little, but they were pretty much good to go. No windows and no doors means we can keep the lights on without being spotted, except at night, when we maintain strict light discipline in the main concourse. As for the defensibility of the building itself, the roof is flat and easily accessible. We keep guys up there on a rotating shift. If the Task Force shows up, we'll be able to see them coming a long way off."

"Then what? What happens if you see them coming?"

"We evacuate through the parking garage," he replied. "There's a road behind the mall that we'd take. Our plan is to escape on the buses while the good guys on the roof lay down suppressive fire to hold the bad guys off. Obviously, that's a worst-case scenario—we won't be outrunning anyone in school buses—but if it happens, we'll get as many people away as we can. The ones who get captured won't be any worse off than they are already."

"But what about your guys on the roof? What happens to them?"

He glanced at her, his dark eyes radiating a fierceness that reminded her of Taylor. "They volunteered for this. They know the risks."

"Okay, so forget the Task Force," she said. "Let's say everything goes according to plan. What do you intend to do with all these people you've rescued from the detention centers?"

"Get them to safety, obviously. Link them up with their families."

To Gemma, Clarke sounded like a robot who'd been taught to repeat certain phrases that meant nothing to him. "But even if you hide these people until you can safely reunite them with their families, they'll be hunted down and rearrested within a few weeks, maybe even a few days. And their family members will be arrested, too."

"Why are you trying to find every excuse not to rescue them?" Clarke demanded, giving her a piercing look. "Aren't you the same girl who went on television, held up a Bible, and promised those people in the detention centers that you were coming to rescue them? *Your salvation is coming.* What did you mean by that, Alcott?"

What Gemma wanted to say—but what she couldn't say

because Clarke wouldn't understand—was that God had been speaking through her that day. She'd gone into the compliance office, intending to make a statement. To share the Truth with a sinful and unbelieving world. To tell them about Taylor and Yost and the sacrifices they'd made for a group of subversives. To encourage other subversives to keep going. She'd intended to put on her jacket, with its upside-down Task Force patch, and read an excerpt from the Bible in front of the world. She'd even intended to give encouragement to the people—like her parents —who were still languishing in detention centers.

But she had *never* intended to give them false hope.

However, something strange had come over her when she'd pulled her cross necklace out of her shirt. The same cross that Mike Yost had clutched in his hands as he'd given his soul to Christ in the last moments of his life. As Gemma stood in front of that camera, with the entire world watching, her eyes had fallen on the flecks of dried blood on the cross's surface, and those infamous four words had spilled from her lips.

Your salvation is coming.

But she couldn't explain any of that to Clarke, so she turned away from him and stared at the calm surface of the Susquehanna River.

After a few minutes, he said, "If you're not too busy moping, you need to see this."

Peeking sideways out of the corner of her eye, she glimpsed Clarke's finger pointing out the windshield. When she looked in the direction he was pointing, she saw a billboard advertising a fast-food restaurant, and her right hand found its way to her heart.

Spray-painted over the advertisement was a symbol she knew well: two swords forming a cross borne upon a dark silhouette of a pair of shoulders. Whoever had spray-painted the symbol had also included a blood-red background, exactly the same color as on the Task Force patch.

"We've passed two other billboards like this one since leaving the mall," Clarke said. "I didn't point them out to you because I didn't think I needed to. But I think maybe you need to be reminded that this fight is bigger than you, Alcott. It's bigger than us all."

Gemma rotated in her seat, staring at the billboard until it disappeared from view.

Just south of Liverpool, Clarke pulled the truck into the center lane and turned onto a secondary road that wound through the woods for several miles. Eventually, the dense border of trees on both sides of the road gave way to fields and rolling countryside. None of the houses showed any signs of activity—it was still too early for most people to be awake and outside—but Clarke had to slam on his brakes in front of a rundown trailer to avoid hitting a flock of hens that were following a single rooster across the road. Even the screech of the truck's brakes wasn't enough to make the rooster pick up his pace, and he cast only the briefest of glances at the truck before continuing across the road.

While they waited, Gemma turned to face Clarke. "So, since we're stuck together, why don't you tell me about yourself? What's your family like? Are you married?"

Clarke tapped his fingers impatiently on the wheel as the last of the hens cleared the highway. "I'm not married. I don't have any kids. My parents are both dead. I've got a younger sister, but I haven't seen her in years."

"How much younger?"

He gave Gemma a pointed look. "That's everything you need to know about me."

"Okay," she said, straightening in her seat. "Good talk."

A few miles down the road, Gemma finally saw someone outside. An Amish woman stood on the front porch of a farmhouse, stringing yards of dark-colored clothing from an old-fashioned pulley clothesline. As the truck drove by, Gemma reflexively raised her hand in greeting. The Amish woman stared back at her, but she did not wave.

That struck Gemma as odd because Amish people *always* waved, even in the worst circumstances. It was a part of their culture. Once, Gemma's family had driven past an Amish church just prior to a funeral, and although they were in mourning, every Amish person in every horse-and-buggy they'd passed along the way had waved at them, including the children.

Perhaps the woman on the porch was just having a bad day.

"They don't go after Amish," Gemma said, more to herself than to Clarke. "Isn't that strange? They're Christians, too...and yet the Task Force leaves them alone."

She didn't expect a response, but Clarke surprised her by saying, "Only because the government doesn't view them as a threat—not yet, anyway. But they will. A few months ago, the Task Force detained a bunch of Amish families out in Ohio. Not for their faith, but because they were hiding subversives on their farms. They'd even given the subversives Amish clothing to wear."

As the Amish woman faded from view in the rearview mirror, it occurred to Gemma that the woman on the porch—who looked the part, but who didn't seem to know the Amish customs—might not have been Amish at all.

Not long after the Amish farmhouse, Clarke turned onto an unimproved road, the truck kicking up gravel and dust as it sped up the hill. They skirted along the side of the ridge, the land to their right sloping down into a valley. Thick groupings of trees interspersed with the occasional house shielded the land below from view. But every so often, the trees would clear enough for Gemma to glimpse a gothic-looking building seated at the base of the valley, surrounded by fields on all sides.

Only when they got closer did she notice the concertina wire.

When they reached a pull-off area that overlooked the building, Clarke parked on the side of the road, shut off the engine, and exited the truck without saying a word. He walked around to her side of the truck and yanked open the passenger door.

This time, she didn't wince at the sound of the rusty hinges.

She couldn't tear her eyes away from the building.

It looked like a gigantic box fan lying on its back in the middle of a field. That was the best way to describe it. A rectangle-shaped perimeter of fencing topped with concertina wire surrounded seven wings that stretched out in all directions from a central hub. The grassy areas between the wings were overgrown and appeared unused. Gemma couldn't see anyone walking around outside—not even any guards. The stone structure looked entirely out of place in the peaceful countryside, like a gothic nightmare that someone had dreamt into reality.

"This," Clarke began, "is our objective. It's one of twelve detention centers currently operating in Pennsylvania. They modeled this particular center after Eastern State Penitentiary."

"That old prison in Philadelphia?"

"Exactly. Eastern State *used* to be a prison, but after it shut down in 1971, the city turned it into a tourist attraction—daytime walking tours, Halloween ghost tours, that kind of thing. The government fixed it up about ten years ago, and Eastern State was the first detention center to open in Pennsylvania. This is one of its little sisters."

Gemma had heard about Eastern State Penitentiary on the news. It was now the Region 1 Detention Center in Pennsylvania, and the government had built it to rehabilitate ministers they deemed problematic. "I remember hearing about the government buying up empty buildings to house detainees," she said. "They also turned the old Harrisburg State Hospital into a detention center, didn't they?"

"That's right. But the powers-that-be liked the architectural design of Eastern State enough to replicate it, because all the newly built centers look like this one."

Gemma shook her head. "I didn't realize they were building new detention centers." She'd always imagined, in the back of her mind, that things would get better. She'd imagined that the world would eventually reach the height of its insanity, and then the pendulum would swing back in the other direction, and all the detainees would be released.

"This one has a max capacity of four-hundred detainees. It might *look* like a prison, but it's not a normal prison. The architectural design wasn't the only thing they stole from Eastern State. They also stole the idea of separate incarceration, so they keep all detainees entirely separated from each other. There's no interaction at all. Detainees do everything in their cells. Sleep, eat, shower...everything. They don't see anyone except for the guards who deliver their meals."

Gemma's eyes landed on the overgrown grassy areas between the wings. "Are they allowed to go outside?"

"The guards are supposed to let them outside, but they don't. The detainees never leave their cells. There's no television. No entertainment. The only thing they ever hear from the outside world are the renouncements."

She blinked at Clarke, certain she'd misunderstood him. "What?"

"It's a tactic designed to demoralize the prisoners. They broadcast the renouncements over speakers directly into each cell. They play them all day long."

She didn't realize she was squeezing her necklace until her fingers ached. "Does that mean—"

"Yes," Clarke said, not even waiting for her to finish. "When you got up in front of the world and made that statement of yours, everyone who was inside a detention center at the time heard it."

Including my parents, Gemma realized. *Is that where they've been all this time? Are they in that awful, wheel-shaped building?*

Huddled in their separate cells, completely isolated from each other and everyone else, for three years?

"How do you know all of this?" she whispered.

"Like I said before, we've got people on the inside. People who are going to help us execute our plan."

With one shaking hand, she braced herself against the rear quarter panel of Clarke's truck. "What is our plan?"

Clarke's eyes lingered on Gemma, studying her intently. Then, he pointed at the valley below. "A nighttime attack on that detention center. But this is only our little piece of the puzzle. There will be other attacks happening concurrently across the state. Now, we might only get one shot at this, so our goal is to liberate as many detainees as possible in one night."

The muscles in Gemma's body tensed as Clarke spoke. She wasn't armed. She did not know how many guards were inside that building. And she certainly had no way of transporting four-hundred detainees back to the mall. But if Clarke had told her he wanted to attack the building right now, in broad daylight, she would've gone with him.

"How long?" she muttered. "How long until we attack?"

For the first time that morning, Clarke smiled at her.

There you are, the smile said.

"Tomorrow."

CHAPTER FIFTEEN

Something was wrong. There was no ignoring it anymore.

Taylor flipped onto his stomach on the bumpy mattress, trying to find a comfortable sleeping position, but the waves of nausea kept coming. It was worse than the worst stomach bug he'd ever had. He'd only received two meals since arriving at the detention center, so there wasn't much in his stomach to throw up, but he'd spent much of the last few hours dry-heaving into the toilet. He kept waiting for the worst of it to pass, as twenty-four-hour bugs typically did. But as time went on, his stomach issues seemed to get worse, not better.

Unable to take lying on his front for another minute, he pushed himself into a sitting position, planted his bare feet on the floor, and wrapped his arms around his stomach.

Not being able to see anything in the pitch-black darkness of his cell made the sickness so much worse because there was nothing for his eyes to focus on. Nothing to occupy his mind. He felt as if he were adrift on an endless sea of black, being tossed around by the waves.

The cycle of light and darkness in his cell continued with no discernable pattern. Sometimes, it felt as if the lights were on for hours. Other times, it felt as if they were only on for a few minutes.

Whenever the light returned, so did the renouncements, and he listened intently for Gemma's voice, *hoping* to hear it. If she was still alive, he wanted her to renounce. Not because he believed they had any hope of a future together—he wasn't naïve enough to still cling to an idea like that—but because he never wanted her to end up in a cell like this one.

That would destroy him.

When darkness claimed his cell, he thought about all the Christians he'd sent to detention centers over the years. People he'd sentenced to imprisonment in a cell just like this one.

People like his father.

Another wave of nausea struck him with the force of a nuclear blast, and he fell to his knees and crawled in what he hoped was the general direction of the toilet. He didn't have far to go—the cell wasn't big—but he barely made it before more bile came lurching up from the depths of his stomach. He didn't realize that it was possible for vomiting to *hurt* this much. Everything between his stomach and his tongue burned. His throat was on fire, and he wanted a drink of water more than anything in the world, but he didn't have the strength to push himself up to the sink to get one. He didn't even have the strength to crawl back onto his bed. Instead, he slumped against the wall, one arm propped on the rim of the toilet, and stared at the red light of the camera.

Wiping the sheen of sweat from his forehead, he imagined the people on the other end of the camera watching him. Laughing at him. Waiting for him to break. To lose his sanity.

To give up.

But here—in this awful place—he had nothing.

Nothing to lose. Nothing to give up.

Only his life. And would it be such a bad thing to give *that* up?

No, he didn't think that would be bad at all.

He tried to distract himself from his nausea by devising various ways to kill himself. There were no blankets or sheets in his cell, and they hadn't given him a belt for his Task Force uniform, so hanging wasn't possible. He could file the end of the toothbrush into a stabbing implement, but that would take days and require strength he didn't possess. If he was lucky, he'd die of dehydration within the next forty-eight hours. Probably less. But that was still a *long* time to wait.

Taylor's head lolled forward as sleep pulled at his ankles, trying to drag him toward the abyss of oblivion. He didn't fight it, but surrendered willingly. Until death came for him, sleep would be his only escape from this hell.

And then his dead mother spoke to him in the darkness.

Her voice was only a whisper, but it was clearer than any other voice he'd heard in his life. "The Lord is close to the brokenhearted," she breathed into his ear, "and saves those who are crushed in spirit."

Psalm Thirty-Four, verse eighteen. Another of his mother's favorite verses.

But his mother was dead. She didn't have favorite verses anymore.

Did that mean he was dead, too? Had he died on the floor of his cell, leaning against the toilet?

"Mom?" he croaked.

With great effort, he lifted his head to look for her, expecting to see her kneeling on the floor beside him.

But she wasn't there.

Taylor choked back a cry. He'd wanted his mother to be there. So badly. He didn't want to be alone anymore. He was tired of being alone.

"Mom?" This time, the word sounded like a plea for rescue. "Are you there?"

The silence that followed made him yearn for the return of the endless, droning renouncements. He needed something to fill his mind. Something to distract him from the silence and the sickness and the darkness and the emptiness that his life had become.

The Lord is close to the brokenhearted and saves those who are crushed in spirit.

Was he brokenhearted?

Yes. He felt brokenhearted for Gemma. For everything they'd lost. For a future they would never share. For the children they would never have. For a life they would never build together.

Even if she evaded capture, even if she never ended up in a cell like this one, Gemma might still do those things—but she would do them with another man.

So, yes, he was brokenhearted. But was he crushed?

Crushed. Annihilated. Defeated.

Yes. He was all of those.

His body slid farther down the wall so that only his upper back and shoulders were touching the concrete. Inside his chest, his heart raced. He felt so hot. Too hot. Every part of him was on fire, as if he already had one foot in hell.

Taylor brought a hand up to his forehead, but it came away dry. He wasn't sweating, and he remembered enough from first aid training in the Task Force to know that wasn't a good sign. He wanted to strip off his uniform jacket and t-shirt and let the concrete cool his body, but he didn't have the strength to sit up straight, much less remove his clothing.

"God, help me."

Three little words. Words that had no business coming out of his mouth...and yet there they were. He'd said them. And now that they'd been said, he couldn't take them back. He couldn't put them back inside himself any more than he could put the bile he'd expelled into the toilet back where it had come from.

The moment the words left his lips, Taylor saw something like a wall in his mind. A sturdy brick wall of his own making, sealed not with mortar but with anger and sadness and pain.

Years of anger and sadness and pain.

But there were large cracks in the mortar. Weaknesses. Light peeked through the cracks in the wall. Not the malevolent red light of the camera, but the blazing white light of hope. Of freedom.

Of salvation.

As he watched, the wall began to crumble. Not all at once, but a little at a time. Several of the cracks in the mortar grew bigger, and the bricks nearest to the cracks gave way first, allowing in more light. Others followed. One by one, they broke apart and shattered to dust on the ground.

Something had changed inside him back in Ash Grove. When Carver had pressed a gun to his skull and threatened to take his life, Taylor had called out to God. He'd prayed. He'd apologized. It hadn't stuck, but that was when the cracks had formed.

But those cracks hadn't brought down the wall, because he hadn't been broken yet.

He hadn't been crushed.

Another brick fell, smashing into powder and blowing away like chaff. And then another. The entire wall was collapsing now. There was no stopping it.

"I'm done...fighting." Taylor hurled the words at the wall like a wrecking ball. "I won't...fight You...anymore."

The wall crumbled like the walls of Jericho.

"Jesus. Please. Help me."

White light exploded all around him.

Taylor was on a gurney.

Overhead, white ceiling tiles flashed by in rapid succession, interspersed with lights that were imbedded within the tiles themselves. Two guards walked on either side of his gurney, pushing him down a seemingly endless hallway.

He vaguely remembered the door to his cell opening. The bright light rushing in, chasing away the darkness. The two dark silhouettes who'd lifted him off the floor and placed him on the gurney. He had a hazy memory of one of the younger of the two guards saying, "Hang in there, buddy." But that couldn't have happened, could it have? He must've imagined it.

Turning his head to the right, he saw steel doors—one after another, spaced evenly apart, each with a food port built into the door. Most of the ports were closed. A few were open, but the hallway was too bright, and the cell was too dark. He couldn't see anything.

Just ahead, a set of double doors swung open, revealing a bright room with a tile floor and arched ceiling. As the guards wheeled his gurney through the doors, Taylor saw hospital beds lining each side of the room. A few were occupied, but most were empty. The entire room smelled heavily of antiseptic.

I'm in the infirmary, he realized.

He scanned the room for Nurse Chin Hair, but she wasn't there.

Sunlight streamed through rectangular windows built high on the walls, just below the ceiling. Based on the strength of the sunlight, it appeared to be midday. But back in his cell, Taylor's internal clock had been telling him it was the middle of his second night in the detention center. How long had he been inside that cell? Two days? Four? Longer? He had no way of knowing for sure.

The guards parked the gurney next to an empty bed, but when the younger guard started to help Taylor off the gurney, the older one jabbed him with his index finger. "Knock it off, Ballentine. He can do it himself. He's awake." The guard turned his attention to Taylor. "Go on. You ain't dead yet. Get on the bed. I don't strain my back for traitors."

The bed they wanted Taylor to climb into was *right there,* only a few feet away, but to Taylor, the area between the gurney and the bed appeared as vast and insurmountable as Mount Everest. They might as well have asked him to run a marathon or swim the English Channel. His legs were too weak. No matter how hard he tried, he couldn't even slide them off the gurney.

A grunt of disgust came from his left side, and then rough hands fell upon his back, forcefully shoving him to the floor. He hit the tiles hard.

The older guard bellowed laughter.

A surge of adrenaline—brought on by the sound of that horrible, braying laughter—compelled Taylor to reach for the bed, grip the sheets, and try to pull himself up. If he didn't want the older guard to hurt him again, he needed to get himself onto that bed. Expending every remaining ounce of energy left in his body, he pulled himself up far enough to fling his left leg over the bed. But the strength in his arms gave out, and he collapsed back to the floor.

The older guard loomed over him, the smile on his rat-like face morphing into a sneer. "You should've tried harder, roach."

Taylor covered his stomach with his hands. A meager defense against the blow he suspected was coming, but then the young guard stepped forward, placing himself between the older guard and Taylor.

"I got it, man."

The young guard slipped his hands underneath Taylor's armpits and hauled the upper half of Taylor's body onto the bed. But when the kid went for his legs, the rest of Taylor's body slid off the bed. The guard grabbed him and leaned over to get a better grip on Taylor's torso. "Come on, man," he whispered. "Help me out."

That was all it took.

Taylor grabbed the mattress with both hands, using his own strength to keep himself from falling while the guard lifted his legs and slid them onto the bed. Then, he fell back onto the hospital bed, panting, his body sinking into the soft mattress. Despite the sunlight streaming into the infirmary, he felt his eyelids growing heavy.

"You ain't going soft on me, are you, Ballentine?" The older guard squinted at his partner, his expression hovering somewhere between curiosity and contempt. "Why'd you help the roach?"

Ballentine stood up to his full height, which was at least three inches taller than his older counterpart, and the other guard backed down a little. "I'm not going soft," he shot back. "This one's already done for, anyway."

Ballentine. Taylor's eyes drifted shut. *Rhymes with Valentine.*

✝

W hen he opened his eyes again, the guards were gone, and the room wasn't as bright. There was an IV in his arm (how had he slept through *that?*) and a saline drip attached to a pole next to his bed. His stomach didn't hurt anymore, which was a blessing because there was no toilet nearby, but now he was sporting the worst headache of his life, probably brought on by dehydration. Hopefully, the fluids they were pumping into him would take care of that soon.

A motherly, gray-haired nurse walked down the center aisle between the beds.

"Ma'am?" he rasped.

The woman gave him a cursory glance—her eyes narrow and filled with hatred—and kept right on walking.

Taylor raised his head to look for someone else—someone who might actually speak to him. At the other end of the room, he saw a doctor in a lab coat. The man stood with his back to Taylor, speaking in a quiet voice to a patient whose face Taylor could not see.

Only one other bed was occupied, and it was located directly across the aisle from Taylor. The bed's inhabitant was wide awake and seated in an upright position. The man's hair—a mixture of gray and black that hung well past his shoulders—looked as if it hadn't been washed in months, and while he was thin, there was a natural physicality about him. Taut muscles rippled beneath his sagging skin. He stared intently at Taylor, moving his jaw from side to side menacingly.

"You're going to die here." The man's voice sounded scratchy, as if he needed to clear his throat. "We're all going to die here."

Then, he raised his arms to show Taylor the open, raw sores covering each of his forearms. They looked badly infected.

Taylor tore his eyes away. "Speak for yourself," he muttered.

"My name is Brimmer. Charles Brimmer," the man rasped. "I used to be a pastor—a *great* pastor. I used to have three-hundred people in my congregation. I renounced seventeen months ago, right after they brought me here, but they won't let me out. They won't ever let me out, so I just scratch at my skin. Every time the doctors fix me up, I scratch them open again."

Taylor swallowed hard, still refusing to look at the man. "Why do you do it?"

"If you have to ask that question, soldier, then you haven't been here long enough."

"Quiet down," the doctor called out from the other end of the room. "No talking."

When Taylor looked back, the man—Brimmer—had dropped his arms and pressed the button to lower his bed. Once he was lying flat, he folded his inflamed arms over his chest and closed his eyes.

Taylor settled onto his own pillow, feeling uneasy. Something wasn't right.

He had no reason to be afraid. His situation had improved since arriving in the infirmary. He wasn't sick anymore. The doctors were giving him fluids and medication to help him. The only thing bothering him now—aside from Brimmer—was his headache.

So why did he want to leave this room so badly?

Why did he feel like he'd be safer in his cell?

✝

Skrrreeettt.

The sound ripped Taylor from sleep.

The moment he opened his eyes, the sound stopped, and he wondered if he'd been dreaming it. But it had been so real—and so *close*. Close enough to wake him out of a dead sleep. He could still hear it clearly in his mind. High-pitched. Scraping. Like metal being dragged across a rock. An abrasive noise that made you want to cover your ears.

There was no longer any light coming through the high windows—day must've given way to night as he slept—but the room wasn't entirely dark. Dim red bulbs built into the walls behind each hospital bed cast a glowing, reddish tinge over the entire area, giving the infirmary the appearance of hell's waiting room.

There was a smell, too. One that hadn't been there earlier. The unmistakable stench of an unwashed body. It reminded him of the recruit barracks at his Task Force basic training. But the beds on either side of him were still empty. He lifted his head to check on the pastor, Brimmer, expecting to see the man's body glowing red beneath the lights.

The bed was empty.

"Hello?" he whispered.

The wild-haired man shot up from the floor like a crazed jack-in-the-box, falling on top of Taylor and clamping a bony hand over Taylor's mouth. The red light made the wet sores on Brimmer's arms appear to be filled with blood. The man's unwashed hair hung in tangled strands in Taylor's face, but Taylor glimpsed a sharp object in the man's other hand. Long and thin, its polished surface reflected the light coming from behind the bed.

A blade of some sort.

Taylor grabbed for Brimmer's other hand, but his reflexes were off—he wasn't fast enough—and the man buried the blade in his neck.

He braced himself for the pain he knew was coming, for the sensation of blood spurting out of his jugular, but he couldn't feel anything. Just the sharp point of the blade pressing against his skin. Whether Brimmer stabbed him or slit his throat, Taylor wouldn't survive a knife wound to the jugular. Not in this place. He thought of the nurse from earlier —the one who'd looked as if she'd wanted to drive nails underneath his fingernails—and realized he would probably bleed to death long before anyone ever noticed he'd been stabbed.

"Please," he gasped, the word muffled by the man's sweaty hand.

The man pressed down on him, using his weight to hold Taylor in place, and dug the blade in far enough to pierce the skin. Warm blood trickled down the side of Taylor's neck.

"You did this," the man rasped into Taylor's ear. "You. Are. Responsible."

The man emphasized each word by driving the tip of the blade deeper into Taylor's neck. How much farther until he hit the jugular? Half a centimeter? Less?

"You deserve this, you coward!" Brimmer shouted at him, teeth bared, spittle spraying from his lips. "You put us in this hell! You deserve to suffer!"

His hand lifted from Taylor's mouth a little. Enough for Taylor to get two words out.

"You're right."

The man pulled back as if Taylor had slapped him, confusion flooding his eyes. Without removing the blade, he removed his hand from Taylor's mouth. "What did you say?"

"I said you're right." Taylor sucked in a few deep mouthfuls of air, his tongue clicking against the roof of his dry mouth. "I deserve to be here. You don't."

A brief internal conflict followed, one where the man's face betrayed every emotion he was feeling. Confusion. Guilt. Frustration. Rage.

And finally…resignation.

"I'm sorry," the man said, and he did sound sorry. "But it's too late for apologies."

The man raised the blade in the air.

Someone grabbed Brimmer from behind, grasping the blade with one hand while the other fastened around the man's throat and yanked him backward with superhuman strength. All at once, the weight disappeared from Taylor's chest, and both Brimmer and the blade dropped to the floor.

Clutching his injured neck, Taylor could feel blood, warm and sticky, against his palm. But there wasn't a lot. The guy hadn't nicked anything important.

Thank You, God.

Taylor's rescuer stood with his back to the bed, his attention on Brimmer, who remained on the floor. He was a large man—at least six-and-a-half feet tall—and every inch of him appeared ready for a fight. "Get back into your bed," the man growled. And Brimmer complied without question, scurrying across the floor and climbing into his bed like a dog who'd been reprimanded by its master.

Slowly, the man who'd saved Taylor's life turned around, his expression morphing from anger to disbelief in a heartbeat. Then, tears filled his tired eyes, and he leaned over the hospital bed and pulled Taylor into a fierce hug that said more than his lips ever could've.

"Son," his father wept.

CHAPTER SEVENTEEN

Five years.

It had been five years since Taylor had detained his father, yet Joseph Nolan seemed to have aged at least twenty years in that time span. Had they passed one another on the street, Taylor might not even have recognized him. The red glow of the infirmary wasn't strong enough to hide the sickly yellow hue of his father's complexion, and although he wasn't as emaciated as the other two patients in the infirmary, most of the excess weight that had once clung to his considerable frame was gone. When they hugged, Taylor could feel bones protruding everywhere.

He's wasting away, Taylor realized. *He's being consumed by this place.*

The only thing that hadn't changed was his height. His father might've lost an inch or two, thanks to poor nutrition and the passage of time, but he was still as physically imposing as ever. He'd certainly struck fear into the heart of Brimmer.

Now, Joseph Nolan towered over Taylor, pressing gauze pads against his son's neck. His father had located the gauze inside the cart at the other end of the room. He'd also brought Taylor the cup of water from his own bedside.

Since arriving at the infirmary, Taylor had been sharing a room with his father, and he hadn't even realized it.

The water in the Styrofoam cup was room temperature but tasted like heaven. Taylor took another long sip. His throat wasn't nearly as dry anymore, and it was becoming easier to talk. "Well?" he asked. "What's the verdict?"

His father pulled the gauze away from Taylor's neck. "The bleeding has almost stopped. The wound isn't deep, thank the Lord. That's a miracle, considering Brimmer was using a scalpel. There are a few butterfly bandages in the cart. Those should do the trick."

"A scalpel? How did he get a scalpel?"

"The nurse probably gave it to him," he replied, leaving Taylor's bedside and heading for the supply cart.

"What?" But then Taylor remembered the look in the nurse's eyes as she'd walked by his bed. She'd hated him for being a traitor as much as Brimmer had hated him for being in the Task Force. He felt lightheaded, either from fear or blood loss or a combination of both. "How did you know it was me?"

"I didn't know it was you." His father returned with more gauze and a butterfly bandage. "I just saw Brimmer attacking some young man in a Task Force uniform, and I couldn't allow that. I didn't know it was you until I turned around."

Taylor lifted his head to see his attacker, but the man was curled up in the fetal position, either asleep or pretending to be. "Why did he attack me?"

As soon as the words left his lips, he realized what a stupid question it was.

"All he saw was the uniform, Son. It inspires quite a bit of ire in here, even amongst professing Christians." He lowered his voice. "There are many people in this place who used to profess Christ, but some of them have changed. I don't know what they are now. But if Brimmer had known you were my son, he wouldn't have attacked you."

"I guess I should've led with that," Taylor said. "So, why are you in here? Are you sick?"

Joseph Nolan sank onto the edge of Taylor's mattress, as if the encounter with a crazy, scalpel-wielding detainee had robbed him of all of his energy. "I could ask you the same thing. Is this where the Task Force sends its soldiers for medical treatment?"

"They transferred me here from an interrogation unit a few days ago. Keeping me in uniform is part of my punishment. I'm sure they were hoping something like this would happen."

"Punishment for what?"

"For going AWOL last spring. And for...a few other issues."

His father's bushy eyebrows shot up, his expression one of genuine surprise. "You went AWOL from the Task Force? Why did you do that?"

Taylor shook his head. "It's a long story."

"We've got plenty of time, Son. They don't check on us much in here, as I'm sure you've figured out. At night, they lock the infirmary and forget about us, probably hoping a few of us will die during the night. The detention center only keeps a skeleton crew on at night. The good thing is, we don't get the same treatment as the people in the cells. In here, it's light during the day and dark at night, and there are no renouncements. But it can get a little boring, so why don't you tell me this long story of yours?"

So, while his father applied the butterfly bandage to his neck, Taylor relayed everything that had happened since they'd last seen each other, only stopping when it became necessary to clear his throat or take a sip of water. He explained how Gemma's parents had been arrested at one of their secret church meetings and how Taylor had visited her a week later to give her Oliver Barnes' phone number so she could link up with his group before they went into the wilderness. He talked about reuniting with Gemma on Dragon's Back Mountain and how she'd practically carried him off the mountain after a member of her group had shot him.

Talking about Colonel Carver and what happened in Ash Grove was much harder, and he left out certain parts of the story because he couldn't bring himself to talk about them. Finally, he told his father about Letty Webb, and Winter's Dam, and how he'd gotten captured helping a group of sympathizers escape before they could be transferred to an interrogation unit.

He didn't mention Patches or Groot for the same reason he didn't mention Carver.

He also left out the fact that he and Gemma had fallen in love, because while that was certainly still true from his perspective, a lot of time had passed since they'd last seen each other in Winter's Dam. If Gemma was still free—and that was a big if, given what had happened to the Sanctuary—she might have found someone else by now.

She might have even been back with Gavin.

After Taylor finished speaking, Joseph Nolan took one of the clean gauze pads and dabbed at the fresh tears shining in his eyes. "So, let me get this straight. You believe that the young man in your group, the one who'd been waiting for you in the tunnel..." His father's voice trailed off. "What was his name?"

"Gavin," Taylor muttered. The name tasted like bile in his mouth, and he took a long swig of water to wash it away. Taylor had made his peace with God, but he hadn't made it with Gemma's ex-boyfriend.

And he never would.

"So, you believe this Gavin fellow deliberately left you behind?"

"Yes. I *know* he did."

"But how can you be sure? You said that you were being chased."

When Taylor closed his eyes, he could still see Gavin pulling the door shut in front of him. Inside his chest, his heart sped up. "They were coming after me, but they weren't right on top of me. There was plenty of time. He didn't have to shut the door."

"But why would he leave you behind if you two were working together?"

Unfortunately, there was no way to explain Gavin's actions without telling his father the whole truth. He breathed a heavy sigh. "Because we're both in love with the same girl."

His father's head tilted to one side. After a few moments, the corners of his mouth ticked upward into a knowing smile.

"Gemma Alcott," he said, shaking his head. "Can't say I'm surprised."

Taylor turned his head away, not wanting his father to see the emotions he was feeling. Instead, he searched the high windows for any sign of light, but all he could see were stars.

Was Gemma sleeping outside underneath that same blanket of stars? Was she looking up at them and thinking of him? Or was she sleeping soundly in Gavin's arms?

"Son?"

"Yeah?"

"How serious is this thing between you and Gemma?"

Taylor kept his eyes trained on the stars as he spoke. "I asked her to marry me, and she said yes."

"Oh, Son." Joseph Nolan's hands closed around his own. Somehow, those gaunt hands still dwarfed Taylor's. "For what it's worth, I always knew Gemma had a crush on you. Your mother knew, too. We used to joke about how obvious it was. Any fool could've seen it—except for you, apparently," he added, lightly squeezing Taylor's hand. "She would always look so happy when she arrived at church. I wasn't naïve enough to think she was *that* excited to hear my sermons. Whenever she walked through the door, she'd lean around me to look for you. And if you weren't there for any reason—like when you were sick or when you stopped coming to church when you got older —I would watch the light in her eyes fade away. The sadness in that poor girl's face made me want to drive home and drag you to church more than once."

Taylor wrenched one of his hands free so he could drape an arm over his face. He wasn't crying yet, but he was close. "Please stop," he whispered. "I can't talk about her, Dad. I'm here now. That part of my life is over now."

But his father continued as if Taylor hadn't spoken. "Do you remember your mother's funeral? How Gemma sat next to you in the front row? Even back then, she was already carrying so much love for you in her little heart, and she couldn't have been more than ten."

"She was nine." The tears were coming now. Taylor couldn't do anything to stop them, so he used his free hand to wipe them away. "Yeah. I remember."

"That kind of love doesn't go away when circumstances change. Your mother has been gone for thirteen years, Taylor, and I still love her as much as I ever did. Maybe more, because I miss her so badly."

Taylor blinked at his father, the frustration building inside of him. "But that's the thing, Dad. It hurts so much to think of her moving on with someone else." *Especially Gavin,* he wanted to add but didn't. "But I also don't want her to have a miserable life because I'm not with her. She doesn't deserve that. They've already told me I'm never getting out of this place because I can't be rehabilitated."

Understanding dawned in his father's eyes. "Because you're not a believer?"

"I wasn't when I got here."

His father's grip on his hand tightened. "And now?"

Taylor should've said that he believed. That he'd never really stopped believing, despite the depths to which he'd fallen trying to deny those feelings. After his mother's death, he'd hated God for a little while, because his young mind couldn't comprehend why a loving God would take away his mother, especially since she'd devoted her entire life to serving the Lord. It made little sense to him, and no amount of Bible verses and sermons could convince him otherwise. In the end, it was easier to tell himself that he'd been wrong about God all along than to admit the hard truth, which was that people who followed Christ had their fair share of disasters, just like those who didn't follow Christ.

Often, they had more than their fair share.

But he couldn't say all of that to his father. So, he said, "I'm working on it, Dad."

The way Joseph Nolan's face lit up with joy, you would've thought that Taylor had just asked his father to take him to the river and baptize him. More tears followed, because of course they did. Another one of his father's quirks was that, despite his formidable appearance, he cried like a baby at the drop of a hat.

That wasn't a trait he'd passed on to Taylor, thank goodness.

When he finally composed himself, his father said, "Son, I'm going to let you in on a little secret about this place. This is something people like Brimmer over there haven't figured out yet. If you're a Christian—and I'm not talking about a *professing* Christian, but someone who *truly* knows Christ—then it doesn't matter what the world does to you. It really doesn't. It doesn't matter if they lock you up and never let you out. That's the beautiful miracle of it all. Jesus has already set you free."

Taylor wished he could share his father's enthusiasm. While he understood the concept of spiritual freedom, he also wanted *actual* freedom. He couldn't imagine living another fifty years without Gemma. He couldn't imagine spending another fifty years in this detention center, even with his father by his side.

But then he looked at his father. *Really* looked, for the first time since their reunion. He took in his father's sunken cheekbones. His jaundiced skin. His severe weight loss. The way he kept reaching back to press on his lower back. Only then did Taylor realize his father might not have forty years left.

He didn't look like he had *forty days* left.

"Why are you in the infirmary, Dad? What's wrong with you?"

The excitement on Joseph Nolan's face withered like dry grass in the scorching sun. His head bobbed up and down in a barely perceptible nod, as if he'd been waiting for this moment and was steeling himself to face it. "I've been in here for the past month," his father said, gesturing to the nearly empty infirmary. "Ever since my diagnosis."

The muscles of Taylor's throat tightened, so he could barely force the words out. "What diagnosis?"

"Pancreatic cancer. Stage four."

A violent rush of fear swept over Taylor, unlike anything he'd ever felt before—not even when he'd watched Gavin close the door to the tunnel. He couldn't move. He couldn't think. Breathing was suddenly difficult. It was a good thing he was already lying down because he felt like he might pass out.

"No." He shook his head. "This isn't happening."

He raised his eyes to the windows. To the stars.

You can't. You can't do this to me again. I just found him.

"I'm afraid it is, Son," his father continued. "There's nothing they can do. Even if they'd caught it earlier, they wouldn't have treated me. Too expensive. But I'm at peace with it. It might sound crazy to you, but when they told me, I was relieved. I've lived without your mother for so many years. I can't wait to see her. I can't wait to be free of this place. And I can't wait to see the Lord face to face." He gave a light chuckle. "Of course, I have to admit that I'm not as eager to leave now that you're back in my life. God has a sense of humor, doesn't He?"

"Are you in pain?"

"Sometimes. My back gets bad sometimes, but they give me painkillers when I need them. The guards treat me well, and the infirmary staff seems to like me. I'm not sure why, since I don't shut up about Jesus. I'll tell anyone who comes near me about what the Lord has done for me. Some of them just roll their eyes, and they scoff, of course. But some of them stay and listen. Some of them are changing."

"But I don't want you to die."

It was a childish thing to say, but Taylor didn't care. Soon, he would be an orphan.

"I know," his father said. "But I'm so tired, Son."

Although Taylor understood his father wasn't referring to sleep, he scooted over as far as he could anyway, making room on the bed for his father to lie down next to him. Joseph Nolan glanced uncertainly at the door to the infirmary, seemed to decide that it was worth the risk, and then tucked his long legs underneath the blanket and eased himself onto the pillow. He wrapped his arms around his only son and held him close.

They remained like that for a long time, not speaking, until Taylor eventually broke the silence. "Do you want to talk about it?" he whispered. "About the day I detained you?"

So much time passed after Taylor asked the question that he thought his father must've fallen asleep. If his father was dying —*especially* if he was dying—then Taylor wanted to ask him for forgiveness. To tell him how sorry he was for taking away his freedom. For imprisoning him when he should've been the one to protect him.

He'd been so wrong about everything. So wrong for so long.

But then his father's voice drifted to him in the darkness, and all the guilt and shame he'd been holding onto for five long years melted away like snow during the first spring thaw.

"There's no need to talk about it, Son," his father said, pulling Taylor into a tighter embrace. "I forgave you that same day."

CHAPTER EIGHTEEN

The school bus sped north on the empty highway, heading for the detention center.

At the front of the bus, Gemma breathed in the smells of exhaust, Lysol, and aging vinyl seats. It was almost midnight, so there weren't many people on the road. Still, the twelve buses had staggered themselves to avoid attracting more attention. That probably hadn't been necessary, however, since any drivers who noticed the group of buses traveling together probably assumed they were a high school sports team returning home from a late game.

The driver, one of Clarke's men, clutched the steering wheel so tightly that it looked like the bones of his knuckles might puncture the surface of his skin. He'd mentioned his name to Gemma back at the mall, before they'd fallen into line behind the other buses and exited the parking garage, but she'd been distracted by all the activity and had instantly forgotten it.

Several times, Gemma had tried to engage the driver in a conversation, but he'd responded to her questions with one-word answers, and she'd soon realized that he had no more desire to talk than she did. He wore a headset with a tiny boom microphone that dangled in front of his mouth, presumably to communicate with someone. Maybe Clarke? Or the other buses? But Gemma hadn't heard him say a word to anyone since they'd left the mall.

She ran a hand across her forehead, wiping away the beads of sweat. It was *stifling* on the bus, but she didn't want to bother the driver by asking him to turn on the air conditioning. He might not have even known *how* to turn on the air conditioning. So, she rested her head against the window, the glass cold and soothing against her head.

She gazed out the window at the Susquehanna River. The river appeared calm and welcoming, but many hidden dangers existed beneath its polished surface. Fast-moving undercurrents capable of overpowering even the best swimmers. Downed tree limbs and other debris sweeping along at bone-shattering speeds. Jagged rocks crouching like predators just beneath the surface. At its angriest, the Susquehanna had torn bridges apart, battering them with ice and water until entire spans collapsed, leaving nothing behind but their concrete support posts.

Gemma imagined herself floating on her back in its current, her limbs extended like a starfish as she allowed the river to carry her far away from Clarke and his crazy mission.

Clarke hadn't allowed the others from Winter's Dam to take part in the rescue. Only Gemma. When Max and Gavin confronted him about it as everyone started loading onto the buses, Clarke had said, in no uncertain terms, that his forces had spent months planning and training for this operation. It *had* to be conducted with military precision, or it would fail. He had no intention of dragging a bunch of civilians along for the ride.

Plus, they would need as many empty seats on the buses as possible.

So, the others had remained behind.

No one—not Gemma's friends nor Clarke's forces—had

questioned why Gemma was the one exception to the rule. That decision appeared to be Clarke's and Clarke's alone.

"Almost there," the driver said in a flat voice, flicking on the left-hand turn signal. There was no traffic, so he rolled right over the southbound lanes of Route 11/15 without stopping and joined up with the same country road that Clarke and Gemma had taken the previous day.

"Great," she said, not really meaning it. "You nervous?"

"Nope." He yawned for emphasis. "Don't get nervous."

Gemma didn't know if the driver was claiming that *he* never got nervous, or if he was telling *her* not to get nervous, so she didn't respond. Leaning forward, she gripped the vinyl seatback in front of her and peered through the windshield. Up ahead, she could see the taillights of one bus. Her bus was bringing up the rear of the procession. She wasn't sure if that made her more or less safe, but this was where Clarke had wanted her.

The detention center was a soft target, according to Clarke, and extremely vulnerable to an attack. There were no guard towers. No sophisticated alarm systems. No major towns nearby from which help could be requested. Since the detainees weren't allowed outside of their cells, the risk of escape was extremely low. Stovington wasn't a maximum-security prison built to house violent criminals and murderers, and the government had not designed it with security as a priority. They designed detention centers with the sole purpose of tormenting Christians until they broke. The detention center's only external security system consisted of a roving patrol—a guard in a Jeep who drove the perimeter of the grounds twenty-four hours a day.

Gemma's role in the operation was simple: wait near the buses. When she saw detainees coming across the open field, she would direct them toward the buses. "Help them, if necessary," Clarke had told her before they left. "Some might need assistance walking. Some might need to be carried. We don't know what kind of condition these people might be in, so be ready for anything."

Be ready for anything. But how was she supposed to prepare herself for anything when she didn't know what was actually going on? Clarke's instructions had sounded simple enough, but there was still so much about this operation that Gemma didn't understand and that Clarke hadn't had time to explain to her. How were a dozen buses supposed to evade detection by the roving patrol? How were Clarke's forces supposed to get the detainees not only out of their cells, but out of the building itself? And if they got the detainees outside, how were they supposed to get them over a fence topped with concertina wire?

Suddenly, the driver pulled the bus to the side of the road and shut off the engine.

Had they reached Stovington already? Gemma searched the landscape below for the lights of the detention center, but she couldn't see anything but rolling farmland punctuated by the occasional barn or house. She couldn't even see the next bus in line, as it had passed over a crest of a hill and disappeared from sight.

"Why are you stopping?" she asked. "We're not there yet."

"This is where we're supposed to wait until the fence comes down."

"Until the fence comes down?" Gemma could no longer control her frustration at being kept in the dark. "Can you *please* tell me what's going on?"

The driver stole a quick glance at his watch and then used his fingers to smooth his mustache. "The attack will kick off inside the detention center in exactly three minutes and forty-seven seconds. There are five guards on duty tonight, including a duty sergeant, a guard stationed inside the control room, and a guard outside, patrolling the grounds in a Jeep. Three of the guards are in on our plan; the other two aren't."

What? Had she heard him correctly? "Wait. Did you just say that three guards are—"

"The duty sergeant will signal the start of the attack," he continued, cutting her off, "by pulling the fire alarm in the basement. Then, he's going to light off a few smoke grenades and throw them into the air ducts. Per fire protocol, the guard in the control room—who is also in on the plan—is going to press a button to override the locks on all cell doors and exterior doors. Then, he's going to throw three tear gas canisters into the main hub."

"Tear gas?" Gemma asked. "Why tear gas?"

"To create chaos," the driver replied. "Smoke will pour out of every vent. The guards who aren't in on the plan are all new guys. Young guys. The sergeant scheduled these specific guys to work tonight because they don't have prior military experience. They don't know the difference between smoke as the result of a fire and tear gas. The duty sergeant is going to command them to go through the corridors and direct the detainees from their cells to the exits. To what they *think* is still a fenced-in yard. They're actually going to be helping detainees escape, and they won't even realize it."

"But what happens once the detainees get outside? Won't they be trapped inside the fence?"

The driver smirked at her. "There won't be a fence. The roving patrol guy is with us. He's going to use the Jeep's winch and pull the sucker down. Well, a section, anyway. Our guys are going to be hunkered down in the field surrounding the detention center, waiting to direct the detainees coming out of each corridor toward the buses."

"What about the police?"

The driver shook his head. "Notifying the authorities is the job of the guy in the control room, and he's obviously not going to make any calls. However, just to be safe, once the attack kicks off, we've got someone who's going to call in a report of a shooting thirty minutes north of here. Multiple victims. Every cop within a fifty-mile radius will head in that direction, which just happens to be *away* from us."

"Clarke won't kill them, will he? The two guards who aren't in on the plan?" It seemed important to clarify this point. Gemma was a willing participant in this operation, and one day, she would have to answer to God for everything that happened tonight. It was one thing to kill in self-defense, but it was another thing to murder people who were just doing their jobs —no matter how terrible those jobs might be.

Until that moment, the driver had treated Gemma like a minor annoyance, like a fly he occasionally had to shoo away. Now he twisted in his seat to face her. "Why? Would it bother you if they died?"

Gemma had spent a lot of time staring at the back of the driver's head, and her mind had constructed its own idea of his appearance from that limited view. So, when he turned around, she felt as if she was looking at a different person entirely. The bushy mustache hid the fact that he was much younger than she'd first realized. He couldn't have been much older than she was—perhaps in his mid to late twenties—and attractive in a menacing way.

"Yes," she replied, lifting her chin as if to meet some challenge. "They don't deserve to die just because they work at a detention center."

The driver gave her a thin, humorless smile, but there was something behind the smile. Something cold and hard and knowing. It made her wonder who this young man had been— and what kinds of things he'd done—before crossing paths with Clarke.

He turned away from her. "I wonder if you'll feel the same way after you see the detainees."

A few minutes later, the driver started the engine back up.

He didn't say another word to Gemma, only started to drive, presumably in response to some command in his ear. If they were moving again, that meant the attack was underway.

She closed her eyes and whispered a prayer.

As the bus crested the next hill, the wheel-and-spoke facade of the detention center came into view on the right side of the road. The other eleven buses were already lined up like football players waiting on the sidelines to be called into the game. On the right side of the access road, the overgrown field provided some concealment for the buses, gradually sloping downward for about fifty yards and ending at the razor-wire-topped fence that surrounded the detention center.

Only, the fence wasn't standing anymore. A large section of it was down, just as the driver had said it would be, but she couldn't see any detainees outside yet. All along the access road, Clarke's men and women were disappearing into the tall grass of the field and creeping toward the perimeter of the detention center. Dietrich would be among them. Gemma had seen the former Task Force soldier climbing aboard another bus back in the parking garage.

When they reached the bottom of the hill, the driver brought the bus to a stop, slipped out of his seat, and clomped down the steps, leaving the door hanging open behind him.

Gemma followed him off the bus and found him standing a few feet away, a pistol in his hand. He cleared the chamber and stuck the gun in his waistband.

"What happens now?" she asked him.

"When you see detainees coming out of the field toward the buses, move forward and help them. Just like Clarke told you back at the garage."

"But I can't see anything from back here, and I don't have a radio to communicate with anyone. I don't even have a gun. What am I supposed to do if something goes wrong?"

The driver's expression turned serious. "If something goes wrong, we're all screwed."

And then he vanished into the field with the others.

CHAPTER NINETEEN

Taylor lay on his bed, staring at the wall—or, rather, at the spot where his wall *should've* been. The lights were off again, and he couldn't see his hand in front of his face, much less the concrete wall a few inches from his nose.

The guards had transferred him back to his cell at dawn, right after the head nurse from the previous evening had come back on duty. When the door to the infirmary opened and she'd walked in, her eyes had darted to Taylor's bed, and she'd been unable to conceal her disappointment that her least favorite patient had made it through the night. But when she'd silently checked him a few minutes later and discovered that he was hydrated and no longer vomiting, she'd perked up a bit, clearly relishing her power as head nurse to sign his discharge paperwork and transfer him back to his cell.

Being escorted out of the infirmary was the worst thing he'd experienced at the detention center, and that was saying something. He missed the peace and the silence of the place. The normalcy and comfort of a bed with sheets and a blanket. Being able to track the passing of time by the amount of light streaming through the windows. But by far, the worst thing about leaving the infirmary had been leaving his father behind. Taylor hadn't even said goodbye because he hadn't wanted to draw any unnecessary attention to his father. And now he didn't know when—or *if*—he would ever see him again.

A guard had delivered food to his cell a few hours later, when the lights—and renunciations—were still on. The gray-tinged contents of the metal bowl appeared to be watery oatmeal, but when he brought a spoonful to his lips, it tasted nothing like any oatmeal Taylor had ever eaten. It was cold and totally bland. Just flecks of rice and what he thought might have been chopped onion. He occupied himself by fishing out the rice and onion, but after he finished, a ton of liquid remained in the bowl's bottom. The liquid tasted like a combination of cold milk and water, and it had a strange aftertaste, but he tilted the bowl to his lips and drank the rest of it down in three large swallows anyway, trying his best to ignore the little particles that accompanied the liquid down his throat. When the guard eventually returned, Taylor had passed the metal bowl through the food port in the door and whispered, "Thank you."

"Shut up," was all he'd gotten in return.

So far, the meal hadn't come back up, which Taylor counted as a good thing. Whatever had been wrong with his stomach was over now, and the food—as disgusting as it had been—had given him a brief burst of energy. When the darkness returned, he tried to distract himself—and build up his strength—by dropping to the ground and knocking out a few pushups. But after just three, he'd collapsed to the floor of his cell, utterly exhausted.

He desperately needed a shower—he could *smell* himself— and if he was going to the trouble of showering, he might as well wash his uniform in the sink and hang it up to air dry. But he couldn't stomach the idea of allowing whoever was on the other side of the camera to watch him bathe, nor did he *want* to lie naked on his bed for hours while he waited for his clothes to dry.

So, instead of showering, Taylor stared into the darkness and thought about the many mistakes he'd made. The many lives he'd ruined. He counted them like sheep, as if they might bring him rest, but they brought him nothing but pain.

One detention stuck out to him more than the others because it was the last one he'd taken part in before reuniting with Gemma on Dragon's Back Mountain. His unit had discovered a small group of subversives hiding in the woods close to the Station, and Taylor had pulled a little girl with blonde curls out of the arms of her sobbing mother. The girl couldn't have been more than five, but she had fought him like a warrior, kicking and screaming and pounding on his back with her fists. When another soldier shoved her mother inside a transport vehicle, the girl had gone limp, sagging against Taylor as if someone had snatched her very soul out of her body. She'd dampened his uniform with her tears until he'd handed her off to one of the Youth Liaisons to be placed with a foster family.

Taylor had taken that little girl from her mother, just as the cancer had taken his mother from him.

"God, forgive me," he spoke into the darkness, covering his face with his hands.

And then the world exploded.

Blaring noise. Intermittent. Some kind of alarm.

Followed immediately by dazzling light that surrounded him on all sides, so bright it cut through his closed eyelids. But he compelled his eyes to open, glimpsing the concrete wall through his splayed fingers.

The wall. He could see the wall.

Forcing his hands away from his face, Taylor rolled over and sat up in bed, blinking rapidly until the room came into focus. There wasn't much to see in his cell, but he could see everything. The sink. The toilet. The camera hanging near the ceiling.

And finally, the source of the light, which *wasn't* the overhead fluorescents.

The light was coming from the hallway *outside* of his cell.

The cell door was hanging open.

People shuffled past his doorway, none of them looking in his direction. Most were clinging to someone else, holding each other up, while others moved entirely on their own. Many had snot dangling from their noses, and all of them were coughing and wiping at their eyes. Even if Taylor hadn't noticed their pale skin and haunted faces, it would've been impossible to mistake the khaki-colored clothing that hung from their gaunt bodies for anything other than a detainee uniform.

Detainees. Outside of their cells.

The blaring noise came back to Taylor, its pitch increasing in intensity as his muddled brain finally put the pieces together and understood what it meant. It wasn't just the alarm. There was something else. Something more urgent. As the detainees rushed past his door—as much as they *could* rush while coughing and hacking like they were—the surrounding hallway was growing increasingly foggy.

Not foggy. Smoky.

The building was on fire.

Taylor pushed himself to his feet, stumbled to the doorway, and peered into the smoke-filled hallway. Immediately, the smoke filled his nostrils, thick and acidic, choking him and burning his eyes, and he doubled over, hacking. He almost pulled the door shut right then, but some survival instinct propelled him into the hallway instead, because this was his only chance.

If he wanted to live, he had to move forward, not back.

Once outside of his cell, he pulled his shirt over his mouth and nose and squinted against the smoke. He looked in both directions—first to the left, then to the right, then to the left again—as if waiting to cross a busy highway. The smoke was thicker to the left, close to the center's main hub. The train of detainees continued past his cell, heading away from the smoke.

But it wasn't normal smoke. The reaction it had triggered in him when he'd first breathed it in had been familiar, but it wasn't a reaction to normal smoke caused by a fire. That kind of smoke didn't burn your skin.

It's not smoke, Taylor suddenly realized. *It's tear gas.*

The Task Force had exposed him to tear gas as part of his training, and he still remembered how the gas had burned everything it touched. His eyes. His skin. His throat. His nose had run uncontrollably for a good ten minutes after the exposure ended. Afterward, he'd sat in the grass, repeatedly splashing water from his canteen onto himself until his skin stopped burning. Then, he'd watched the next batch of recruits come staggering out of the gas house. All of them had been hacking and crying, with ribbons of snot dangling from their nostrils.

Exactly the same way the detainees looked.

But why was the fire alarm going off when it was tear gas—not smoke—filling the hallways? Whatever was happening, Taylor was pretty sure it wasn't a fire. This was something else altogether.

With his shirt still over his mouth, Taylor turned away from the hub—and the worst of the gas—and followed the detainees in the opposite direction. He didn't know what—if anything—might have been waiting for them at the far end of the hallway, but hopefully there would be an exit that way. Once he got outside, he would find a guard and ask them where they'd taken the patients from the infirmary. He needed to make sure his father was—

At night, they lock the infirmary and forget about us.

As detainees filed past him, confusion etched on their faces at the sight of his uniform, Taylor's father's words came rushing back, blaring louder in his ears than the fire alarm. He stopped in his tracks and turned in the other direction, toward the center hub and the worst of the smoke.

Toward the infirmary.

What if none of the guards checked the infirmary?

It was nighttime—at least, it *felt* like nighttime—which meant there were no nurses or doctors on duty. Would the guards remember to check the infirmary in all this chaos?

Someone grabbed his arm.

Taylor spun around and came face to face with a guard.

The guy was wearing a riot control gas mask, which made it difficult to see his face clearly, but Taylor was pretty sure this was the same guard who'd helped him onto his bed in the infirmary.

"What are you doing?" the guard shouted in his face, the mask muffling his voice. There was a look of urgency in the guy's eyes that Taylor didn't particularly like. "Follow the others! Get outside!"

Forgetting himself for a moment, Taylor dropped the shirt from his mouth to be heard clearly. "Has anyone checked the infirmary?" Then, he sucked in a deep breath of the tear gas and hacked. "There were...patients...in there!"

On both sides, people continued to flood toward the end of the corridor, moving around Taylor and the guard like water around a pair of rocks.

"I'm sure someone got them out!"

But the guard didn't look sure. He didn't look sure at all.

Something pulled Taylor in the opposite direction. A force much stronger than he was. Even if he had wanted to follow the guard, he couldn't have done it. He pulled his shirt back over his face and shouted, "We have to go check!"

Through the foggy face shield, Taylor saw the guard's eyes narrow as he considered his options, neither of which was very good. Finally, he said, "Take this." He took his mask off and handed it to Taylor, who immediately pulled the straps around his own head. "The infirmary is in the other direction." The guard pointed toward the main hub, his eyes already watering. "Last door on the right, just before you reach the hub. But it's probably empty, man."

"Is it unlocked?"

The guard nodded. "Everything's unlocked now."

"Okay." Taylor gave the guard a quick nod and turned toward the infirmary, but the guard grabbed his arm.

"Come back this way," he sputtered, tears flowing down his face. He released Taylor's arm to wipe them away. "There's an exit at the end of the corridor. Hopefully, it will still be open. If you make it outside, head west through the field. Keep moving until you reach the buses."

Buses?

"Wait!" Taylor shouted. "What's going on?"

But the guard was already gone, jogging down the corridor toward the exit.

Every part of Taylor wanted to follow him. Not only to get away from the tear gas and whatever might have been happening closer to the hub, but also to find out what was happening outside.

But then he heard God's voice for the first time in years.

Go back. Go back.

He spun around and headed for the infirmary.

CHAPTER TWENTY

An alarm was going off inside the detention center.

Even from a hundred yards away, Gemma could hear it blaring, high-pitched and urgent, as if the building itself were crying out for help. The alarm had only been going off for a few minutes—maybe only five or six—but those minutes had felt like an eternity. She did not know if she was listening to the detention center's fire alarm system, as the driver had said, or if the guards inside the detention center had realized they were under attack and activated an emergency system.

And she hadn't seen a single detainee yet.

Casting a nervous look at the gravel road that stretched out behind the bus, Gemma expected a line of police cars to come roaring over the hill at any moment. But so far, there was nothing. No approaching vehicles. No distant sirens. Even the ever-present night songs of the insects and frogs had ceased until nothing remained except for the incessant wailing of the alarm coming from inside the detention center.

Adding to Gemma's sense of unease was the fact that it was *very* dark in the field. Clarke had chosen a moonless night for the raid, probably because he wanted as much conceal-ment as possible for the detainees. But the darkness also meant that the good guys were going to have trouble seeing the detainees. If it weren't for the faint lights coming from the detention center, Gemma wouldn't have been able to see anything at all.

In front of her, the overgrown grass of the field danced in the night air, swaying lazily back and forth. At first, she'd assumed the movement in the weeds was the detainees coming toward the buses, and she'd rushed forward to help them. But when no one emerged from the field, she'd retreated to her spot next to the bus's front right tire, more convinced than ever that Clarke's plan would fail. That certainty increased with every shriek of the alarm.

She almost couldn't believe her eyes when she glanced to her left and saw detainees stumbling out of the field farther up the road, heading for a different bus. At first, she thought they were Clarke's forces returning from the failed raid, but the people wore light-colored clothes instead of dark, and some of them were limping.

Then, the tall grass in front of her parted and ghosts drifted out of the field.

At least, she *thought* they were ghosts at first, not only because of their pale complexions, but because they all seemed as fragile and insignificant as wisps of smoke. But instead of white shrouds and chains, these ghosts wore filthy khaki uniforms that were far too big for their thin bodies. Their faces were beet red, either from the exertion of the walk, or the tear gas, or a combination of both.

"This way!" she cried, rushing toward the field. "Over here! Get to the bus!"

They moved past her, a group of five, followed by a group of three. None of the people were running, but they were all moving at a clip that showed they knew how precarious their situation was. They found their way onto Gemma's bus as if they had been part of Clarke's plan all along.

Turning back to the field, she saw a middle-aged woman struggling to make her way out of the weeds. The front of her uniform trousers was damp, and Gemma realized the woman had lost control of her bladder at some point. Grabbing the woman's bony elbow, Gemma helped her navigate the uneven terrain between the field and the bus. "Grab any seat you want. It's okay. We're going to get you out of here."

"Thank you," the woman whispered as she climbed the steps.

No sooner had Gemma left the bus than the tall grass in front of her parted once again, and a younger man stepped out of the field, carrying an elderly gentleman in his arms. The elderly man's legs dangled over the ground, and his head tilted back at an impossible angle.

The old man could've been asleep or dead.

She rushed up to the young man. "Can I do anything to help you?"

The young man walked past her as if she hadn't spoken, his cheeks shining with tears.

The flow of people exiting the field continued for another five minutes. After the first group of five, it was mostly pairs traveling together, helping one another, or people moving on their own, struggling to find their way through the field. Aside from the elderly man, everyone Gemma encountered could walk on their own, and although most of the detainees were skinny, they didn't seem to be injured in any other way. But the faraway expressions on their faces betrayed the truth of their situation. To Gemma, they looked like a group of soldiers coming back from war. Whatever they'd endured inside the detention center—whether over months or years—it might not have harmed them physically, but it had clearly taken a terrible mental and emotional toll.

Gemma helped whenever she could, going into the tall grass,

guiding people out, and directing them to the nearest bus. She searched every haunted face for her parents, certain that if they were inside this detention center, they would somehow find their way to her.

Eventually, the flow of detainees coming out of the field and filing onto the buses stopped as suddenly as it had begun. When Gemma saw her driver stepping out of the field, she rushed up to him. But she halted in place when another young man stepped out of the tall grass.

Not a detainee. He was wearing a uniform.

A guard.

"Don't worry," the driver said as he brushed past her and bounded up the stairs of the bus. "He's with us."

Gemma returned her attention to the guard, who hesitated in front of her as if waiting to be granted permission to board the bus. He kept rubbing at his watering eyes. "Do you have any water?" he asked. "Something I can use to flush out my eyes?"

"There are bottles of water on board." When he tried to move around her, she grabbed his wrist. "Did you get everybody out? Was anyone left behind?"

"No," he replied quickly. Too quickly. "We got everyone."

The man was a liar, and he wasn't even very good at it. Gemma could see the truth written all over his face. But the guard wrenched his wrist out of her grip, jogged to the bus, and climbed the steps.

"Let's go," the driver called to her through the open door. "If those other guards haven't figured out what's happened yet, they will soon. And then they're going to come this way. We've got no time."

Up and down the gravel road, the buses started their engines. Then, one by one, they pulled away from the detention center with their human cargo in tow. Gemma remembered Clarke saying that the bus drivers were going to stick to the back roads, with each bus taking a different, predetermined route until they reached the bridge that would carry them across the river and back to the mall.

As the other buses disappeared from sight, Gemma stood her ground, halfway between her bus and the field. She saw the terrified faces pressed up against the glass, peering out at her, silently pleading with her to get on. If she got on the bus, she might be leaving people behind. But if she didn't get on, she was risking the lives and freedom of all those other people.

She climbed onto the bus.

The driver closed the door and pressed the gas pedal before Gemma made it halfway up the stairs, the momentum throwing her sideways into the handrail. She grabbed onto the rail and pulled herself the rest of the way up. Instead of returning to her seat, she walked down the center aisle, grabbing each seat for balance, and peered through the rear doors.

Three men broke out of the field just behind the bus, hobbling toward the road. The one in the middle was holding the other two up. One man raised a hand in the air to flag down the bus.

"Stop!" She rushed forward to the driver. "There are people back there!"

But the driver didn't slow down. He didn't even tap the brakes. "We can't stop," he said, his voice cold and robotic. "Sorry. It's too risky."

Without thinking—because there was no time to think—Gemma threw herself on top of the driver and drove her boot down hard onto the brake. The bus lurched to the left, its passengers crying out as it nearly ran off the gravel road and plunged into the ditch. But the driver reacted quickly, jerking the wheel back to the right and bringing the bus to a stop in the middle of the road.

The bus driver shoved Gemma away. "You stupid—"

But she didn't hear the insult because she was already hitting the lever to open the door and rushing down the steps and into the night. She searched the darkness and saw all three men in the distance, a good twenty-five yards behind the bus, nothing more than shadows moving at a steady clip in her direction.

She listened for the sound of the bus pulling away. She fully expected the driver to leave her and the three strangers behind on the deserted road, but when the engine continued to idle, she picked up her pace, fueled by the hope that she might get these three men safely aboard the bus. They were so close. One of them had crazy hair, going in all directions, and one was very tall. And the third man...she could almost see his face...

A sharp sound rang through the night air, and Gemma didn't realize it was a gunshot until one man—the one closest to the field—collapsed to the ground, writhing in pain.

A moment later, a young guard burst out of the field, his pistol aimed at the remaining two men. "Stop! One more step and I'll shoot you both!"

Three more gunshots rang out, and the guard dove headfirst into the field.

She spun around and saw the driver standing outside of the bus, returning fire.

Gemma glanced back at the field. She didn't know where the guard had gone or if he was planning to circle around and take another shot at the detainees. Or maybe he would try to shoot her this time. Or the tires on the bus.

She had to get the detainees to safety.

But the men were so close. Only a few dozen feet away.

Gemma ducked her head and sprinted toward the detainees. The other two were trying to help the man on the ground, but judging by the pool of dark blood surrounding the man's body, he was going to bleed out. Even if they got him aboard the bus and took him to a hospital—which they obviously couldn't— they would never get him there in time.

As she ran up to the detainees, one of them stood up and moved away from the body, but the other one—the really tall one—remained on the ground, crouched over the dying man. He pressed one hand over the exit wound in the man's lower abdomen, while his other hand rested on the man's forehead.

The tall detainee was praying. And his voice was as familiar and comforting as a lullaby.

It was a voice Gemma hadn't heard in years.

Dropping to her knees beside him, she put a hand on the detainee's shoulder and whispered, "Pastor Nolan?"

As the crazy-haired man lying on the ground exhaled his final breath, the tall man dropped his head in a soft nod. He turned and looked at her, his eyes widening in surprise. Despite all the terrible things he must've suffered over the past five years, he still managed to smile. "Hello, Gemma."

"Get on the bus right now, or I'm leaving you behind!" the driver shouted.

Only after she'd helped Pastor Nolan to his feet did she steal a glance at the third detainee—the one who'd stepped aside as she approached. And when her eyes met his, her peripheral vision diminished until all that remained was a tiny circle with his beautiful face illuminated in the center.

Her legs grew weak beneath her, and she might've fallen, but Taylor reached out with one arm and caught her.

CHAPTER TWENTY-ONE

On the bus ride back to the mall, Gemma remained on her feet, nervously pacing up and down the aisle, assisting the freed detainees in any way she could. She passed out bottles of water, handed blankets to those who looked cold, and kept reassuring them they were safe. But each time she passed Taylor's seat, she double-checked to make sure he was still there. That she hadn't imagined their reunion on the gravel road.

She also spent much of her time watching the highway unfurl behind the bus, certain that, at any moment, flashing lights might appear on the horizon. The lumbering bus could not outrun the police—or a Task Force vehicle.

Only after they drove into the parking garage did Gemma allow herself to relax.

Every bus had made it back.

The driver pulled into a spot next to the other nine buses, which appeared to be empty, their passengers having already departed for the main level. He hit the lever to open the door. When he stood, the cushion of his seat made an audible wheezing sound, as if exhaling its relief at their good fortune.

"Alright, folks," he said. "Welcome to your new home."

He clomped down the steps and disappeared from sight, his part of the operation over. Some detainees hurried for the exits, trailing the driver like chicks following a mother hen. Others hung back to assist their weaker counterparts, slim arms wrapping around bony shoulders, working together to remain on their feet.

Pastor Nolan had spent the entire ride with his head bowed in prayer, and he continued to pray until all the other detainees had disembarked. Then, he rose from his seat, gave Gemma's shoulder a gentle squeeze, and clutched the vinyl seatbacks for support as he made his way down the aisle. Despite his weakened appearance, he still had to tilt his head to keep from knocking it against the roof of the bus.

When she and Taylor were the only two people left on the bus, Taylor took her hand and pulled her to him. Without saying a word, she climbed onto his lap and wrapped her arms around his shoulders, overwhelmed by the need to be as close to him as possible—a need she had put off for an unbearably long bus ride. Taylor's arms encircled her waist, and he pressed his face into her neck.

"I'm worried you're not real," he whispered, his voice breaking a little.

She raked her fingers through his sweat-dampened hair. "I'm real," she reassured him. "I'm right here, and I'm not going anywhere."

She hadn't allowed herself to focus on Taylor during the ride back to the mall, as if dwelling on the fact that he was not only alive but *with her* again might have been enough to break the spell and make him disappear forever. Part of her expected to wake up and find herself back in her bed at Letty's and that everything that had happened over the past few days—meeting Clarke, the rescue, reuniting with Taylor—had been nothing but a vivid dream.

But she hadn't woken up. And every time she'd checked Taylor's seat, he'd still been there, his head resting against the glass of the window, his eyes squeezed tight as if to block out the world. Dark blood coated his hands, but it wasn't his blood.

It was the crazy-haired detainee's blood. The one who'd died back on the gravel road.

Now, wrapped up in Taylor's arms, she had so many questions. Why had he been in the detention center in the first place? He wasn't a Christian. Was it some sort of punishment for helping their group? And if he was a detainee, why was he wearing his Task Force uniform instead of the tan-colored prison uniform worn by all the other prisoners?

And she wanted to know what had really happened with Gavin back in Winter's Dam.

Finally, reluctantly, they drew apart, but only far enough so that they could look into each other's eyes. Taylor brought his hands to Gemma's face and gently guided her lips to his in a slow, hesitant kiss. It wasn't the kiss she'd imagined for their reunion—when she'd allowed herself to imagine such a thing. It was awkward and distant, as if something existed between them now. An invisible barrier that neither of them could cross.

"I'm sorry," he said, pulling away from her and dropping his head.

He'd felt it, too.

Putting a hand under his chin, she gently lifted his head, forcing him to look into her eyes. "It's okay. We're going to be okay."

But Taylor looked away again. "What is this place? Where are we?"

"An old shopping mall," Gemma replied. "About twenty minutes north of Harrisburg. The guy who organized the rescue got us out of Winter's Dam right before the Task Force destroyed half the town. He's got a bunch of former cops and military people working with him. Even some former Task

Force. His people also raided other detention centers last night. Yours wasn't the only one."

"What's going to happen to the detainees?"

"The plan is to reconnect them with their families," Gemma said, "but I'm not sure how that's going to work. The Task Force is going to hunt down the escaped detainees, and their relatives' homes will be the first place they check."

Taylor passed a hand through his damp hair, pushing it away from his face. "What about Letty? Could she help us find a place for them?"

That was when it hit her.

He doesn't know Letty's dead. He probably thinks she escaped Winter's Dam with the rest of us. And he doesn't know about Yost, either.

"I know the Sanctuary is gone," he continued when she didn't respond. "But my dad is in bad shape. He needs medical care. I know Letty has money. Maybe she'd be able to pay a doctor to treat him—and to stay quiet about it?"

Pastor Nolan had looked terrible, but Gemma had just assumed that had resulted from five years in a detention center. "What's wrong with your dad? What kind of treatment does he need?"

He tapped a fist against his lips, as if trying to keep the words from coming out. "Pancreatic cancer," he said, finally meeting her eyes again. "Stage four. I don't know if he needs radiation or chemotherapy, but there has to be *something* the doctors can do. He couldn't get any kind of treatment in the detention center, but maybe Letty could help him? With her connections?"

The childlike hope in his eyes gutted her. Taking his face in her hands once again, she pressed her forehead against his. "I'm so sorry," she whispered, closing her eyes so she wouldn't have to see his reaction. "But Letty's dead. She died back in October, the same day the Task Force attacked the Sanctuary. Mullen found her somehow. He forced her to call the Sanctuary and pretend she had a pick-up, and then he killed her. When Kyle and Yost showed up, Mullen followed them back to the Sanctuary, and then he shot them both. Kyle survived, but Yost didn't make it."

Gemma couldn't see Taylor, not with her eyes closed, but she felt his face crumple beneath her hands. Feeling his raw pain brought Gemma's emotions back to the surface, and she dropped her face to his shoulder and cried along with him.

But Taylor was strong. After a few moments of weakness, he pulled himself together and wiped his face on his sleeve. "What happened to him?" he demanded. "What happened to Mullen?"

The answer would not satisfy him, because it hadn't satisfied her, either. "He fell into a vertical shaft in the coal mine. According to the news, he broke most of the bones in his body and then slowly died of dehydration." She deliberately left out how Mullen had kidnapped Sophia and blown up the mine's entrance to bury Gemma and Sophia alive. She only hoped that Taylor wouldn't ask what Mullen had been doing in the coal mine.

Thankfully, he didn't. "Death isn't good enough for him," he muttered. "Even a slow death isn't good enough."

"I know."

"Letty was a good woman. She didn't deserve to die."

"Neither did Yost." Gemma reached inside her shirt and pulled out the cross necklace, tiny flecks of Yost's blood still affixed to its surface. "But he died protecting our friends. I gave him this necklace the day he died, and he had it in his hands when we found him. Before he passed away, he told me he'd given his life to Christ."

She'd expected more of a reaction to this news, but Taylor didn't seem all that surprised about Yost's last-minute conversion. He nodded thoughtfully, in a way that reminded her a lot of Pastor Nolan.

"I'm really going to miss his jokes," he said.

"Yeah. Me too."

Taylor brought his blue eyes up to meet hers. Red veins formed squiggly lines in the whites of his eyes. He looked exhausted. "I want to go to bed."

"Okay."

But instead of rising from the seat, Gemma wrapped her arms around his shoulders and held him close, determined to never let him go again.

CHAPTER TWENTY-TWO

Detainees filled the mall.

At the spot where the corridor opened into the main concourse, Gemma stood with her hand interlaced with Taylor's, watching as Clarke's people moved among the detainees, handing out protein bars and bottles of water, directing some people to cots and others to the restroom. Despite the late hour, the vast majority of detainees remained awake, huddled in small groups and chewing on their protein bars. Some prayed quietly while others joined hands and sang hymns of praise, their voices rising above the din. Only a few people were actually trying to sleep through the chaos, the gentle slopes of their thin bodies barely visible beneath the thin blankets.

Gemma went up on her tiptoes, searching the concourse for her parents, hoping against hope for one more miracle. It was a long shot, of course. There were plenty of other detention centers, and it was possible that the people Clarke was working with had rescued her parents tonight. She also wanted to find Clarke. She hadn't seen him since before the rescue began, and she wanted to find out what came next in his plan. Because this was too many people in one small space. The mall had felt exposed before, but with so many people now huddled in one location, it felt downright claustrophobic.

Noticing the discomfort on Taylor's face, Gemma said, "We've been staying in the old theater. It's in a different section of the mall. It'll be much quieter there."

He nodded. "I should find my dad first."

"Okay." Pastor Nolan's height should've made him easy to spot, but Gemma couldn't see him anywhere. Not among the groups that were huddled together and singing, nor among the people gathered in prayer. "He might already be asleep. You don't have to worry about him tonight. He's safe. Let's rest for a few hours, and then we'll find him in the—"

"Gemma!"

Glancing to her right, Gemma saw Max jogging toward her, an unopened bulk package of bottled water in his arms. The color drained from his face at the sight of Taylor. "What?" His eyes darted to Gemma. "How?"

But Gemma wasn't ready to talk about the rescue yet. Not when Taylor looked so anxious. He needed to rest. "We're both exhausted," she said. "I'll tell you everything in the morning, after we get a few hours of sleep."

Max gripped the back of his neck, his expression morphing from confusion into astonishment. Unable to help himself, he lunged forward and pulled Taylor into a hug. "This is incredible. I'm so glad you're here, man."

"Thanks." Taylor tried to smile, but he looked relieved when Max released him.

"So, how is everything going?" Gemma asked Max, nodding toward the crowd gathered in the concourse. "Do you guys need anything?"

Before Max could respond, she heard Taylor's sharp intake of breath. Sensed his body stiffening. Felt his hand tighten painfully around her own.

"Taylor? What's—?"

She looked up and saw Gavin standing only feet away. The pillows he'd been carrying slipped from his hands and tumbled to the floor. He looked utterly terrified, as if he'd just seen a ghost.

"Nolan?"

One look at Taylor's face told her everything she needed to know. Any lingering questions she'd had about what really happened back in the tunnel evaporated the moment she saw the look in Taylor's eyes.

He wanted to *murder* Gavin.

She reached for Taylor, tried to grab him, but he was too fast.

He plowed into Gavin like a defensive end sacking a quarterback, knocking into him with such force that it looked like Taylor was trying to knock the life right out of Gavin's body. Together, they went down to the ground, landing in a heap in the center of the concourse, crashing into several empty cots on the way down. Gavin's head slammed into the metal leg of one cot, sending it screeching across the tile floor, but he had no time to recover before Taylor straddled him and began raining punches on his face.

"Taylor!" Gemma cried. "Stop!"

After a few punches, Gavin's police training kicked in, and he hooked his arm around Taylor's left leg and rolled to the side, taking Taylor with him. In a flash, the roles reversed, and Gavin was on top, delivering a powerful blow to Taylor's face. The sickening sound of flesh against flesh echoed throughout the now-silent concourse. He pulled back his arm to strike again.

"No, Gavin! Please don't hit him!"

Instead of landing the punch, Gavin hesitated at the sound of Gemma's voice, his fist clenched over Taylor's face. His eyes darted from Taylor to Gemma and back again. Finally, he dropped his hand to his side, climbed to his feet, and stumbled backward.

Taylor clambered to his feet, blood leaking from his nose.

Gemma rushed over to him, took his face in her hands, and forced him to look at her. "Please," she begged him. "Please, Taylor. Just stop."

But he took her by the arms and eased her away from him. "Keep her back," he said to Max before turning back to Gavin.

The two men faced each other in the center of the concourse, inside a crude semicircle of rescued detainees, most of whom looked too shell-shocked to know what to do. Both men were bleeding—Taylor from his nose and Gavin from his split lip—and their blood intermingled on the floor in a pattern of droplets and smears, like an abstract painting.

"Why?" Taylor demanded, his pale-blue eyes growing dark. "Why did you do it, Bonnar? Why did you close the door?"

Gavin brought a hand to his lips and looked at the blood-stained tips of his fingers. "What are you talking about?"

"Just admit it. Just admit why you left me there."

"I didn't leave you there," Gavin shot back. "I was doing *exactly* what you told me to do, Nolan. The Task Force was right behind you. So, I closed the door. If I wouldn't have closed it, we would've all been finished."

"You're lying." Taylor's nostrils flared, and he pointed a finger at Gavin. "I was *right there*, Bonnar. I saw your face when you closed the door. You knew exactly what you were doing. From the beginning, this has always been about her. She's in love with me, so you left me there to die."

Gavin's head snapped back as if Taylor had punched him again. He spun his finger in a circle near his ear. "You're crazy. You know that? Paranoid and crazy."

"Crazy?!" Taylor bellowed. "You think I'm crazy? Do you have any idea what they did to me?" He launched himself at

Gavin again, but this time Max was there, grabbing him from behind and holding him back.

"Let go of me!"

Gavin's eyes locked with Gemma's over Taylor's shoulder. "Why?" he demanded. "Why did you bring him here? Why couldn't you have just left him wherever he was?"

Furious, Gemma charged forward, raising her hand to slap Gavin, as she had in the basement of the elementary school. But he caught her wrist in mid-air and held it there, his eyes boring into hers. Challenging her.

"KNOCK IT OFF!"

A roaring voice, so ear-splittingly loud that, for a moment, Gemma thought she was hearing the voice of God Himself, shouting down from heaven.

But it wasn't God.

It was Clarke.

Gavin released Gemma's wrist and stumbled away from her.

"What *exactly* is the problem?" Clarke shouted. His eyes shot between Gavin and Taylor before finally landing on Gemma, as if he knew she was the answer to this equation. "Haven't you idiots had enough excitement for one night?"

Gemma's face burned with embarrassment and anger. She had to get out of this situation now, before she and Taylor got themselves kicked out of the mall. Moving around Clarke, she linked her arm with Taylor's and pulled him away.

"It was just a little misunderstanding," she called over her shoulder. "But it's over now. We're leaving." She walked faster, dragging Taylor along with her.

"Alcott."

At the sound of Clarke's voice, she stopped and turned around.

This is it, she thought. *He's going to kick us out. Where are we going to go? Where* can *we go?*

"I don't know what this was about," Clarke said, pointing at the streaks of blood beneath his boots. "But this is your only warning. If anything like this happens again, you're out of here. Not just you two, but your entire group, including the little girl. You got me?"

Gemma said nothing, only nodded, but that seemed to be good enough for Clarke.

"Let's go," she muttered to Taylor. "Now."

He followed.

CHAPTER TWENTY-THREE

David Ogden slid out of the back seat of his Mercedes SUV and stood on the sidewalk in front of Elevation Ministry Center. He tilted his head back and closed his eyes, basking in the heat of the early morning sunshine and the glory of his own achievements.

The building didn't just look brand new—it looked better than new. A phoenix rising from the ashes. As far as he could see, no evidence of the bombing remained, nor was there any sign of the large resistance symbol that had been spray-painted on the front sidewalk.

The symbol had been Lydia Grimes's idea.

He strolled the sidewalk, hands shoved deep into the pockets of his designer suit, scrutinizing the building for any imperfections. When he was satisfied that the building was perfect, he knelt down and visually inspected each of the cracks in the sidewalk for spots of blood or shards of glass, but found neither.

The contractor he'd hired—funded by Lydia Grimes, of course—to oversee the repairs had done a marvelous job.

Ogden gazed up at the building, overwhelmed by the pride he felt at the sight of his creation.

With its modern exterior, glass-facade entrance, and the word *Elevation* adhered to the pale-gray exterior of the building in bright-purple letters, the building managed to be both understated and extravagant, like Ogden himself. Once, Elevation Ministry Center had been a dilapidated furniture warehouse intended for demolition. When Ogden had first walked the property, he'd found used heroin needles strewn around the interior of the warehouse. But despite the property's run-down condition, Ogden had seen its potential, just as he could see the potential of each one of his new converts.

People from all religious backgrounds flocked to him, but most of his followers had once followed Christ. Now, they were eager to serve a new god, and Ogden was happy to be that god.

He glanced back at the idling Mercedes, where his driver waited to take him back home. Beyond the vehicle, two teenage boys circled the lawn on riding lawnmowers. He didn't know who the boys were. He hadn't seen them around before, but then again, he didn't know most of the staff who worked in his building. They were part of the invisible folks—the people who did the work and then crawled back into the walls prior to showtime.

Ogden continued his stroll along the sidewalk, following it around the side of the building to a botanical garden that featured several wooden benches. At the climax of his comeback show in two short days, he would announce to the world his intention to build a memorial fountain in the botanical garden. He would dedicate the stone fountain to the victims of the Elevation bombing and engrave all forty-seven of their names on it.

It was the least he could do.

The victims of the bombing had given their lives for a greater cause. They hadn't known what they were doing—they'd only been running for their lives like sheep—but they still deserved to be remembered.

He continued through the garden, looking for a place to rest, but droplets of dew coated the surface of each bench. Ogden retrieved a handkerchief from his suit pocket and wiped off the bench as best he could, making a mental note to have one of his staff wipe down the benches every morning. Then, he sat down, careful not to lean against the damp backrest.

Aside from the Mercedes, there were about a dozen other vehicles in the parking lot, all parked in the spaces closest to the building. The cars belonged to the staff members inside the building right now, rushing back and forth, making sure everything would be perfect for Ogden's comeback. He was forgoing his usual Friday night schedule for a Sunday evening show on the one-month anniversary of the bombing.

A special Sunday service. The beauty of it brought a smile to his face.

His phone vibrated in his back pocket. He pulled it out and glanced at the name he'd programmed into the contacts. *Dragon Woman / Lydia Grimes.* Of course Lydia was calling. Until now, Ogden had been enjoying his morning, and Grimes could probably sense his contentment all the way from her apartment in Washington. It was her nature to destroy happiness. He considered sending the call to voicemail but then vetoed the idea. Knowing Grimes, she probably had some of her goons watching him right now.

He answered in a chipper voice. "Lydia! What a lovely—"

"David?" She was practically panting. "Have you heard?"

He rolled his eyes. To Lydia Grimes, every situation was a crisis. He always tried to respond to her breathless dramatics with extreme calm. "I haven't heard anything today, Lydia. I came straight to the ministry center this morning. Everything looks wonderful, by the way. Your team did a phenomenal job. We're all ready for Sunday night."

"That's wonderful, David." But Grimes's tone indicated she thought it was anything *but* wonderful. "I'm thrilled that you're having a relaxing morning, but can I suggest something? Just because you're not on the news anymore, that doesn't mean you should stop watching it."

Forgetting himself, Ogden leaned against the backrest and ran a palm over his forehead. It took him a few seconds to notice the icy dampness seeping into his expensive suit jacket. Cursing, he launched himself to his feet as if someone had doused him with a bucket of cold water.

"What?" Grimes sounded alarmed. "What's wrong?"

Ogden clenched his jaw. "Everything's fine, Lydia. Just got some water—and who knows what else—on my suit. So, spit it out. What's so terrible that it warranted an early-morning phone call?"

"I can't believe you haven't heard yet. The rebels raided seven detention centers last night."

He blinked, not understanding at first. "Raided? What does that mean?"

"Raided! Attacked! Plundered!" Grimes shouted the words, her voice so loud he had to hold the phone away from his ear. "Use whatever word you wish! They all apply!"

A somewhat comical image formed in his mind: a detention center ablaze, flames licking the night sky. In the image's foreground, a band of marauding pirates sprinted away from the fire as fast as their peg legs would carry them. "Lydia, please stop with the hysterics and tell me exactly what happened."

"Some group—part of this rebellion that's gone unchecked for too long—broke into seven different detention centers last night and rescued the detainees. Most of the compromised centers were in Pennsylvania and Ohio. One was an hour north of Harrisburg." She said this last part accusingly, as if he should've been guarding the center himself since it was in his neck of the woods.

Stepping around the corner of the ministry center, out of sight of the boys on the lawnmowers, Ogden leaned against the building and closed his eyes. "I don't understand. How could something like that even happen? How does anyone break into a detention center? Isn't it like a prison?"

Grimes said nothing for a few moments, which probably meant she was reluctant to tell him something. Finally, she exhaled and said, "They had help on the inside."

"You mean the guards?"

"That's exactly who I mean."

Ogden could no longer hear the lawnmowers. Peeking around the side of the building, he saw the boys seated on their lawnmowers, drinking bottles of Coca-Cola and eating sandwiches. "How many detainees escaped?"

"We don't have an exact count yet. Everything is very chaotic. There were a few casualties, and some detainees were too sick to be moved. But my best guess is that somewhere north of three-thousand detainees escaped last night."

Three-thousand. The number flashed in Ogden's mind, too large to comprehend. It wasn't the idea of all those subversives back in the world that made the remnants of his breakfast curdle inside his stomach. It was the realization that this escape would be a huge news story for days to come. Maybe even weeks. How was he supposed to go onstage Sunday night and proclaim victory over the subversives now?

"Good Lord, Lydia. What are we supposed to do?"

"We round them up; that's what we do. The detainees aren't the problem. We know who they are. They can't return to their lives. In most cases, after we detained them, the government seized their homes and sold them. Where are they going to go? Some will try to reconnect with family, but that's fine, because we'll know exactly where to find them. I hope they enjoy their freedom because it will not last long."

"I sense a 'but' coming."

"A *huge* but," Grimes agreed. "The real problem is public perception. This is a great big stain for the Bureau of Compliance. It makes us look weak. Incompetent. We have to be very careful how we proceed. If we handle this situation correctly—and by correctly, I mean with a great show of strength—we can still come out on top."

Ogden pulled the damp handkerchief from his pocket and ran it over his forehead, wiping away the beads of sweat that had accumulated there. "Do you think I should postpone my show?" He wasn't sure how the public would respond to him postponing his comeback at the last minute. Even if he claimed the delay resulted from health issues, people would talk.

"Your show?" He could almost hear Grimes rolling her eyes. "You're such a narcissist, David. I've just told you that three-thousand subversives are out there, some of them joining up with this rebellion as we speak, and you're worried about your stupid show."

Instead of slipping the handkerchief back inside his pocket, Ogden released it and watched it flutter to the grass. "So, what are you going to do about this, Lydia? This is *your* train, after all. I'm just along for the ride."

"Like I said, we're going to respond with extreme force, starting with speeding up the unbindings. In the past three weeks, we've administered shots to nine-thousand detainees, most of them on the West Coast. I think we can double that number by this time next week."

Ogden nodded, barely listening. His mind was elsewhere, trying to figure out how to salvage his comeback show. "Alright."

"I'm going to address the nation tonight. I'm going to encourage everyone to stay strong in the face of this subversive threat, and I'm going to reiterate that our nation will prevail if we stick together. All the usual garbage. I'm also going to announce the unbindings to the public."

That got Ogden's attention. "Lydia, are you absolutely certain that's a good idea? You think the public will be on board?"

"People aren't as squishy as they used to be, David. The Bureau of Compliance receives thousands of calls every day from people who suspect their friends, neighbors, or even family members are housing subversives. They're practically foaming at the mouth, some of these people, and even if the squishier members of the public don't like the idea of the unbindings at first, they won't care once I tell them about the dead guards."

"What?" Ogden nearly dropped the phone. "The subversives killed the guards?"

That certainly didn't square with what he knew about Christians.

Grimes responded with that strange, hissing laugh that made his skin crawl. "Are you kidding? The subversives didn't kill anyone. Frankly, I wish they would've. There were some shots fired and a few injuries, but that's about it. The guards who were in on it fled with the subversives, but since we have no way of knowing if the ones who remained behind had anything to do with it, my people took care of the problem as soon as they arrived on scene."

Although there was no one nearby, Ogden lowered his voice to a whisper. "Are you saying your people executed them?"

When Grimes spoke again, he could hear the smile in her voice. "Didn't you hear me, David? I said the subversives did it."

Ogden walked around the side of the building, heading for his Mercedes. He didn't particularly care what Lydia Grimes did —or who she had killed—as long as no one ever connected him to any of it. But he wanted to be finished with his call. He needed to go home and mentally prepare for his show. "Finish what you were saying, Lydia. You're going to announce the unbindings..."

"I'm going to spin the unbindings as the only way of truly eradicating the subversive threat. I'm also going to let the nation know that we have video footage of some suspects in the detention center raids, thanks to the surveillance cameras. The turn-coat guards were smart enough to shut off the interior cameras, but some of the exterior cameras remained operational throughout, and our office is working diligently to identify any suspects we've captured on video. We've already identified one, and I'm going to put her picture up and announce her name at the press conference."

He waited for Grimes to continue, but she remained silent, clearly drawing out the suspense as long as possible. Finally, he asked, "Well? Who was it?"

"You're never going to believe this, David. It was *her*. Gemma Alcott. The girl from the compliance center. The girl the nation thinks bombed your building. She was there last night, at Stovington, the detention center north of Harrisburg. We've got her on video! We had to enhance the video a lot—it's very grainy—but there's no doubt it's her. I'm going to show her face to the nation."

Now, Ogden's stomach felt like a washing machine on spin cycle, its contents swishing round and round. "Do you think that's wise, Lydia? I've seen the chatter online. Even after the attack on Elevation, she still has a great deal of support among the public. You don't think putting her face on television as a brave rescuer of detainees might inspire more people to join the rebellion?"

"Not when I tell them we have evidence that suggests she executed three guards at Stovington. We're going to show photographs and video footage of the guards with their families. Really play to our viewer's emotions. One guy had three young children. I'm working on setting up an interview with his wife, but she's still quite distraught."

She gave the order to execute those guards, Ogden realized, *and now she wants to interview their widows.*

"Maybe we can invite a few of the family members to your show on Sunday?" Lydia sounded excited, as if this was the first time the idea had occurred to her. "Although, I'm not sure if they would come. I imagine they're busy right now with funeral preparations. I'll see what I can arrange. Anyway, to close out the press conference, I'm going to speak directly into the camera to Miss Alcott herself. Give our little troublemaker an ultimatum."

"What kind of ultimatum?"

Another hissing laugh. "You'll just have to tune in, David. But let's just say that I'm going to make her an offer she can't refuse."

With that, Grimes hung up on him.

Ogden stared at the black screen of his cell phone, feeling as if he'd just gotten off a call with the devil himself. He briefly entertained the idea of chucking his phone into the woods, driving to the nearest bank, withdrawing all of his money, and going on the run to a non-extradition country, like Mexico. But who was he kidding? There would be no escaping from Grimes.

The Dragon Woman would find him sooner or later.

Walking back to his Mercedes, Ogden deliberately strolled across the section of sidewalk where the rebellion's symbol had been spray-painted. It wasn't there anymore, but it gave him a little thrill to imagine the cross beneath his feet, where it belonged.

He didn't like the messiness of killing—he wasn't a sociopath like Grimes—but it would all be worth it in the end. Revolutions took time...and they took sacrifice. Soon, Grimes would have her country free from the influence of the Christian church, and Ogden would have more fame and power than he could've ever imagined.

And if a little blood had to be spilled for that to happen, so be it.

When Ogden reached the SUV, the driver hurried around to the back. "If you don't mind me saying, sir," he said, pulling open the door, "the building looks good. As sturdy as the day she opened."

Glancing at his reflection in the tinted rear windows, Ogden saw Elevation Ministry Center rising up behind him like a fortress. And he realized he was smiling.

"Nah," he said, sliding into the backseat. "She's even stronger now."

CHAPTER TWENTY-FOUR

aylor's gone.

The first thing Gemma noticed when she opened her eyes the morning after the rescue was Taylor's empty cot. The second thing she noticed was the time. According to her digital watch, it was already eleven-thirty.

Taylor's first day back and she'd slept half of it away.

Dressing quickly, she exited the theater and headed for the lobby. She could hear people out there, talking in animated voices, and she picked up the pace, straining to hear any signs of tension or anger. She had to make sure that Taylor and Gavin stayed away from each other so they didn't get into any more fights.

But it wasn't anger she heard coming from the lobby.

It was laughter.

As she reached the end of the hallway, her eyes landed on the group occupying the semicircle of folding chairs in the center of the lobby, and she froze in place. Taylor wasn't there, but Max, Brie, and Sophia each had a seat in the circle. The other people had their backs to her, but Gemma didn't need to see their faces. She recognized their voices. Their laughter. When her legs grew weak, she leaned against the wall for support. Then, an audible gasp escaped her lips, and the people in the chairs turned in her direction.

For the first time in seven months, she saw the faces of her friends.

Oliver Barnes. Mia Weber. Kurt Horst. Jerry Andrews. Abram Cleary.

They all looked a little older and a little thinner, but they were alive.

Not just alive, but *right in front of her*.

Mia Weber sprang to her feet, her mouth hanging open in an expression of surprise that would've been comical if not for the tears pouring down her cheeks. "Oh, honey. I didn't think I was ever going to see you again."

With tears blinding her vision, Gemma ran across the lobby into Mia's waiting arms. Over Mia's shoulder, Gemma saw the men from the Sanctuary rise to their feet, but they remained at a distance, as if they understood that this moment was just for the two women.

"Taylor's here," Gemma whispered into Mia's ear. "We found him. He was at the detention center." Then, she added, "*Your* detention center, I guess."

Mia nodded. "I know, honey. We saw him earlier this morning. He's still as handsome as ever, isn't he?"

Gemma smiled through her tears. No one could ever take the place of her mother, but over the past few years, Mia had become a second mother to her. Someone she could go to for advice and guidance. Someone who cared if she ate her dinner or brushed her teeth. Gemma hadn't realized how much she'd missed having that maternal presence in her life.

But seven months in a detention center had taken its toll on Mia. She appeared to have aged at least ten years in that time. Her hair was now entirely gray with a few streaks of white, and her once-tanned skin had morphed into the same deathly pallor

Gemma had seen on the other detainees. Like the others, she'd lost a significant amount of weight when she had had little to spare in the first place. Gemma could feel bones jutting out of Mia's back and shoulders, and she loosened her grip on the woman a little, not wanting to cause her any pain.

But Mia compensated by hugging her tighter. "Don't worry, honey," she said. "You won't break me. If that awful place couldn't do it, neither can you."

"But you're so thin."

"Oh, I'm fine. Nothing a big pot of ketchup spaghetti won't fix. Do you guys have ketchup here?"

A laugh burst from Gemma's throat. "I'm sure we can scrounge some up for you."

Hovering over his chair, Abram cleared his throat. "What about the rest of us?" he said in that gruff voice of his. Just hearing that voice again made Gemma feel safer. "What are we, chopped liver?"

Gemma wiped her eyes and headed for Abram. "You're definitely *not* chopped liver," she said, going up on her tiptoes to hug him. "You're more of a boiled turkey neck."

"Still funny as ever, Alcott," he said, giving her a hug that could crush bones.

After Abram let her go, she made her way around the circle, hugging the others from her old group, until she finally came to Oliver. Despite being reunited with his wife, Mia, he didn't look happy. Instead, worry clouded his eyes.

"What is it?" Gemma asked. "What's wrong?"

He reached up to stroke his beard. "There are more people from the Sanctuary out in the main concourse. But we haven't found everyone yet. They sent some people to different detention centers, I guess. We haven't found Coop. Or Pastor Jenson."

"That poor man," Mia said, nervously tugging at the hem of her donation bin sweater. "Pastor Jenson's health wasn't great to begin with. What if he didn't survive the center?"

"They could be here somewhere," Kurt interjected. "There's a lot of people here, and it took us a while to find each other. It's possible we just haven't stumbled across them yet."

"That's right." Gemma grabbed onto the idea like a sailor clinging to a sinking boat. "I'm sure they're here somewhere. What about Susan Richardson and Marcus Derrick?" Those were the only other members of what had once been the Sanctuary's leadership council who weren't present in the lobby. "Are they here?"

Oliver and Abram exchanged a look that told Gemma everything she needed to know.

"The Task Force executed them at the Sanctuary," Abram said. "At that point, I'd been beaten, handcuffed, and shoved onto a bus, but I saw it happen through the window. Marcus and Susan were trying to stop the soldiers from setting a cabin on fire. I don't know why. Maybe they thought there were people inside. Or maybe they just didn't want to watch the soldiers burn down the campground. But I watched a Task Force soldier pull out his gun and execute them both."

Gemma reached for her necklace, twisting the chain in her fingers. She remembered hiding in the woods that Sunday afternoon and listening to the gunshots. She'd felt so powerless knowing that she was probably listening to her friends die. On the opposite side of the lake, people were being killed, and there had been nothing she could do to stop it.

She turned to Max. "Where's Taylor? I need to talk to him."

"Up on the roof."

"The roof? Why is Taylor on the roof?"

Max shrugged. "He was in the mall earlier, when Brie and I were passing out breakfast to the detainees. He said he wanted to do something—to be useful—so I took him to Clarke. Once Clarke found out that he used to be a soldier, he assigned Taylor to guard duty on the roof."

Of course. Taylor couldn't enjoy a single day of freedom without playing soldier.

"Okay. I'm going to talk to him."

But when she turned to leave, Oliver's voice stopped her. "Gemma, before you go, would you pray with us? We were actually waiting for you to wake up. Now that you're here, all the leaders from the Sanctuary are present, except for Marcus and Susan. And Taylor, of course. I'm sure things are going to be busy the next few days, and I don't know if we'll be able to assemble like this again. I really feel like we should use this opportunity to pray together."

Gemma couldn't believe that Oliver and the others saw her as a leader. She'd been through a lot over the past year, and she'd tackled many difficult things on her own, but that didn't change the fact that she still felt like a kid around the older members of her group. *They* were in charge, not her. She only followed. However, somewhere along the line, she must've graduated to a place of leadership without even realizing it.

"Sure." She hurried over to join the others. "Absolutely."

In the center of the lobby, the survivors from the Sanctuary joined hands.

And they prayed.

CHAPTER TWENTY-FIVE

After ten minutes of searching, Gemma finally located Taylor on the rear extension of the roof that jutted out to accommodate the movie theater.

He'd exchanged his uniform for a black t-shirt and a pair of dark-gray cargo pants. He leaned against the concrete wall, one hand wrapped around a sweating water bottle, and peered into the dense cluster of trees that separated the mall's rear parking lot from a small housing development. A handheld radio hung from his belt, and a rifle laid on the wall in front of him.

He'd been through so much, and now he was sporting new bruises from last night's fight with Gavin, but Taylor still looked incredible, as if he'd just stepped out of Gemma's dreams. She hesitated near the roof's ventilation system and closed her eyes, silently thanking God for bringing her love back to her.

After she finished praying, she walked closer to Taylor, opening her mouth to say his name. But then her eyes dropped to his bare forearms, and she saw dozens of angry red lines carved into his flesh. Scars that hadn't been there before. They continued up his arm and disappeared into the sleeve of his t-shirt.

"So, how'd you find me?"

She jumped at the question. "Huh?"

Taylor turned to face her, that understated smile she knew so well playing at the corner of his lips. "Who told you I was on the roof?"

She glared at him, annoyed that he'd somehow known she was sneaking around. "I have informants. By the way, it was nice of you to tell me where you were going this morning so that I didn't worry about you."

"I didn't want to wake you," he said. "I thought you needed to rest after last night."

"Well, what about you? It's your first day of freedom, and you're already back on duty. You could take a few days off. You don't *always* have to be a soldier."

Gemma tried to keep her voice light, but she couldn't stop looking at those scars. They made her so angry. She would ask Taylor about them someday, but not now. For now, she just wanted to be near him. To know he was okay.

He tilted his head to the side, his smile growing a little wider, as if he found the mild scolding amusing. Then, he left the wall and moved closer to her, not stopping until they were a few inches apart. "If I didn't know you better, I'd think you weren't happy to see—"

Before he could finish, Gemma flung herself into his arms, and although he looked weak, he caught her and held her as if she weighed nothing. Wrapping her arms around his neck, she hugged him fiercely, not caring if she caused him pain. Because he would survive. Taylor *always* survived. She kissed the rough stubble of his cheek, his jawline, and inched her way closer to his lips. Being back in his arms felt like home. A home she never wanted to leave.

Finally, he brought his lips to hers, and he still tasted the same—like cinnamon gum. The kiss was nothing like the awkward one they'd shared the previous night. That kiss had made her think that something had broken between them. Something that could not be repaired. But this kiss held nothing back. It was both an apology *and* a promise. Using only their lips, they said everything they hadn't been able to say during those long seven months of separation. As they held each other on that sunbaked roof, both smelling a little like sweat and dirt, Gemma cried, her tears running down Taylor's cheeks.

When they came up for air, Taylor whispered against her lips, "Why are you crying? This is a good day, remember? We're together."

"The scars on your arms," she said. "There are so many of them."

"Oh. Those. Interrogators love their knives." He said it as if it were nothing. As if they were discussing the weather instead of torture. "There's a bad one on my chest. But at least they didn't mess up my handsome face."

Running her fingers through his sweat-dampened hair, her smile faded a bit as she noticed dark specks of dried blood on the right side of his neck. He probably didn't even realize they were there. Without saying a word, she rubbed at the dark splotches with her thumb, trying to erase them and, along with them, the memory of the detainee who'd died in his arms.

When the blood disappeared, she whispered, "Taylor, tell me about the tunnel." She hadn't planned to ask him about it yet, not so soon after the fight with Gavin. But she couldn't wait any longer. She needed to know the truth. "You're sure about what happened?"

At the mention of the tunnel, Taylor's jaw instantly stiffened, so Gemma put her hands on either side of his face to calm him down. "I already know what happened, but I just need to hear it from you."

Taylor spoke slowly, his voice as cold and hard as marble. "I spent the first six weeks after they captured me reliving those few seconds over and over in my mind. I wanted to make sure I was right. That I hadn't imagined things. To be honest, I wanted to be wrong, because I knew you were probably still with him, and I didn't want to imagine you trusting someone who could do something like that. But I'm one-hundred percent certain about what happened in that tunnel, Gemma. I saw the look on his face right before he shut the door. He left me there on purpose."

"Okay," she said, biting back her anger. It was one thing to suspect Gavin of leaving Taylor behind, but it was another thing to have it confirmed. "That's all I needed to hear. So, what happened afterward? Where did they take you?"

Taylor's hands dropped to her waist, and he tore his eyes away from hers and stared into the distance. "They took me to an interrogation facility. The same type of place the Task Force held Max after they captured him. They wanted to know who was running things in Winter's Dam, but I never told them. Eventually, they interrogated the sympathizers from Winter's Dam—the ones they'd captured at the Sanctuary. One of them must've told them about Letty."

"But that's something I never understood. Why did it take the Task Force so long to connect the Sanctuary to Letty? She owned the property. Couldn't they just have looked it up and found out that she was the owner?"

"Yes, but Letty was a smart woman." A smile played at the corner of his lips. "I asked her once if she worried about the Sanctuary being raided and everything being traced back to her. She'd just smiled and said that when she bought the camp-ground, she'd paid for it in cash and put the property into a land trust so her ownership wouldn't be part of the public record."

Gemma shook her head. "Letty was always a few steps ahead, wasn't she?"

"Many steps ahead," he replied, his voice thick with sadness. "Anyway, after the Task Force found out about Letty, they sent me to a detention center. I was only there for a few days before I got sick and ended up in the infirmary. That was where I found my dad. He actually stopped one of the other detainees from stabbing me in the throat with a scalpel."

Gemma gasped. "Someone tried to stab you?"

Tilting his head to the side, he pointed at the butterfly bandage partially covered by his t-shirt. "I guess he didn't like my uniform." He gave her a little shrug, as if that were a perfectly justifiable reason to stab someone in the throat. "I've spent a lot of time thinking about this over the past few days, and I realized that if my dad hadn't been in that infirmary—if he hadn't gotten cancer, or if I hadn't detained him in the first place—I wouldn't be alive right now. It's like everything that happened, including the bad things I've done, have all worked together for good."

She stared at him, searching his face, trying to decipher him like a code. "Taylor?" she finally managed. "What are you saying?"

Instead of answering her, he brought his hand to her neck, sending chills down her spine as he traced his fingers along the chain of her necklace. His fingers stopped where the silver chain disappeared into her shirt. Then, gently, he tugged the cross out of her shirt and let it fall across the palm of his hand. The sun reflected off its surface, its light overpowering the dark specks of blood, erasing them, if only temporarily.

Taylor looked at her. "God found me in that detention center, Gemma." He closed his fist around the cross and tugged on it to draw their faces closer together. "I don't know how, but He found me."

Tears spilled down her cheeks.

Years of prayer. Years of waiting. Years of hoping.

She closed her eyes. *Oh, God. Thank You, God.*

She kissed him again. Deeper this time. More meaningful than any of their previous kisses. As they kissed, he kept his hand wrapped around her cross necklace, his knuckles brushing against her sternum.

When they reluctantly pulled apart, Taylor said, "I want my dad to marry us. He loves you, and I know it would mean the world to him. But if he's going to do it, it should be soon. You've seen him, Gemma. I don't know how much time he has left."

"Okay—"

"But we don't have to get married if you're not ready," he interjected. "The last thing I want to do is pressure you. We haven't seen each other in seven months. If you want to give it a little time, I totally respect that."

A little time? Gemma almost laughed. She probably would've laughed if he hadn't looked so serious—and so hopeful. He was even blushing a little. She took his face in her hands, his cheeks rough beneath her palms. "Taylor Nolan, I've been waiting to marry you since I was eleven. If you're *finally* ready to get hitched, I'm free later today. Do you think you can make time in your roof-guarding schedule to marry me?"

"Today?" His cheeks flushed an even deeper shade of red. "Okay. That's faster than I was thinking, but I can make today work. There's just one thing I have to do first."

"Ugh. What now?"

He laughed. A genuine Taylor laugh. A rare but amazing sound, like the hoofbeats of zebras. "You know that old fountain just outside the entrance to the movie theater? Does it still work?"

The rest of the mall had running water. Gemma couldn't see a reason why Clarke wouldn't be able to get the fountain working. "I don't know. Probably. Why? Do you want to go swimming?"

He responded with a conspiratorial wink.

"Something like that."

CHAPTER TWENTY-SIX

"Wow. You look amazing."

Standing in front of the full-length mirror, with Sophia seated cross-legged at her feet and the lingering smell of chocolate filling her nostrils, Gemma used her hands to smooth out the wrinkled fabric of the dress.

Her wedding dress.

"Thanks, Soph." She glanced down at the girl. "This is the one."

Sophia giggled. "Don't you mean the *only* one?"

"Eh, good point."

Gemma hadn't expected to find a dress in the donation bins, much less one that could pass for a wedding dress. But when she'd glimpsed white buried at the bottom of one bin, she'd pushed aside a faded flannel shirt, reached deep into the bin, and carefully extracted a wrinkled ivory dress with three-quarter length sleeves. Not a wedding dress, by any means, but also not a dress that had any business being at the bottom of a donation bin.

Yet, it was there, as if it had been waiting for her to find it.

Without saying a word to Private Dietrich or Sophia, who'd

still been rifling through other clothing bins, Gemma had snuck behind the counter to try it on. She hadn't wanted to get her hopes—or theirs—up. Holding the dress up to her body, it had seemed a little small. But after she'd tugged it down over her hips and realized that it fit, she'd let out an excited little squeal that had caught the attention of Dietrich, Sophia, and several of the people walking by.

When Dietrich and Sophia spotted her, and their mouths had dropped open in identical expressions of shock, Gemma had known she'd found the right dress.

It fit a little snug in the waist, and the bottom hem ended just below her knees instead of just above them, but she didn't care if she looked short and chubby on her wedding day. There was also a bright-red stain on the front of the skirt that she *hoped* was spilled wine, but she could just cover it up with her hand. And there was a small hole in the right armpit, but no one was going to be looking at her armpits.

Her dress wasn't perfect, but so what?

She was marrying the perfect guy, and that was all that mattered.

"But does it twirl?" Sophia hopped to her feet and spun in a circle to demonstrate. "Not all dresses twirl, but twirling is really important. Just in case there's dancing."

Although Gemma didn't think there would be any dancing tonight—such revelries would certainly stretch the limits of Clarke's already-strained patience—she obliged Sophia with a few quick twirls. The dress billowed around her hips, and at once she felt like laughing and crying because, for those precious few seconds, she felt normal.

When she stopped spinning, Sophia beamed at her. "It twirls."

Oblivious to the twirling that had just taken place, Dietrich let out a frustrated groan and shoved a shoe bin to the side. "I'm sorry, but you're probably going to get married barefoot," she said before moving onto the next bin. "There's nothing but ratty old sneakers and boots in these boxes. I can't find a single pair of dress shoes. Not even a fancy pair of flip-flops."

"Dietrich—"

"It's fine. We'll just make Taylor go barefoot, too. And the guests. We'll lean into the whole bohemian vibe."

Gemma laughed. "You don't have to look anymore. I already found a pair."

Dietrich raised her head from the shoe bin, her eyes narrowed into slits. "Please don't tell me you're planning on wearing those ugly boots of yours. That only looks cute in the movies."

"No. I found something better." In fact, Gemma had found the shoes *before* she'd found the dress. With a smile on her face, she bent over and slipped on a pair of low-top Chuck Taylor All Stars. The fronts were a little scuffed, but the shoes were her exact size. And they were white. Once she had them on, she straightened up and extended one foot in front of her. "Well? What do you think?"

Dietrich stared at her for a few seconds, clearly struggling not to cry. Her lips pinched together so tightly they seemed to have disappeared entirely from her face. Finally, she took a deep breath, wiped furiously at her nose, and said, "You know what? It's perfect. The whole thing. The dress. Those shoes. Even that nasty red stain. It's you."

"You forgot the hole in the armpit." Gemma held up her right arm, putting the hole on full display.

Dietrich bellowed laughter. "Oh, that's *definitely* you." She grabbed a bag off the counter, dug inside, and pulled out some lip gloss, some powder foundation, and a pink tube of mascara. "I'm not much for makeup, but I keep this on hand in case of an emergency. Let's see if we can make you look halfway presentable."

"Halfway presentable is good enough for me," Gemma agreed.

After Dietrich finished applying her makeup, Gemma turned to the mirror for one last look. The dress, the makeup, the shoes...everything was better than she could've ever hoped for. Reaching inside the neckline of the dress, she pulled out the cross and allowed it to fall over her chest.

"Perfect," she whispered.

The only thing that caused her heart to ache—and the one thing she would not allow herself to dwell on for more than a few seconds—was that her parents would not be there to watch her marry the love of her life. Her father would not walk her down the aisle. He would not say the words, "Her mother and I do," when Pastor Nolan asked, "Who gives this woman to this man?" Her parents would not be present to give their approval of this union. Even if Gemma found them again one day, she could never give this moment back to them.

Behind her, Dietrich cleared her throat. "Gemma? If you're ready, it's time to go."

"Already?" Gemma had taken her watch off, so she lifted Sophia's wrist and looked at the time. "We still have a half-hour."

"Taylor asked me to bring you to the fountain at six-thirty."

Six-thirty? But the wedding wasn't until seven. "Why? What's going on?"

Dietrich gave her a dramatic sigh. "I told Taylor you'd be annoying about this. Look, your fiancé swore me to secrecy, so I can't tell you anything. I'm supposed to bring you to the fountain at six-thirty, but we have to stay back a bit because Taylor doesn't want to see you."

Gemma could feel her anxiety threatening to rear its ugly head. What if Taylor was getting cold feet? What if he was stalling because he didn't want to marry her? The idea was ridiculous, given everything he'd done for her, but fear wormed its way into her mind. "I don't get it. Why does Taylor want me there at six-thirty if he doesn't want to see me?"

Sophia folded her arms over her chest and plastered a scowl on her face. "I agree. You need to tell us why he doesn't want to see her."

Dietrich raised an eyebrow at Sophia. "Not you, too." Then she turned to Gemma. "Look, I know it's your wedding day, so you're allowed to be a little crazier than usual, but don't go all Bridezilla on me. It's not that Taylor doesn't want to see you. It's just tradition to not see the bride until she walks down the aisle" —she shrugged her shoulders—"Or...mall, I guess."

Frustrated and unable to think of a more mature way to show her displeasure, Gemma stomped one Chuck Taylor-clad foot on the floor. "So, why does he want me there early?"

"Because," Dietrich said, taking Gemma by the arms, "he wants *you* to see *him*."

✝

By the time Gemma reached the theater annex, dozens of people had gathered in the area surrounding the water fountain. The sun was almost down, and the lights in the annex weren't on, so the entire area was crowded and dim. But there was a purplish light near the fountain, although Gemma couldn't see its source. The size of the crowd —which included members of Clarke's forces as well as recently liberated detainees—made it nearly impossible for her to see *anything.* Glimpsing the top of Pastor Nolan's head, she went up on her tiptoes and searched the area in front of the fountain for Taylor, but if he was there, she couldn't see him.

Dietrich uttered an exasperated sigh and seized Gemma by the hand. "This way."

Not wanting to lose track of Sophia in the darkness, Gemma used her free hand to grab the girl's arm. Then, she allowed

Dietrich to pull them both through the crowd. There weren't as many people on the far side of the fountain, which would hopefully make it easier to see whatever Taylor wanted her to see.

Before they'd left for the fountain, Dietrich had grabbed a ratty old sweater—foul-smelling and several sizes too big—and approached Gemma tentatively, the sweater held out in front of her like an equestrian approaching a wild horse with a saddle. Before Gemma could protest, Dietrich lunged forward and flung the sweater over her head, effectively covering up her entire bridal ensemble. "No arguments," she'd said with a shake of her finger as Gemma reluctantly slipped her arms into the sleeves. "You're going incognito tonight. We can't have people realizing you're the bride before it's time. If someone draws attention to you, Taylor might see you."

Gemma wanted to argue that the *smell* of the sweater would certainly draw attention to her and that it was bad luck to get married in clothing that someone had died in, but she kept her mouth shut.

But the sweater was working. As Dietrich dragged her toward the metal bench that sat outside the entrance of the theater, no one paid any attention to Gemma—except to take a few steps back to distance themselves from the odor that surrounded her. When they reached the entrance to the theater, the ex-soldier held out a hand and helped Gemma climb onto the bench. Sophia clambered up beside her, and Gemma wrapped an arm around the girl's back to keep her steady.

"The wishing fountain!" Sophia cried, her voice swallowed up by the noise of the crowd. "Gemma, look at it! It's beautiful!"

And it was. Water cascaded down each of the three marble tiers, passing over dozens of forgotten copper wishes before tumbling into the basin below. It was beautiful to see water flowing in the once dried-up fountain, but the water wasn't even the best part. Now that Gemma was high enough to see the source of the light in the annex, she realized it was coming from the fountain itself—from color-changing lights hidden inside the basin and each of the three tiers. As she watched, the color of the water changed from purple to green. A few seconds later, it changed again, this time to pale blue.

Gemma chewed on her lower lip, determined to not wash away her makeup with her tears. She couldn't imagine the effort that had gone into getting the fountain working again, much less fixing any of the color-changing lightbulbs that had probably burnt out long ago, and she made a mental note to give Clarke a big hug when the evening was over.

Reluctantly, she tore her eyes away from the fountain and searched the area where she'd glimpsed Pastor Nolan earlier. She needed to see Taylor, to know that he was there, waiting for her, and that he hadn't changed his mind. She saw Pastor Nolan standing on the opposite side of the fountain, no longer in his detainee uniform but wearing a pair of wrinkled slacks, a sweater, and sneakers. On Pastor Nolan's tall frame, the donation-bin slacks ended just above his ankles, but the sweater fit him just fine.

A few feet away from Pastor Nolan, Gemma's friends from the Sanctuary stood in the front row of the rapidly expanding crowd. Mia, Oliver, Max, Brie, Kurt, Jerry, Abram. They were all present. Even Teresa was there, looking a little awkward and out of place, but she was there just the same. The only person who was missing was Gavin, but Gemma hadn't expected him to attend.

But no matter how hard she looked, she couldn't see Taylor anywhere.

As Gemma watched, Pastor Nolan climbed onto the elevated platform that surrounded the fountain. He looked wobbly, and for a terrifying instant, Gemma was certain that he was going to tumble backward into the water, smacking his head off the tiers on his way down.

But he steadied himself, cleared his throat, and lifted his hands in the air.

"Good evening, ladies and gentlemen," he said, raising his voice to be heard over the crowd. "Could I have your attention for the next few minutes?" The crowd instantly quieted down. Even though he was rail-thin and terminally ill, Pastor Nolan still carried himself in such a way that people listened when he spoke. Not out of fear or intimidation, but from respect.

"Where's Taylor?" Sophia whispered to Gemma. "I don't see him anywhere."

"Me neither."

"My name is Pastor Joseph Nolan, and I was liberated from Stovington Detention Center last night. Some people gathered here tonight were my rescuers. You saw an injustice being perpetrated and decided you could not look the other way. I can never thank you enough for—" He stopped talking mid-sentence, his face contorting in obvious pain, and put a hand on his lower back.

Oliver and Abram stepped forward, ready to assist him if necessary.

But Pastor Nolan waved them off. "I'm alright," he said, but he didn't sound alright. Not at all. "I apologize, but I'm afraid I'm not feeling my best tonight. However, the Lord has called me to do this, and He will carry me through this."

Behind him, the light in the fountain changed from yellow to red.

"Throughout my ministry, I've always preferred performing funerals to weddings." Several in the crowd chuckled at this statement, probably assuming it was a joke, but Pastor Nolan remained straight-faced. "The reason is that, at weddings, people are happy. They are celebrating. Everything is right with the world. Funerals are very different. At funerals, people are at their lowest. They're grieving. They're looking for answers. Answers that many of them could not find despite years of searching. Funerals bring people face to face with their own mortality in a way that nothing else can. You might not remember the first wedding you ever attended, but I bet you remember the first funeral."

Many in the crowd nodded their agreement.

"As a minister, God has called me to speak to people in their bleakest moments. To provide them with a bit of light as they walk in the darkness. To speak to their souls—to that part of themselves that is aware, on some level, of its own immortality —and to comfort them. But my greater purpose is to give them hope through the Gospel. At funerals, people are open. They're ready to receive that message of hope. Many of you are not believers, and this is not a funeral, but you've all seen your share of death and pain. My prayer is that your hearts are open now. My prayer is that, tonight, you're ready to not only hear the Truth, but to receive it."

Everywhere Gemma looked, there were people crying, including a few of Clarke's people. Even the unflappable Dietrich pulled a wad of bunched up toilet paper out of her pocket and dabbed at her eyes. Pastor Nolan had that effect on people.

But Gemma gritted her teeth, determined not to ruin her makeup.

As the fountain changed from red to purple, Pastor Nolan said, "I don't know how much longer God will keep me on this earth, but I can feel my time growing short. I've spent the better part of the last few years begging Him to take me home." Then, he turned so he was facing the bench. His eyes landed on Gemma, as if he'd known where to find her all along, and his lips stretched into a smile. "But I'm so thankful that the Lord didn't take me on the hundreds of occasions I asked Him to, because then I wouldn't have gotten to watch my son, Taylor, marry his childhood sweetheart, Gemma. Thirteen years ago, I had the honor of performing the funeral service for my beautiful wife, and Gemma was by my son's side on that difficult day. And now, I have the honor of joining her to my son by marriage. So, do I prefer funerals to weddings? Yes. But this—this moment right here—is the one exception to that rule."

That was all it took. Gemma lost her battle to preserve her makeup.

Dietrich handed her some toilet paper. "Here."

"Thanks."

Pastor Nolan continued, "The only thing on earth that could bring me more joy than this wedding would be for my son to accept the Truth and allow Jesus Christ into his heart. So, you can imagine my overwhelming joy when Taylor came to me this afternoon and asked me to baptize him."

Gemma's heart skipped a beat. "What?" she whispered.

Beside her, Sophia uttered a choked sob and threw her arms around Gemma's waist.

"Son? Come forward."

The crowd parted, and suddenly, Taylor was there, standing between Abram and Oliver. He wore the same dark t-shirt and cargo pants he'd been wearing on the roof, the scars on his arms made more vibrant and beautiful by the ever-changing light of the fountain.

Gemma wanted to run to him. To hold him. To tell him how much she loved him. To tell him how she'd been praying for this moment for as long as she could remember. Marrying Taylor had always been her dream, but she had always wondered what it would be like to marry an unbeliever—something the Bible specifically warned against. What would that mean for their marriage? For their children?

Never in all of her fantasies had she imagined Taylor being baptized moments before their wedding.

Pastor Nolan stepped down into the fountain, the water reaching to his knees. If the water in the fountain was cold, which Gemma was almost certain it was, he gave no indication of discomfort. He motioned for Taylor to join him.

With one hand still pressed over her heart and the other wrapped around Sophia, Gemma watched as Taylor joined his father in the water. Both men went to their knees in the water.

"Ladies and gentlemen," Pastor Nolan began, "baptism represents the beginning of a new life with Christ. While it is not a requirement for salvation, it represents our acknowledgement that we have been broken by sin and that we need a savior. It represents our desire to turn away from sin and to put our faith and trust fully in Jesus." He looked at his son, his eyes lighting up with pride. "Taylor Joseph Nolan, do you know and accept Jesus Christ as your personal savior?"

Except for the sound of trickling water and the steady pounding of Gemma's heart, the entire annex was quiet, as if the whole assembly was waiting for Taylor's answer.

Taylor's eyes glistened, his unshed tears reflecting the green light of the fountain.

"Yes," he finally said. "I do."

With tears running down his cheeks, Pastor Nolan put one hand on Taylor's upper back and the other on his chest. "Then, it's my privilege," he said, barely able to choke out the words, "to baptize you in the name of the Father, the Son, and the Holy Spirit."

He dipped Taylor backward, submerging his head beneath the surface of the water before bringing him back up.

For just a moment, both men remained perfectly still, and Gemma closed her eyes and seared the image into her mind. A snapshot of Taylor with water pouring down his cheeks like tears, dark hair plastered against his forehead, back-lit by a fountain that had just turned the same shade of blue as his eyes.

When she opened her eyes again, Taylor was pushing the wet hair away from his face. He looked up at his father and smiled. Not the understated half-smile that Gemma loved, but a wide, joy-filled smile she had never seen before.

The two men embraced in the water, and the crowd applauded.

"Thank you, God," she whispered.

Sophia, the only one who'd heard, squeezed her waist harder.

Somewhere in the crowd, a woman began to sing.

Abram extended his arms to help Pastor Nolan and Taylor out of the water, while Kurt and Oliver met them with towels. The others from the Sanctuary stood nearby, holding hands.

As her eyes passed over the faces of her friends, Gemma realized it was Mia's voice she'd been hearing. The woman was singing the hymn "Fight the Good Fight," her voice rising over the dying applause. When the crowd heard her, many of them joined in.

"Run the straight race through God's good grace,

Lift up thine eyes, and seek His face;

Life with its way before us lies,

Christ is the path, and Christ the prize."

The people from the Sanctuary joined hands with those around them. Before long, everyone in the annex was holding hands, creating an endless chain with Pastor Nolan at its start. Clarke's people didn't know the hymn, but they joined hands with the Christians, closing their eyes and swaying as the voices swelled around them.

Something drew Gemma's gaze to the rear of the crowd, and she saw Clarke standing all the way in the back, apart from everyone else. He wasn't holding anyone's hand. He hadn't connected himself to the chain. Instead, he stood alone, hands clasped behind his back, head tilted back, his eyelids pressed tightly together.

He was singing.

CHAPTER TWENTY-SEVEN

After Taylor disappeared into the bathroom to change out of his wet clothes, Gemma left Dietrich and Sophia standing on the bench and made her way through the crowd toward her friends. With the hem of her ivory dress barely protruding from the bottom of her sweater, she couldn't have looked much like a bride, but the crowd parted around her, creating a makeshift aisle for her to walk down.

As she drew closer to the group, Gemma noticed Taylor's father perched on the ledge of the fountain, resting after the exertion of the baptism. The yellow glow from the color-changing lights made him appear older and sicker than he was, but when he saw Gemma approaching, excitement filled his tired eyes, and he rose to his feet.

"My dear." The minister gave her a broad smile and pulled her into a powerful hug. "Please tell me you saw what just happened."

Gemma nodded, blinking the tears away. "I didn't think this day would ever come."

Pastor Nolan held her at arm's length. "It wouldn't have

come if not for you, Gemma. My son has done so many things wrong, but you never gave up on him. You never stopped loving him. You're the only believer that my son didn't cut out of his life, and I think God used you to show him a Christlike love that he might otherwise never have known. It's the greatest honor of my life to join you two together in marriage."

Emotions bubbled up inside of Gemma, threatening to spill over like a pot of boiling water. But if she lost it now, before her wedding even began, she wouldn't be able to get through the ceremony. And nothing—absolutely *nothing*—was going to stop her from marrying Taylor.

"What's going to happen to us in the future, Pastor?" she asked.

Pastor Nolan bowed his head as if in prayer, seeming to consider her question for a long time before answering. "I don't know," he finally said. "But just remember that we already know how this story ends. Whatever happens to us in the future, we must never lose faith in the end of the story."

Before Gemma could respond, Mia appeared at her side and put an arm around her shoulders. "Honey, I don't quite know how to tell you this, but your sweater is ugly as sin, and it stinks to high heaven."

Gemma laughed. "Yeah, I know."

"Okay, good. So, why don't we take it off and get you married?"

✝

Gemma carried no bouquet in her arms, but that didn't matter because she had no free arms with which to carry a bouquet. One arm was linked with Abram's, and the other was linked with Oliver's. No organ processional announced her arrival, but that didn't matter because she could hear the processional in her mind. *Trumpet Voluntary in D-Major.*

The song the little-girl version of herself always imagined would play on the day she married Taylor. No bridal party preceded her down the aisle, but that didn't matter because her friends were all present. Smiling at her. Supporting her. Loving her.

She had no father to escort her down the aisle, but when the two father-figures in her life moved, she moved with them, trusting them to usher her along the narrow path, through a sea of strangers, toward her future.

And there, standing at the end of the aisle, was Taylor.

Their eyes met, and in those few moments as she made her way down the aisle, everything else—and everyone else—faded away, until only the two of them remained, their eyes locked on each other.

Holding each other up, as they always had.

Giving each other a reason to keep moving.

As she drew closer to him, Taylor's eyes traveled down to her feet and back up again, taking in her dress, her makeup, her scuffed Chuck Taylor All Stars. There were stains. There were holes. There were imperfections. But his eyes saw none of them.

They only saw her.

Instead of a tuxedo—because most people didn't throw their old tuxedos into donation bins—Taylor was wearing a pair of black pants and a white button-down shirt with a tie. Probably the nicest outfit he could find. His hair remained damp from his baptism, and he'd pushed most of it behind his ears, but a few wet tendrils dangled over his forehead. He gave her one of his signature half-smiles, and he looked almost shy as he pushed the hair away from his face.

He'd never been more handsome.

As she stared into his eyes, Gemma allowed herself to travel back to that night, years earlier, when the carnie had found her cross necklace. She remembered the fear she'd felt. The humiliation of falling into the mud. The anger at seeing her necklace dangling from the carnie's meaty hand. She remembered how everyone had stood there and watched the scene play out, some of them pulling out their phones to film the interaction. And she remembered the immense relief she'd felt when Taylor had charged into the scene, coming to her defense, positioning himself between her and her attacker. He'd been the only one to stand up to the much-larger carnie. The only one to defend her when no one else had.

It was *that* Taylor she saw standing in front of the fountain. Not the handsome twenty-five-year-old man he would eventually become, but the fourteen-year-old boy with a broken heart and an instinct to protect the innocent when no one else would.

"I can't believe I get to marry him," she whispered, and Oliver squeezed her hand.

When she reached the fountain, Pastor Nolan smiled down at her with tears in his eyes. "Who gives this woman to this man?" he asked.

Oliver and Abram responded in perfect unison. "We do." But Abram's voice cracked a little as he said the words.

Both men gave her a kiss on the cheek. Then, they released her hands.

And she stepped forward, placing her hands into Taylor's.

✝

After the ceremony, there was dancing.

Gemma hadn't thought there would be—not under the circumstances—but then one of Clarke's guys had shown up with a laptop. He'd hooked it up to a set of small external speakers and turned the volume up as loud as it would go, which wasn't very loud. But the crowd—many of whom hadn't heard music in years—quieted down and listened.

Gemma instantly recognized the song as Don McLean's, "American Pie."

At first, no one danced. And then, slowly, like the dead coming back to life, people started to move. Some only bobbed their heads up and down to the music, while others held each other and swayed on their feet. Some danced alone, tears streaming down their cheeks.

But *everyone* sang along with the chorus.

Taylor took Gemma's hands and pulled her close, pressing her hand to his heart and covering it with his own. "This is our first dance."

She rested her head on his chest. "I can't believe I'm officially Gemma Nolan."

"I always thought your name was beautiful," Taylor spoke the words into her hair. "But I like it even better now."

Lifting her head from his chest, she brought her eyes up to meet his. Her hands crawled up the back of his neck, her fingers tangling in his still-damp hair. "Did you do this for me?" she asked, nodding at the fountain.

"No," he replied without hesitation. "I did it for me."

As the song slowed in its last verses, Gemma pressed her lips against Taylor's and kissed him deeply. And there was something wonderful about kissing him now that he was finally hers in the eyes of God. He was her husband, and she was his wife, and there was something so beautiful and powerful about that union.

After they pulled apart, she went up on her tiptoes and whispered into his ear, "I don't want to be here anymore," she said. "I want to be alone with you."

It was dark in the annex, so she might've imagined the way his cheeks flushed. But she definitely *didn't* imagine the way he tensed up and pulled away from her slightly. "We probably shouldn't leave yet," he said. "It's our wedding reception. It wouldn't look good if we just disappeared."

He was making excuses. Not because he didn't want to be with her, but because he *did*. The truth was written all over his face. He wanted to be with her as much as she wanted to be with him. But even though they were husband and wife, something was holding him back.

"What is it?" she asked. "What's wrong?"

They stopped dancing and stared at each other.

"Gemma..."

"We're married now," she said. "We're not doing anything wrong. And I'm certainly not going to—"

"I never got your father's permission to marry you," Taylor blurted the words out. He glanced nervously over her shoulder, as if expecting her father to materialize out of the crowd and charge at him. When he looked back at Gemma, there was guilt in his eyes. "Your parents are out there somewhere, and they don't even know you're married. I didn't think it would bother me this much, but it does. My father's here, but your parents aren't. It's not right."

At that moment, "American Pie" gave way to "Wonderful Tonight" by Eric Clapton—one of the most romantic songs ever written, in Gemma's opinion. And while those familiar opening guitar chords made her want to launch herself into Taylor's arms, she grabbed both of his hands. "Promise me you'll help me find them," she demanded. "Even if we have to do it alone. Even if these people abandon us. We won't stop searching until we find them, no matter what. We never stop. If you want to make it right, Taylor, *that's* how you can make it right. Help me find my parents."

Resolve filled Taylor's eyes. She'd given him a mission—one that mattered more to her than anything else she'd ever asked of him—and he would fulfill it or die trying. "Okay," he said when she finished speaking. "We'll find them. No matter what. I promise."

Behind them, the fountain lights changed to yellow, the color of happiness, and Gemma fell into her husband's arms, her sneakers briefly leaving the floor as he lifted her off her feet. Then, he kissed her until the color changed to red.

The color of love.

When Taylor put her back down, Gemma asked, "Did we just have our first fight ten minutes into our marriage?"

Taylor shrugged. "I'm surprised it wasn't sooner."

They finished dancing to "Wonderful Tonight," and then Taylor took her by the hand and led her away from the fountain. Away from the lights. Away from the crowd. They snuck back into the movie theater to find a place to be alone, the sound of music and dancing and laughter fading as the door closed behind them.

Anything might happen in the future.

But for tonight, they were together.

CHAPTER TWENTY-EIGHT

For the first time in months, Gemma dreamt of dragons. Instead of orbiting the sky above Dragon's Back Mountain or creeping into the mine to attack her in the darkness, the dragons circled in the air above the shopping mall, exhaling acrid black smoke from their nostrils, their leathery wings casting sinister shadows over the desolate parking lot.

Thousands of them. More than ever before.

After a year of searching, their savage instincts had led them back to Gemma. To the mall where she'd been hiding. She stood on the far corner of the roof, watching in horror as the dragons dove at the mall, their cavernous mouths hanging open to breathe fire on any soul unfortunate enough to be caught between them and their target.

She wasn't alone on the roof. Clarke's soldiers were with her, firing their weapons into the sky. But their bullets bounced off the beasts, unable to pierce the impenetrable armor of the dragon's scales.

One by one, each soldier burst into flames.

Falling to her knees, Gemma unleashed an animalistic howl.

Her arms dropped onto her legs, palms facing the sky in supplication. There was nothing to do but wait for the attack to be over.

And then she saw him.

Taylor. Running toward her.

The last remaining soldier. Her only hope, still wearing his Task Force uniform. As if sensing the approaching horde, he stopped in the center of the roof and pivoted to face the squadron of dragons as they finished their strafing run and circled back for one last attack.

Gemma tried to scream at him to run, to get out of the way, but he wasn't looking at her. And he couldn't hear her voice over the thunderous sound of beating wings. But she couldn't let them kill him. The dragons wanted *her*, not him. Because, although they were aiming for Taylor, they fixed their eyes on her.

Offer yourself to us, they seemed to say, giving her a choice. *Sacrifice yourself, and no one else has to die.*

Gemma leapt to her feet and sprinted across the roof, waving her arms in the air, doing everything she could to draw attention to herself, giving herself to the beasts. She would willingly hand over her life if they would allow the man she loved to live.

"Take me!" she screamed. "I'm right here!"

The dragons understood her. One by one, they shut their massive jaws and swooped away from the mall, the violent wind from their wings nearly tossing Gemma backward onto the roof. But she remained on her feet and kept running, determined to reach Taylor before the monsters consumed her.

Risking another glance at the sky, she watched as the lead dragon pulled away, retreating to the edge of the parking lot where it could circle the mall at a distance. The remaining dragons followed suit, abandoning the attack and joining the makeshift holding pattern.

They had accepted her conditions. They were waiting for her.

All except one.

One last dragon, which had only been a pinprick in the sky moments earlier, was now bearing down on the roof with malicious intent.

The creature was heading straight for Taylor.

She kept running, kept waving her arms, but there was no time. There was nothing she could do but watch as the blue spark in the beast's throat ignited, sending forth a column of heat and fire that lifted Gemma off her feet and tossed her backward. She landed hard on her back, the impact knocking the breath from her body.

When she opened her eyes again, Taylor was no longer standing. He was on all fours on the ground, wailing in agony as the heat from the fire melted the Task Force uniform onto his blackened skin. Even as his screams faded to pitiful moans, the lone dragon circled back for one last strike. The beast's objective was clear.

It intended to take everything from her, once and for all.

The dragon dove toward the roof, mouth agape, the heat of a thousand furnaces spilling forth from its belly.

And Gemma could only scream as Taylor turned to ash and blew away.

✝

She awoke, gasping for air, as if she'd been the one on fire instead of Taylor.

The projection room was pitch black, and she extended a shaking hand into the darkness, fumbling for the Maglite they'd carried upstairs with them after they had snuck out of the mall. Her fingers knocked into something hard, and she grabbed it, located the switch, and turned it on.

The projection room was empty. There were no dragons. Nothing lurked with them in the darkness, waiting to attack. In fact, there was nothing in the room at all, except for a few dust-covered boxes of old film reels on the other end of the room, stacked neatly beside the stairway.

And when she spun around and directed the flashlight at the floor, Taylor was there, lying next to her on a bed of blankets.

Safe.

If she'd been crying or moaning in her sleep—which she sometimes did, according to Sophia—the sound hadn't disturbed him. He was sound asleep, one arm still outstretched to support Gemma's neck.

Gradually, Gemma felt her breathing return to normal. It helped to see Taylor alive and unharmed, but the horrible image of him from the dream, where he'd blown apart like ash, was impossible to forget. Reaching out, she touched him on the shoulder, reassuring herself that he was real. She considered waking him up so he could hold her—she knew he wouldn't have minded—but he looked so peaceful that she couldn't bring herself to do it.

Instead, she slipped out from underneath the warm pile of blankets and pillows they'd set up in the room's corner and climbed to her feet. Immediately, her arms erupted in goose-bumps. The projection room had grown chilly since they'd come upstairs, and her tank top and pajama shorts offered little protection against the cold. She reached for her backpack, which was lying nearby, pulled out her gray utility jacket, and slipped it on. She needed to use the bathroom, but she didn't feel like wasting time putting on her shoes, so she left her sneakers beside the backpack, grabbed the flashlight, and headed downstairs.

As soon as she stepped into the dimly lit lobby area, she switched off the Maglite. The others from the Sanctuary lay scattered around the room, fast asleep on their respective cots.

Even Sophia, Max, and Brie had carried their cots into the lobby to sleep with the others. Gemma couldn't see Gavin or Teresa anywhere, which meant they were probably still huddled away in their own theater, isolating themselves from everyone else.

She could've used the lobby bathroom, but she didn't want to wake the others when she flushed the toilet. So, she padded back down the hallway toward the other bathroom, her bare feet sinking into the soft carpet.

As she walked, memories of the past few hours came back to her, and she smiled to herself as she remembered how it had felt to be with Taylor as husband and wife. Their wedding had been amazing, but being with Taylor physically, finally crossing that threshold and experiencing the one thing they had never shared with each other, had been everything she'd ever imagined and more. She was so glad they'd waited, so glad they had taken nothing away from that moment by experiencing it before marriage. And Taylor had been incredibly sweet with her—so gentle and loving. At least twice, he'd asked her if she was okay. Over and over, he'd whispered into her ear how much he loved her. Afterward, he'd held her in his arms, and they'd talked for hours, until they both fell asleep.

She felt closer to him now than ever before.

When she reached the bathroom, Gemma stepped inside and flicked on the overhead lights, bathing the room in a harsh fluorescent glow. She glimpsed her reflection in the mirror—still smiling—and then hurried into the closest stall. The cold tiles of the bathroom floor didn't feel nearly as nice as the hallway carpet, and she regretted not slipping on her shoes before leaving the projection room. Eager to get back to Taylor, she used the restroom quickly then washed her hands at the sink. She bent over and splashed cold water on her face, trying to wash away the sweat left behind by her nightmare, which was rapidly fading from her mind.

There are no dragons, she reassured herself as the water

cascaded down her face. *You're married to Taylor. You're safe now. Everything is okay.*

Without opening her eyes, she reached for the brown bath towel she knew was hanging over the divider for the nearest bathroom stall. Her hands closed around it, and she pulled it down and felt around for a dry area. She used the towel to blot the water from her face, and then stood up, her eyes falling on the mirror...

...and the man reflected within it.

A half-gasp, half-scream escaped her lips, and she dropped the towel on the floor and spun around to face him. Every muscle in her body coiled up, ready for a fight.

But it wasn't a stranger.

It was Gavin.

"What are you doing in here?" she demanded, her voice part shriek, part whisper. "You almost gave me a heart attack!"

He sat on the tile floor, just inside the bathroom's entrance, his legs bent in front of him, his elbows resting loosely on his knees. There was something in his hands, something small that he was passing back and forth between his fingers, but Gemma couldn't see what it was. He looked her up and down with bloodshot eyes, his face wrinkling in revulsion as his eyes passed over her bare legs and feet. "Well? How was your wedding night, Mrs. Nolan?"

Her hands balled into fists. She wanted to punch him. Not just for frightening her so badly, but for staring at her like that. Like she disgusted him. Like she'd done something wrong. "Gavin, answer me. What are you doing in here?"

"Sorry I couldn't be at the ceremony," he continued, slurring his words. "Teresa begged me to come. She said it was the right thing to do and that it would prove to her I didn't still have feelings for you." He uttered a bitter laugh. "I guess I screwed *that* up, didn't I?"

The slurred speech. The bloodshot eyes. The slight flush of

his cheeks. The fact that he was even speaking to her. "Are you drunk, Gavin? Seriously? Where did you even find alcohol?"

"Most of Clarke's guys are former cops," he said with a shrug, as if that was enough of an answer. "Look, I wanted to come tonight, Gem. I really did. Not just for you, but for Teresa. But I just couldn't do it. I couldn't bring myself to watch you marry him."

The way Gavin said *him*—with the same disgust she'd just seen in his eyes—made Gemma want to shake him and force him to acknowledge that *he* was the bad guy in this situation. *He* was the one who'd abandoned Taylor in the tunnel back in Winter's Dam, not the other way around. But she drew in a deep breath and swallowed back those words. No good would come from saying them. "Gavin, I understand you not wanting to be at the ceremony. Honestly, it's probably better that you weren't there. You and Taylor shouldn't be in the same room together."

"But I wanted to come," he said again. "It's just...that was supposed to be us, you know? At least, I always thought it would be us. I guess I thought that someday you'd figure out that you'd made a mistake in picking him over me."

Unable to look Gavin in the eyes, she bent to retrieve the towel from the floor. As she shook it out and hung it over the divider, she contemplated what she wanted to say next. "Gavin, I didn't make a mistake in picking Taylor," she said in a soft voice. "I've been in love with him since I was a kid. He's been nothing but good to me. If you even tried to get to know him, you would see what a great guy he is. Yes, he's made some mistakes, but so have I. Like how I treated you back at the Station. I never should've led you on like that. I should've told you I was in love with someone else. That was my mistake, and I'm so sorry for hurting you, Gavin. I really am."

As the words left her lips, she felt an incredible sense of relief. She'd tried to apologize to Gavin a year ago, back in Oliver's farmhouse, but Gavin had silenced her with an unwanted kiss. This apology would not magically fix everything, but she'd avoided taking ownership of her role in the whole Gavin situation for far too long.

She stared at him, waiting for him to accept her apology—or to say he never wanted to talk to her again. Neither response would've surprised her.

Instead, he said, "Teresa's pregnant."

He blurted it out, just like that, as if the news didn't have life-changing implications for both of them. For their entire group.

Teresa. Pregnant. The pieces of the puzzle came together in Gemma's mind. Gavin and Teresa had been distancing themselves from the group since Winter's Dam. Gemma had just assumed that Teresa was struggling with the loss of her father or that she didn't feel as if she fit in.

But pregnant?

They had gotten Addie through her pregnancy without an obstetrician or prenatal care, but the pregnancy had still been difficult. Plus, they'd been at the Sanctuary when Addie had given birth, and Letty had made sure that Oliver and Claudia had everything they needed to bring Weston safely into the world. Still, it had been a rough delivery.

Gemma braced herself against the countertop with both hands, using it to hold herself up. "How far along is she?"

He dropped his eyes to his hands, as if to count out the days on his fingers. "Almost three months. That's our best guess, anyway. She took a test a few days before the Task Force raided Winter's Dam. We hadn't even told her father. She was too afraid to tell him. She thought we should get married first."

"And what do you think?"

"I'm not sure what to think." He raised two fingers to his face and rubbed the space between his eyes. "I want to be there for her, and for the baby, but..."

"But what?"

Pulling his fingers away from his eyes, Gavin opened his hand and showed her the pearl ring laying on his palm—the promise ring he'd given to Gemma back at the Station. The one she'd returned to him at the Sanctuary after Taylor came back into her life. "The day you gave this back to me was the worst day of my life," he said. "It probably sounds terrible, but losing my mother didn't hurt as much as you handing this ring back to me. I never expected my mother to stay in my life, but I thought you would be around forever."

His expression shattered her heart. He looked so lost. So devastated. No matter how happy she was with Taylor, and no matter how certain she was of her choice, she'd made Gavin an unfortunate casualty in her love story. She'd hurt him and pushed him away, and he'd retaliated by running into someone else's arms. And now, there was going to be a baby. Another innocent life brought into a scary and uncertain world.

She crossed the room and crouched beside him. The floor was freezing, and she was wearing pajama shorts, but she barely noticed the cold as she wrapped an arm around Gavin's shoulder and pulled him close. Ignoring the smell of alcohol that permeated the surrounding air, she rested her head against his, closed her eyes, and remembered how it had felt to be loved by him. To be his friend. So much had happened between them, but she couldn't forget that, when she'd needed someone to save her, Gavin had been there. He'd reached down and pulled her back from the brink.

Now, it was her turn to save him.

"You know what to do." Although there was no one else around, she kept her voice low, because these words were just for the two of them. "Take this ring and put it on Teresa's finger. Love her—and your baby—as hard as you can. Protect them. Watch over them. And never give either of them any reason to doubt that they're the most important people in your life."

Beneath her arm, she felt his shoulders rising and falling

with silent sobs, and that made *her* want to cry. But she had to be strong for Gavin, as he'd once been strong for her. She had to lift him up, as he'd once lifted her up.

"I mean, the genetics alone are enough of a reason to be excited about this baby," she said. "Just think about how gorgeous he or she is going to be with you two as its parents."

Gavin nodded and wiped the tears from his cheeks. "That's true. At least it won't be an ugly little troll like your future kid."

"Careful, or I'll encourage my ugly little troll to date your supermodel baby just to mess up your perfect genetic line."

That made them both laugh. And it felt good to laugh with Gavin again. To no longer see him as an adversary. To put aside the past and remember what had once brought them together.

When their laughter died down, he looked at her, his expression turning serious. "I'm so sorry, Gem," he said. "I need you to know that. I'm so sorry for what I did back in the tunnel. That wasn't me. I don't know who that guy was, but that wasn't me."

Gemma stared at him, stunned. It was the first time he'd admitted to doing anything wrong back in Winter's Dam, and although she still had unanswered questions, she didn't ask any of them. Hopefully, one day, he would also make things right with Taylor, but he didn't need to do anything else for her.

She'd already forgiven him.

"Okay," she said, nodding. "It's okay. I forgive you."

And then she pulled him close and held him tight.

CHAPTER TWENTY-NINE

Gemma left Gavin alone in the bathroom to sober up and headed back to the lobby, emotionally exhausted and eager to return to the projection room. She wanted to crawl under the covers with her new husband and sleep for hours.

Halfway down the hallway, a voice called out to her.

"Alcott."

Gemma turned and saw Clarke rapidly approaching her from the bend in the hallway. The soft lighting of the hallway made it hard to see him clearly, but as he drew closer, his expression made her uneasy.

"Where've you been?" he demanded. "I've been looking everywhere for you. You weren't in the theater you've been sleeping in, and you weren't in the lobby with the others."

"I got married last night, Clarke. I was with my husband," she replied, feeling a little embarrassed, like a teenager who'd gotten caught sneaking in after curfew. "Why? Is something wrong?"

When Clarke opened his mouth, Gemma heard an audible click deep in his throat, like a padlock snapping closed. "It's better if I show you."

Zipping up her jacket to cover her tank top, she followed him out of the theater. When they passed the wishing fountain, she saw that someone had turned off both the water and the color-changing lights. The fountain no longer looked magical, like something transported to the mall from a faraway, happier world. Whoever had turned it off hadn't taken the time to drain the basin, and in the shadowy annex, the still water appeared dark and thick, like a pool of blood.

The fountain looked menacing. A harbinger of things to come.

When they reached the main concourse, they silently wound their way through hundreds of sleeping bodies. Despite the early hour, some people were already awake—or perhaps they hadn't gone to sleep. They lay on their cots, their eyes focused on the ceiling, as if they could see straight through it into heaven.

Clarke led Gemma back down the hallway to the security room. She had no watch on—she'd left that in the projection room—but she knew it wasn't quite five o'clock yet, because the overhead lights in the hallway weren't on. The door to the security room hung open just a little, letting light into the hallway, and Gemma could hear people talking in low, tense voices inside the room, but she couldn't make out what they were saying.

He pushed the door open and stepped inside with Gemma following on his heels. The sound of the door clicking shut behind her drew the attention of the four people huddled around the laptop. When they saw Gemma, the room fell silent.

Dietrich was there, her hands thrust into her pockets, and Gemma gave her a pleading look—*how bad is it?*—trying to communicate the question with her eyes, hoping Dietrich would read her mind and offer her a calming smile.

But Dietrich shook her head, her lips drawing into a fine line.

Bad.

The door pressed against Gemma's back, hard and unyielding. She hadn't even realized she'd been slowly walking backward until the door stopped her from going any farther.

Clarke nodded at the man seated in front of the laptop. "Play it from the beginning."

"Yes, sir." The man began punching buttons on the computer.

Leaning close to Gemma, Clarke said, "This recording was livestreamed and broadcast on all channels last night, just after nine o'clock. We don't normally monitor television or social media in here. We use these laptops for security, but one of my guys was screwing around online and stumbled across the video an hour ago. He promptly informed me, and I came looking for you."

An hour? Clarke had been searching for her for an hour, and yet he hadn't thought to ask the people in her group where she was? That made no sense at all, unless he didn't want the others to know what was going on.

Gemma glanced at Clarke. "Whatever this video is, why are you only showing it to me?" she asked. "What about Taylor? What about the others? Why aren't they here?"

"You'll see," he replied, folding his arms over his chest. "Just watch."

The video began to play. On the screen was a podium featuring the insignia of the Federal Bureau of Compliance—a gilded yoke on a royal-blue background. Then, the disembodied male voice of a news reporter spoke in a hushed tone. "We're going live now to Washington D.C., where the Director of the Federal Bureau of Compliance, Lydia Grimes, is about to address the nation."

The camera zoomed in closer, and Grimes appeared on the left side of the stage, striding toward the podium in a pair of Louboutin stilettos that looked almost as dangerous as the woman herself. When she reached the podium, she turned and looked directly into the camera. Like her sensible black pantsuit, her makeup was simple and understated.

All except for her lips. They were the color of blood.

"Good evening, ladies and gentlemen," she began, addressing the camera. "As many of you are aware, last night, a group of rebel subversives conducted a large-scale attack against seven detention centers in our East Coast region. Nearly three-thousand detainees escaped because of these coordinated attacks, and we have every reason to believe that additional attacks are being planned in other sections of the country. While last night's attacks are still under investigation, I can tell you that the rebels had help from some guards who were working inside the detention centers. Those guards escaped with the rebels. We've also learned that members of the rebel force executed any guards who weren't in on the plan."

"Executed?" Gemma shot a look at Clarke. "What is she talking about?"

"Keep listening."

"While I understand that the events of the past twenty-four hours have been alarming," Grimes continued, "we're asking the nation to remain calm and not to panic. Our Task Force soldiers are working diligently with local law enforcement officials to track down each detainee who escaped last night, as well as those individuals who carried out these senseless attacks against our country. Let me assure you, we will *not* stop—we will not rest—until we have recaptured every one of these domestic terrorists. We've already sent federal officials to question the close family members of every escapee. We intend to arrest any friends or relatives who aid or house subversives and charge them with treason, which I don't have to remind you, is punishable by death."

Gemma couldn't think. Even the act of breathing was becoming difficult. From the beginning, the plan had always been to reunite the rescued detainees with their relatives. But even if they could find relatives that the Task Force wasn't already surveilling, who in their right mind would take in a detainee when their punishment would be death?

But the four-hundred people currently sleeping under the roof of this abandoned mall couldn't stay here forever. There were too many people and not enough supplies. They had a few days—a week at most—before they would have to find somewhere else to take everyone. "Clarke? What are we going to do with all these people?"

In true Clarke fashion, he showed no visible signs of emotion. Instead, he rubbed at the two days' worth of dark scruff that had accumulated on his chin. "Alcott, that's the least of our problems."

On the screen, Lydia Grimes glanced down as she flipped to the next notecard in her pile, and when she looked at the camera again, her expression had become even more grave. "Tonight, I'm asking every American to join with us. Help us by reporting any suspicious activity you observe, especially over the next few weeks, when these extremists might try to make their way into your neighborhoods. If you see anything out of the ordinary, do not—I repeat—*do not* intervene. I cannot stress enough how unstable some of these detainees are, which is why they haven't been granted release. Over the past few years, we've discovered that many Christians unfortunately cannot be rehabilitated. They are extremely resistant to our treatment methods, and many have become more dangerous and manipulative during the rehabilitation process. Clearly, these detainees manipulated some of the detention center guards into helping them escape. I say this not to frighten you but to warn you. If you see anything suspicious, call the authorities. Let us handle it. It's our job."

"Smart," Clarke muttered. "Turning these people into a bunch of Machiavellian boogeymen. 'The Christians might look normal, but don't be fooled…'" He shook his head. "That woman is a demon wearing human skin."

Gemma felt her arms erupt in goosebumps. "And the entire nation is listening to her."

"We have tried to play nice," Grimes continued. "We have wasted extraordinary amounts of time and money trying to rehabilitate the people who still cling to the tenants of Christianity. But we've reached a point where we can no longer play nice. With the senseless attack on *Elevation Ministries* and these recent attacks on our detention centers, our adversaries have left us no choice. In order to protect this nation and its citizens from any further threat, we must act. And we must act now."

Act now? What does she mean?

"One week ago, the Federal Bureau of Compliance—under the authority of the President of the United States—implemented the first phase of our Unbinding Program. In phase one, any Christian detained for longer than three years, and who has shown absolutely no sign of being rehabilitated, will be unbound from the constraints of their religion via a humane and painless injection that will stop their hearts."

"What?" Gemma rushed toward the desk, shoving her way through the group and grasping for the laptop. She wanted to destroy it. To slam it to the floor and smash it into a thousand pieces—as if, by doing so, she could destroy Grimes herself. But her fingers barely grazed its cold surface before Dietrich grabbed her and pulled her away from the desk.

"Let go of me!"

"Cool it, Alcott!" Dietrich said. "You're going to wake everybody up."

"I don't care! Do you really think I care?"

Her gaze dropped to the floor, and she saw Grimes's words scrawled there in bold, fiery-red print.

A painless injection that will stop their hearts.

A sound burst from Gemma's lips—something otherworldly, the cry of a phantom.

On the screen, Grimes continued to speak, and although Gemma didn't want to hear anything else, Dietrich was still holding her back, so she could do nothing but listen. "We've administered these injections in several detention centers, and so far, everything is going well."

"Three years," Gemma whispered, her body going slack.

"I know," Dietrich said, removing her arm from Gemma's waist.

"My parents, Amy. My parents."

"I know."

On the screen, the camera zoomed out, and a picture appeared just over Lydia Grimes's left shoulder. "This image was taken from an exterior security camera during the attack on the Stovington Detention Center. The young woman in this photograph brutally executed three guards at point-blank range during the Stovington attack. All three men were on their knees when this woman shot them in the backs of their heads. As some of you may have already noticed, this young woman appears to be the same person who initiated last month's attack on Elevation Ministry Center, which resulted in the deaths of forty-seven civilians."

The image was dark and a little grainy, but there was no mistaking the identity of the person standing at the edge of the field, the silhouette of a school bus behind her. Even if her face hadn't been identifiable, the jacket she'd been wearing—with its upside-down Task Force patch sewn onto the shoulder—certainly was.

"The young woman in the photograph has been positively identified as Gemma Alcott, age twenty-two, originally of Ridgefield, Pennsylvania. You'll remember that Miss Alcott and her contingent of subversives attacked a Pennsylvania compliance office last fall and broadcast their traitorous message to the world."

A clear image of Gemma replaced the image taken outside the detention center. This one was from the compliance center broadcast. Somehow, they'd captured a shot of her looking threatening. Her nostrils were flared, and her head was dipped slightly so that she was looking up menacingly at the camera. "During that broadcast, Miss Alcott issued a message to those individuals still in detentions centers. Her message was, 'Salvation is coming.' We now believe that this was a direct threat against our nation's detention centers, and it appears Miss Alcott and her fellow subversives have followed through on that threat. We believe their plan is to liberate as many detention centers as possible in order to form an army, with the goal of overthrowing the government. Once they've accomplished that goal, they can install their own government and force all citizens to adhere to Christianity under threat of reprisals and imprisonment. Possibly even death."

With nothing else to do, Gemma lowered her head and prayed for strength, keeping her voice so low that no one except Dietrich could hear it.

"Miss Alcott's parents are currently being held in federal custody."

Gemma's entire body jolted at the mention of her parents, as if she'd just grabbed onto an electrified fence with both hands. All lingering traces of self-pity disappeared as terror turned the blood in her veins to ice.

"No," she whispered. "Not them."

"Detained three years ago for conducting illegal religious services in their home, Miss Alcott's parents have been in federal custody ever since. Although they are not combative or manipulative toward the staff at their detention center, they also have shown no signs of rehabilitation. In fact, both have consistently performed poorly on their bi-annual reintegration reports, which isn't surprising, considering their connection with Miss Alcott."

The muscles in the center of Gemma's chest tightened until it felt as if she were having a heart attack. The familiar pull of anxiety ratcheted up to a ten. She'd dealt with anxiety before, especially after she'd first arrived at the Station, but it had felt nothing like this.

"Because both of Miss Alcott's parents meet the criteria for inclusion in phase one of the Unbinding Program, I've ordered the staff at their detention center to perform their unbindings. As the saying goes, desperate times call for desperate measures."

Dietrich gripped Gemma's shoulder and squeezed, probably trying to communicate her support, and Gemma resisted the urge to jerk her body away. She didn't want to be touched—not by anyone. Not even a supportive touch. Her stomach twisted and rolled, and thankfully, she had eaten nothing in the last six hours or it would've made a reappearance on the security room floor.

Stop it, Gemma told herself. *Calm down.* If she didn't get control of herself quickly, she was going to have a full-blown panic attack, and then she would be useless.

Useless to herself, and useless to her parents.

"However, if Miss Alcott surrenders to authorities within the next twenty-four hours, and if she assures us that her followers will not carry out any further attacks against our federal detention centers or any civilian targets, we are prepared to offer both of her parents a full pardon, along with an immediate release from their confinement."

Grimes paused with her eyes on her notecards, allowing time for her words to sink in.

"Now, I'm going to speak directly to Miss Alcott. If you're listening to this broadcast, do the right thing and turn yourself in. This is a one-time offer, and it goes away in exactly twenty-four hours. If you have not surrendered to your nearest compliance office by nine p.m., eastern standard time, tomorrow night, your parents will be unbound. When you turn yourself in, we expect you to renounce your faith." Grimes cast a final, grim look into the camera. "Do the right thing, Miss Alcott. We just want this madness to end. Thank you, and good night."

After the laptop screen went black, Clarke's men glanced at Gemma, searching her face. Waiting for her to speak. To say something profound. To inspire them all with an epic-war-movie speech.

But she said nothing.

Instead, she shrugged Dietrich's hand off her shoulder and slipped into the hallway.

While she was in the security room, the hallway lights had switched on, and the sudden brightness made her head hurt. Her chest felt uncomfortably tight, but she took several deep breaths until the pain abated. She didn't walk very far down the hallway—only far enough to get out of earshot of Clarke's people—and then she waited.

Dietrich and Clarke joined her a few seconds later, as she'd known they would.

She didn't wait for them to speak. "I'm going to need your truck."

"Alcott—"

"I don't want to take Taylor's car," she said. "He loves that car, and he hasn't even gotten to drive it again. Plus, your truck is a piece of junk. I'm going either way, Clarke. But driving will be easier than walking."

Dietrich grabbed her by the elbow. "Gemma, listen to me. You can't turn yourself in. They won't let your parents go unless you renounce, and if you renounce—"

"What?" Gemma spun on the ex-soldier, her face hot with anger. "What terrible thing is going to happen if I renounce? Is the world going to stop spinning? Are planes going to fall from the sky? Because, as far as I can tell, the only thing my renouncing is going to do is save my parents."

"But what about everyone else?" Dietrich demanded, gesturing toward the mall. "Those people out there know you. I talked to them yesterday, and dozens of them said they'd heard your voice when they were at their lowest point. For many of them, your voice was the only voice they'd heard since being detained that gave them any hope. You gave them the will to keep fighting. To stay alive."

Gemma snatched her arm away from Dietrich. "You know what? That's wonderful. If they needed that broadcast to stay alive, then I'm glad they had it. But they're safe now. They don't need me anymore. Maybe that was God's plan for me all along. To give those people hope."

"So, is it God's plan for you to turn yourself in, publicly renounce, and take away every ounce of hope you've ever given them?"

"They don't need me anymore," Gemma repeated. "They're free."

"Are they?" She gave Gemma a hard stare, challenging her. But when Gemma said nothing, Dietrich muttered, "What a disappointment," and walked away.

Gemma looked back at Clarke. "So, can I have the keys?"

He rubbed his forehead, the tip of his little finger brushing against a patch of gray that Gemma was certain hadn't been there a few days ago. "What about your husband? What about Taylor?"

The sound of Taylor's name jarred her, and she realized she hadn't thought of him at all since hearing Grimes's offer. Her mind had done the impossible and completely blocked him out, probably because he was the one person in the world who could change her mind.

"He'll understand," she finally said.

Clarke raised his eyebrows. "So, you're going to tell him? Before you go?"

But that wasn't possible, and Clarke knew it.

"No," she replied. "You're going to tell him. And before you argue with me or try to change my mind, I want you to imagine yourself in my shoes, Clarke. Imagine it's *your* parents who are going to die for *your* crimes, but you have the power to stop it. If you give yourself up, they get to live. Not only that, but they get their freedom. You would do the same thing, and you know it."

He wanted to argue with her—she could see it in his eyes—but what could he say that she would believe? What could he say that would make any difference?

Finally, Clarke gave her a sigh of resignation. "The keys are above the visor," he said. "If you need the truck, take it. But I'm begging you...don't do this, Alcott. Don't make me tell these people—including your new husband—that you're gone and you're not coming back. Don't put me in that position. Whether you like it or not, Dietrich is right. These people needed hope, and you gave it to them. Don't take it away from them now."

Just then, a memory came rushing back to Gemma. In her mind, she saw Clarke singing after the baptism, his lips forming the words to "Fight the Good Fight."

"You're a Christian, aren't you?" Before he could deny it, she added, "I saw you singing with the others at the fountain, right after Taylor got baptized. You knew every word of that song. You never would've known it unless you'd grown up in the church."

He didn't deny it. "And? What's your point?"

"You're a fighter, Clarke. Much more than I am. Without you, none of those people out in the mall would be here. They would still be locked up. Why can't you be their leader? Why can't you give them hope?"

"Because I'm not the same as you, Alcott," he said. "I renounced."

Gemma stared at him, certain she'd misheard. "You what?"

The admission shattered Clarke's hard-candy exterior, and he melted into the wall, knocking his head against it once, as if trying to inflict pain on himself. "My family was very religious. We attended church every Sunday. We read the Bible together in the evenings. We prayed together. Our faith was a huge part of our lives. When I renounced, I did it to keep my job. I thought I could somehow help Christians if I was still a cop. But they fired me anyway. I was the only member of my family to renounce. My parents were detained pretty early on, and they both died in the centers. But my little sister was the strong one. She refused to renounce. I tried to convince her—believe me, I tried—but eventually she went on the run. I don't know where she is or if she's even alive."

He didn't cry, but his body tensed with the effort of suppressing his emotions, his muscles stretched as tight as the string of the bow she'd once hunted with at the Sanctuary.

"Talk to Pastor Nolan," Gemma whispered after a few moments. "Tell him you renounced. He'll help you, okay? He'll help you find your way back."

Clarke nodded. "Yeah. Okay."

"And tell Taylor I love him. Tell him I had no choice."

"Alcott—"

"I'm going to get dressed now," she said, loosening her grip on his shoulders. "And then I'm going to leave. Please don't try to stop me."

Thankfully, Clarke didn't know about the projection room. He couldn't find Taylor now, even if he'd wanted to. God was giving her the opportunity to leave without giving the one person who could stop her the opportunity to intervene. Which meant that God wanted her to go.

Clarke and Dietrich might not have understood, but that didn't mean it wasn't true.

"Thank you," she said, giving Clarke a quick hug—one he didn't return.

And when he dropped his head into his hands, Gemma quietly slipped away.

CHAPTER THIRTY

The blue pickup rolled into the empty parking lot of the Region 7 Compliance Office, an endless cloud of noxious fumes spewing from its exhaust pipe into the cool morning air.

Gemma backed the truck into a parking spot with a good view of the front door. Then, she shut off the engine, relaxed into the driver's seat, and waited.

The dumpy building with the stone facade had changed little since she'd last seen it, except that it looked smaller, as if it had shrunk under the intense pressure of the media spotlight. But there was one notable difference. Random splotches of what looked like black spray paint littered the laminate siding, as if someone had attempted to scrub the paint away but hadn't done a good job. Gemma couldn't be certain, but the general shape and position of the splotches indicated they had once formed a cross.

She touched the patch on her left shoulder, rubbing her thumb over it, as if for luck. But it wasn't luck she needed today.

It was courage. And faith.

Is this the right thing, God? she asked herself for the hundredth time. *Am I doing the right thing?*

Her body certainly didn't think she was doing the right thing. She couldn't stop shaking. The trembling had begun in her hands immediately after she'd left the mall and had quickly spread to her arms and legs. Zipping up her jacket hadn't helped, so she'd cranked the truck's heater up to full blast. But even the blast of hot air on her face hadn't made a difference, because she wasn't cold.

She was terrified.

Before leaving the mall and heading north toward Snyder County, she'd taken off her pajamas and thrown on her boots, a pair of jeans, and a black sweater—the same sweater that Dietrich had given her in Ash Grove. She didn't know why she'd chosen that sweater in particular. It had just felt like the right choice. She'd also taken her utility jacket with the Task Force patch. But her backpack and its contents—including the Bible she'd found in Ash Grove—were still in the projection room. She hadn't wanted to risk going up there. If Taylor had woken up, he would've asked her what she was doing. Even if she'd tried to lie, he would've figured out the truth...and he would've stopped her.

Leaving her backpack behind was probably for the best. Once she surrendered, the Task Force would've confiscated and destroyed her Bible. At least now Taylor could have it.

With her left hand nervously tapping the steering wheel, she clutched the cross necklace in her right hand. She had considered leaving the necklace behind—it was just one more precious thing for the Task Force to destroy—but taking it off had felt wrong on too many levels. Despite the inherent danger of placing a Christian symbol around his child's neck, her father had still chosen to gift her with the necklace all those years ago. He wouldn't have given it to her if he hadn't wanted her to wear it.

Plus, the necklace had somehow escaped the notice of both Carver and Mullen, which had to mean something. She knew better than to think of it as a mystical amulet capable of offering her protection from people like Lydia Grimes. Plenty of Christians had been detained—and worse—while wearing crosses. But it was still around her neck after so many close calls, and that had to mean that God wanted it there, so there it would stay.

She glanced at the digital clock on the dashboard.

8:01

The Region 7 Compliance Office opened its doors at eight-thirty. Any minute now, employees would begin arriving to prepare for another full day of renouncements.

Would they force her to renounce here? Or somewhere else?

Gemma wasn't struggling with the idea of turning herself in. She was more than willing to surrender her own freedom to save her parents' lives. But when it came to renouncing, the choice wasn't as clear. Logically, what Addie had said when she'd visited the bookstore sounded right. She'd said that God knew people's hearts and motives. So, if someone renounced, not because they truly believed what they were saying, but because it was what they *had* to do to save their own life or someone else's, then God would understand.

But it also said in the Bible that Christ would deny those who denied him.

What would Lydia Grimes do if Gemma turned herself in but refused to renounce? Would she still release her parents? Gemma had a sinking feeling that it would not satisfy Grimes until Gemma stood in front of the camera, just as she'd done last fall, and renounced her faith in Christ.

Just then, a gold Toyota Camry pulled into the parking lot, traveling at a fairly high rate of speed. The older woman behind the wheel cast a cursory glance at the pickup before swinging the Camry into a marked spot directly outside the main door.

The sign planted in front of the concrete wheel stop read: Beatrice Mosely, Director of Operations.

The Camry's taillights blinked out, and the driver's door swung open.

Gemma watched as Beatrice Mosely emerged from her vehicle, one hand raised to shield her eyes from the sun. The woman looked just as Gemma remembered, except that she'd put on weight since November. Not just a little, either. Mosely wasn't a large woman, so a little extra weight went a long way. The difference was most obvious in her face, but her body had also grown noticeably rounder.

Mosely squinted at the pickup, trying to see who was inside, but the sunlight reflecting off the windshield concealed Gemma from view. Finally, the woman gave a little shrug and slammed her door. Shuffling around to the passenger side, she yanked open the passenger door and unloaded her belongings. She tossed a leather handbag over one shoulder then reached back into the car and pulled out a large box of donuts and a frozen coffee drink. With the donuts in one hand and the drink in the other, she bumped the passenger door shut with her bottom and headed for the building.

It's not too late. It's not too late to go back. She hasn't seen me yet.

She moved her foot to the brake pedal. Her right hand released the necklace and dropped to the keys hanging from the steering wheel.

I can drive back to Taylor right now, and he'll tell me I did the right thing. He'll tell me that my parents wouldn't want me to turn myself in. He'll tell me they would rather die than watch their daughter surrender her faith.

Gemma prayed. "Your will, Father. Whatever Your will is, give me the strength to do it. Your will, not mine."

When she opened her eyes again, Beatrice Mosely still hadn't entered the compliance office. She'd placed her frozen coffee drink on the sidewalk—the same sidewalk that Gemma and the others had lined up on last fall—and she was fumbling in her handbag for something. Probably the keys to the building.

Gemma knew what she had to do.

Her hand fell away from the ignition.

As if sensing that a decision had been made—one with ramifications for both of them—Mosely stopped fumbling with the door and glanced back at the truck.

Put the keys above the visor. Tuck in your necklace. Open the door. Hop down. Close the door. Start walking. Don't stop.

Gemma completed one task after another, each step carrying her closer to a future that had always been inevitable. No world existed in which she got to live a happy life with Taylor. She'd sealed her own fate months ago—the day she'd broadcast herself to the world.

The Region 7 Compliance Office was where her rebellion had begun, and it was a fitting place for it to end.

As Gemma approached the building, Beatrice Mosely watched her like a hawk eyeing a field mouse. Perhaps it was Gemma's auburn hair that gave her away. Or maybe it was the jacket with the upside-down Task Force patch. But a sound came from the depths of Mosely's throat—a guttural inhale, as if she was choking on something—and the donuts slipped from her hand. The flimsy box flew open in mid-air, sending a dozen colorful donuts splattering onto the pavement. One of them—chocolate-frosted with sprinkles—landed frosting-side-down on one of Mosely's white orthopedic shoes.

The woman didn't kick it away. She didn't even appear to notice it.

Her eyes darted from Gemma to the pickup truck. Seeing nothing, she whipped her head around, scanning the parking lot, probably expecting Gemma's friends to be sneaking up on her.

Stopping a few feet away from Mosely, Gemma held both

hands in the air, palms out, trying to appear as non-threatening as possible.

"It's okay," she said. "It's just me."

When Mosely realized she wasn't about to be ambushed by an army of subversives, her expression morphed from shock into something else: a look that went beyond anger, to a deep and bottomless hatred that knew no bounds.

"You," she sneered.

It came out sounding like a curse word.

Three years of running. Three years of fighting. Three years of hoping and praying for freedom.

It was all over.

"I'm Gemma Alcott," she said. "And I'm here to surrender."

CHAPTER THIRTY-ONE

*G*emma's gone.

When Taylor awoke, his brain immediately registered the absence of weight on his outstretched arm. Still half asleep, he reached for Gemma, fully expecting to find her sleeping next to him. But the space beside him was empty. Not just empty, but cold.

Wherever she was, she'd been gone for a while.

Something about her absence made him uneasy.

"Mrs. Nolan?" he called into the darkness, his voice still gruff with sleep.

No answer.

He sat up and blinked into the darkness, waiting for his eyes to make sense of the room, to settle on the vague outline of the boxes of old movie reels or one of the folding chairs the beam of his flashlight had passed over the previous night as they'd made their way to the far corner of the room. But he couldn't see a thing.

Where's the flashlight?

And then it hit him: *Gemma must've taken it with her.*

The realization brought a smile to his face. When he eventually found her, he would give her a hard time for leaving him to stumble around in the darkness, where he might have fallen down the stairs and broken his neck. He'd accuse her of being a black widow, already trying to off her new husband and make it look like an accident so she could get the insurance money.

Of course, there was no insurance money. But that was beside the point.

Since Taylor was only wearing sweatpants, he felt around for his t-shirt and pulled it over his head. He couldn't locate his sneakers—the only shoes he found were Gemma's—so he went barefoot.

Taylor moved through the darkness of the projection room, running one hand along the wall, the timeworn carpet rough beneath his bare feet. He inched closer to the exit, moving slowly to avoid tripping over the raised rubber mats that had once sat underneath the projectors. The door to the stairwell was on the other end of the room. He was probably being overly cautious by feeling his way along the wall, but he didn't want to go stumbling around in the darkness, trip over one of those rubber mats, and end up tumbling headfirst down a flight of concrete stairs.

The darkness of the projection room hadn't been a big deal last night—they'd brought a flashlight along with them—but now it made him a little uncomfortable. As if the darkness was complicit in hiding something from him.

Finally, his reaching fingers found the doorframe, and the sense of unease that had been nagging at him grew even stronger. He gripped the railing and hurried down the stairs. Shoving open the heavy door at the bottom of the stairs, he stepped into the kitchen, where he was assaulted by bright light and the smell of stale popcorn. He stood there for a few moments, rubbing his eyes, giving them time to adjust to the light. The tile was freezing beneath his feet, and as soon as his vision cleared, he headed for the lobby, eager to trade the cold tile for carpet.

Noise and laughter drew his attention to the lobby, so he headed in that direction. Laughter was a good sign. They wouldn't have been laughing if something bad had happened to Gemma. How late was it, anyway? Out of habit, he glanced at his watch, but his wrist was empty. The guards had taken his watch at the detention center, and he hadn't found a replacement yet.

When he emerged from the kitchen, Taylor saw the group from the Sanctuary gathered in the lobby. They were all seated around a long folding table, each with a group of playing cards splayed out in front of them. Some cards were laying face-up, while others were laying face-down. There were two more piles of cards in the center of the table, one stack turned face-up and the other turned face-down. Everyone was playing, including Teresa and Gavin. In fact, Teresa had more cards turned face-down than anyone else at the table—only one remained face-up —and she looked happier than Taylor had ever seen her.

Taylor's first thought was to wonder where they'd found the folding table, because it hadn't been there yesterday. His second thought was that Gemma wasn't with them.

Abram flipped over another card in the center of the table. A smile formed on his lips, and he hesitated only a moment before saying, "Jack of Clubs."

Teresa flipped over her last card and screamed, "Bingo!"

Beside her, Gavin groaned and slumped back in his chair. "I challenge."

"You can't challenge!" Teresa huffed. "What's there to challenge?"

"Relax, babe. I'm not challenging your win. I'm challenging the game. Card Bingo is an insult to other card games and should not exist."

"Don't be a sore loser." Teresa slugged Gavin in the arm. She turned to Abram, her eyes sparkling with excitement. "So, what do I win?"

Abram reached into the paper bag at his feet. "As the winner of this round of Card Bingo," he said, pulling a rectangular box from the bag, "you win an expired pack of Sour Patch Kids!"

By Teresa's reaction, you would've thought she'd won a million dollars. She jumped out of her seat and pumped her fists in the air, her little celebratory dance causing her baggy t-shirt to ride up high enough for Taylor to glimpse her stomach, which was noticeably rounded in a way that could only mean one thing. At first, he thought he'd imagined it, but then he glanced at Mia, and the look of shock on her face revealed that she'd seen it, too.

Taylor wasn't content to just stare daggers at Gavin. If he could've launched missiles from his eyes and blown the guy up, he would've done so in a heartbeat.

As Teresa danced over to Abram to collect her prize, Taylor moved closer to the table. The others were so absorbed in gathering their cards into piles and reshuffling them for the next game that they still hadn't noticed him standing there.

"Abram? Can I talk to you a minute?"

The group glanced up at the sound of Taylor's voice.

"Well, well, well," Abram announced, returning his attention to his cards. "Looks like the newlyweds are finally awake. We weren't sure if we'd see you two today or not."

"Did you get the license plate off the truck, Taylor?" Mia asked.

"Huh?" He had no idea what she was talking about.

She walked over to him and put an arm around his shoulders. "The one that spun its tires in your hair."

Taylor gave her a nervous smile and self-consciously ran a hand through his hair, trying to smooth it down. He could only imagine how terrible it looked, especially since it was longer than it had been in years. "Have you seen Gemma?"

Mia's smile faded, replaced by a look of confusion. "Shouldn't she be with you?"

"Yes, but I can't find her. I haven't seen her yet this morning."

"Morning? Honey, it's one-thirty in the afternoon."

One-thirty. That sense of unease continued to gnaw at him, like a rabid dog chewing on his insides. His thoughts were coming too fast now, all jumbled and disorganized.

After the wedding, they'd snuck off to the projection room, their hands intertwined, eager to be alone. To him, those next few hours had been more beautiful than he could've ever hoped for. He remembered everything. How good it had felt to be with Gemma as his wife. How he hadn't shrunk away from her when she'd run her fingers along the terrible scar on his chest. How it had felt to touch her without guilt. He'd been with other women before her—not many, but a few—and he regretted every single one of them. He hadn't loved those women, and it killed him that he hadn't been able to give his wife the same gift she'd given him. Had that upset her? Or had he hurt her in some other way?

"Honey?" Mia's voice broke into his mind. "Are you all right?"

He shook his head. "No. I think something's wrong."

"Wrong?" Oliver asked. "You mean with Gemma?"

"I don't know. Maybe. But she wasn't there when I woke up. And if she's not with you guys, then where is she?"

Brie spoke up from her spot next to Teresa. "There are lots of places she could be other than here. It's a big mall. Maybe she's helping to serve lunch or something?"

"That's right," Max agreed. "Do you want me to help you look for her?"

"No. Don't worry about it. I'll be back in a few minutes. I'm sure she's around here somewhere." Actually, he wasn't sure of *anything* anymore, except that he wanted to get away from them. From *all* of them. Because their presence somehow made Gemma's absence even more obvious and disturbing.

He just wanted to find her.

To find her as quickly as possible so he could put to rest the feeling that something terrible had happened to his wife while he'd slept.

CHAPTER THIRTY-TWO

Taylor didn't bother with shoes. Or his hair. Instead, he left the others in the lobby and headed for the annex. Maybe Gemma would be at the fountain. He could picture her there, seated on its ledge, auburn hair hanging in loose waves down her back. Maybe reading a book. Or praying. But when she saw him, she would jump to her feet and run into his arms, and everything would be okay.

The picture he'd built in his mind was so vivid that when he emerged into the annex and Gemma wasn't at the fountain, her absence physically jarred him.

There was no one in the annex, so he continued into the main concourse, weaving his way through the maze of scattered cots and unwashed bodies, searching every face for the one he knew better than all others. When he reached the intersection at the main hub, he saw his father in the middle of a circle of believers, leading them in prayer as the afternoon sunlight beat down on them from the skylight above their heads.

Taylor kept walking, not knowing where he was going, until he ended up outside the closed door to the security room. He turned the knob, but the door wouldn't budge. There were people inside—he could hear them talking in low voices—but he couldn't hear Gemma.

He only meant to knock, but his fist took over, pounding the wood hard enough to rattle the door in its frame.

One of Clarke's lackeys opened the door, but only enough to poke his head through the crack. Not enough for Taylor to get a good look at the room or its inhabitants. The lanky kid who'd opened the door couldn't have been over twenty, and the sneer on his face seemed to indicate that the interruption annoyed him. "Yeah? Who are you?"

Taylor slid his foot across the threshold in case the kid tried to slam the door in his face. But he hoped it wouldn't come to that, since he wasn't wearing any shoes. "Where's Clarke?"

The kid surprised Taylor by saying, "Wait here. I'll get him. But a word of warning: I'm closing this door whether your foot's still there or not."

"Okay." Taylor snatched his foot away from the threshold just as the door slammed shut.

He waited in the hallway, arms folded over his chest, for at least ten minutes before Clarke emerged from the security room and pulled the door shut behind him.

The ex-cop looked completely drained, as if the lanky kid had just dragged him out of bed.

Taylor uncrossed his arms. "Where is she, Clarke?"

"First, I need you to do something for me, Nolan. I need you to calm down."

Rage bubbled up inside of Taylor, threatening to erupt out of him like lava and consume everything in its path. But he held it at bay. Not for himself, but for Gemma. Because Clarke knew where she was. "Don't tell me to calm down. I've never been calmer in my life. All I want to know is where she is. Where's Gemma?"

Clarke used his thumb and forefinger to rub at his eyes, and his eyes made a noise like someone squeegeeing a windshield.

Finally, he dropped his hand to his side and blew out a breath. "She wanted me to tell you she loves you," he said. "And that she didn't have a choice."

The boiling pot of rage bubbled over—Taylor could no longer contain it—and he grabbed Clarke by his shoulders and slammed him into the wall. "Where is she?!"

The door to the security room burst open, and two of Clarke's guys rushed into the hallway. Both went straight for Taylor, each latching onto one of his arms. Together, they easily wrenched him off of their boss and put him on the floor. One goon knelt on his spine while the other pressed his face into the tile.

"Let him go."

It was Clarke's voice, calm as ever.

Immediately, the hand pressing his face into the ground disappeared from his head, and the weight lifted from his back. Pushing himself to his feet, Taylor moved to the opposite side of the hallway from the three men, eager to get away from Clarke's goons in case they jumped him again.

But they didn't look like they wanted to jump him. They looked like they felt sorry for him, which was even worse.

Feeling warmth on his neck, Taylor reached up and touched the butterfly bandage, and when he glanced at his fingers, they were coated with blood. Somehow, the scalpel wound had opened up again.

"I'm sorry about your neck," Clarke said. "We'll get someone to patch that up."

"Where is she?" Taylor repeated, wiping his bloody fingers on his sweatpants. "What do you mean, 'she didn't have a choice'? What did she do, Clarke?"

To Taylor's relief, Clarke pressed his lips together and nodded, gesturing for one of the goons to open the door to the security room.

"Okay," he said. "But it's probably better if I show you."

✝

The next thirty minutes passed by in a blur.

First, Clarke had one of his guys—a former Army medic—clean and stitch the wound on Taylor's neck. The cut only required three stitches, but the medic didn't have any numbing agent, so Taylor had felt the needle sliding in and out of his skin. After Taylor's neck was stitched up, Clarke sent everyone else out of the room and closed the door behind them. Then, he sat Taylor down in a folding chair in front of a laptop and started clicking through videos on the screen.

The first video he played featured the Federal Bureau of Compliance Director Lydia Grimes discussing the newly announced *unbindings*. Even the word made Taylor want to be sick. The government was great at taking something truly awful —like the mass murder of millions of innocent people—and prettying up the language to make the pill easier to swallow.

He'd never expected it to come to this. Never in his wildest dreams had he imagined the government would begin executing Christians who refused to renounce. Like so many others, he'd simply chosen to believe the Bureau of Compliance when they claimed to be successfully rehabilitating Christians inside the detention centers. Yet, he never thought to question why so few were actually released.

Now that it was happening, he realized these unbindings had probably been part of the Bureau of Compliance's plan all along. After successfully turning the country against Christians, they had appealed to the more sensitive folks by promising to rehabilitate and reeducate Christians in detention centers. By turning in your neighbors, you were actually helping them. And when the government's *rehabilitation program*—which Taylor had witnessed first-hand at Stovington—inevitably failed, they would convince the public that no option remained but to execute the people who refused to renounce their faith.

And because of Taylor's ignorance—and his own issues with God—he'd played a pivotal role in their evil scheme. He'd joined the Task Force and detained hundreds, if not thousands, of Christians. How many people had he committed to death by detaining them? How many Christians was he responsible for killing?

Taylor lowered his head into his hands, not wanting to see anymore, but then Lydia Grimes said something he'd never expected to hear come out of her mouth—Gemma's name—and his head snapped up.

The grainy image of Gemma waiting outside the detention center quickly gave way to an image he'd never seen before. According to Grimes, the photo was taken on the day Gemma had seized control of the compliance office. Taylor's gaze dropped from her face to the Task Force patch sewn upside-down on the left shoulder of her jacket.

His Task Force patch.

His mind flashed back to the strange symbol he'd noticed spray-painted on billboards and bridge overpasses along the highway as they'd driven back to the detention center. It had seemed so foreign to him at the time—the outstretched arms bearing the cross on its shoulders—and all along, it had been his own patch turned on its head.

"...footage shows the young woman in this photograph brutally executing three guards at point-blank range during the attack on Stovington. All three men were on their knees when this woman shot them in the backs of their heads."

"What?" Taylor gripped the metal sides of his chair. "What is she talking about? Gemma didn't shoot anyone. She didn't even have a gun!"

Clarke nodded, his face grim. "I'm sure Grimes ordered her people to kill the guards so she could pin everything on Gemma."

"Now, I'm going to speak directly to Miss Alcott. If you're listening

to this broadcast, please do the right thing and turn yourself in. This is a one-time offer, and it goes away in exactly twenty-four hours..."

Taylor understood why Grimes wanted Gemma so badly. The government saw her as a threat to their cause, and all threats needed to be eliminated. Someone had tried to frame Gemma for the bombing of Elevation Ministry Center. Had Grimes been involved in that, too? If so, the bombing clearly hadn't had the impact she'd been hoping for. But Gemma's involvement in the plot to liberate the detention centers and the fact that she supposedly executed several guards at Stovington was all the ammunition Grimes needed to justify the need for the unbindings to the public—and to move Gemma's parents to the top of the list.

When Gemma turned herself in—and when she renounced her faith to the world—the rebellion would end. And Grimes would win.

Clarke clicked the X in the upper corner of the video to shut it off.

Taylor touched the tender stitches in his neck. "Is that it?"

"Not yet," Clarke replied, pulling up another video. "Believe me, I wish it was."

The last video was a short news clip, filmed earlier that morning at the Region 7 Compliance Office in Snyder County. The news footage showed two Task Force soldiers leading a handcuffed Gemma from the compliance office to the rear door of a transport vehicle. She had that jacket on again—the one with the upside-down patch. Taylor couldn't believe they hadn't taken it off her. In the shot's background, a heavy-set woman stood just outside the door to the building, pudgy arms crossed over her chest, a satisfied smile on her face. An overturned box of donuts laid on the ground near the woman's feet.

"What's with the donuts?" It was the only thing Taylor could think to say as he watched the love of his life being escorted toward a black SUV.

"I don't know," Clarke said. "But I'm certain your wife had something to do with it."

The newscaster spoke over the video: *"Early this morning, Gemma Alcott, 22, of Ridgefield, Pennsylvania, surrendered to authorities at the same compliance office that she and her fellow subversives overtook by force last November. We believe her surrender to be a direct response to Federal Bureau of Compliance Director Lydia Grimes's recent announcement of the Unbinding Program, in which any subversive held in federal custody longer than three years will have their suffering ended via a humane and painless injection. At a news conference last night, Ms. Grimes stated that Alcott's parents would be among the first to be unbound unless the subversive, wanted in connection with the murder of three detention center guards, turned herself in within twenty-four hours. Alcott surrendered early this morning to Beatrice Mosely, the Director of Operations for the Region 7 Compliance Office, bringing a quiet end to six months of violence and tyranny."*

Clarke uttered a sharp laugh. "Six months of violence and tyranny? These people truly have no shame."

As Gemma disappeared into the back of the SUV, the pudgy woman appeared on the screen. *"We're relieved to know that this subversive, who has proven herself to be a real danger to our community, is finally in federal custody,"* she said. *"We hope that this senseless violence will now end."*

Taylor continued to prod at his neck wound, trying to feel pain, but the skin around the laceration had gone numb.

Right now, he wished every part of him could feel that numb.

Clarke closed the laptop. "We don't know where they've taken her, but it's probably not a detention center—not someone like her, and especially not after what we did a few days ago. They're going to take her somewhere where there's zero chance she'll escape." He lifted his eyebrows and gave

Taylor a pointed look. "And zero chance of anyone breaking her out."

Taylor slumped back in his chair and put a hand over his face. "Clarke, if you've got something to say to me, just say it."

"Okay." Clarke nodded. "Your wife knew exactly what she was doing when she turned herself in. She was doing what she *had* to do to save her parents. You might not like the decision she made, but you need to respect it. Even if we could rescue her—even if that were possible, which it's not—how is she going to feel when Grimes retaliates by executing her parents?"

"They're *still* going to be executed!" Taylor launched himself to his feet, the metal chair clattering to the floor behind him. "You honestly think Grimes is going to release them? She might tell the public that she's going to honor her end of the bargain, but then she's going to execute them anyway, because that's who she is. Morals and ethics and pinkie-swear promises will not constrain someone who developed a plan to execute millions of innocent Americans. This whole thing was one big setup—a trap to capture Gemma—and you let her walk right into it. You're probably glad to be rid of her, aren't you? She's become too much of a liability."

Clarke rose from his chair, bringing himself eye-level with Taylor. "You know that's not how I feel, brother."

"Don't call me brother," Taylor snapped. "I'm not your brother. I don't even know you."

He left the office, slamming the door shut behind him.

He walked with his head down, not knowing where he was going or what he was going to do, only that he needed to do *something*.

As he neared the entrance to the mall, he could sense someone just ahead, blocking his path, so he glanced up, ready to plow straight through whomever it was.

Gavin.

"What happened?" he asked, putting an arm up to prevent Taylor from slipping past him. "Where's Gemma?"

"What do you care?"

Gavin glared at him. "Because I care about *her*. No, she's not my girlfriend anymore, but I still care about her. Who do you think watched out for her for two years while you were off arresting Christians?"

On a different day, he might've punched Gavin for a comment like that, but the guy was right. Taylor *could've* gone into hiding with Gemma when she'd left for the Station, but he hadn't. Back then, his job—and the mission—had been the most important thing in his life. What an idiot he'd been. How different would things have been now if he'd gone with her?

Would she still be with him? Would she be safe?

Just when Taylor thought things couldn't get any worse, his father appeared behind Gavin, looking even more sickly than he had the previous night. When he noticed Taylor in the hallway, a smile brightened his pale face, but the smile faded when his gaze fell to Taylor's bare feet.

"Son? Where are your shoes? That floor must be freezing." Joseph Nolan shook his head. "Honestly, if your mother could see you walking around like that, she'd have a fit. Do you want to get sick?"

My father is dying of cancer in front of my eyes, Taylor thought, *and he's concerned I might catch a cold from walking around barefoot.*

"Is something wrong, Taylor?"

"No, Dad. Everything's fine."

"Everything is *not* fine," Gavin interjected. "Gemma's missing."

"Gemma?" His father's bushy eyebrows pressed toward each other. "I don't understand. We're not allowed to leave, so she's got to be around here somewhere, doesn't she?"

"He knows something," Gavin said, nodding at Taylor. "Just look at his face. He knows where she is."

"Son? Where is she?"

Taylor couldn't take it anymore. Their expressions. Their questions. He had to get away from them right now before he said or did something he'd regret. Without another word, he barreled through the outstretched arm of Gemma's ex-boyfriend, walked past his dumbfounded father, and headed for the annex.

He wanted to be alone.

CHAPTER THIRTY-THREE

The room was completely white.

Bone white.

Not an ounce of color existed in the space, except for Gemma, who sat with her back pressed against the opposite wall, as far away from the room's only door as she could get. She wasn't stupid. She understood the purpose of a room like this one—a room so blindingly white it was disorienting. A room with pristine tile floors and no furnishings, save for a single chair planted in its center. A chair she would never, ever willingly sit on.

Someone would come for her, eventually.

They would make her sit on that chair, and then they would hurt her.

Nearly a full day had passed since she'd surrendered to that miserable woman at the compliance office, and so far, very little had happened. The soldiers who'd picked her up had transported her to some kind of military installation. She wasn't surprised that they hadn't taken her to a detention center—not after the things she was accused of doing. A detention center was no place for a high-value prisoner. She *had*, however, expected an extensive in-processing procedure. But the female guard who'd accepted her from the Task Force soldiers hadn't asked her to change out of her civilian clothes into a detainee uniform before escorting her to her holding cell. Aside from the cursory search by the transport soldiers, no one had even checked to make sure she wasn't carrying a weapon.

The female guard had locked her inside of a cell, and she'd spent hours with her head bowed over her knees, silently praying for strength. Over and over, she'd prayed for the courage to face what was to come. She'd prayed that she could save her parents. And she'd prayed that Taylor would understand why she'd left him.

Then, a few hours ago, the female guard had returned and escorted Gemma to the white room. The woman's passivity and silence had somehow been worse than if she'd cursed at Gemma and shoved her through the door. After the guard left, locking the door behind her, Gemma had stared at the chair for a long time, debating whether to sit on it. She didn't want to make her situation—or her parents' situation—worse by coming across as defiant.

But then she noticed tiny flecks of red marring the chair's immaculate surface. And when she listened hard enough, she thought she could hear the screams of the people who'd occupied that chair before her.

In the end, she'd given the chair a wide berth and crossed to the other side of the room, where she would have the best view of the door and the greatest reaction time when it opened.

She watched the door, listening carefully for the sound of voices. For any approaching footsteps in the corridor. For the sound of doors opening and closing as the soldiers went about their business. But she couldn't hear a thing. Not that they weren't out there—she'd passed at least a dozen soldiers on her way to this room, all of whom refused to make eye contact with her—but the white room was likely soundproof, which made sense when one considered its intended purpose.

Her stomach rumbled.

Gemma almost laughed. How could she be hungry at a time like this? She was going to be interrogated, likely tortured, possibly killed...and yet her body was still demanding to be fed. She had eaten nothing since surrendering, and although her hunger had come and gone over the past twenty-four hours, it had gotten much worse since her arrival in the white room.

A sound broke the silence. A soft click. The door on the other side of the room opened.

Gemma's appetite vanished.

Lydia Grimes stood in the doorway, dressed in a black pantsuit and her signature stilettos, not flanked by bodyguards, as one might've expected, but completely alone. Yet, there was no fear in her eyes. No trepidation about being in a room with a supposed terrorist and murderer.

Instead, the look on the woman's face was one of satisfaction and pride, like the proverbial cat that swallowed the canary.

"You look different from what I imagined," Grimes said, closing the door behind her. "Shorter...and not nearly as intimidating. How does that old saying go? Don't meet your heroes because they will disappoint you."

Gemma understood that the woman was baiting her, but she went for it anyway. "I'm your hero?"

"Oh, you've been my hero since the day you stepped in front of that camera and implied to the world that you were going to liberate the detention centers. And then you did it! Believe it or not, I see shades of myself in you. Neither of us is afraid to fight for the things we believe in. It's unfortunate we're on opposite sides of this fight because I think we'd work well together." She gave a little shrug. "Oh, well. Perhaps in another life."

The idea of being compared to someone like Grimes

repulsed Gemma almost as much as the idea of working with her. "I'm nothing like you," she muttered. "You're a killer."

"As are you, Miss Alcott. Or haven't you been watching the news?" Grimes made a *tut-tut* sound with her tongue. "Those poor guards and their families. One of them had young children. Did you know that? A little boy and a little girl, ages three and four. Not to mention all the innocent people you killed when you bombed *Elevation Ministries*."

"I had nothing to do with—"

"We differ in other ways, too," Grimes interrupted, waving a hand to quiet Gemma down. "For instance, I never would've surrendered. Not for anything...or anyone. When I heard about how you marched right up to that chubby woman from the compliance office and put your hands in the air... Well, I can't describe exactly how I felt at that moment. Victorious, yes, but also a little sad. Kind of like when you're watching a football game, and your team is winning but only because the other team's star quarterback just got hauled off the field on a stretcher. But you did the right thing for your parents, Miss Alcott. Please don't feel bad about deciding to sacrifice your mission to save them. Most people would've done the same."

When Gemma said nothing, Grimes began walking along the perimeter of the room, her hands clasped behind her back. "On the day the president appointed me as the director of the Federal Bureau of Compliance, I made a vow to myself that I would do whatever it took to protect this great country from people like you. You know, most people don't possess the resolve necessary to do my job. Most people are weak, easily swayed by emotion. Just look at those ridiculous symbols popping up along the highways." She gestured to the walls of the white room, as if the symbols were scrawled there in ink visible only to her. "I can't drive to work without seeing that stupid cross scribbled on half a dozen different billboards. All because some stupid girl in a ratty jacket went on television and tried to start a rebellion. I suppose people will always root for the underdog, even if the underdog is just a former top dog who got overthrown."

Gemma's eyes swung from Grimes to the chair in the center of the room. How many people had bled there? How many had died there? Giving no thought to what she was about to say, Gemma blurted out, "Why do you hate us so much? We're human beings, the same as you. How can you hate us enough to kill us?"

Grimes came to a sudden halt along the far wall and turned to face Gemma. She looked genuinely offended at the accusation. "I don't hate you, Miss Alcott," she said. "I don't hate Christians any more than I hate the spiders that spin their webs in the corners of my house or the snakes that make their homes in my garden. It's not about hatred. It's about annihilation. Christianity is like an infectious disease that needs to be eradicated. The ideas written in that book of yours by long-dead men are outdated and no longer applicable to our modern world. Yet, some of you cling to those ideas as if your very lives depend on it. And as we've seen in recent months, exposing the weak-minded to that level of devotion only causes the disease to spread."

"Is that why you televise the renouncements?" Gemma asked. "To keep the disease from spreading?"

"Of course!" A laugh that sounded more like a hiss slipped out of Grimes's lips. "What better way to show Christianity for the fraud it is than by having so-called believers renounce their faith in exchange for five minutes of airtime? Even the ones who sob through the entire thing are ratings gold."

"Funny." Gemma tilted her head defiantly. "I heard your ratings have been slipping."

That seemed to strike a nerve, and for the first time, the mask Grimes wore briefly slipped, giving Gemma a glimpse of the ugly creature that lurked behind those blood-red lips and perfect smile.

Just a glimpse, and then it vanished.

Grimes composed herself, forcing a smile onto her lips. "We're marching toward a new world, Miss Alcott," she said, resuming her leisurely stroll around the room. "A world free from the hateful tenants of Christianity, and I refuse to let anything—or *anyone*—slow that progress. Certainly not some stupid girl from the backwoods of Pennsylvania." She paused, letting the insult hang in the air. "My purpose for this visit is simple. I'm letting you know that you're going to be appearing on David Ogden's comeback broadcast tonight."

What?

"I'm going to be on *Elevation Ministries*?" Without thinking, Gemma reached for her neck. Her fingers found the metal chain and tugged it out of her shirt. "Why?"

"Because millions of people watch Ogden's show, Miss Alcott," Grimes said as if it should've been obvious. "This is the first show since the bombing, so I expect his ratings may double. Or even triple. Given all that's happened over the last month, I couldn't think of a better place for you to renounce your faith to the world."

Gemma lowered her voice to a whisper. "You want me to renounce?"

"Of course. That was the deal, wasn't it? You had to turn yourself in, and you had to renounce your faith. To save your parents, you must walk onto that stage tonight willingly. My soldiers will not drag you in front of the cameras. We will not tie you up. We will not force you to do or say anything. The public must understand that you are doing this of your own free will. Once onstage, you will take responsibility for the detention center attacks and last month's Elevation bombing."

"But that's not true!" Gemma cried. "I had nothing to do with the bombing!"

"The public doesn't care about the truth, Miss Alcott. They used to, but not anymore. All they care about is having their beliefs affirmed. So, you *will* take responsibility for coordinating these attacks, and you will renounce your faith to the world. You will finish your confession by ripping that traitorous patch off your jacket and tossing it to the ground. This rebellion of yours ends tonight."

No. She couldn't do it. She could claim responsibility for the attacks, if that was what Grimes wanted, but she couldn't renounce her faith to the world. Could she?

But Addie had done it. Both Addie and Kyle had done it for Weston, comforting themselves with the knowledge that God knew their hearts. That He wouldn't hold it against them. That He would love and forgive them.

Would He do the same for Gemma?

She released her necklace and climbed to her feet. With her hands outstretched, she took a step toward Grimes, who grimaced and stumbled backward on her heels as if Gemma were infected with some contagious disease—which, she supposed, was exactly how Grimes saw her.

"Please," Gemma begged, lowering her hands. "Please. I'll take responsibility for the bombing, if that's what you want, but don't ask me to renounce. That's the one thing I can't do. I don't care what you do to me. Punish me on live television. Make an example out of me. Kill me if you want to. But just let my parents go. They have done nothing to you. I'm the one you want."

Grimes's nose wrinkled in disgust. "Oh, stop begging. It makes you look even more pathetic." Her gaze fell from Gemma's face to her chest, and her eyes widened. "What's that?"

By the time Gemma realized her mistake, it was already too late. In a flash of movement, Grimes grabbed the cross necklace and gave it a hard yank. The chain broke, and the necklace fell away.

"You won't be needing this anymore," Grimes said, stuffing it into the pocket of her suit jacket. She turned and headed for the door, moving as swiftly as her heels could carry her.

"No!" Gemma cried, rushing after her. "Please! Don't take that!"

The door swung open, and two guards raced into the room, positioning themselves between Gemma and Grimes. Even then, Gemma kept running, but the guards grabbed her arms and pulled them behind her back. A pair of handcuffs snapped over her wrists.

Only after she made it safely to the hallway did Grimes turn to face Gemma. She was trying hard to look composed, but her face was red, and she was breathing heavily. One hand slid down the front of her suit, coming to rest on the suit pocket that contained Gemma's broken necklace.

"Just remember our deal, Miss Alcott," Grimes said, patting her pocket. "If you choose not to renounce tonight, both of your parents will die."

With that, Grimes pulled the door shut behind her.

Since the room was soundproof, she probably couldn't hear Gemma's screams.

CHAPTER THIRTY-FOUR

Taylor couldn't bring himself to leave the projection room.

Over the last twenty-four hours, he'd tried to work up the motivation to go downstairs. To check in with his father. Maybe put a little food in his stomach. But the farthest he'd gotten was the top of the stairwell before the idea of seeing everyone else—except Gemma—overwhelmed him, and he'd circled back to the patch of blankets in the corner of the room and collapsed to the floor.

He leaned against the wall, legs bent in front of him, arms draped over his knees, shivering despite the abundance of blankets underneath him. He ran his fingers over the phone number tattooed on his inner wrist, barely able to see the numbers anymore because the battery-powered lantern he'd grabbed out of a box of supplies on his way to the projection room grew dimmer with each passing hour. Eventually, it would blink out altogether, and if God were merciful, perhaps Taylor would blink out, too.

"I can't save her," he whispered. "I'm supposed to protect her, but there's nothing I can do, Father. Not when I don't know where she is."

He'd spent much of the last day talking to God. Not praying exactly, but *talking*, as if God Himself were there in the dark with him. After his mother died, Taylor had gotten used to blaming God for everything bad that happened to him. He'd discovered that it was easier to blame God—and eventually deny His existence altogether—than to accept the fact that sometimes things just didn't make sense.

Why had God allowed him to find his father again, after all these years, only to discover that he was dying of cancer? Why had God brought Gemma back into his life, time and time again, only to rip her away from him?

Before, those questions would've incited anger within Taylor. But not anymore.

Now, he just wanted to understand. What was the point of it? Hadn't Gemma done the right thing by speaking to the world and giving Christians hope? Hadn't she done the right thing by helping to liberate the detention centers? So why was she being punished? Why, after everything she'd done, had God allowed her to fall into the hands of the enemy?

Only she hadn't fallen, had she?

She'd walked.

Taylor dropped his head into his hands, his palms muffling his next words. "I know You're listening to me. I can feel You here with me. But I need You to answer me. I need You to show me what to—"

A loud buzzing sound, like static, shattered the silence of the room.

And then it was gone.

Taylor's head snapped to the right, searching the immediate area for the source of the sound, and his eyes landed on Gemma's backpack.

Until that moment, he'd forgotten it was there. Gemma

carried that navy-blue backpack with her everywhere. So why was it here?

He crawled across the blankets and pulled the backpack onto his lap. When he unzipped it, the first thing he pulled out were the clothes she'd packed two nights earlier: a pair of jeans and a green sweater. He brought the sweater to his face, but it smelled nothing like Gemma. She'd never worn it. She'd probably gotten it from one of the donation bins. He tossed it aside.

Underneath the clothing was Gemma's Bible—the one she'd found in the old church in Ash Grove. At the Sanctuary, Taylor had often found her sprawled on her bed or seated underneath a tree, reading from that Bible. Even then, when his faith had been nowhere close to what it needed to be, he'd admired her for believing in something so strongly. Yes, he'd been a Task Force soldier, but he'd also been raised by a pastor, so he knew more about the Bible than many Christians. But Gemma's knowledge of the Bible had always impressed him. He'd never admitted it to himself until now, but her strong faith was the thing he'd found most attractive about her.

He opened the Bible.

As a soldier, he'd seized many Bibles. Torn pages from them. Burned them over his campfires. But he hadn't *read* from a Bible in years. So, he flipped to a random page and found himself in the first chapter of Philippians. That book contained the Apostle Paul's words to the Philippian church, written during his imprisonment in Rome. Taylor's eyes landed on a passage Gemma had underlined in pen.

"Now I want you to know, brothers and sisters, that what has happened to me has actually served to advance the Gospel. As a result, it has become clear throughout the whole palace guard and to everyone else that I am in chains for Christ. And because of my chains, most of the brothers and sisters have become confident in the Lord and dare all the more to proclaim the Gospel without fear."

It wasn't the first time Taylor had read that passage in

Philippians. He'd read the Bible three times by the age of thirteen. But this time, the passage nearly bowled him over. Even while imprisoned for preaching the Gospel, Paul had continued to share the Good News with everyone who would listen, including the Roman guards who were chained to him day and night. Paul's boldness for the Gospel while in prison had not only inspired other Christians to continue sharing the Good News, but it had also likely led to the conversion of many of the guards and officials during his imprisonment.

Leaning his head against the wall, Taylor gazed up at the ceiling. Was that what had happened at Stovington? Was that why so many guards had betrayed their own mission to help the detainees escape? How many of them had been introduced to the Gospel by the very Christians they were guarding?

He wanted to read more—to see what else Gemma had found important—but then he remembered the strange noise. Placing the Bible next to him on the blanket, he reached inside the backpack, and his hand closed around something at the bottom of the bag.

Instantly, he knew what it was.

He pulled the tactical radio out of the bag and turned it over in his hand, examining the broken clip. Then, he glanced at the serial number. He recognized it immediately. All Task Force soldiers had to maintain control of their equipment, and maintaining control meant knowing your radio's serial number by heart.

This wasn't just any radio. It was *his* Motorola SRX-2200.

His Task Force radio.

The last time Taylor had seen it, he'd been pulling Gemma out of the escape hatch at the mine. The clip had broken during the rescue, sending the radio plunging into the darkness. As far as he knew, Gemma had never returned to the mine after that night.

So, how did his radio get inside her backpack?

He turned the dial at the top of the radio and heard a sharp blast of static—the same sound he'd heard coming from the backpack minutes earlier, even though the radio hadn't been turned on. How could it still have been working? The battery should've been long dead. That it was still working, after all this time, was a miracle.

"How?" he repeated.

He didn't expect anyone to answer him, but someone did.

"She found it at the bottom of the ladder."

Taylor glanced up at the sound of Sophia's voice.

The girl stood a few feet away from him. She wore an outfit he'd never seen before: green leggings and a purple hoodie so big it appeared to be swallowing her up. Tears shimmered in her eyes.

He'd been so focused on the radio that he hadn't heard her approach.

"Gemma went back to the mine?" When Sophia nodded, he asked, "But why would she do that?"

"The soldier with red hair. After he shot Yost and Kyle, he came after me."

Mullen, Taylor realized, his fingers tightening around the radio. "Then what happened?"

Sophia stuffed her hands inside the pockets of her hoodie. "I ran as fast as I could. I even made it to Neverland, but he still caught me. He took me back to the mine. But it wasn't me he wanted. It was Gemma. He kept talking about her. He said she'd come for me eventually, and she did. Then, he tied us both up. He wanted to blow up the mine and trap us inside." Her voice broke, and she started to cry. "He wanted us to die slowly."

Taylor opened his arms, and Sophia ran into them, sobbing. He held her as she cried, amazed at how much love he could feel for a young girl who was not his own. It horrified him that something like that had happened to Gemma and Sophia, and he wasn't there to help them. "It's okay, Soph. That guy is dead now. You don't have to worry about him ever again. He's done hurting people."

"But there are more bad guys," she cried. "There are more soldiers out there."

Taylor felt a pang of guilt, as he always did when he tried to distance himself from soldiers—from the *bad guys*—like Mullen. No, he hadn't been sadistic like Mullen, and he hadn't murdered anyone, but he'd ruined his share of lives. He'd torn families apart. He'd burned churches to the ground. He'd condemned his own father to spend the final years of his life in a detention center.

When the girl's cries subsided, Taylor drew in a deep breath. "Okay. I need you to do something for me. I need you to tell me what else happened in the mine. You said that Gemma found my radio?"

Sophia nodded against his chest. "We got away from Mullen, but then he blew the entrance to the mine. We couldn't get out that way. I thought we were going to die, but then Gemma remembered the escape ladder. She got us to the ladder, and that was when she found your radio. I saw her holding it against her body like this." She closed her eyes and mimicked clutching something over her heart.

Taylor lowered his head, forcing the image from his mind. He needed to stay focused. "Thank you for telling me, Soph. That's all good information. But how did you know I was up here?"

"Max told me where to find you." She lowered her head, a guilty look passing over her face. "But I had to lie to him. Otherwise, I don't think he would've told me. You know how Max is."

"Yeah, but you still shouldn't have lied. We never *have* to lie," Taylor responded, sounding so much like his father that it floored him. He softened his voice. "What lie did you tell him?"

"I told him I wanted to cheer you up, but that's not the real reason I came up here."

"Okay... So, why did you come up here?"

Sophia sat back on her heels and wiped her eyes on the sleeve of her hoodie. "Because I heard some people talking about Gemma. Abram and Oliver and Gavin went into a theater. I didn't think it was a big deal until I saw that other guy —Clarke—go into the same theater, and then I knew something was going on. So, I snuck inside and hid where they couldn't see me." She glanced up at him. "And yes, I know I'm not supposed to lie and sneak around, but Gemma is my friend. I wanted to see if they were talking about her."

Taylor felt his heart rate increase. "And? Did those guys say anything about Gemma?"

The girl cast an uneasy glance at the stairwell, as if she were expecting someone to come racing up the stairs and tackle her before she could get the words out. When no one did, she turned back to Taylor and lowered her voice to a whisper.

"They said she's going to be on TV."

CHAPTER THIRTY-FIVE

With Gemma's backpack slung over his shoulder and Sophia following close behind, Taylor moved down the theater's main hallway, going from theater to theater, grabbing doors and throwing them open hard enough to send them slamming into the exterior walls. At each theater, he leaned into the darkness and shouted Clarke's name.

But every theater was empty.

He'd checked the lobby first, of course, but the folding table had been empty, discarded playing cards and half-empty bottles of water littering its surface.

"They must be in the mall," Taylor muttered, after they checked theater twelve. He pushed open the exit door and stepped into the annex. Stagnant water rippled in the fountain as he marched past, his boots pounding against the tile floor.

There was no one in the annex, either. The mall felt dead, as if Armageddon had occurred in the last twenty minutes, and he and Sophia were the only survivors. Taylor glanced distrustfully at the vacant stores, their gates hanging halfway down like metal teeth. If he were in a zombie apocalypse movie, this is when one of the undead would come bounding out of the darkness and leap on him, tearing hungrily at his flesh with its rotting teeth.

When they reached the mall, Taylor spotted Private Dietrich standing among a group of detainees, jotting information down on a clipboard.

He made his way over to her. "Where's Clarke?"

"Good morning to you, too." Dietrich tipped her clipboard toward him. Names and phone numbers filled the paper. "Not sure where Clarke is. Yesterday afternoon, he ordered us to move the detainees out of here as quickly as possible. We've been going all day and all night, connecting people with their families—the ones that would take them, at least. We've been using the vans to transport them a few at a time, dropping them off at gas stations and places like that. It's not ideal, but it's the best we can do under the circumstances."

This was a waste of time. He didn't care about Clarke's little operation. It had nothing to do with Gemma. "Is Clarke in the security room? I need to talk to him."

"Talk to me about what?"

He turned to see Clarke approaching him, flanked on either side by Abram and Oliver. Taylor's father trailed behind them, his eyes overflowing with concern.

Taylor marched up to Clarke. He let the backpack drop to the floor and jabbed a finger in the guy's chest. "I want to know what's going on, and I want to know *right now*."

"Back off, Nolan," Clarke growled. "Let's not do this again."

"Take it easy, brother," Taylor's father said, wedging his large body between the two men. He put a hand on Taylor's chest. "We were just coming to find you."

"Why didn't you find me right away?" he demanded, clenching his hands into fists. He looked past his father at Abram and Oliver. "You included Gavin in your little meeting, but not me? She's my wife."

"We thought it would be better to have your father with us," Oliver said, giving Sophia a pointed look. The girl lowered her head and stared at the ground. "We weren't trying to hide anything from you."

"My father has nothing to do with this."

"Son..."

"Where is she?!" Taylor shouted, his patience gone. "Tell me what's going on!"

"Calm down," Clarke muttered, glancing at the detainees. "Stop scaring everyone. She's going to be on *Elevation Ministries* tonight. The first live broadcast since the bombing. According to the news, she's going to renounce her faith. There's also speculation that she's going to take responsibility for the bombing, as well as for the deaths of the guards at the detention centers."

Taylor couldn't believe what he was hearing. Forty-seven people had died in the Elevation bombing, plus now they were accusing her of executing those guards. If she publicly accepted responsibility for everything, her life would be over—literally.

And Clarke had done nothing. He'd just stood there and watched her leave.

"Why did you let her go?!" Taylor shouted, launching himself at Clarke, but his father caught him and held him back.

"Son, please. Calm down."

"They're going to execute her!" Taylor struggled to break free from his father's grip, but even in Joseph Nolan's cancer-weakened state, he was very strong. "Let go of me!"

His father squeezed him tighter, a Boa constrictor tightening around his chest, and brought his lips to Taylor's ear. "You must get control of yourself," his father whispered. "Losing control won't help the carnival girl. She *needs* you."

The carnival girl.

The words broke through the frenzy in Taylor's mind, and he stopped fighting and blinked at his father, trying to make sense of what he'd just heard. Those words—carnival girl—had thrust him back in time, back to the Mountain View Medical Center, where Taylor had recovered after being shot in the thigh by Brie. He'd been dreaming about detaining his father, and in the dream, his father had referred to Gemma as the carnival girl.

But he wasn't dreaming now.

"What did you say?" Taylor whispered.

His father's arms loosened a little. "I said that losing control won't help your wife. She needs you."

Taylor didn't know what to believe. Nothing in his father's face indicated he was lying—or at least that he *knew* he was lying. But Taylor hadn't misheard him. His father had said the words *carnival girl.*

He felt his rage toward Clarke dissipating. Whatever his father had called Gemma, his words had been true. She needed him. He couldn't lose control now. "So, what are we going to do?"

"What *can* we do about it?" Clarke asked, rubbing the back of his neck. "Elevation is going to be a fortress tonight. The news report said that Lydia Grimes has ordered the Task Force to handle the security tonight. We've got no forces of our own, and even if we did, we still wouldn't be able to get Gemma out of there."

"But we have forces here, don't we?" Oliver interjected. "Your people—"

"My people have other responsibilities," Clarke cut in. "Our mission isn't to rescue every subversive who gets herself captured. Our mission has always been to liberate the detention centers. Even if we *could* help Alcott—which we can't—we don't have the manpower or the weapons necessary to stage a full-scale assault against the Task Force. And even if we had the manpower, such an attack would only create more bloodshed, which would give the government more ammunition to use against Christians. I hate to say it, but our hands are tied."

"So, we're just going to let this happen?" Abram demanded. "Look at what she's done for these people." He pointed to the detainees scattered around the mall. "Some of them wouldn't be alive today, if not for her. She gave them hope when they had none. And now we're not going to help her?"

"What choice do we have?" Clarke shot back. "Believe me, brother, I don't like it any more than you do."

Task Force, Taylor thought. *Security.*

As the men argued, an idea took shape in Taylor's mind—dark and formless, at first, like the world before God had molded it into being. But there was something there. Something lurking in the darkness, waiting to be revealed. Even as God took over, sliding the pieces together in his mind, Taylor didn't know if this plan—if you could even call it a plan—would work, but if God wanted him to do it, then he would do it.

"I'll go."

The other four men looked at him.

"What?" his father asked. "Go where?"

Taylor ignored the question and turned to Clarke. "No one else has to go. Just me. I'm not asking you to be involved. I'm just asking that you don't interfere or try to stop me. And if you have a vehicle and a gun to spare, that would be helpful."

"Now, wait just a minute," his father interrupted, his voice taking on that deep baritone that Taylor remembered from his childhood. It was the no-nonsense voice he reserved for when his son got out of line. "Getting yourself killed or captured will solve nothing, Taylor. That's not going to help Gemma."

But this wasn't Joseph Nolan, the pastor, speaking. This was Joseph Nolan, the father. Taylor couldn't fault him for that. "I understand what you're saying, Dad, but I saw how hard you fought to save Mom. You would've given anything, including your own life, to save her. And I'm willing to do the same for Gemma."

Joseph Nolan grimaced as if Taylor's words had caused him

actual pain. Or perhaps it was the pain from the cancer. His mouth dropped open as if to argue further, but then he pinched his lips together and remained silent.

"I'll go," Abram said. "Someone's got to keep an eye on Nolan. Might as well be me."

Taylor shook his head. "I won't put anyone else in danger. Plus, I *know* these guys. I used to be one of them. Maybe I can use that to my advantage. Maybe I can infiltrate the Task Force that's pulling security at Elevation."

Clarke scratched at his five o'clock shadow. "And just how do you plan on accomplishing that?"

"I've still got my uniform," Taylor replied. "My interrogators made me wear it when they sent me to the detention center." He glanced at his father. "They intended for it to harm me, but I think God intended it for good. I think He wanted me to have my uniform for tonight." He picked up Gemma's backpack and pulled out the radio. "I've also got this."

Oliver wrinkled his nose. "A radio?"

"Not just a radio. A Task Force radio. *My* radio. Apparently, Gemma found it months ago in the coal mine, and she's been carrying it around ever since. The battery should be dead by now. There's no reason this thing should still work, but it does. I think God wants me to use it tonight."

It was the radio that convinced the others to let him go. There was no more arguing after that.

Clarke stepped forward and grasped Taylor on the shoulder. "Alright. If you're sure you want to do this, then I'll see you get a gun and a vehicle."

"Hopefully, you'll get them both back."

"I don't care about that. Just get your girl and come back safely. Stop by the office before you go, and I'll have everything ready."

"Okay. Thanks."

After Clarke walked away, Abram stepped forward. "Since

you don't want my help, I'll stay here and get everybody praying. I'll use force if necessary."

Taylor smiled. "I'm sure you will."

Oliver glanced at his watch. "We don't have much time, so I'll put Mia in charge of organizing a prayer meeting. If there's one thing that woman is good at, it's getting people moving."

After both men walked away, Taylor crouched down and opened his arms, and Sophia ran into them, nearly knocking him over. Holding the girl tightly, he could feel her tears dampening the fabric of his shirt. "If you see Gemma tonight," she said, "please tell her I love her."

"You can tell her when I bring her back, Soph. Just pray for us, okay? We won't be alone out there if you're praying for us."

"I won't stop praying until you both get back. I promise."

Sophia ran off, leaving Taylor with one more goodbye.

The hardest one of all.

As he rose, he tried to think of something funny to say. Something that would make this goodbye a little easier. But when he turned around, he saw that Joseph Nolan was no longer alone.

Gavin and Teresa stood beside him.

It surprised Taylor that he didn't feel the same anger he'd once felt at the sight of Gavin. It just wasn't there anymore. His hostility tank was on empty. Had he forgiven Gavin in the last two days without realizing it? Despite the strange absence of any resentment in his heart, he still didn't know what to say to the guy, so he ended the awkwardness with a statement.

"I'm going to bring her back."

"I know," Gavin said. "We overheard you talking to the others. And if it's okay with you, I want to go along."

Taylor waved him away. "Absolutely not."

"Please," Gavin said in a pain-choked voice. And for once, there was no challenge in his eyes. No enmity. Only the same desperation that Taylor felt in his own heart. "Please. Let me go with you. I have to make this right."

Taylor considered his options. If he refused, there was really nothing Gavin could do about it. But if he said yes, he would have to trust the guy. Not only with *his* life, but with Gemma's. And that was something he never would've considered doing a few days ago.

So why was he considering it now?

Silently, Gavin watched him. Waiting. Hoping.

Taylor ran a jerky hand through his hair. He couldn't believe what he was about to say. "Alright. Check with Clarke's guys. Some of them used to be Task Force. See if any of them can wrangle up a uniform for you. If you don't have a uniform, you don't come along. Do you have any issues with wearing a Task Force uniform?"

"None at all," Gavin assured him. "I'll do whatever it takes."

Yeah, Taylor thought. *We'll see about that.*

"Okay." Taylor glanced at his watch. "Meet me in the garage in an hour."

Gavin nodded and then turned to Teresa, who was already crying. He reached down and took Teresa's hand, bringing it to his lips and kissing her knuckles. Then, he stepped closer and kissed her on the lips. His hand came to rest on her stomach, confirming what Taylor already knew.

Taylor turned away from them and locked eyes with his father. Without speaking, the two men embraced, holding each other longer than ever before. When they reluctantly separated, Joseph Nolan retrieved a handkerchief from his pocket and wiped at his eyes.

"What can I do, Son?" he asked. "I have to do *something.*"

"You can pray, Dad," Taylor said without hesitation. "Please. Just pray for us."

And then, instead of saying goodbye, Taylor said something else. Something he never thought he'd say again.

"I love you, Dad."

CHAPTER THIRTY-SIX

Locked inside a dressing room at the Elevation Ministry Center, Gemma's hand kept drifting up to her neck, her subconscious mind forgetting that the cross necklace no longer hung there.

It was gone. Grimes had it now.

Gemma felt naked without it, unprotected, as if she were riding in a speeding car with no seatbelt. Except for the few hours when the necklace had been in Yost's possession, she hadn't taken it off since the night Taylor had returned it to her—the same night he'd professed his love to her for the first time.

Despite the loss of her necklace, the memory brought a smile to Gemma's face. When she closed her eyes, she could still see Taylor dropping to one knee in her parents' living room, looking nervous and unprepared and blindingly handsome all at the same time. She'd spent the last few hours reliving each of the memories she'd shared with Taylor. There were so many to choose from. He'd been a huge part of her life, long before he ever realized it. Yet, there would never be enough memories, not even if she lived a thousand lifetimes and spent every one of them with Taylor.

It was her way of saying goodbye. To him. To their shared past. To the life they might've had together. Because whatever happened on that stage tonight, one thing seemed certain.

She would never see Taylor again.

She felt no bitterness toward God for giving her Taylor for such a short time. Instead, she felt incredibly thankful to have had him at all. Many people went their whole lives without finding their true love, and yet Gemma had grown up with hers. He'd been in her life from the very beginning. She'd watched him transform from the cute boy with the disheveled hair and the broken heart to the handsome soldier with the disarming blue eyes and the good heart. Their time together hadn't been nearly long enough, but God had answered every one of her prayers. Taylor had loved her back. He'd rediscovered his faith in Christ. He'd married her. He'd been her first and her last. Her best friend. Her everything.

God is so good, she thought, tears blurring her eyes. *He's been so good to me.*

A faint click drew her attention to the door of the dressing room—the sound of a key turning in a lock—and then the door opened.

Gemma jumped a little, her nerves more frayed than the clothing in the mall's donation bins. She expected to see soldiers on the other side of the door. Or perhaps that Bureau of Compliance woman, Lydia Grimes, intended to escort her onto the stage.

Instead, a plain-looking woman stood in the doorway, holding a clipboard against her chest. She wore a coffee-colored dress that hit just below her knees, and her dark hair was pulled back in a ballerina bun. There was nothing at all remarkable about the woman, as if God had designed her specifically to blend in. And although Gemma was certain she'd never seen the woman before, there was something so familiar about her face. Something she couldn't quite pinpoint.

"Good evening, Miss Alcott," she said. "I'm Tara Wilkinson."

There was no animosity in the woman's voice. She was all business.

"Good evening?" The statement came out sounding like a question. Gemma had no idea what else to say to this woman.

"Are you ready?" Tara asked. "Do you need anything?"

Despite her hours of mental preparation, Gemma still wasn't ready. She could already feel the heat of the lights and the dark eyes of the cameras that would soon be pointed at her, broadcasting her renouncement to the world.

But this woman, whoever she was, couldn't help her.

"I don't need anything," Gemma finally said. "I'm ready."

Rising from the chair, she followed the woman out of the dressing room and into the hallway. They passed several employees on their way to the main stage, and none of them spared Gemma a second glance. They were all too busy, hurrying from one place to another, each playing their own role in making tonight's broadcast a success. Gemma had seen Ogden's show before, and although she hated everything he stood for, the beauty of his stage had always impressed her. Even driving up to the building tonight, handcuffed in the backseat of a Task Force transport vehicle, Gemma had been awestruck at the sight of Elevation's newly renovated exterior. The front of the building looked perfect, the array of windows sparkling in the waning light of the day, as if the bombing had never happened.

Now, as they reached the entrance to the left side of the stage, Gemma could hear the thunderous applause of the crowd, loud enough to drown out the orchestra music. Through a gap in the curtains, she saw Ogden on the Jumbotron, larger than life, head tilted back toward the ceiling, his arms outstretched in his trademark, Christ-like pose. On the screen behind him were the words: *Be Elevated to a Place You Never Dreamed Of.*

The backstage area wasn't cold, but Gemma couldn't stop

shivering. She brought her hands up to eye level. Her fingers were visibly trembling. No matter how hard she concentrated, she couldn't make them stop.

It's the fight-or-flight response. Your body is preparing to do one or the other.

But tonight, neither was an option.

Tonight, the only option was surrender.

Finally, Ogden dropped his arms, signaling for the audience to quiet down. "Folks, let me just tell you...I couldn't hold my arms up like that a few weeks ago!" And the audience roared with laughter, as if this was a comedy show. As if forty-seven of their own hadn't died in this very building one month earlier.

"Thank you, ladies and gentlemen," Ogden continued after the laughter died down. "Thank you so much for coming out tonight to celebrate the grand reopening of Elevation Ministry Center. For those who wanted to attend but could not, I apologize. We couldn't have a full auditorium tonight because of security concerns, but please know that you're here in spirit. Thank you for your continued support. It means the world to me." His voice deepened, growing more serious. "This has been an extraordinarily difficult time, not only for myself, but especially for the families and the victims of last month's senseless attack on our worship center. But with this broadcast tonight, we are showing the world that they will not shut us down! They will not silence us! We are just...getting...started!"

This time, Gemma didn't just hear the audience, she *felt* them. The ground shook beneath her as thousands of Ogden's followers leapt out of their seats to applaud their leader. The roar of the crowd sounded like an approaching army.

"He's on fire tonight," Tara commented dryly, clipping a small microphone to the lapel of Gemma's utility jacket and slipping the transmitter inside her pocket.

After the crowd grew quiet, Ogden continued, "As I'm sure

you're aware, we have a very special guest with us tonight. She's the Director of the Federal Bureau of Compliance. This woman has dedicated her life to keeping us safe from these domestic terrorists known as subversives. Ladies and gentlemen, please join me in welcoming Lydia Grimes to the stage!"

On the Jumbotron, Gemma watched as Lydia Grimes strolled out from the opposite side of the stage, her smile broader than the lake back at the Sanctuary. She hugged David Ogden and kissed him politely on the cheek, and although Gemma wasn't certain, she thought she saw Ogden flinch when Grimes's lips touched his skin.

As if it burned.

"Lydia, thank you for being here tonight," Ogden said. "Please, take a moment and bring us up to speed on what's going on regarding the investigation into the bombing."

"Thank you, David." Grimes turned to face the audience. "As I'm sure you're aware, yesterday morning, Gemma Alcott surrendered to authorities. This young woman is wanted in connection with several incidents of domestic terrorism, including the recent coordinated attacks on several detention centers, as well as last month's bombing of this building. So far, fifty people have died because of her actions. She has caused our great nation a great deal of heartache, but all of that is about to end. Gemma Alcott is here tonight, and in a few brief moments, she's going to take the stage and publicly accept responsibility for her actions. She's going to call off her followers and bring an end to this rebellion. And finally, she's going to renounce her faith in Jesus Christ."

The crowd launched themselves to their feet again, clapping and cheering.

Gemma's hands continued to shake, but now she also felt sick to her stomach.

After they took their seats, Grimes nodded at a producer on

Gemma's side of the stage. "It's time," she said. "Please send her out."

"This is it," Tara spoke the words directly into Gemma's ear. "When you get out there, walk up to David but don't touch him. Don't shake his hand. Just stand in front of him and face the crowd. Answer his questions. Do whatever you have to do." When Gemma didn't move, Tara gave her a little push. "Get out there."

But Gemma didn't move.

Not because she was terrified but because it had suddenly occurred to her why her female escort looked so familiar. It wasn't just the woman's eyes. It was also her lips. Her nose. The slight New Jersey inflection in her voice. It was like one of those visual illusions where you stare and stare at a picture, but there's nothing there. And then, finally, once your eyes adjust and make sense of what they're seeing, the image becomes crystal clear. And you're left wondering how it took you so long to see what was staring you right in the face.

"What are you doing?" Tara's eyes darted between Gemma and a very frustrated-looking producer who'd just poked her head through the curtain and was waving frantically. "We're live! Get out there!"

But instead of walking onto the stage, Gemma spun around to face Tara. "I'm going," she said, "but first, tell me your name."

"I already told you my name. It's Tara Wil—"

"No. Your *real* name. Please. I won't say anything, but I need to know."

Tara didn't demand to know how Gemma had figured it out, nor did she ask what had given it away. Only a few seconds ticked by before the woman finally answered, but in those few seconds, Tara's countenance went from mousy to menacing, her nostrils flaring, irritation blazing like a fire behind her brown eyes. Irritation not at Gemma, but at being discovered.

This is the side of herself, Gemma realized, *that she keeps carefully buried underneath those frumpy clothes and ballerina buns. It's intentional. She's hiding. It's a disguise.*

And then, finally, she said...

"My name is Tara Clarke."

CHAPTER THIRTY-SEVEN

Gemma knew her legs were moving, but she couldn't feel them.

As she walked onto the stage, the entire lower half of her body seemed to be disconnected from the rest of her, as if her upper body might float away like a balloon and get lodged somewhere high in the ceiling. With no power over her own body, she felt as if she were being carried along by one of those moving walkways in airports, except this walkway was taking her somewhere she didn't want to go.

When she reached the center of the stage, it felt as if she'd been transported inside her own television. Everything looked exactly as she'd expected, only bigger. The stage was enormous and draped in reds and purples—the color scheme of royalty.

Even though she'd hated Ogden's broadcasts, Gemma had always thought that the Elevation stage looked majestic, if not a tad garish, on television. But in real life, the reds and purples were obscenely bright, intensified by the blinding lights that hung overhead and peeked out from the floor at the front of the stage. She felt half-sick at the sight of so much color, and the heat of the lights beating against her skin only intensified the feeling.

She continued toward the spot where the tip of the stage jutted into the audience like a shelf. That was where Lydia Grimes and David Ogden stood waiting for her. They both held microphones against their chests, but only Ogden's was gold.

Gemma already knew that Grimes hated her, but she'd expected a certain level of kindness from Ogden. He'd been a pastor once, and he'd often spoken of forgiving subversives and welcoming those who've renounced back into society.

But there wasn't even a hint of benevolence in Ogden's dark eyes. He regarded Gemma with a strange concentration that wasn't hatred exactly but something more sinister. Something more akin to hunger.

The look a snake might give a baby rabbit just before striking.

Ogden's gaze dropped to the patch on her left shoulder, and the hunger in his eyes gave way to disgust.

As instructed, Gemma had worn her utility jacket to the broadcast. She could feel the upside-down Task Force patch growing hot against her shoulder, as if the very threads that held it together had caught fire under the intense scrutiny of the audience. She'd spent some of her time in the dressing room, working at the seams, loosening them so the patch would be easier to rip off when the time came.

Which she fully intended to do.

She was still ten paces away from Grimes when the woman held up a hand, indicating for her to stop. Obediently, Gemma froze in place and waited for her next instructions. She knew what they expected of her. She'd been rehearsing the words in her head all afternoon.

God will understand, she repeated to herself for what must've been the hundredth time since leaving the white room. *He'll understand that I'm only doing this to save my parents. They don't deserve to die in a detention center. They deserve to be free.*

"Welcome back to *Elevation Ministries*, Miss Alcott," Ogden spoke into his gold microphone, his tone uncharacteristically serious. "If you'll recall, the last time you were inside this building, you attempted to take my life. You put a bullet in my shoulder, but you did not kill me. Our loving creator prevented you from harming me. He would not allow me to be killed, despite your best efforts."

Ogden hadn't asked her to admit anything yet, so Gemma remained silent.

Leaving Grimes at the front of the stage, Ogden moved closer to Gemma, his eyes darting to the Jumbotron overhead, as if to check his appearance. He stopped a few feet away from her. "The creator protected me because I've devoted my life to freeing people like yourself from the chains of your divisive religion. I don't do this because I hate Christians, Miss Alcott. I do it because Christianity is dangerous. It's predicated upon a falsehood, and that falsehood is the belief that there is only one way to salvation."

Ogden closed his eyes and held his hands in the air. "*I am the way and the truth and the life. No one comes to the Father except through me.*" He shouted the words in an exaggerated Southern accent that brought to mind TV evangelists of days past. Then, he opened his eyes and glared at Gemma. "That's what Christianity teaches, doesn't it, Miss Alcott? It teaches that a person's salvation depends on their belief in the death, burial, and resurrection of Jesus Christ. And no matter how good a person is, or what kind of life they've led, they will spend an eternity in hell if they don't worship a carpenter who died over two-thousand years ago. Tell me the truth now, Miss Alcott. Is that what Christians believe? Do they really believe they are the only people worthy of heaven?"

"No." She shook her head. "That's not true."

Ogden's mouth twisted into a bitter smile. "Oh, Miss Alcott. It *is* true, and you know it. Look at these people in the audience. Your religion teaches that they're all going to hell. All of them. Myself included. But I assert that any god who would condemn most of his creation to hell for not bowing down to him sounds more like a tyrant than a god."

The audience leapt to their feet and applauded their leader. Some pumped their fists in the air. One young man in the front row bared his teeth at Gemma.

"Christianity is a plague on this world, Miss Alcott," Ogden continued after the noise of the crowd died down. "We have fought wars over it. We have lost millions of lives over it. Right here, in this building, forty-seven lives ended because of your religion. There is no longer a place in this world for those who believe as you do: that the rest of the world is evil and deserving of eternal punishment."

"That's not what I—"

"Quiet!" Ogden commanded in a voice that Gemma had never heard him use in any of his broadcasts. He nodded at Lydia Grimes. "The stage is yours."

Striding in front of Ogden and blocking him from view, Grimes raised her own microphone. The hint of a smile on her blood-red lips showed that she'd been patiently waiting for her moment in the spotlight. "Miss Alcott, when we spoke earlier today, you relayed you are ready to renounce your faith. You stated that you no longer believe in this rebellion, and that you intend to confess your involvement in last month's attack on this building, as well as your participation in several coordinated attacks on area detention centers. You told me that you're doing this of your own free will, and in exchange for your confession, you've asked that your parents—scheduled to be unbound later this evening—would be awarded their freedom. In a gesture of good faith, the Federal Bureau of Compliance is prepared to honor those terms. Are you prepared to proceed with your renouncement?"

Gemma opened her mouth, tried to force the words from her lips, but nothing came out. It felt as if her tongue was stuck to the roof of her mouth.

The perfect silence of the auditorium only amplified the fact that she hadn't answered. Over Grimes's shoulder, the crowd waited, staring at her with the same predatory hunger she'd seen in Ogden's eyes. They hated her. She could *feel* the anger radiating off their bodies like steam. The air was positively thick with it—so thick Gemma found it difficult to breathe. Minutes earlier, she'd been cold, but now she was sweating underneath the heat of the overhead lights and the wrathful stares of the audience who looked as if they wanted to rip her apart.

After a few moments, Grimes nodded at one producer. "Bring up the live shot, please."

On the Jumbotron overhead, the stage disappeared, replaced by a security camera view of what looked like a hospital infirmary. Rows of beds lined the wall on either side of the room, but only two of the beds were occupied. A small group of medical personnel huddled around the beds.

As Gemma watched the screen, her heart thudding against her ribcage, the wide shot of the infirmary switched to an overhead shot of the beds...and the two patients with an array of tubes hooked up to their arms.

A noise escaped Gemma's lips. Somewhere between a gasp and a scream.

Her parents.

For the first time in three years, she was looking at her parents.

CHAPTER THIRTY-EIGHT

Gemma knew the devastation that years in a detention center could wreak on a person's body, but nothing could've prepared her to see those same drastic changes exhibited in the people she loved.

When her father was detained at fifty-five, he'd had a full head of hair. Now, he was completely bald. Gemma didn't know if he'd lost his hair naturally or if they had made him shave it off, but it wasn't a look her father would've ever chosen willingly. He'd also lost all of his muscle mass. The man on the hospital bed looked nothing like the strong, invincible father who used to throw her over his shoulder and carry her, squealing and laughing, up the stairway to her bedroom at night.

But her mother looked even worse. Her hair—which had once been the same length, thickness, and shade of auburn as Gemma's—was now short and choppy, as if someone inexperienced had taken a set of kitchen shears to it in a fit of rage. And her hair appeared to have skipped gray altogether and gone straight to white. Dark age spots riddled the thin skin of her hands and arms, the spots made even more apparent by her

"

ghostly complexion. Her mother's lips hung slightly open, and when the camera zoomed even closer, Gemma saw a thin line of drool extending from the corner of her mother's mouth to the pillow.

Ogden pulled the microphone away from his mouth. "Lydia," he muttered through clenched teeth. "What is this?"

But Grimes ignored him. "Miss Alcott's parents have already been sedated for the unbinding procedure," she explained to the audience. "As you can see, detainees experience no pain during the unbinding process. There is no stress. No anxiety. Our doctors conduct these unbindings with great compassion and respect for the detainee."

"Please," Gemma whispered. "Don't do this."

"There's no need to beg, Miss Alcott. Their fate is in your hands. You're very lucky in that regard. We do not afford most subversives the opportunity to exchange their own freedom for the freedom of their loved ones."

Gemma tore her gaze away from the screen, away from the medical personnel gathered around her parents, waiting for the go-ahead to inject death into their veins.

She closed her eyes.

God, please don't let them die.

"Your parents do not have to die," Grimes said, as if she'd heard Gemma's prayer. "They can return to their home and live out the rest of their years in peace."

I don't know what to do, God, Gemma continued to pray. *But You promised to give us the words to say when we're brought before governors and kings.*

"No one has to die tonight. We brought you here because we want this rebellion to end. We only want peace."

Please, Lord. Put the words in my mouth. Tell me what to say. Tell me how to save them.

OPEN YOUR EYES.

The words filled Gemma's mind, and an eerie feeling of calm

—unlike anything she'd ever felt before—washed over her. She opened her eyes, expecting to see Grimes standing in front of her, but the woman was gone. So was Ogden.

Gemma was alone on the stage.

She whirled around to face the audience, but they were gone, too.

The auditorium was empty. Every seat was vacant.

All except one.

In the center of the auditorium, halfway down the center section, a woman rose from her seat, a smile smoothing out the fine lines of her face. The woman standing before Gemma was dead—or at least she *had* been dead—but now, somehow, she was alive. A crown of light encircled her, illuminating her dark hair and casting a youthful glow on her chocolate skin. All around the woman, the darkness tried to close in on her like an enemy force, threatening to sweep over her, but the light—the light from which Gemma could see no source—formed a protective barrier around her.

The darkness could not defeat it.

Remember what I said, Stormy.

Letty's lips never moved, but it was the old woman's voice in Gemma's mind, as clear as day. She lifted her hand and pointed at the Jumbotron.

Gemma didn't want to turn away from Letty. She didn't want to turn her back on that beautiful light. But she did as the woman asked, only because she could still see the reflection of light on the polished floor of the stage. Slowly, she raised her eyes to look at the screen. Her parents were there, lying lifeless on their beds, drifting side by side in a dreamless sleep, unaware of the nearness of death.

They're already safe. Letty spoke the words into Gemma's mind. *The folks I worry about are the ones who still need saving.*

The statement catapulted Gemma back in time to Winter's Dam, seven months earlier. The day the Task Force released

Letty. Gemma had urged the old woman to abandon the book-store and move to the Sanctuary, but Letty had nixed the idea, saying that the people at the Sanctuary were already safe, and that she was only concerned with the ones who still needed saving.

My parents are already safe, Gemma realized, her eyes locked on the screen. *No matter what happens to them, they're already safe. I need to worry about the people who still need saving.*

On the stage in front of her, the light began to fade. Letty was leaving.

"Wait!"

Gemma spun around, desperate to catch one more glimpse of the woman, but it was too late.

The light was gone.

Letty was gone.

Once again, a myriad of nameless faces stared back at Gemma. No matter how hard she tried, she couldn't find an ounce of kindness in anyone's eyes. Instead, she saw varying levels of impatience, indifference, hatred, and disgust.

The darkness had returned.

On either side of the stage, like cruel bookends, Ogden and Grimes watched her. Nothing in their faces indicated that they'd seen Letty. Like the audience, they were waiting to see what Gemma did next.

But the thousands of people inside Elevation Ministry Center weren't the only ones waiting for Gemma. The eyes of the world had fallen upon her. The viewership for this broad-cast had to be astronomical. Millions of people had likely tuned in tonight, livestreaming the broadcast from their phones or computer screens, or watching on their television sets, all of them hoping to see a rebellion fall.

They were all watching her. Listening to her words.

"Well?" Grimes prodded her. "Have you decided?"

The folks I worry about are the ones who still need saving.

Suddenly, Gemma knew what she had to do. Because Grimes wasn't in control. She thought she was, but she wasn't. It wasn't Grimes who'd given Gemma a worldwide audience tonight—an audience that desperately needed saving.

God had done that.

Okay, Lord, she silently prayed. *I trust You. Whatever happens, I'm putting my trust in You. No matter what.*

Straightening her back, she turned to face Grimes. "I've decided," she said, "that I will not say I bombed this building, because I had nothing to do with it. And while it's true that I took part in the rescue of hundreds of Christians who'd been wrongly imprisoned in your detention centers, I did not kill *anyone* during or after the rescue."

Every ounce of fear had left Gemma's body. With each word, her strength grew.

"Finally—and write this part down so you don't forget it—I want you to know that I will *never* renounce my faith. Never. Not to you, and not to anyone else. And I don't care what you do to me or to my parents. Because for me—and for them—to live is Christ, but to die is gain."

Silence.

Gemma's words were met with total silence. From the audience. From Ogden. From Grimes. No one seemed to know what to do with her.

No one had seen this coming.

Finally, Grimes cleared her throat, clearly eager to regain control of the situation. "That's very unfortunate, Miss Alcott. I'd hoped you were strong enough to do the right thing for your parents. Now, they'll have to pay the price for your cowardice. For your weakness."

I trust You, Lord. She repeated the words over and over. *I trust You. I trust You.*

"You're right. I *am* weak. But God is strong." Gemma closed her eyes, and one of her favorite Scripture verses tumbled from her lips. *"We have this treasure in jars of clay to show that this all-surpassing power is from God and not from us."*

When she opened her eyes, she saw Grimes recoiling from her words, as if Gemma had just spat on the stage.

"Stop speaking this instant," the woman snapped, her eyes wide. She shot a desperate look at Ogden. "Don't just stand there, David. Do something."

But Ogden remained still, a mannequin in an expensive suit. He looked incredulous, as if he couldn't believe that someone was actually quoting Scripture on *his* show.

The audience shouted at Gemma from their seats. Some stood up and lobbed insults and curses at her like baseballs. Three men in the front row charged the stage, but the Task Force soldiers below the stage—who Gemma hadn't even noticed until that moment—sprang forward and intercepted them.

Gemma saw the irony in the soldiers holding those three men back. *The Task Force is protecting me right now. They're the reason I'm still speaking.*

She fixed her gaze on the camera. She had very little time. Someone was going to cut her microphone or pull her off the air soon—if they hadn't done so already. This was her chance to reach the world. Her only chance.

Please, God. Show me what to say.

And then He did.

The words rolled off her tongue. "Ogden, you said before that Christians believe they're the only people worthy of heaven, but that's not true. We believe *no one* is worthy of heaven and that it's impossible for anyone to be good enough to earn their salvation. But we also believe that God loved His creation so much that He wanted to make a way for them to be with Him forever. And he did that through His Son, Jesus Christ. Our salvation comes not through our own works, not through anything we can do, but through our faith and belief in Christ's finished work on the cross."

"Shut up," Ogden muttered into his gold microphone, his dark eyes blazing.

But Gemma wasn't finished. Not yet.

"We don't have to do anything to earn our salvation. It's already been done for us."

When Gemma finished speaking, the crowd was no longer shouting at her. They were no longer cursing. No one was trying to rush the stage. Even the Task Force soldiers were staring at her, confusion etched on their stony faces.

That was the Gospel, she realized. *Millions of people just heard the Gospel for the first time.*

The audience sat in stunned silence, many of them looking to their leader for guidance.

But it was not Ogden who broke the silence.

It was Grimes.

"Do it," the woman said, turning toward the Jumbotron. "Kill her parents."

CHAPTER THIRTY-NINE

"I can't believe I'm wearing this."

Taylor glanced over at the passenger seat where Gavin was tugging at the collar of his uniform jacket, as if trying to free himself from it. For once, the guy wasn't being dramatic. The uniform was several sizes too small for him, but it was the only one they'd been able to find on such short notice. An ex-soldier named Kaminsky—the shortest and skinniest private Taylor had ever seen—had found one of his old uniforms in the trunk of his car, badly wrinkled and buried underneath a mountain of fast-food wrappers.

"It doesn't look that bad," Taylor said as they exited the highway and turned onto the road that led to Elevation Ministry Center. "But you smell like a rotten hamburger."

"I *feel* like a rotten hamburger."

The Ford Expedition they were driving was Private Dietrich's personal vehicle. She'd offered it up to Taylor at the last minute, pressing the keys into his palm and saying, "Just bring it back. And while you're at it, bring your girl back, too." Then, before she walked away, she'd said, "At night, you can almost mistake my Expedition for a Task Force vehicle."

She was right. There were obvious differences between the navy-blue Expedition and the black Suburbans commonly used by the Task Force—including no government license plates—but those differences wouldn't be as obvious in a crowded parking lot at night.

Taylor was counting on it.

According to the news reports, Ogden's comeback show was supposedly a "limited seating event," but when they pulled into the parking lot, it was nearly full. The show had started ten minutes earlier, at seven o'clock, but Taylor didn't think Ogden would put Gemma onstage right away. He was the star of the show, and he'd want to relish in the adoration of his audience for at least a few minutes.

Taylor drove the Expedition around the perimeter of the parking lot, his eyes passing over the line of Task Force vehicles parked in front of the building. Instead of wasting time looking for a spot in the main lot, he circled around to the back of the building. There were only a handful of vehicles in the rear parking lot, and most of them probably belonged to Ogden's staff. He parked the Expedition underneath one of the parking lot lights.

"Okay," he said, shutting off the engine and tucking the keys inside his pocket. "Check the radio. Let's see if we can hear what they're saying."

Gavin picked up the SRX-2200 Task Force radio from the center console and turned the volume knob to switch it on. He twisted the channel knob, pausing on each frequency to listen for voices. Since there was a significant Task Force presence at Elevation and the building was so huge, the soldiers would have to communicate via radio.

Taylor observed the LED indicator light at the top of the Motorola. It was already blinking red, indicating a critically low battery. Of course it was critically low. The thing hadn't been charged in over a year. There was no way it should have still been operational, but he'd accepted that some things were beyond his understanding. The radio was still working, and he prayed it would continue to work long enough for them to get some intel.

Gavin continued twisting the dial, his frustration growing more evident with each dead channel. "We're wasting time, Nolan. What exactly are you hoping to hear?"

"Anything," Taylor replied. "Anything that will—"

"Unit Four, external check complete. Building remains secure. Over."

Gavin's hand leapt off the dial and hung in mid-air, as if he was afraid that touching the radio might make the voice disappear.

Another equally robotic voice replied, "TOC, good copy. Unit Four, continue your patrol of the mezzanine. Next check-in at nineteen-thirty. Report to Captain Steele in the TOC to relieve Unit One."

"Unit Four, good copy."

"TOC, copy. Over and—"

The indicator light at the top stopped flashing.

The radio went silent.

"It's dead," Gavin muttered, twisting the volume knob. He switched the radio off and back on again, but there was nothing. No static. No light. Nothing. "That's it?"

Taylor unbuckled his seatbelt and opened the driver's door. "It's going to have to be enough. Let's go."

He stepped out of the SUV and straightened his uniform jacket. A soft bumping sound came from overhead, and Taylor glanced up to see a cluster of moths circling the parking light, repeatedly bouncing off its surface. For some reason, those moths made him think of Ogden's followers. They were the moths, and he was the light. They couldn't get enough of him. He was their savior. The brightest point in their universe.

But the moment the light burned out, all the moths would be gone.

"They're called bugs, Nolan."

Gavin limped around the side of the SUV. Not only was Kaminsky's uniform too small for him, but the private also had tiny feet. "They're not that impressive. I saw a ton of them when I was in the woods, hiding from people like you." It was a dig, but Gavin's voice lacked its usual sharpness.

"Don't forget your cover." Taylor grabbed Kaminsky's hat from the center console and tossed it to Gavin. "Good luck getting this thing to fit on your enormous head."

As they headed toward the building, Taylor couldn't get over how strange it was to be walking side by side with Gavin. Three days earlier, they'd been at each other's throats. They'd wanted to kill each other. But somehow, they'd been able to put their differences aside for Gemma. Two former enemies united by a common goal.

Keeping his eyes on the glass doors, Taylor said, "You know, Bonnar, just in case we both die or get captured tonight, I want to say that I'm sorry for the things I've done to you. Not only in my position as a soldier, but..." He wasn't exactly sure how to say this next part, so he just forged on. "I'm sorry for the hurt it caused when I showed up in Gemma's life. I should've sat down with you and explained everything. I should've given you that much respect. I hated you for being with her, but I should've been thanking you for watching over her."

The silence that followed felt like it went on forever. Taylor could hear the faint sound of applause coming from inside the building, and he imagined that the applause was for him. He'd said what he'd needed to say. It didn't matter if Gavin accepted his apology.

At least, that was what he was telling himself.

And then, a few dozen feet from the glass doors, Gavin came to a stop.

Slowly, he brought his eyes up to meet Taylor's. "I left you behind," he said, his voice barely more than a whisper. "I did it on purpose. I saw an opportunity, and I took it. That's the truth. And I know it's not enough to apologize, after what you've been through. I know that. But I'm so sorry, man. I never should've closed that door. I'd do anything to take it back."

Taylor couldn't believe what he was hearing. Had Gavin just admitted that he'd intentionally left Taylor behind? That decision had led to seven months of grief for Gemma and seven months of pain and torture for Taylor. That decision had led to the White Room. To Patches and Groot. To Stovington Detention Center. To nearly getting his throat slit by another detainee. And all of it could've been avoided if Gavin hadn't closed that door.

But as he saw the sincerity in Gavin's eyes, Taylor realized something.

He'd already forgiven him.

"It's over, brother," Taylor said, extending his right hand. "It's forgotten."

Gavin reached out and shook his hand. "Alright." His voice cracked a little, and he cleared his throat. "Thanks."

They continued toward Elevation's rear entrance, not speaking.

There was nothing else to say.

When they approached the glass doors, Taylor saw two soldiers—one heavy-set and one skinny—seated at a folding table just inside the door. Both of them were scrolling on their phones, totally oblivious to the two men approaching the entrance their superiors had assigned them to guard.

"This feels wrong, man," Gavin whispered. "They haven't seen us yet. Shouldn't we at least try to sneak in?"

But Taylor was a soldier again—not out of desire, but necessity—and it felt like coming home. He'd slipped back into the role as easily as a business executive might slip into a comfortable pair of joggers after spending all day in a suit. And it wasn't putting on the uniform that had done it. It was having a mission.

But for the first time, he was on the right side of this fight.

He was fighting for the good guys.

"We're soldiers, Private Kaminsky," Taylor said. "Soldiers don't need to sneak in. Soldiers use the door. Just follow my lead."

"Quit calling me Kaminsky," Gavin mumbled without moving his lips. "My name isn't Kaminsky."

"That's not what your nametape says."

Finally, the skinny soldier glanced up from his cell phone and spotted them through the glass. He jumped to his feet, startled, and the chubby soldier followed suit, nearly knocking over his folding chair. But when they noticed the uniforms, they appeared to relax a little. They pocketed their cell phones, came around the table, and pushed the glass doors open.

"Good evening, Sergeant," the chubby one said. "What can we do for you?"

Taylor tucked a hand in his pocket and tried to look casual. He stood with the left side of his body canted away from the soldiers so they wouldn't notice his missing patch. "Sergeant Nolan and Private Kaminsky. We're with 2nd Battalion. Captain Steele sent a dispatch requesting a few additional patrol units, and we're the lucky ones who were *volun-told* to do it. This was supposed to be our night off," he said, trying to sound put-out by the whole thing. "Anyway, we're supposed to report to the TOC, but this building looks big, and I have no clue where that is. You guys mind pointing us in the right direction?"

"Sure, Sarge, no problem." The skinny guy gestured at the long hallway that stretched out behind them. "Down at the end of this hallway, there's an elevator. Take it up to the mezzanine level. The TOC is in the coffee lounge."

Taylor smirked at this. "Of course it is. Captain Steele likes his coffee." He walked down the hallway. "Thanks for the info, gentlemen. You boys have a good night."

"You do the same, Sarge."

When they reached the elevator, Gavin hit the up button, and Taylor glanced back at the table. Both privates had returned to their seats, retrieved their phones from their pockets, and resumed their idle swiping.

"How are we going to sneak Gemma past those guys?" Gavin whispered.

Taylor responded with a shrug. "We'll figure that part out when the time comes. But if we make it this far, those two knuckle draggers won't be stopping us."

A high-pitched ding. The elevator doors opened, and both men stepped in.

As the elevator rose, Taylor said, "We're not leaving here without her."

Gavin nodded. "No way."

The elevator let out another ding as it came to a stop, but Taylor barely heard it.

Because when the doors opened, all he heard was screaming.

CHAPTER FORTY

"Kill them now."

Grimes's command shocked Ogden out of his stunned state. He had no intention of allowing two people to be executed—or unbound, as Grimes called it—on *his* broadcast, especially since many of his followers (and biggest donors) were former Christians. He certainly hadn't been aware of the live video feed from the detention center, and if he had, he never would've allowed it to be shown. When the show ended, he planned to fire whichever producer had rolled over for Grimes and put that shot on the air.

He lifted the gold microphone to his lips, intending to bring a swift end to this madness before it went any further, but movement drew his attention to the Jumbotron.

Ogden didn't know how, but the medical personnel on the screen seemed to have received Grimes's execution order. A nurse pulled a rolling cart into the shot and positioned it between the two beds. Two hypodermic needles rested on its surface, their metal tips winking at the camera.

Half of his audience cheered at the sight of those needles.

The other half looked horrified.

Ogden's gaze shifted to the girl. Alcott.

She was no longer standing. Now, she was crouched on the floor beside the podium, her face buried in her hands, rocking back and forth and repeating the same prayer over and over. Since she was still wearing her microphone, her words echoed throughout the auditorium.

"Oh God, I trust You. Whatever happens, I trust You. Please, God. Please help me trust You. Whatever happens. Whatever happens."

Not just the auditorium. Fresh horror swept over him. *That prayer of hers is going out to the world.*

The realization only made him angrier. Alcott should have been begging God to rescue her parents, but instead, she was putting her faith on display for the world. Nothing was going according to plan. He hadn't expected the girl to put up any resistance tonight—not after she'd willingly turned herself in. Why had she surrendered if not to save her parents? Had this been her plan all along? To hijack *his* stage?

Did she think there wouldn't be consequences?

"Just do it already!" Grimes screamed at the Jumbotron, a maniacal look in her eyes. "What are you idiots waiting for?"

No. He couldn't allow the girl's parents to be executed on his broadcast. It would ruin everything. It would ruin him. He would rather die than lose his audience.

Finally, he found his voice. "Cut the feed!" he shouted into the microphone, hoping someone in the control room would react quickly. "This is obscene! I will not allow this to be—"

The screen went black.

Finally.

One of his producers must've finally grown a brain and pulled the live shot. He breathed a sigh of relief, his gold microphone capturing the faint whistle of air through his lips. But his relief was short-lived.

Immediately, another video appeared on the screen.

This one wasn't a live shot. It was a shaky cell phone video shot in a different detention center infirmary. He knew exactly what it was because he'd seen this video before. Unlike Alcott's parents, none of the patients on the screen had been sedated, and restraints held them on their hospital beds. It did not surprise Ogden when the detainees were told they were going to be injected with a cure for Christianity. It did not surprise him when they struggled. And it did not surprise him when, one by one, the detainees were injected with potassium chloride.

Their awful, guttural screams of agony were broadcast to the world.

"David?" Grimes ran up to him, her heels clicking on the stage. Somehow, she'd had the wherewithal to turn off her microphone. "Why are you playing this? How did you get it?"

He wanted to punch her. To knock those nasty fangs of hers right out of her ugly mouth. Did she honestly think he had anything to do with this? Was she that stupid? And why were these videos playing? Who was in the control room?

"Ladies and gentlemen," he said, struggling to navigate his way through these strange waters. If he handled this correctly, he might still salvage his career. "I assure you, I had nothing to do with what happened in that detention center. These unbindings…they were Lydia Grimes's idea—"

"David!" She slapped him across the face. Hard.

In a reflexive movement, Ogden shoved the woman away. She stumbled backward on her mile-high heels and landed on her bottom. She gaped at him from the floor, her expression a hybrid of rage and disbelief, and then she climbed to her feet and ran offstage.

With Grimes no longer an issue, Ogden turned back to his audience. He squinted into the bright lights, trying to read faces to determine how many of his followers had turned on him. A few of the weirder ones were smiling, even laughing, at the horrors playing out on-screen, but the vast majority appeared shaken by the video. Some people in the first few rows had tears in their eyes. But what upset him the most was that the aisles were rapidly filling up with people leaving the auditorium.

This is bad, he realized. No. Not bad. *This is terrible.*

But it was nothing compared to what came next.

An interior shot of a bedroom replaced the infirmary scene.

It was *Ogden's* bedroom.

And he was there, stretched out on his bed. But he wasn't alone. Lydia Grimes was with him, perched on the chair right next to his bed.

Ogden's brain couldn't quite process what he was seeing. There were plenty of security cameras on his property, yes, but none in his bedroom—for obvious reasons. But based on the angle of the shot, the camera had to have been hidden on the left wall of his bedroom, somewhere on his bookshelf.

"To be honest, David," on-screen Grimes was saying, *"you've really impressed me over the last few weeks. There was so much that could've gone wrong with the bombing, and the risk of it being traced back to us was huge. But you executed everything perfectly."*

Ogden's hand dropped to his side, the gold microphone dangling a few feet above the floor. "No," he muttered, wishing he could wake up from this nightmare. "Oh, hell."

But this was real. This was actually happening.

Those people in the aisles who hadn't exited the auditorium yet stopped to watch the video. Bizarrely, the sight made Ogden think of those stinger scenes at the end of movies, after the credits stop rolling. The ones where the people exiting the movie theater pause in the aisles, empty popcorn boxes in hand, to watch the surprise bonus scene.

That was what this was. A surprise bonus scene.

"When you suggested taking a bullet in the shoulder, I thought you were crazy," Grimes continued. *"I thought the bomb would be more than enough to accomplish our mission, and I saw no need for you to take such a personal risk. But you were right. That bullet turned you*

into a hero. Everyone loves you now. And do you want to hear the best part? Those forty-seven deaths have forced the president to act..."

The microphone slipped through Ogden's fingers and clattered to the stage.

The video shut off. The screen went black.

Ogden sensed people rushing toward him before he actually saw them. His primal instincts alerted him to danger before the sound of running feet and grunting registered in his mind. Risking a glance at the audience, he saw dozens of his most-devoted followers charging the stage, hurling themselves at him like rabid animals, determined to rip him to pieces for what he'd done.

In his peripheral vision, he saw the girl—Alcott—crawling behind the podium, trying to hide from the crowd.

Good luck, he thought. *After they're done ripping me apart, you're next.*

But the well-trained Task Force soldiers stationed at the front of the auditorium formed a last line of defense, intercepting the people charging the stage and taking them to the ground with brutal force. One soldier, who looked to be about fifteen, clambered onto the stage and positioned himself in front of Ogden. He drew his rifle and leveled it at the audience, ready to kill anyone who made it past the line.

More soldiers flooded in through the side entrances. With their rifles drawn, they bellowed commands, forcing the remaining audience members from their seats and out of the auditorium. Meanwhile, the soldiers stationed at the base of the stage were now herding Ogden's would-be attackers—some with their hands zip-tied behind their backs—toward the exits.

"Everybody out! Let's go!"

Ogden hadn't been happy when Grimes had pulled Levins and the rest of his personal security guys off this detail and turned the whole thing over to the Task Force, but now he realized what a good call that had been. Levins and the other brutes he employed wouldn't have been able to handle this mess.

He didn't believe in the Loving Creator he so often talked about, but if he had believed, he would've fallen on his knees right now to worship the guy.

"David?"

He spun around, expecting to see Grimes.

But it was his assistant, Tara.

She stood in front of the podium, and she looked so different that Ogden hardly recognized her. Her clothing remained the same—she still resembled a misshapen brown amoeba—but everything else about her was different. It was the first time he'd ever seen her without a clipboard in her hands. And there was a level of confidence and self-assuredness that— only a few hours ago—Ogden would've sworn the woman didn't possess. She no longer looked the least bit mousy. Instead, she looked like a cat who'd just eaten a mouse.

"It's over, David," Tara said. "It's finished. *You're* finished."

Even her voice was unfamiliar. Ogden was having a hard time reconciling the woman in front of him with the woman who'd brought him coffee every day for the past two years.

In his mind, the pieces of the puzzle clicked together. When Grimes had visited him that day, the security team had seized her laptop—the same laptop that contained the video of the unbindings that had just been broadcast to the entire world. Ogden remembered calling Tara and asking her to bring the laptop to the bedroom, and she'd done so.

But how long did she have it? He struggled to remember. Not very long, but certainly long enough to transfer its contents to an external hard drive.

"You?" He could barely get the word out, could barely comprehend it himself. "You did this? What are you, some kind of spy?"

But Tara wasn't a spy. She was nothing. She was invisible.

She didn't matter. Someone as insignificant as her couldn't bring down someone like him, could she?

No. It simply wasn't possible.

Tara took a step closer to him. "I wish I would've known what you were planning. I would've killed you myself before you could do it. You murdered those people, David, and you're going to pay for it."

Ogden glanced at the young Task Force soldier, but the kid's attention was on the rear of the auditorium, where the last few soldiers were directing the remaining audience members through the rear doors. Outside those doors, people were screaming, hurling expletives at the Task Force, demanding to be allowed back inside.

Ogden's eyes dropped to the soldier's duty belt—to the black pistol that hung on the young man's right hip—and Tara's words filled his mind.

It's over, David. You're finished.

As much as he hated to admit it, Tara was right. He was finished. Even if Grimes found some clever way to spin that bedroom video, his career would never recover. Everything he'd spent years building had been destroyed in less than thirty minutes.

But Tara was wrong about one thing.

He would not pay for any of it.

When the doors at the rear of the auditorium clicked shut, the soldier protecting Ogden turned toward him, probably to tell him that the coast was clear, but he never made it all the way around.

In one swift movement, Ogden grabbed the kid's pistol and gave it a sharp twist, freeing it from its holster. Then, he shot the soldier between the shoulder blades. As the kid collapsed to the stage, Ogden whirled around, leveled the gun at his traitor assistant's unimpressive chest, and pulled the trigger.

The impact of the bullet knocked Tara backward. She landed

beside the podium, her legs splayed wide, a red flower blooming on the front of her blouse.

Finally, Ogden thought with a smile. *A little color in her wardrobe.*

And then he stuck the still-smoldering barrel against his temple and pulled the trigger.

CHAPTER FORTY-ONE

Chaos.

Taylor could think of no other way to describe the scene on the mezzanine level.

Throngs of people streamed past the open elevator doors, driven away from the auditorium by Task Force soldiers armed with M-4 carbine rifles. Some were sobbing. Others kept turning around to scream profanities at the soldiers. A few of the angrier attendees tried to fight their way back toward the auditorium, but the forward momentum of the crowd kept pushing them toward the front exit.

Stepping off the elevator, Taylor hesitated at the edge of the crowd, sensing Gavin's presence behind him. A river of people flowed past them, but the walls on either side of the elevator protruded far enough into the crowded corridor to keep them out of sight. As the mass of people continued through the exit and emptied into the parking lot, the soldiers lined up just outside the main doors, their weapons at the ready, to prevent anyone from coming back inside.

The building was emptying quickly, and Taylor still had no clue where Gemma was. Where would Grimes be holding her?

Backstage? Obviously, something had happened during the broadcast to create the pandemonium he was now witnessing. What if soldiers had whisked Gemma away the moment things went downhill? An image appeared in his mind: the group of transport vehicles lined up along the front of the building. Why hadn't he parked out front and watched those vehicles until they brought Gemma out? What if he'd made a crucial mistake by going inside the building?

The forward motion of the crowd suddenly ceased, and Taylor glanced to his left and saw a bottleneck at the exit doors. The entrance hall had been loud before, but the noise increased exponentially as agitated soldiers shouted at the crowd to keep moving, and the crowd responded with expletive-laden shouts of their own.

"What should we do?" Gavin shouted over Taylor's shoulder. "Which way?"

Three sharp cracks drew Taylor's attention to the auditorium. He'd heard those sounds many times before and recognized them immediately.

Gunshots.

If there was even the slightest chance that Gemma might be in there, he had to check it out.

Suddenly, the bottleneck cleared up, and the crowd moved again. The last wave of soldiers trailed behind the group, herding them forward like sheep. As the soldiers passed by the elevator, one of them—a female corporal—glanced to her left and saw Taylor. She rolled her eyes, gave him an exasperated headshake, and kept right on moving. Whether she was exasperated with the crowd or with him—a sergeant who wasn't doing anything—Taylor didn't know. And he didn't care.

Now that the crowd had cleared out, there was nothing between him and the auditorium.

"Watch our six," Taylor said to Gavin. Then, he drew the Glock 22 that Clarke had given him and started moving toward the closed auditorium, staying as close to the wall as possible. He glanced back and saw Gavin following behind him, walking backward to watch for any threats coming from their rear.

Four different double doors led into the auditorium, all of them painted the same nauseating shade of purple. Taylor took the farthest doors on the right, trying to stay out of the line of sight of any soldiers who might have still been inside the building. He pushed the door inward and poked his head inside. There was a narrow walkway with black walls and black carpeting leading down a ramp into the auditorium. On either side of the walkway, yellow lights trailed along the base of the wall, reminding Taylor of the emergency lighting on airplanes. Up ahead, he saw where the walkway opened up into the auditorium, and he thought he could hear someone talking.

"Come on," he whispered, gesturing for Gavin to follow him. But Gavin turned away, his attention on something else.

"Someone's coming," he said.

And then Taylor heard them, too—voices coming from behind them.

They were getting closer.

"How many did you see, Corporal?"

Corporal. The female soldier who'd rolled her eyes at him.

"I think just one, sir."

Just one? But Gavin had been standing right behind him at the elevator. She hadn't seen him?

Peeking through the partially closed door, Taylor saw four soldiers range-walking down the hallway, heading directly for the auditorium.

The corporal, two privates, and an officer with gold bars in the center of his chest.

That must be Captain Steele, Taylor realized.

All of them carried M-4 rifles.

There was nowhere to go. They could hide inside the auditorium, but Taylor didn't know what was happening in there—

only that someone had been firing a weapon a few minutes ago. Plus, even if they were lucky enough to stumble across Gemma, Steele and his soldiers would be right behind them.

Gavin glanced at him, and despite the dim lighting inside the walkway, Taylor had no trouble recognizing the look of steely determination in the guy's eyes. "Find Gemma and get her out of here," he said. "I'll hold them off as long as I can."

"Wait. What are you going to do?"

"They think there's only one of us," Gavin said, a glimmer in his eye.

And then he spun on his heels and barreled into the mezzanine, racing toward the approaching soldiers.

Before the doors slammed shut, Taylor saw the soldiers drawing their weapons. Aiming them at Gavin. Shouting for him to stop.

The doors closed. Taylor waited for the inevitable sound of gunshots, but there was nothing. The shouting stopped, replaced by an eerie silence.

He didn't wait around to find out what had happened to Gavin.

Instead, he drew his weapon and continued down the walkway toward the distant sound of voices.

CHAPTER FORTY-TWO

Three gunshots, one after another, each followed by a sickening thud.

Gemma cringed against the podium, making herself as small of a target as possible, silently praying that the few inches of cherry-stained wood between herself and the shooter would be enough to stop a bullet. She considered making a run for it, trying to get backstage, but she wasn't willing to risk taking a bullet in the back.

Seconds passed with no gunshots. Indescribably long seconds while Gemma imagined the shooter—in her mind, it was Lydia Grimes—peeking around the side of the podium, her lips peeling into a wicked smile when she discovered Gemma's hiding place.

But if Grimes was the shooter, where was she? What was she doing? Gemma strained to listen, trying to figure out what might be happening on the other side of the podium. She could hear plenty of noise, but it was the muffled sound of chaos coming from outside the auditorium.

And then she heard it.

A soft moaning coming from somewhere nearby. Gradually, the moan formed into words.

"Help...me..."

She still didn't know who the shooter was—or where they were—but Gemma couldn't ignore that voice. Carefully, she poked her head around the side of the podium.

Less than four feet away, Tara Clarke lay in a rapidly expanding pool of blood, her arms extended to her sides and moving up and down, creating her own bloody version of a snow angel. Both of her heels had come off her feet. One of her legs was bent at the knee, her stockinged foot sliding back and forth across the floor as if trying to push herself away from danger.

Gemma no longer cared if the shooter was still hunting her. She abandoned her hiding place and crawled toward the injured woman, her eyes darting nervously around the stage, hoping to spot the shooter before they spotted her.

That was when she saw the bodies.

Two of them, lying side by side on the stage.

One was a Task Force soldier.

The other was David Ogden.

She didn't know if the soldier was alive or dead, but he wasn't moving at all. However, the *Elevation Ministries* leader was definitely dead. Gemma didn't have to get any closer to him to know.

Half of his head was missing.

A pistol laid on the stage beside his right hand. Ogden must've shot the others before turning the gun on himself.

But he hadn't killed Clarke's sister. She was still alive, still moving, still trying to get away from her dead attacker. Her blood-coated lips opened and closed as she pleaded for help.

Gemma had no idea how anyone could lose that much blood and still be alive, but Tara was a fighter.

Just like her brother.

When she reached Tara, she pressed down hard on the woman's chest to stop the bleeding, her knees slipping in the pool of blood. But Tara was already turning the kind of pale that no human being should ever be. She looked like the victim of a ravenous vampire that had drained every ounce of her blood.

Clarke's sister would not survive the night.

She probably would not survive the next five minutes.

Hooking her hands underneath Tara's armpits, Gemma lifted the woman's blood-soaked body onto her lap and held her close, doing anything she could to comfort Tara in her last moments. To let her know she wasn't alone.

"Tara?" she whispered. "I know your brother."

The woman's lips stopped moving, and her searching eyes locked with Gemma's.

"My friends and I would be dead or detained if not for him. And those detention centers that were just liberated? That was your brother, too. He organized the whole thing. He's the reason those people are free. And because of what you did here tonight, the Christians who are still locked up might have a fighting chance."

Blood dripped from the corners of Tara's mouth as she tried to smile. Then, she reached for her neck, the tips of her fingers lightly brushing against the heart-shaped locket hanging there, before her hand fell limply back to her chest.

Gemma picked up the locket and opened it.

Inside was a picture of two children, a boy and a girl, both laughing.

The boy couldn't have been older than ten when the picture was taken. His eyes were focused somewhere above the camera, probably looking at whoever took the picture.

The girl was much younger. Only three or four.

Her eyes were on the boy.

"Don't worry," Gemma whispered as Tara breathed her final, hitching breath. "I'll tell him you love him."

And then the woman's body went limp.

Gemma gently removed the locket from around Tara's neck and tucked it inside the pocket of her jeans. She bowed her head protectively, almost reverently, over the body, and allowed the tears to spill from her eyes. She hadn't known Tara Clarke, but she knew the woman's older brother, and she knew that this death was going to wreck him. But she also knew how proud Clarke would be to know that his baby sister had taken down a man like David Ogden. Like David slaying Goliath.

"How touching."

Gemma's head snapped up, her arms reflexively tightening around the body.

Lydia Grimes loomed over her, her hands behind her back, a maniacal look in her eyes. One of her high heels was missing, which caused her body to list to one side like a ship about to capsize. "Typical David. Leaving me to clean up his messes."

Gemma had no weapon. No way to defend herself. And there was a body lying across her lap, preventing her from attacking Grimes *or* attempting to escape.

Once again, Grimes had the upper hand.

But this time, Gemma wasn't afraid of her.

"I don't understand it." Grimes brought her left hand around to scratch at a run in her stockings. "All you had to do was renounce. Countless others have done it before you. It's not a big deal. Why couldn't you just do it? We could have avoided all of this."

"What does it matter if I renounce?" Gemma shot back. "I'm a nobody, right? Just some stupid girl from the backwoods of Pennsylvania. But what I'm wondering is...how can one stupid girl be such a big problem for the Federal Bureau of Compliance?"

Grimes smirked at her and brought her other hand out from

behind her back, revealing the pistol in her right hand. "Don't worry, Miss Alcott. I intend to put an end to this problem tonight."

Gemma's eyes darted to Ogden's body, but the gun was gone.

Of course it was gone. Grimes had it now, and she was aiming it at Gemma's head.

"Tell me something, Miss Alcott. How does it feel to be a few seconds away from death?"

Rage flooded Gemma's veins. Rage not only for the senseless death of the woman in her arms, but for the senseless deaths of all those people she *couldn't* hold in her arms. For the people who Grimes had sentenced to die in the detention centers. For the victims of the bombing. For the executed detention center guards. For the countless people the Task Force had murdered over the years.

For her parents.

"I'll answer your question," Gemma said, "but first you have to answer mine."

Grimes raised her eyebrows. "I'll bite. What's your question?"

Gemma smirked at her. "How does it feel to have lost?"

The woman's face twisted with disgust. "You think this is a loss, Miss Alcott? This isn't a loss. This is a setback. There are a thousand other Ogdens waiting to take David's place. After you're gone, the networks will have me on their shows, and I'll explain everything away. And the nation will believe me because they *want* to believe me. They'll forget everything they've seen here tonight because they *want* to forget. Because it's easier that way."

"You're wrong," Gemma said. "They won't forget what you did. Not after they've seen you for what you really are. If you're going to shoot me, then shoot me. It doesn't matter if I die because this rebellion was never about me. That's what you don't get. There are plenty of others like me. People who will fight—and sacrifice—to win this nation back from people like you. And after tonight, there will be thousands more. A few spray-painted billboards will be the least of your problems. You tried to destroy the rebellion, but you just poured fuel on the fire. So, enjoy your power while it lasts, Grimes, because your time is ending."

Grimes tilted her head to the side to examine Gemma, as if she were some strange specimen from another planet. "Is it, now? Too bad you won't be around to see it."

"Just do it, you coward," Gemma muttered. "Stop talking about it and do it."

Keeping her eyes open, Gemma focused on the barrel of the gun.

She would not close her eyes. She would not show fear.

She wasn't afraid to die.

"You know, Miss Alcott, I was hoping to turn you into a villain tonight," Grimes said, her finger tightening around the trigger. "But I'll settle for turning you into a martyr."

Gemma never heard the shot, and she never saw the bullet.

All she saw was a burst of red as the front of Grimes's blouse exploded.

Then, the woman crumpled to the floor like a puppet with its strings cut.

Seconds later, a Task Force soldier appeared beside Gemma, wrapping his arms around her and pulling her close, his chest shaking as if he was crying. And maybe he *was* crying. She couldn't be sure because she wasn't looking at him.

She was still looking at the barrel of the gun. Only, it wasn't pointing at her anymore.

It was on the floor, pointing at the empty auditorium.

And then the soldier spoke her name, his voice like a bullet that ripped through her chest and shattered her heart into a million pieces. But his voice...it made no sense because it belonged to someone who couldn't possibly have been holding her right now.

Am I dead? she wondered. *Did Grimes kill me?*

Finally, she brought her eyes up to meet his. "Are you real?"

"I'm real," Taylor assured her, lightly kissing her lips. "It's going to be okay."

Only then did she release her grip on Tara and grab onto the front of Taylor's uniform shirt, clinging to him as if her life depended on it.

"How?" was all she could say.

Gently, he lifted Tara's body off Gemma's lap and then helped her to her feet. "Later. We need to get out of here." He wasn't lying. Gemma could hear the distant sound of sirens.

The police were on their way.

Taylor pulled Gemma toward the rear of the stage, away from the bodies.

"Wait," she said, resisting his efforts to drag her toward the exit. Finally, she pried her hand out of his. "I'll be right back."

"Gemma, we have to go *right now.*"

She ignored him and ran to the body of Tara Clarke, peeling off her blood-stained jacket as she went. Carefully, she lowered the jacket over Clarke's sister, covering her face and upper body, making sure the patch was visible for all to see.

"Thank you," she whispered. "You saved us."

Then, kneeling over Lydia Grimes, she reached inside the woman's suit pocket and felt around, hoping it was still there. *Praying* it was still there.

The sirens grew louder.

"Gemma!" Taylor whisper-shouted at her. "Let's go!"

Finally, buried deep inside the pocket, her fingers closed around a metal chain. The one she liked to work between her fingers whenever she got scared. She pulled out the silver cross necklace and gazed down at it, unable to believe that she hadn't lost it forever. Then, she closed her palm around the necklace, holding onto it so tightly that it would surely leave a cross-shaped imprint in the flesh of her palm.

But no one would ever take it from her again.

No one *could* ever take it from her.

Taylor jogged up beside her, grabbed her other hand, and pulled her to her feet.

And they both ran.

CHAPTER FORTY-THREE

The Expedition bounced along a grassy access road that was hemmed in by trees on either side. The road ran from the rear parking lot of Elevation Ministry Center to...somewhere. Gemma had no idea where, and she didn't think Taylor did either, but she didn't care where the road went. Anywhere was better than Elevation.

Escaping from the building had been relatively easy. They'd avoided the chaotic mezzanine altogether by taking a staff stairwell down to the lower level. Gemma kept expecting to encounter soldiers along the way, either in the stairwell itself or in the hallway leading to the exit, but the ground floor was totally deserted. All the action was upstairs. The last obstacle had been the rear exit, and when they found that unguarded, they'd thought they were home free.

But moments after they'd stepped outside, a pair of Task Force soldiers had appeared from out of nowhere, coming around the side of the building.

"Hey!" one of them had called out. "What are you doing back here?"

As the soldiers jogged up to them, their weapons drawn,

Taylor had reacted quickly, stepping around Gemma and tugging her arms behind her back so that he appeared to be escorting her.

When the soldiers—two privates—got close enough to see Taylor's rank, they lowered their weapons.

"Oh. Sorry, Sarge," one of them rushed to say. "It's too dark back here. We couldn't tell who you were."

Taylor donned his stern soldier's voice. "Captain Steele gave me orders to sneak the girl out the back," he said, nodding at the dark-colored SUV parked a few yards away, underneath a parking lamp. "It's a train wreck out front, and he's worried about the crowd coming after her. I'm going to take her back to the Gap. But only if that's okay with you boys?"

The two soldiers had quickly apologized and walked away, Taylor's rank distracting them enough that they'd never even noticed his missing patch.

They'd made it to the SUV, but as they drove toward the front of the building, they'd realized the entire area was swarming with police and emergency vehicles. It was a miracle that Taylor noticed the access road, given how dark it was in the rear lot. "There," he'd said, veering the SUV onto the heavily rutted dirt road while Gemma clung to the door handle, her eyes on the red and blue flashing lights in her side-view mirror, praying that they wouldn't come any closer. She watched two police cars drive into the rear parking lot, but instead of pursuing the SUV, they pulled to a stop outside the exit Gemma and Taylor had used only moments earlier.

Finally, the flashing lights disappeared from view, and Gemma's iron grip on the door handle relaxed.

Eventually, the access road dumped them onto a side street, directly across from a closed Dollar General store. Taylor turned right, and in another half-mile, the side road linked up with the main highway, with its fast-food restaurants, grocery stores, and law offices. He brought the vehicle to a stop at a red light, and both of their heads turned south, toward Elevation, where emergency lights flashed against the night sky.

When the light changed, Taylor turned away from those lights and everything that came with them. He drove with one hand on the steering wheel and the other intertwined with Gemma's.

We made it, she realized. *We got out.*

Gemma tugged nervously at her necklace. She'd put it back on as soon as they'd climbed inside the vehicle. "So, you saw Gavin get detained? You're absolutely sure he didn't get away?"

Taylor's hands tensed on the steering wheel. "He ran right at them, Gem. I don't know if he got detained or what happened, but he gave himself up so I could find you."

"Will it be worse for him because he was wearing a Task Force uniform?"

After a few long seconds, Taylor shook his head. "I don't know."

Turning away from him, Gemma gazed out the window. She couldn't focus on the buildings that lined each side of the highway, because they were zipping by too fast. Taylor was speeding, and she understood why. He wanted to get away, to put as much distance between themselves and Elevation as possible. But soon they would be back at the mall, and Teresa would be there, waiting for any word about Gavin. How was Gemma supposed to tell Teresa that the father of her unborn child wasn't coming home?

She wasn't ready to do that. She didn't even know *how* to do that.

"Pull over," she said.

Taylor glanced at her. "What's wrong?"

"Please. Just pull over right now."

Gemma knew Taylor didn't want to stop, that it violated every single instinct he possessed, but he did it anyway. For her.

After another quarter-mile, he turned into the parking lot of an Exxon gas station. There was a single car at the pumps, its driver seated inside her vehicle and scrolling through her phone as the digital numbers on the pump's display continued to climb. Taylor drove around to the back of the building and pulled the SUV behind a dumpster, where it couldn't be seen from the road. Then, he shut off the engine.

Gemma reached down to unfasten her seatbelt, but she couldn't get it. Her fingers wouldn't stop shaking enough to work. Tears of frustration burned behind her eyes as she struggled with the stupid thing...until Taylor reached a hand across the center console and unfastened it for her.

Freeing her.

In that moment, she needed to be close to Taylor, and there was nothing keeping them apart except the center console. So, she crawled over it—this last hurdle between them—and climbed onto his lap. The steering wheel pressed against her lower back as she flung her arms around his shoulders and cried.

He didn't ask her what was wrong because he didn't have to ask. He didn't offer her words of comfort because he knew that his words—no matter how well-intentioned—wouldn't have meant much to her. She only wanted to be held. To be loved.

The Gospel message had gone out to the world tonight. She wanted to believe that it might change things. She wanted to count tonight as a victory.

But Gavin was gone.

And her parents were dead.

This victory had come at a substantial cost.

Gemma would tell Teresa how brave Gavin had been. How he'd sacrificed his freedom for a man who had once been his mortal enemy. She would promise to take care of Teresa and her baby. She would find Clarke and tell him how brave his sister had been. How she'd sacrificed her life to expose the awful truth about Ogden and Grimes. Finally, she would place Tara's locket in his hand, and she would explain that, although his sister had left the family behind, she hadn't left her older brother behind. She'd carried him with her everywhere.

Gemma would do all of those things later.

For now, she only wanted to cling to Taylor.

Her husband. Her best friend. Her lover. Her rock.

Taylor held her as tightly as he could, one arm wrapped around her waist. His other arm stretched up her back, his fingers entangled in her hair. There wasn't an inch of space between them anymore. But that might change in the future. Lydia Grimes had been wrong about a lot of things, but she'd been right about one. There were others out there—others like her and Ogden—who would rise up in their place and try to destroy everything good in the world. It would always be that way…until the end.

Even after tonight, Gemma and Taylor would still be hated, and they would still be hunted. For them, tomorrow wasn't a promise, but a wish.

Whatever happened in the future, Gemma would not lose faith in the end of the story.

When she finally stopped crying, Taylor kissed all of her tears away, one by one, his lips moving down her cheeks. Eventually, their lips found each other in the dark, and when he kissed her, all the pain and heartache of the world fell away, as it always did.

Because in Taylor's kiss, there was love.

There was truth.

And there was freedom.

They clung to each other long after the distant blare of sirens faded to a memory, until nothing remained but the two of them.

Two souls, breathing as one.

In a world overcome by darkness, they were the light.

EPILOGUE

Frank Diggs *really* had to use the restroom.

His eight-hour shift in the exterior guard shack of Elmhurst Detention Center had only begun fifteen minutes earlier, and already, he had to take a leak—the kind of leak that men in his particular age bracket would not do well to ignore. Lately, even if he used the bathroom right before he left the main building, he still had to go by the time he reached the guard shack. He shifted in his seat, trying to shake the feeling away, but that didn't work. He imagined himself as one of those cartoon characters, his eyes filling with yellow liquid.

It wasn't the coffee, either. Shirley liked to nag him about the huge thermos of coffee he packed when he went to work, but the coffee wasn't the problem. He hadn't even drunk much of it yet—only a few sips on his drive in—and that certainly wasn't enough to justify this kind of urgency. Maybe he was getting the sugars? Diabetes made you pee a lot, didn't it? Plus, it ran in his family. He'd watched his own father battle the disease for years, losing four toes, but Frank wasn't in any hurry to call the doctor —especially if it meant changing his diet.

Trying to find a comfortable position that also lessened his need to urinate, Frank leaned back in his seat and propped his feet on the metal desk. Chunks of mud crumbled off his boots onto the desk. He considered brushing it away with a quick sweep of his hand but then left it for the two night-shift boys. Those twenty-something punks thought they could boss Frank around just because he was new. He'd only been at Elmhurst for two weeks, while the punks had been there for two years, which technically meant that they outranked him.

And they never let him forget it.

Telling the little twerps about his past had made no difference. His first day on the job, when he'd met them at shift change, he'd mentioned that he'd been a corrections officer at the United States Penitentiary in Lewisburg for thirty-two years, eventually retiring as a shift supervisor. He'd told them he'd only come out of retirement because the Federal Bureau of Compliance was in such dire straits. Across the country, detention center guards were quitting right and left, and there were rumors that many of them were joining up with the rebellion, although Frank didn't believe that for a second. Either way, the centers were looking for people like him. People with experience. People who didn't like subversives. And people willing to accept the three-thousand-dollar sign-on bonus that was currently being offered.

In other words, he was there because Uncle Sam needed him.

And because a part-time job would get him away from Shirley for at least thirty-two hours a week.

But the punks hadn't cared about his past. They'd looked at him as if he'd accidentally stumbled into Elmhurst on his way to the senior lunch special at Golden Corral.

Frank glanced back at the main building, searching for his partner, Tom Bosco, who was currently patrolling the perimeter of the detention center. Unlike the punks, Bosco wasn't a bad guy. He was in his late thirties and kept mostly to himself, which was good because Frank didn't care to know the details of his partner's life. He didn't lie awake at night, wondering if Bosco had kids or what sports they played or what colleges they wanted to attend. The two men didn't talk unless they absolutely had to. Usually, Bosco brought a book along and spent the whole shift reading, which was just fine by Frank, who preferred to spend the hours reading the newspaper, solving crossword puzzles, and taking the occasional nap.

Detention centers hadn't had exterior guards until recently, and Frank had always thought that was a mistake. He'd been proven right after the rebels attacked the centers last spring, freeing over three-thousand detainees. In response to the attacks, the powers-that-be had augmented their security measures, increasing the number of guards inside the building and stationing two additional guards outside in a guard shack to radio back to the main building if an immediate lockdown became necessary.

So, four days a week, Frank sloughed off his sweatpants like a snake shedding its skin, pulled on his uniform, and reported to work. After punching in at the main office, he went to his locker and cinched on his duty belt, which was too small, but he wasn't about to ask for a bigger size. He'd worn the same size belt for thirty-two years at the prison. His duty belt at Elmhurst consisted only of a flashlight and a baton, so it was a sad imitation of his old duty belt, but it was better than nothing. After he was in uniform, Frank would trudge down the muddy road that ran from the main building to the guard shack, carrying his thermos in one hand and his leather handbag in the other.

That was another thing the little twerps made fun of him for. They called his handbag a purse, which infuriated him to no end.

Two nights ago, unable to take it any longer, Frank had

finally lost his temper. "It's not a purse, you morons!" he'd shouted, shaking the bag at them. "Look! It doesn't even have a shoulder strap. It's more of a briefcase, see? I clutch it by the handle."

"Sorry, Frank," one of them had said sheepishly. "It's not a purse; it's a *clutch*."

And then they'd both fallen over themselves laughing.

Finally, the urgency to urinate subsided a little, and Frank whistled his relief. He knew the feeling would return soon enough, but for now, the universe had granted him a brief reprieve, like a death row inmate who'd just received a last-minute stay of execution from the governor. However, if Bosco didn't show up by the time the feeling returned, Frank would have no choice but to write his name in the slush-covered field right next to the guard shack. No one was around anyway. Let his shift supervisor try to say something to him. Just let him try.

A shiver passed through his body—an odd feeling since it wasn't cold inside the shack. Winter had come early this year. It was only November, and already, Pennsylvania had seen two snowfalls, one of them fairly significant. But it wasn't cold inside the shack. With the two industrial-sized space heaters humming away, the small building was practically stuffy. Frank wasn't the type of man to complain about the cold—he ran pretty hot—but he wasn't exactly a young buck anymore, either. Wasn't always being cold a symptom of old age? He'd always assumed that was a woman thing, but maybe it happened to men, too.

Frank reached back and slipped his arms into his uniform coat. Then, digging into his handbag—which was most defi-nitely *not* a purse—he pulled out the newspaper. He shook it open and gaped at the headline on the front page.

More Subversives Emerge from Hiding, Evangelize in the Streets.

The accompanying pictures made Frank want to vomit up

the two slices of toast slathered in apple butter that Shirley had prepared for him that morning.

One picture showed an older man standing on the steps of a courthouse. He held a Bible in his hands—a Bible, of all things! —and was reading it to an enormous crowd of people. Another photograph showed a group of young people huddled around an elderly woman in a wheelchair. They appeared to be praying over her.

But the last image infuriated him.

As snow fell around them, two groups faced off in the middle of the street like the Sharks and the Jets from *West Side Story*. Only, these groups didn't appear to be at odds with each other. One group stood with their hands locked together, their mouths hanging open as if they were all talking at the same time. Every one of them had the upside-down Task Force symbol sewn, drawn, or written somewhere on their clothes.

The caption underneath the image said: *A group of subversives forces cold, confused locals to stand in the snow and listen to the banned hymn, "Amazing Grace".*

Now, Frank hadn't been there when the picture was taken, but the locals sure didn't look cold or confused to him.

In fact, they appeared to be singing along.

Dropping the paper onto his lap, Frank grabbed his thermos and poured himself a cup of black coffee. Adding more fuel to the fire didn't seem like a good idea, especially since he could feel the need to urinate creeping back up on him, but he needed to take the edge off his anger, and coffee usually did the trick.

Ever since the Elevation debacle, as he thought of it, the news kept getting worse every day. Not only were the detention centers short-staffed because guards kept walking off the job, but now there was talk of trouble *inside* the Task Force itself. Like the guards, more and more soldiers were defecting and joining up with the rebellion. The main news channels said little about it, but Frank had heard rumblings on social media about the brutal tactics that some Task Force soldiers had employed during detentions.

There were supposedly images floating around the Internet. Images of beaten and bloodied subversives, tortured at the hands of the Task Force. Images of homes torched by the Task Force, with entire families still inside. Images of subversive children falling ill from malnutrition in makeshift orphanages, the photos supposedly taken by undercover journalists. Frank hadn't seen the pictures himself. By the time he sought them out, the social media sites had already deleted them, citing misinformation.

Whether or not the pictures were real, Frank didn't want the government policing what he saw on the Internet. He could think for himself, and he assumed the pictures were a crock. An elaborate hoax perpetrated by the rebellion to swing public opinion their way. Just like that video of the unbindings that aired during the Elevation debacle. The video of the subversives struggling and fighting during their unbindings had upset the snowflakes in the public so much that the Federal Bureau of Compliance had temporarily halted the unbindings.

They *still* hadn't been reinstated.

He downed the last of his coffee and twisted the empty cup back onto the top of his thermos. Bosco still hadn't shown up, but Frank's need to urinate had returned with a vengeance, and it could no longer be ignored.

As he pushed himself off the chair, his left knee made a terrible crunching sound. That wasn't unusual. It made that sound anytime he bent it. "Snap, crackle, pop, Frankie," Shirley had said that morning when he rose from the breakfast table. "That knee of yours makes me want a bowl of Rice Krispies."

Opening the door to the guard shack, he stepped into an unseasonably chilly November morning. He swiftly pulled the door closed behind him, not wanting to lose any of the precious heat. His boots slid a little on the well-trampled snow leading up to the shack, but he grabbed onto the side of the building and caught himself before he went down.

"Can't believe I gave up retirement for this," he grumbled, pulling down his zipper and unleashing a torrent of urine against the closed door of the guard shack. Hopefully, the door would freeze shut when the temperatures dropped tonight, and the night-shift boys would be forced to chisel their way through Frank's urine to get inside.

Movement caught his attention. He quickly zipped up his fly and squinted into the distance, trying to figure out what he was looking at.

Like most detention centers, the government had built Elmhurst in a remote location. The nearest town was a thirty-minute drive, and there was nothing but cornfields for miles on either side of the road that ran past the center. But the yearly harvest had come and gone, and now the field consisted mostly of broken corn stalks and a whole lot of nothing else. Across the road, the snow-covered field sloped upward for approximately a hundred yards before falling away on the other side.

It was there, at the crest of the hill, that he'd seen movement.

There were people standing there.

Only, they weren't standing. No, they were *moving* down the hill, trudging through the ankle-deep snow like a herd of animals.

As he watched, people continued to appear at the top of the hill. Hundreds of them. Too many to count. Men and women of all ages and races. Even a few children walked among them. As the front of the group edged nearer, he realized that some of them were wearing Task Force uniforms.

They were all heading straight for him.

No. With dawning horror, Frank realized what this was. *They aren't coming for me. They're coming for the detainees. Elmhurst is under attack.*

Oddly enough, his first thought was of those two night-shift punks. What would they say if they found out the rebels had attacked the center on Frank's watch? They'd probably say that they'd been right about him all along. That he was too old to protect a kennel of puppies, much less a building filled with subversives. They'd say that if he wanted to serve his country, he should've done so by staying retired and continuing to enjoy the senior lunch special at Golden Corral.

As more people appeared on the horizon and Frank remained frozen in a river of his own urine, he wondered if those two young punks hadn't been right about him all along.

With a trembling hand, he pulled his baton free from his belt.

Idiot, Frank thought. *What do you intend to do with that?*

No, he didn't need his baton. What he needed was to communicate with the main building. There were protocols for this. If he called down to the main building right now, they could easily lock everything down. That crowd on the hill—actually, they looked more like an army than a crowd—could huff and puff all they wanted, but they would not blow this house down.

Not by the hair on Frank's chinny-chin-chin.

He ripped the door open and slipped inside, closing it behind him. Then, he bent over the desk, picked up the phone, and dialed the main office. With the phone pressed against his ear, he kept his eye on the approaching crowd. The front edge of their group had almost reached the road now. They weren't close enough for Frank to see the whites of their eyes yet, but they soon would be.

The phone rang seven times, but no one picked up.

"You idiots!" he shouted into the phone, slamming it down on the receiver. "You bunch of incompetent idiots!"

There was only one other thing he could do.

He could make a run for the main building. That was his only chance. If he reached the building before the crowd, he could get the guys inside to lock everything down. In fact, it would probably be better if Frank made it inside. If he stayed in the guard shack, the rebels would probably take him hostage and try to use him to get inside.

Keeping his eyes on the front window of the guard shack, Frank abandoned the desk and ran for the exit, his boots skidding on the wet floor.

He shoved the door open...and crashed right into someone's chest.

"Hey!" he cried, hitting a note several octaves above his normal vocal range.

Bosco stood right outside the guard shack, a strange expression on his face. "Where are you going in such a hurry, Frank?"

"What do you mean?" Frank huffed, so angry he could barely get the words out. "Haven't you seen what's happening?"

"Hurry, man!" Bosco said, pushing Frank back inside the shack. "We have to get inside!"

Frank stumbled back into the shack, but Bosco didn't follow inside. Instead, he pushed the door shut and broke his key off in the lock, effectively sealing Frank inside the guard shack.

"Bosco!" Frank slammed his fist on the window, but since the glass was bulletproof, he only succeeded in hurting his hand. "Just what do you think you're doing?"

"Sit tight, Frank. I'll be back for you in a little bit."

No sooner had Bosco jogged off than Frank heard a distant rumbling. It was growing louder. He ran to the front windows and looked toward the country road.

Buses.

An entire fleet of school buses.

Oh, no, he thought, hurrying over to the rear-facing windows. *It can't be.*

But it was.

Somehow, the front doors of the detention center were standing wide open, and hundreds of detainees in khaki uniforms were pouring outside. None of them were running for their lives, as Frank would've expected, but they were all walking, some of them even *ambling* along, as if they had all the time in the world. And several of his coworkers—including the Benedict Arnold himself, Bosco—were actually *helping* the weaker ones by slinging the detainees' arms over their shoulders for support, even carrying them onto the buses when necessary.

As the buses parked along the country road, Frank dropped into his chair, his knee crunching even louder than before.

Snap, crackle, pop, Shirley whispered in his mind.

And then, among the crowd of people currently surging past the guard shack, Frank saw someone he recognized. Someone walking at the front of the pack.

It was the young woman. The one from the Elevation broadcast a few months back. At least, he thought it was her. People from television always looked different when you saw them in real life. But it sure looked like her. That thick, reddish-brown hair was hard to miss.

What was her name? He couldn't remember.

There was a young girl with fiery-red hair walking on one side of her. On the other side was a Task Force soldier with short, dark hair. Only, this soldier, like the others in the crowd, wore his patch upside-down. He carried a rifle slung over his back, but he didn't look as if he had any intention of using it.

The young woman and the soldier were holding hands.

This is only the beginning, Frank realized. *This isn't going to stop.*

He left his chair and walked to the shack's rear-facing window, following the young woman's progress toward the main building. In this same group that formed the center of the crowd, there was a punk-rock-looking girl holding hands with a guy with curly hair and a horrible scar running down his cheek. There was also a stunning young woman with jet-black hair that reached down to her waist. She was visibly pregnant, and she walked with one hand clasped protectively over her stomach.

Suddenly, the pregnant woman stopped in her tracks, her already-fair complexion turning as white as the snow on which she walked. Frank turned his head to see one of the freed detainees—a young man—jogging up to her. They met in the middle of the field, and for a few seconds, they only stared at each other. Then, the young detainee put a hand out and touched the woman's stomach. Tears poured down his face.

Despite everything, Frank's eyes misted over. *That's his child.*

When the detainee took his hand away, the woman fell into his arms.

Something about this reunion touched Frank in a way he couldn't describe. He knew these were subversives and that they needed to be locked away from society. But he was still a human being. How long had that young woman been waiting for her man to be freed? And judging by the size of her baby bump, his freedom hadn't come a moment too soon.

Frank stole one last look at the other woman—the one he knew from the TV. She, along with the Task Force soldier and the little redheaded girl, were so busy watching the reunion between the pregnant woman and the detainee that they hadn't noticed two detainees approaching them. An older man and woman. They both looked very frail, but they were practically running through the snow, heading straight for the girl with the auburn hair.

The Task Force soldier noticed them first, his mouth falling open in obvious surprise. He said something to the young woman and pointed at the approaching couple.

Frank wasn't much of a lip reader, but some part of his brain must've remembered the young woman's name, because when the soldier's lips moved, Frank knew exactly what the guy had said.

"Gemma."

The young woman glanced at the soldier first, confused, and then she looked in the direction he was pointing. When she saw the older couple, her legs buckled beneath her.

But the soldier was right there to catch her, and he only let her go when she fell into the older couple's arms. The three of them held each other, crying and laughing. When they finally composed themselves, the young woman with the auburn hair stepped back and presented the little girl and the dark-haired soldier to the older couple.

"Her parents," Frank whispered as the couple embraced the soldier. He brought a hand up to wipe at the corner of his right eye. Sometimes that eye leaked a little, especially on cold days. "I just bet those are her parents, and that soldier is the guy she loves. And I bet the little girl is their daughter."

Tearing his eyes away from the reunion, Frank slumped into his chair and put his hands behind his head. Might as well take a nap while he waited for Bosco to let him out. He felt the guard shack trembling as the crowd surged around it, as hundreds of rebels led hundreds of detainees to freedom. Frank heard their prayers as they walked past his door, giving thanks to God for their freedom.

For their salvation.

Their prayers didn't bother him too much.

In fact, now that he thought of it, they didn't bother him at all.

Hopefully, Bosco would come back soon to let him out of the shack. He just wanted to go home. To see his beautiful Shirley. Maybe give her a good, long hug and rub her feet while they watched television. He'd take the rest of the afternoon off and return to work in the morning.

Eh, who was he kidding? He wasn't coming back.

Not after today.

He'd leave this job for the two young punks.

Tomorrow, Frank Diggs would rejoin the world of the happily retired. He'd stay in his sweatpants all day and drink his coffee without guilt in a warm house with a bathroom nearby. And maybe, if he was feeling really spunky, he'd even take Shirley out in the afternoon and show her off a bit.

It *had* been awhile since they'd eaten at Golden Corral.

THE END.

NOTE FROM THE AUTHOR

From the bottom of my heart, I want to thank all of you for accompanying Gemma and Taylor (and their many friends and enemies) on this journey. I pray that you've been blessed by this series.

If you're ready for more adventures, check out my new *Reverence Trilogy*.

To receive information about future book releases, click HERE to sign up for my email newsletter.

Or you can use this newsletter link: https://raenaroodbooks. ck.page/736c40c31a

Also, if you've enjoyed this book, please consider leaving a review on Amazon, Goodreads, BookBub, your book blog, or wherever you wish. Reviews are so important for indie authors as we try to compete in an increasingly crowded market space. I truly appreciate each and every review!

Thank you and happy reading!

—Raena

ACKNOWLEDGMENTS

I usually list my husband at the end of the acknowledgements because that's what all the fancy writers do. But this time, I'm giving him top billing because he deserves it.

To my husband, Scott: I wouldn't be able to write without your love and support. You work so hard to provide for our family, and I don't want a single day to go by without you knowing how much I love and appreciate you. You're the most wonderful man I know—my real-life Taylor—and I'm forever grateful to God for bringing you into my life.

To my boys: As much as I love writing, the most important job I will ever have is being your mom. I love you all so much, and my constant prayer is that you will love and serve God in whatever He calls you to do.

Big hugs to my early readers/beta readers/proofreaders: Kimberly Murphree, Judy Kissinger, Lori Thomas, Pastor Joseph Mott, Joyce Mott, and Emily York. These books wouldn't exist—or at least they wouldn't be very good—without you. And to my eagle-eyed best friend from South Africa, Tandy Oschadleus: I can't wait to visit you someday and *not* get eaten by lions.

To my fellow Christian writer, my encourager, and my friend, Jamie Lee Grey: Somehow, you always know when I need to hear from you. Thank you for walking with me on this journey (and sometimes dragging me along). I'm so thankful for our friendship. I still owe you lunch!

Finally, to God: Thank You for giving me this incredible opportunity. Thank You for inspiring me, renewing me, and encouraging me. And above all else—Thank You for my Salvation.

To God be the glory, great things He hath done.

ABOUT THE AUTHOR

Raena lives with her husband and three children in rural Pennsylvania, where her hobbies include raising chickens, singing off-key while cleaning, and introducing her kids to cheesy 80's movies. When she's not writing, she spends way too much time thinking about buying more chickens. And possibly a goat.

BOOKS BY RAENA ROOD

The Subversive Trilogy

Subversive: Book 1 of The Subversive Trilogy

Sanctuary: Book 2 of The Subversive Trilogy

Salvation: Book 3 of The Subversive Trilogy

The Reverence Trilogy

Reverence: Book 1 of the Reverence Trilogy

Rebellion: Book 2 of the Reverence Trilogy

Ransom: Book 3 of the Reverence Trilogy